I0762099

Praise for Christopher Andrews' *Triumvirate* series

Pandora's Game

"Christopher Andrews is an exceptional writer and a master of storytelling ... his characters have complex and often unexpected traits that give them a strong emotional resonance ... completely engrossing ... Rarely does a book come along that is so well written that I can't tolerate interruption. A book that's so well written that I can't tolerate it interrupting *itself* is unheard of. To maintain this level of complexity for twenty-one chapters is an incredible storytelling feat."

— Marcus Alexander Hart, Author of *The Oblivion Society*

"Andrews is a brilliant writer and a wonderful storyteller. I started and finished it without putting it down."

— Julianna Smith, Author of the *Dream Catcher* series

"Andrews shows versatility ... as much competence and style as Poppy Z. Brite or Anne Rice ... Book Of The Month."

— Lesley Meade, *Booknet*

"... a spellbinding novel ... fascinating, riveting ... hard to put down ... a talented writer ... would convert wonderfully to the screen ..."

— Grabbermcgrew, *Sharp Writer Reviews*

"*Pandora's Game* is written in a unique way ... Christopher Andrews writes like an author with much more experience ... fantastic ..."

— Pat McGreal, *Horror Novels Online*

"An interesting story ... I couldn't wait to see what happened next ... the characters are appealing and the concept is absorbing ..."

— Conan Tigard, *Book Browser*

"... incredible ... sharp ... creative ... original and interesting ideas driving the plot and drama ... an ending like a kick in the gut."

— Alex Zawacki, *Class-B*

“Connexion”

(collected in *The Darkness Within*)

“ ‘Connexion’ was ... completely worth the five bucks on [its] own ... Very highly recommended ...”

— Grimlock, 5-star Amazon review

Of Wolf and Man

(Bronze IPPY winner for Horror)

“Better than ‘New Moon’ ... Andrews is amazing with character ... [won] an IPPY award bronze [medal] ... should have won the gold.”

— Marcus Alexander Hart, Author of *One Must Kill Another*

“Outstanding sequel! ... everything that a sequel should be ... interesting and creepy ... addresses some bold issues, and does so very well.”

— John Howard, *Book Reader 222*

Araknid

“… worth the wait! … another 5 stars … Andrews’ writing has matured … outstanding … creepy, compelling, clever, and even stronger on the horror …”

— John Howard, Book Reader 222

“… will not disappoint … Andrews shows his strength for character building … made my skin crawl. In a good way! … a treat …”

— Marcus Alexander Hart, Author of the *Galaxy Cruise* series

PULSE OF THE EARTH

A TALE FROM THE TRIUMVIRATE UNIVERSE

Other Works by Christopher Andrews

TRIUMVIRATE SERIES

Pandora's Game
The Darkness Within
(collection)
Of Wolf and Man
(Bronze IPPY winner for Horror)
Araknid

PARANORMALS SERIES

Paranormals
Paranormals: We Are Not Alone
Paranormals: Darkness Reigns

NOVELIZATIONS

Dream Parlor
Hamlet: Prince of Denmark
Night of the Living Dead
Macbeth
Julius Caesar

SCREENPLAYS

Thirst
Dream Parlor
(written with Jonathan Lawrence)
Mistake
Vale Todo / Anything Goes
(written with Roberto Estrella)
Adrift in the Darkness

WEB SERIES

Duet

VIDEO GAMES

Bankjob

PULSE OF THE EARTH

A TALE FROM THE TRIUMVIRATE UNIVERSE

A Novel by
CHRISTOPHER ANDREWS

Pulse of the Earth: A Tale from the Triumvirate Universe

ISBN: Hardcover #978-1-7361983-4-6

This book was printed in the United States of America.

Rising Star Visionary Press hardcover edition: November, 2025

A Rising Star Visionary Press book
for extra copies, please contact by e-mail at
risingstarvisionarypress@earthlink.net
or send by regular mail to
Rising Star Visionary Press
Copies Department
P O Box 9226
Fountain Valley, CA 92728-9226

Thank you to my wife, editor, and Imzadi,
Yvonne Isaak-Andrews,
for all the ways you make life better.

Thank you to my friend and colleague,
Daniele Serra,
for producing another marvelous Triumvirate cover.

And thank you to my daughter,
Arianna Kristina Andrews,
for making fatherhood such a dream come true.

The following story takes place approximately six months after the events depicted in the Triumvirate novel, *Araknid*.

Consciousness trickled into her, like some perverse water-torture device, bringing the pain searing through her back, scorching its way through her nerve endings. She was somewhere dark and cold, lying on her side on a hard floor and breathing in a rancid stench. Her head throbbed with each heartbeat, and she could feel the stickiness of drying blood matted in her hair.

Pain? Oh, yes. But clarity? No, clarity shunned her.

Time ticked by; it might have been minutes, or even hours, as far as she knew. The agony in her back seared hot and deep — burning lines of it, like ... like ...

Like I was cut, she thought. *No, like I was* clawed.

Some lucidity returned then, and with it, fear. Enough to know she was still in danger, and that she needed to remain absolutely silent.

She attempted to open her eyes, but the drying blood in her hair had oozed onto her eyelids, gumming her lashes together. And even after forcing them apart, she saw little more than darkness — the main lights were out, replaced by insufficient red-tinted emergency backups. It didn't help matters that her ears felt clogged as well.

She swallowed, prompting a *click* within her eardrums. A droning hum all around her continued, but one sound cleaved through it, a grotesque noise that churned her stomach with revulsion and dread: *Chewing*. And beneath that, a brief, weak, horrible moaning.

She turned her head and, squinting through the murky half-light, swallowed a gasp when she saw the first dead body, a man sprawled on his side, whose face looked the way her back felt. Past him, a lifeless woman, her throat ripped to shreds.

The awful chewing noises arose from the shadows beyond them.

A new thought flitted across her mind: *But when did it—?*

That was as far as she got. As soon as the word "it" formed, more of that elusive clarity returned.

She regretted longing for it. It was all she could do not to whimper, to sob aloud. She trembled, and that intensified the pain in her back.

But she bit her lip and forced herself to concentrate.

The chewing emanated from somewhere past the dead man and woman. So, if she stayed low, if she kept absolutely quiet, she might be able to ...

To what? To fight or escape it? Probably not.

To thwart it, somehow? Maybe.

Turning her head the other direction — and God, how even that slight movement prompted yet another spike from her ragged back! — she blinked her eyes several times and scanned her surroundings until she spotted it: Her solid steel steamer trunk. Expensive as hell, so heavy it was a pain in her ass, and, right now, worth every penny.

If she could pull this off before she died, before it killed her.

It had come for her trunk, for the contents therein. Why else would it be here, now?

She drew a preparatory breath, yet still aborted her first attempt to move when the anguish threatened to force a scream past her clenched lips. She knew she could make *no* noise at all, but given the wretched state of her back, that was easier said than done.

Come on ... this might be the last thing you ever do, so make it count!

Steeling herself, her second effort succeeded insofar as she managed to roll from her side onto her stomach. The pain was exquisite, every movement torture, but it also helped her stay focused. So long as those abhorrent chewing sounds continued unabated, she had a chance.

In short, careful, precise movements, she crept onto all fours and inched her way forward, away from the dead people and the chewing, toward her trunk. For an intense heartbeat, she questioned whether or not she had her keys with her, but then she felt them digging into her hip.

Thank God I actually wore slacks with pockets *today; otherwise, they might've been back in my handbag.*

This notion was mildly amusing, at best, but in her current state, she almost let slip a giggle. She froze, holding her breath — *had* she let it out?

The chewing carried on, and so did she.

She was almost there, so near she could almost touch the trunk's cold metal front, when her palm slipped on a puddle of blood — her own or someone else's, she had no idea. Her hand skidded forward out from under her, and her upper body cracked down onto her elbow with a painful *thunk*.

A small sound, little more than what she had already been making.

Yet the chewing halted, replaced a second later by a low, heavy growl that sent an icy chill down her agonized spine.

This is it. This is how I die.

But not yet!

Embracing the jolt of adrenaline that shot through her system and dulled the pain, she lunged, collapsing against her trunk even as she shoved her hand into her pocket.

A dark shape beyond the two bodies rose into view, the red emergency lights throwing it into silhouette. Its growl crescendoed, its shoulders hunching as it prepared to launch itself at her.

She jerked the keys free, and God smiled upon her as she gripped the correct one on the first try.

Death descended upon her with a thunderous bark, but not before she stabbed the key into the lock and jerked her hand sideways, snapping it off inside.

With her dying breath, she gasped aloud, "Take that."

They weren't the best final words, but as the claws and teeth tore through her flesh, they offered her some, minuscule satisfaction.

AIRPORT EXCLUSIVE

Damn, I'm out of shape, Jason Bakari Samir grumbled, his chest heaving way too much as he huffed through the parking garage toward the terminal. *Guy my age shouldn't get winded from a short little run.*

Internal griping aside, Jason considered himself lucky to be navigating one of the smaller airports in Southern California. He preferred to avoid the headache of LAX, or even John Wayne Airport, whenever possible.

One upside to his brief hustle was that it warmed him a bit. "Sunny California" was known for its mild climate, but this year's winter weather was lingering longer than he had come to expect. Chilly drizzle dampened his hair, and cold evening air nipped at his long-ago thinned skin through his too-light jacket; Jason had been born in New Jersey, but his family moved to California before he was in Kindergarten, and thirty-ish years later, he barely remembered the snow. Now it just seemed wrong to have these kinds of temperatures loitering into springtime.

Scooting into the welcoming warmth of the dry terminal at last, and displacing a small flock of white-crowned sparrows picking over some discarded food as he rushed by, Jason shook the rainwater from his lanky hair like a dog just as his phone announced a telltale *ping!* His damp sneakers squeaking and slipping on the tile floor, he shuffled to one side to let an older, weary couple pass by as he tugged it from the back pocket of his jeans, then pulled a face as he read the text from his nominal boss, known online only as "Trey Romero":

FLIGHTAWARE SHOWS CHARTERED PLANE ARRIVING LATER THAN EXPECTED. GET COMFORTABLE FOR NOW.

Great, he groused some more. *I rush in here, thinking* I'm *gonna be late ...*

But Jason wasn't going to complain to Trey about getting this assignment, or any assignment, so he headed for an available concourse chair to settle in. At least until the good doctor's plane arrived, he would be out of the crappy night.

He collapsed into his chosen seat and released a resigned sigh. All he could do now was wait.

What he really wanted was to have a beer and maybe watch some basketball or whatever, but he knew from past experience that airport bars were a little too pricy for his wallet; given the growing size of his gut of late, that was probably for the best. He thumbed through his phone for a minute, then got bored with that and put it back in his pocket. Instead, he indulged in a little people-watching — which, for him, was somewhat more than the idle pastime it might be for others.

What was he watching for? Anything weird. What else would a distinguished reporter for *Watchdogs of the Weird & Unusual* seek?

But tonight, he couldn't fight disappointment at the lack of any strange or extraordinary airport clientele; the individuals on display were too mundane for his professional needs:

Over by the restrooms, a short Latina wearing a gaudy purple shawl appeared to be talking to herself, but these days he had to assume she was wearing a Bluetooth earpiece he couldn't see ...

Seated not too far away, a lanky, older white guy with bright blue eyes and reddened, wind-chapped cheeks — he looked like he could be a fishing buddy of Robert Shaw from *Jaws* — was tapping out an odd, intricate rhythm with his right foot and left hand; Jason imagined he could be a retired drummer ...

Not far past the hypothetical-drummer, a skinny white girl, no older than twelve and sitting apart from her presumed parents, was holding up a *Ranger Rick* magazine — Jason noted the black-legged white-tailed mongoose locked in combat with a black mamba snake on the cover — and peering at it with a faint glow in her eyes, a glow Jason suspected came from a phone hidden from her parents' view ...

Leaning against an open stretch of wall, an androgynous individual with dark hair, pockmarked skin, and ambiguous features gazed up at the ceiling, without blinking or otherwise moving, but that could be heavy daydreaming, the product of simple, sheer boredom — most people could sympathize with that, as Jason could this very moment ...

He hoped that tonight's assignment proved worth his time, but even Trey could never guarantee that. This scientist he was meeting, Doctor Aimée Hellqvist, was an anthropologist so obscure that even Google had trouble finding anything on her. She got her Ph.D. from Cambridge, but since then she had published no major papers and only held a few positions before dropping off the map years ago; she just sort of wandered off on her own, with her wealthy-ish family footing the bill. Now, according to Trey, she claimed to have made some sort of earth-shattering discovery and wanted to share it with the media. But flash forward a couple of months, and she had gone from trying to get interviews with *National Geographic* and other, more reputable channels, to pandering to organizations like the Watchdogs.

Far be it from Jason to shit on his own affiliated publication — if "publication" applied to their niche website — but he never deluded himself that the Watchdogs were anything more than an esoteric curiosity to most of the general public; a ragtag collection of paranormal-obsessed weirdos. If it hadn't been for their coverage of and exclusive interviews pertaining to the "Arach-mageddon" last year, *Watchdogs of the Weird & Unusual* would still be a tiny blip on the greater digital landscape of the World Wide Web.

And if Doctor Hellqvist were suffering such a giant step down the media ladder to reach out to the Watchdogs, he had to question the veracity of her vague claims: Just how "earth-shattering" could her alleged discovery be?

I guess I'll find out, he thought as he pulled his phone out again to check the time. *Eventually.*

So Jason waited. And waited. And he started to have second thoughts about maybe treating himself to one of those overpriced beers—

"Excuse me ...?"

It took a second for Jason to absorb that the female voice was addressing him. Then he looked up, and up.

A breathtaking white woman awaited his response. Even from his seated viewpoint, he could tell that she stood well over his own five-foot-nine — she towered over the other women, and a few of the men, who passed by — and her long red hair flowed like a river of fire. She sported a tight, emerald dress that peeked from beneath her black leather coat; the color complemented her beguiling green eyes. And she had those extraordinary eyes focused on *him*.

The first thing Jason did was suck in his gut. Then he responded with a suave and delightfully Freudian, "... tall?"

The instant the word passed his lips, his dark cheeks burned in mortification.

Luckily, her sympathetic smile suggested she found this endearing. "Yes, I know," she returned with a slight trace of an accent he didn't recognize. She gestured to the chair opposite him. "May I join you?"

No way, he thought. *No way I'm this lucky.*

But his eyes darted around the concourse, confirming that there were an abundance of open seats. Yet, this super tall, super attractive woman was asking to "join him."

And she still awaited his answer.

"Yeah," he finally spat out. "Yes. Please. Do."

The Junoesque woman nodded — a regal gesture, which matched her majestic, Eastern European features that seemed carved from perfect marble, except for a light powdering of freckles across her nose — and lowered herself into the chair. She crossed her long legs — her heels were tastefully short, which made sense given her Amazonian stature — and rested her small purse upon her lap, folding her graceful hands atop it.

And then she looked at him with an expectant gleam in her eyes and an enigmatic smile on her lips.

Jason floundered for something, anything to say. He couldn't remember the last time he had made small talk with a woman, and he was pretty sure that he had never been in conversation with *any* woman so alluring. Californians didn't normally chit-chat much about the weather — traffic was the typical substitute — but ...

"Cold outside," he commented, offering what he hoped was at least a passably charming grin.

She shrugged, the shoulders of her supple leather coat shifting alongside her lithe neck. "I don't mind," she returned, with a sly grin of her own. "I find the bite quite invigorating." God, her voice was smooth as silk.

No way, he thought again. *No way this is really happening, a woman this exotic and attractive, talking to* me. *I'm being punked, that's the only explanation. This is probably being streamed to YouTube or TikTok or something.*

He looked around again, figuring he would catch some young assholes giggling while pointing their phones at him. But he spotted nothing out of the ordinary.

The woman raised an eyebrow. "I apologize. Were you expecting someone?"

Jason shook his head, trying to maintain his composure. "No, no," he assured her, "not at all. I, uh ... I just ..."

She waited for him to finish the thought, her grin spreading another few degrees.

Feeling foolish and clumsy, he tried again. "I was— I ..."

She cocked her head a little, still waiting.

Well, buddy, you wanted weird, you got weird. Except it's you who's making a buffoon of himself.

Jason released a resigned sigh. He wasn't suave or sophisticated; never had been, never would be. So rather than play this woman's game — or attempt to, anyway, with his own embarrassing brand of "debonair" — he might as well cut to the chase. If he was right, if this was some kind of prank, some fucked up "social experiment" or whatever, at least he could go home tonight knowing he had not fallen for it.

"Look," he said, spreading his hands wide in a show of affable surrender. "I promise, I'm not trying to be rude here. And I don't mean this to be the weirdest pickup line in history, either. But you're so ... " He gestured at her, up and down. "... and I know I'm not. Maybe five, ten years ago, but probably not then, either. Let's be real here: You're outta my league. Anybody in this airport would know that in a heartbeat."

As it happened, he glanced around again and spotted another guy, a white dude about his age, making this exact assessment: Gaping back and forth between Jason and this amazing "hottie," all while giving a little disbelieving, disapproving shake of his head. Then he noticed Jason looking at him and zeroed in on his phone screen with extreme focus.

Rather than embarrassing him further, this confirmation of his position actually amused Jason, and made this whole awkward exchange that much easier.

"Yeah," he continued. "So, again, I'm not trying to be crude or disrespectful or whatever, but, with this whole concourse available, why would *you* choose to sit down and chat with *me*?"

There. He'd said it. Now she could laugh, or slap him, or just get up and walk away, and he could relax. Hell, he would have a funny story to share with the other Watchdogs tonight.

But she didn't laugh. Or slap him. And she made no move to stand and walk away. During his little monologue, her expression had not changed, but the gleam in her eyes, if anything, had grown warmer.

"I appreciate your honesty ..." she began. Then she paused and raised one inquisitive eyebrow.

When he finally realized she was waiting for his name, he provided, "Uh, Jason."

"I appreciate your honesty, Jason," she repeated. "I truly do. I think you are being a little downtrodden on yourself, but I'm also worldly enough to know how I am viewed." She flexed those amazing, long legs for just a second—

God, those calves*!*

—then smiled and shook her head. "So I apologize if I gave you the wrong impression. I didn't sit here, across from you, to imply anything other than this: I'm in the mood for conversation, and you're one of the few people sitting here who isn't glued to their phone." She cocked her head again. "But, if you'd prefer solitude, would you rather I go sit next to that gentleman?" She pointed toward the guy whom Jason had designated a retired drummer, still beating that rhythm with foot and hand.

Jason found himself much more at ease as he told her, "No. I would not rather you sit anywhere else."

She nodded. "Good. I'm glad that's settled." Then she leaned forward and extended her hand across the aisle to him; a simple effort, given her height. "My name's Regina, by the way."

Jason leaned forward to accept her hand. "Nice to meet you, Regina."

She held on to Jason's hand a moment, then sat back and settled into her chair as though it were the finest, softest, luxury leather. "So, Jason, what brings you here tonight? Picking up a friend? Family?"

Jason held on to a sliver of skepticism a touch longer, then decided, to hell with it, he would take her at her word. And if he were wrong, who knows — maybe going viral as the butt of a joke could help the Watchdogs' readership.

"No, I'm not picking anyone up," he told her, "but I am here to meet someone. I'm a journalist, and I'm supposed to interview her."

He had expected Regina to just nod, or say something simple like "I see" or "Interesting." He was therefore surprised when her beautiful green eyes widened, and she flashed the biggest smile yet.

"Really? Well, now I'm beside myself! This is an extraordinary coincidence."

Jason refrained from his knee-jerk response of, *I'm always suspicious of "coincidences"* — he avoided offending her before, and he didn't want to push his luck. Instead, he asked, "How so?"

"I don't suppose by any chance this interviewee of yours would be the Swedish anthropologist, Doctor Hellqvist?"

Jason's jaw dropped.

This prompted a delighted laugh — almost a girlish titter — from Regina. "I'll take that as a 'Yes.' I'm *also* here to interview Doctor Hellqvist."

He shook his head in disbelief. "No fu— ... no way."

She nodded. "I'm also a journalist, though I've only been working for a short time. In fact, this'll be my first 'solo' interview."

"What publication?"

"I'm with the *Register*."

Jason's jaw almost dropped again. So much for the larger

publications showing no interest in Hellqvist's announcement. "That's ... wow. That's awesome."

"What publication are you representing?"

"I, uh ... I'm with *Watchdogs of the Weird & Unusual.*"

Regina cocked her head, something he was starting to find familiar. "I'm sorry, I don't know that one."

He resisted the urge to clear his throat in chagrin. "I'm not surprised, honestly. We're not exactly on par with the *Register.*"

She picked up on his self-depreciation. "Don't feel bad, Jason. This'll be my first interview because the *Register* wasn't interested enough to send a more experienced reporter. I'm really only one step up from an intern. Believe me, my position — my assignment here tonight — is no cause for professional intimidation." She smirked and offered a conspiratorial wink. "Not yet, anyway."

Mollified, Jason matched her smirk and nodded his appreciation.

"So, what exactly is *Watchdogs of ...?*"

"*... of the Weird & Unusual,*" he finished for her. "We're a website that shines a spotlight on the stories the mainstream media outlets skip or treat with skepticism. We're apolitical; we don't do conspiracy theories or anything like that. And we're not interested in clichéd tabloid bullsh— tabloid nonsense, either; no 'the government captured aliens' or 'Bill Gates is really Elvis' or whatnot. But when something truly bizarre happens and no one at ABC or FOX or whatever wants to give it air time, and the *Times* might stick it on the very last page ... well, we give it its fair due — if our leader, Trey, deems it worthy. And we try not to commentate; we stick to the facts as we uncover them, no matter how outlandish they may seem to most people." He shrugged. "Almost no one had heard of us until we broke the story on 'Arach-mageddon.' That finally put us on the map, earned us a little more recognition, and landed a few more bucks in all of our pockets."

"Forgive me, but what is 'Arach-mageddon'?"

"You know, that 'cute' nickname the media eventually gave to the spider freak-out in Los Angeles last year."

Regina communicated her ignorance with a little shake of her head and parting of her hands.

This reaction surprised Jason. The incident had garnered a lot of attention — the Watchdogs had only "broken" the story ahead of the mainstream by a matter of hours, and only because it took time for all the horrifying individual accounts to come into focus as one big related event. Trey demonstrated some real foresight on that call.

Jason's consternation must have shown on his face, because Regina explained, "I traveled quite a lot last year, mainly in Europe. I must've missed this spider news from California."

But that excuse didn't quite sit right for Jason — this had been *big*, coast-to-coast news, and he knew for a fact they heard about it up in Canada, and even over in England. But under the circumstances, he stowed his dubious attitude for the time being and described it to her.

"About six months ago, something — everybody has their own pet theories about it, but no one really knows for sure — caused spiders in the Los Angeles area to start breeding like crazy and become unusually aggressive. In retrospect, a bunch of exterminators claim there had been warning signs in the weeks and days leading up to it, but *one* night in particular, the critters swarmed like angry killer bees. They invaded homes, they bit people left and right, and there were a number of deaths. Black widows and brown recluses can always be dangerous to kids and the elderly, but the sheer number of bites had a few people dying from common household spiders. Dozens of tarantulas marching across your kitchen floor were the scariest to look at, but the smaller ones could crawl through vents, gaps, under doors — it was a whole thing. And scary as hell, I'll bet."

Aghast, one hand raised near her mouth, Regina asked, "And this happened all in one single night?"

Jason nodded. "The worst of it, yeah. Like I said, exterminators saw some buildup, but no one could've predicted what those warning signs meant. So that night the spiders went nuts, but by morning—" He snapped his fingers. "—it was all over. Their unexplained aggression vanished. In fact, most of the spiders themselves disappeared, back to wherever spiders usually hang out, I guess."

Regina returned to clasping her hands atop her purse. "Did you experience this yourself?"

Jason shook his head. "No, thank God. Whatever caused it, the epicenter was somewhere up in Los Angeles. It didn't reach this far south. But everybody knows somebody who was affected by it."

She drew a deep breath, held it a second, then released it with a shudder. "Terrifying."

"Yeah. Anyway, Trey got the Watchdogs working on it before the crack of dawn. The *Times* and the *Register* and all the morning news shows jumped on it, of course, but this was the first time we got a few of them quoting *us*. I don't know exactly where Trey lives, but I'm guessing he was in the middle of it."

Regina shook her head in disbelief. "I'm surprised I hadn't already heard about this ..."

Jason held back a *No shit* remark.

"... but I imagine you're grateful that your website earned professional respect over it."

He shrugged. "One of those 'silver lining' things. But I wouldn't have wished it on anyone."

"Of course." She shuddered again, but this time it was a little more theatrical. "May we please change the subject?"

"Sure."

"I'm sort of new to journalism," she began, "but what about you? Have you been doing this long? Have you always wanted to be a reporter?"

He smirked. "No, not at all. When I was younger, I wanted to be a wildlife photographer."

"Really?"

"Oh, yeah. Big time. Not long after my family moved to California, I saw a red-tailed hawk in our backyard — they're pretty common around here, but I didn't know that, then. Seeing that gorgeous bird swooping out of the sky with an effortless grace left my young mind spellbound. When it snagged its prey in its talons, I was transfixed, unable to take my eyes off it. I guess a lot of little kids might've been freaked by the sight of a mouse dying like that, but for me, it was ..." A look of wonder lit his eyes. "... it was like a switch had been thrown inside my head, something waking up for the first time. I mean, I'd seen plenty of dogs and cats and stuff before, of course, but the beautiful grace of that wild, free red-tailed hawk ... all of a sudden, I couldn't get enough of wildlife — not just birds, *all* of 'em. I saw all animals differently from that day forward. I begged my parents to take me hiking in the Santa Ana Mountain Range, and when I saw my first mountain lion, it was *magical*."

When Jason realized that he had gotten a little carried away, he blushed. But thankfully, Regina did not seem bored or put off by his unexpected gushing; instead, she appeared genuinely charmed by his effusion.

"After that," he continued with a shrug and a grin, "I was hooked. I read books, watched documentaries, and eventually joined a local wildlife photography club for kids. I wanted everyone to see wildlife like I did, from a family of deer wandering through the forest to a bald eagle soaring above. I felt like I was a part of something greater, a small piece of this intricate puzzle of nature, and I wanted to capture that splendor with my camera and share it with the whole world. I used to daydream about shooting pics for, you know, *National Geographic*." His grin grew more whimsical. "I imagined getting my own coffee table books, featuring all my pics of wildlife — or maybe, at least, a series of calendars ..."

But he held up his hands in defeat, then dropped them onto his lap.

"When reality finally set in, I had to accept that the paying jobs were too few and far between. I no longer lived with my parents, and I needed to make rent, you know?"

She nodded in sympathy. But between how she was dressed, how she carried herself, and that remark about traveling "a lot, mainly in Europe," he wondered if she had any idea what he was talking about.

"Anyway," he continued, "setting aside wildlife photography, I've also always been fascinated by bizarre, unexplained phenomena — like Arach-mageddon. I had my own blog, which was really just a hobby for me, and I wrote a few entries that somehow caught Trey's attention. He reached out, asked if I'd be interested in joining the Watchdogs, which was a pretty new group at the time. The website wasn't getting much traffic yet, but Trey still made it worth my while. You know, we've never even met in person — almost none of us have, really — but after my first few articles, Trey upped my base pay, threw me a couple of bonuses, and here I am now. Waiting at the airport for an unknown anthropologist. And chatting with you." He smiled.

Regina made a show of checking the seats on either side of him and the surrounding floor. "No camera tonight?" she asked with a playful smile.

He chuckled. "No, for something like this, my phone's good enough. I'm not expecting any wild animals to make a cameo."

She smiled. "True."

"What about you? Have you always—?" But he was cut off when his phone *pinged!* an incoming text from Trey. "Excuse me, please, that'll be my boss."

She nodded her understanding. "Of course."

The new text read: PLANE LANDING SOONER THAN LAST EXPECTED. BUT KEEP YOUR EYES & EARS OPEN. OTHER SIGNS THAT SOMETHING UNUSUAL IS GOING ON WITH THE AIRCRAFT.

"Something unusual"? Jason thought.

He started to type out a reply, asking for more details, when he noticed several airport officials, two of them from Security, hustling toward the runways. Their expressions were neutral, but their body language denoted concern.

Jason supposed that if he were in a movie or TV show, or even if he were a traditional reporter, he would attempt to sneak away from Regina to search for a possible "scoop" ahead of her. But his easy-going personality, not to mention his hormones, decided otherwise.

Leaning forward, he lowered his voice a bit to say, "Looks like something's up with Hellqvist's plane. Wanna go check it out?"

She looked as though she wanted to ask follow-up questions, but instead smiled and said, "That's an interesting proposal. I accept."

They stood together, and he was reminded just how damn tall she was. Then she slipped her free hand under his arm, linking them.

Looking down to meet his eyes, she prompted, "Shall we?"

Once upon a time, it would have been no big deal for them to step outside and onto the airport's apron to await an incoming plane. That was before 9/11 and the TSA, but with an airport this small, Jason had a few options. Reaching into his jacket pocket, he gripped his rudimentary PRESS pass, but as he saw more of the airport staff getting distracted by whatever was going on, he wondered if he might not need it.

Of course, it was difficult not to draw attention with someone like Regina on his arm — given their height difference in her favor, they were kind of the opposite of "inconspicuous" — but he wasn't going to ditch her now.

Then the PA system kicked in. The low rumble of conversations and clattering luggage faded to a hushed murmur as the words echoed throughout the airport. *"Ladies and gentlemen, may we have your attention, please ..."*

This had an almost comical effect on the people milling around, as everyone shifted into a kind of slow-motion as they paid attention to the announcement without actually halting their activities.

The PA continued, *"We must ask everyone in the terminal to please relocate to the parking garage ..."*

This time the scattered crowd reacted with less curiosity and more belligerence. Lamentations of "But it's raining outside!" and "I've already been waiting here for—!" and "I paid good money for—!" rose all around them, drowning out the details that followed through the PA and kicking all employees into crisis mode. Whatever might be going on with Hellqvist's plane, from a Public Relations standpoint, the airport staff were in for a big headache.

Most of the people were, more or less, shuffling toward the exit and the parking garage, but a fair number of determined individuals marched the opposite direction toward the security gates. Jason heard raised voices, angry and demanding to know what was going on, when would their flights depart, when would their loved ones' planes arrive, and the word "lawsuit" got thrown around a few times.

Jason whispered to Regina, "Follow my lead."

Swinging around to the outer edge of the security gates, Jason watched for the most harried TSA agent, and he found her, hair already slipping free from her tight bun and veins popping in her forehead. Her eyes darted around for backup, but that wasn't coming anytime soon, as all agents were inundated with pissed-off members of the public.

"I paid for this flight months ago!" an angular, frumpy man was shouting in a reedy voice, right into the poor TSA agent's face.

"I understand that, sir," the TSA agent returned, struggling to maintain her composure; to her credit, her voice held firm even as her eyes darted toward her fellow agents.

"*No*, I don't think you do!" bellowed Mister Frumpy. "I came out here in this shitty weather, and I do *not* expect to—!"

Regina in tow, Jason moved forward so that he was alongside Mister Frumpy. "Sir, you need to back the fuck up, *now*."

Frumpy regarded the brown man suddenly standing next to him in something close to shock. "Wh-what? *What*?! Just who the—?!"

"This young woman," Jason overrode him, nodding toward the TSA agent (who was anything but "young"), "is just doing *her job*. And if you don't take a step back *right now*, I'll see to it that you're not only arrested, but that you'll be able to read an exposé about yourself in the morning edition."

Frumpy blinked at that several times, his slack cheeks quivering in equal parts rage and confusion as he attempted to process this turn of events. But he did take a step back.

Jason turned to the TSA agent. "Anderson cleared me," he told her as he whipped out his PRESS pass and flashed it, a little too quickly for her to get a good look at it.

The woman, while wearing an appreciative smile, looked almost as confused as Frumpy. "I'm sorry, who cleared you?"

"Sanderson," Jason blurted, giving Frumpy a dirty look. "He cleared me through, but I couldn't just walk by and let this asshole abuse you like that."

The TSA agent's smile, while still thankful, wavered as she shook her head in bafflement. "I ... *who*?"

"Alderson cleared me, damn it," he slurred, behaving as though he, too, were starting to get frustrated with her. "He cleared me. Us.

He cleared us through."

The TSA agent looked up at Regina, taking her in for the first time and gawking at her height.

Regina smiled at her. "He's telling the truth. I heard it for myself." Releasing Jason's arm, she produced her own, more impressive PRESS pass and waved it around, not only to the agent, but also to Frumpy just as he was taking a breath to start blustering again.

The agent shook her head. "I'll need to, um ... just let me ..."

Jason huffed in forced patience. "Listen ..." He read her name badge. "... 'Glenda,' I promise I'll put in a good word for you. But I gotta get through here before Sanders hands me my ass. And if certain *assholes* don't behave themselves," he directed this last bit back at Frumpy, "you just let me know, and we'll give this idiot a public thrashing like he's never seen."

Frumpy had finally had enough. His reddened face twisting up like he was sucking on a lemon, he unleashed an exasperated sigh, spun on his heel, and stomped away. But when another upset guest took his place, Glenda was ready to throw in the towel, too.

"Okay, go, go," she waved Jason and Regina through. "Just tell, um ..."

"Anderson."

"... right, tell him I was helpful, okay?"

"I promise," Jason assured her as he and Regina moved past her and away from the milling crowd.

"Well done," Regina praised as they left security behind.

Jason smiled. "Thanks. I hate doing that to people like her, but I love doing it to dickheads like him." He realized that the PA system was still going, but couldn't make out if it was sharing anything new. "We'll only be able to get away with that once or twice, though. We need to get outside onto the apron and find out what's going on." He clipped the PRESS pass to his jacket; Regina did the same. "I hope you meant it when you said you find the cold 'invigorating.' "

"Oh, I do."

Her expression was inscrutable, but he didn't have time to analyze it. In his peripheral vision, he spotted someone approaching them from the left.

"Sir?" a male voice said; Jason made a point of not turning to get a better look. "Ma'am? Sir?"

Jason shifted his jacket around toward the speaker, tapping his PRESS pass with his fingertip. "We got cleared by Sanderson," he stated with confidence as he led Regina straight for the apron's sliding doors.

"Sir!" the voice demanded.

Regina, too, angled her own pass around as Jason had. "Anderson cleared us, damn it! Now back off unless you want your name on record!"

The doors opened, Jason and Regina hurried out into the rain and chilly night air, and whoever had been calling after them did not follow.

"Nice," Jason grinned at her.

She returned his smile. "Thanks, I got it from the best. Any more professional tips for me?"

He laughed. "Watch and learn!"

But the question taunted him: What the hell comes next? The rain had escalated to more than just a drizzle (he wished he had thought to bring his umbrella), the night was colder, and while this airport was small, it still had three different runways, their lights a glowing haze in the dreary night. If a real story were brewing here, he needed to know which way to go.

Pulling out his phone, he texted Trey: ?4U, KNOW WHICH RUNWAY HELLQVIST WILL BE USING?

"Texting your boss? Trey?" Regina asked.

"Yeah. He used to be the slowest typist in the world, but thank God, he's gotten a lot better over the past few months. I'm hoping he can point us in the right direction, and quickly."

Regina nodded, easing her hands into her jacket pockets as a wistful smile graced her lips. "I wish my editor offered that kind of hands-on support."

"Trey's pretty great, most of the time. Every once in a while he disappears for a stretch, but the rest of us can't really ..."

Jason's voice trailed off as he saw that a text from Trey was incoming.

ON IT. HANG ON.

He hung on, gritting his teeth as he tried not to shiver from the cold — especially since, true to her word, the frigid air did not seem to bother Regina.

Then, *ping!* GOT IT. HELLQVIST'S PLANE SET TO LAND ON THEIR LONGEST RUNWAY. DYK WHAT'S GOING ON?

NOT YET. WILL UPDATE. THX

Grateful that he had been to this airport before, he gestured and led Regina forward. "This way."

Outside the terminal, Jason would never have known that any sort of emergency was underway; for the most part, aside from the rain, everything seemed like business as usual. Two baggage handlers looked their way, one of whom ogled Regina for a crude stretch of time, but they were never approached — their PRESS passes may or may not have had anything to do with it.

Jason's phone *pinged!*, from Trey: FYI, SHOULD LAND ANY MOMENT.

Jason replied, THX

Sure enough, as they slogged toward the near end of the runway, they could hear the incoming plane and make out its navigation lights through the rain. No baggage handlers here; instead, several emergency vehicles were lined up with engines running — though the accompanying staff looked more focused than worried. One of them, a woman with short hair, glanced over at Jason, then up at Regina, then down to each of their PRESS passes before dismissing them altogether.

"Now," Jason whispered as they came to a halt, "we watch and listen, for anything out of the ordinary."

"Anything 'weird'?"

Jason smiled. "That's our mission statement."

When the plane itself appeared through the precipitation shortly thereafter, Jason was a little surprised — it was bigger than he had expected; since it was a chartered flight, he had pictured a private jet, but this was more like a cargo plane. He wondered which was more expensive to charter, and just how much money Doctor Hellqvist's family had at their disposal.

The next thing he noticed was that the plane was coming in a little faster than seemed prudent to him. But what did he know?

The plane descended and touched down in one harsh plunge, then braked hard. Whoever was flying sure wasn't putting a lot of consideration into their passengers' comfort — or, if they were actually hauling cargo, the contents on their manifest. That landing was so rough, Jason would not have been shocked if sparks had showered the runway.

The emergency vehicles surged forward to meet the aircraft as it skidded to a stop, and airport security and local police units joined them; fortunately, the latter group did not take notice of Jason and Regina's uninvited presence.

"Here we go," Jason said, and each of them took out their phones.

"Bet you wish you'd brought your camera tonight after all," she commented.

He acknowledged her words with a distracted, "Mm-hm," but his attention was locked onto Hellqvist's plane.

But after an initial burst of action, the event's momentum ground to a snail's pace. The emergency vehicles, lights flashing, reached the aircraft and bustled about its engines ... and then all of them appeared to stand down from Red Alert, their urgency replaced by evident confusion and uncertainty; a series of radio and phone calls followed, though Jason and Regina were too far away to hear anything specific. Several attempts were made to communicate with the pilot via exaggerated hand signals, but based on their behavior, they received no responses. A stair vehicle joined the scene, and attempts were made to open the aircraft's side door, to no avail. The collective activity drifted toward the back of the plane, where the larger cargo door was located.

"Let's see if we can get any closer," Jason suggested. "Just be slow and casual."

Regina slipped her arm around his again, and they inched their way forward.

As with the side entry, the cargo door put up a stubborn fight against their efforts, but this time the emergency crew did not give up. Tools were applied to the inside of an access panel, accompanied by a liberal amount of cursing.

Fuck, Jason groused to himself. *How much longer do we stand around out here, watching them try to open the goddamn thing?* He was losing his battle against shivering as the rainfall grew heavier, and with their linked arms, Regina couldn't help but notice. *If this is all nothing more than a complicated maintenance issue, we could've just waited back at the damn terminal. Well, okay, sure, the PA asked everyone to relocate to the garage, but since we used our passes to bluff our way out here, maybe we could've—*

A deep grinding noise distracted him from his woes; looked like they were finally getting the cargo door open. Once the passengers disembarked, Jason and Regina could identify Doctor Hellqvist, get her somewhere dry and warm, and at last get down to actually—

One of the emergency staff hollered, "*Shit!*"

That was their only warning.

A dark form exploded from the belly of the plane, bursting out with ferocious speed that caught everyone off guard; some kind of animal, but enormous, and moving fast for something its size, *too* fast in Jason's experience. It barreled through the emergency crew, knocking three of them from their feet, and took off down the runway. Between its shocking speed and the rain, Jason couldn't identify it — a massive dog, maybe? Like a Newfoundland, or a rare Saint Bernard with black fur? Or a large wolf? Except, how in the world would a *wolf* end up on the plane—?

But he had no opportunity to ponder further. The animal, whatever the hell it was, disappeared into the night. It was just ... gone.

All of that happened in a flash, and the beast never made a sound.

For several long seconds, every soul on the tarmac of the runway stood in motionless silence; even the people knocked to the ground remained where they sat.

Then someone declared in a raised voice, "Well, boys and girls, *that'll* wake you up in the morning."

Only one person laughed at the joke, but everyone got moving again. The three were helped up, their coworkers making sure they were uninjured, which they were for the most part. One of them rubbed his ass, forcing a chuckle and asking no one in particular, "Was that a fucking *bear*?"

Jason snorted at that. The animal had been damned big, no question, but no bear could run that fast. *No* animal that large should have been able to, to his knowledge. That thing had been, like, cheetah-fast, but cheetahs were lanky and this thing had some serious bulk.

Jason realized that he had not taken stock of Regina's reaction to all this. Looking up, he found her staring with somewhat widened eyes at all the commotion, but otherwise, her expression was neutral.

When she realized he was looking at her, she asked, "What do you think that was?"

He shrugged, his mind still processing what they had seen. "Honestly, I have no idea. I wish we'd gotten a better—"

But his thoughts were again interrupted. Not by a curse this time, but by a scream.

At some point, two members of the emergency crew had gotten around to actually entering the aircraft; now both of them fled down the ramp, shouting incoherent blather and pointing back inside. Then one of them bent at the waist and vomited.

More crew entered, only to retreat as well. They were all babbling, their voices intermingling in an unintelligible mess; Jason wished he could make out what they were saying, but as the situation evolved into something ever more complicated, getting any closer seemed unwise — at the very least, they might finally get noticed for real and escorted away.

Security took their turn entering the cargo plane, and while they lingered inside longer and exited in a less panicked state, they were all on their radios and, when one of them barked orders into hers, Jason caught the phrase: "Get the Feds out here!"

Regina leaned over to comment, "Our little 'interview' has developed into something a lot more interesting."

Jason nodded. Cold and rain be damned, he wasn't budging.

* * *

He was soaked to the bone, but Jason's determination held true. He could be stubborn that way.

A myriad of authorities had swarmed the aircraft. Local police and county sheriffs milled about, and even a few FBI agents showed up. Jason had expected the FAA and/or the National Transportation Safety Board to put in appearances, but then, the plane had not actually crashed.

Another conspicuous element: Not only did Doctor Hellqvist never appear, *no one* emerged from the plane — no passengers, no flight crew; every person who exited, Jason had seen enter from this end of things.

Also, some coroner vans materialized, but no ambulances. This, too, spoke volumes. But there were no body bags. Not yet.

Jason attempted using his credentials to get closer, to get a quote, to get information, to get a photo, *something*. It was maddening. But they all shut him down, hard and repeatedly; in fact, he would have already been removed from the scene if he hadn't done a little voice-raising of his own ("Are you blocking out *the press*?!" and so on). In that regard, Regina was a blessing — if they looked like they were going to start manhandling him, she aimed her phone at them and offered a polite warning of, "Uh-uh-*uh*, boys!" and would wave her own PRESS pass in their faces.

No one attempted manhandling Regina. In fact, one of the city cops tried hitting on her. But, to Jason's amusement, she just stared at him with a flat, somewhat disgusted look in her eyes that was colder than the rain. Jason stifled a chuckle when the jackass slunk away, his tail between his legs.

Jason had texted Trey a few times, updating him on the lack of progress. Trey was stoked that he was one of only two journalists on the scene and wanted him to find out everything he could about the plane and the fate of Hellqvist, but he had been especially, almost specifically, curious about the large animal. Sure, Jason wanted to know about that, too, but Trey was asking about its size, its speed, its strength, what noises had it made, which direction had it gone ... it almost made Jason long for the days when Trey was a slow typist.

Finally, just when Jason's perseverance was faltering, he

spotted the proverbial ray of light. "Thank God," he mumbled.

Regina perked up. "What? What is it?"

Jason nodded toward a specific police officer, a county sheriff's deputy who had stepped away from the thick of things to take a phone call. "The Black deputy over by himself — name's Derek. He's a friend and one of my sources, sometimes. Cross your fingers and toes."

The deputy ended his call as Jason and Regina approached him. His eyes widened in mild surprise, and Jason's wasn't sure if it was in a good or bad way.

"Deputy," Jason greeted with a deferential nod.

Derek shook his head. "Jesus, Jason ..." He glanced at Regina, and even though he stood roughly eye-to-eye with Jason, he seemed less impressed with her height and more interested in her PRESS pass. "Together, huh?"

"Yeah," Jason smiled, "we've kinda 'joined forces' for the evening."

"Delightful. You know there's nothin' I can tell you, right? You gotta wait for the official statement like everyone else."

Jason looked around. "Come on, man, it's not like you're swamped with the paparazzi."

"Not yet," Derek grumbled.

"Deeereeek ..."

Derek scratched the back of his neck under his uniform hat as he considered. He then made a big show of shaking his head. "Okay, so far as anyone's concerned, I'm just givin' you a bunch of 'No comments,' okay?"

Jason offered a few desperate gestures of his own. "Understood. No direct quotes."

Derek looked to Regina, who nodded her agreement. "No direct quotes."

Peering back at Jason, Derek added, sotto voce, "You gonna make it worth my while later?"

"Of course."

Derek snorted at that. "Don't give me 'of course.' You already owe me a couple, remember?"

"I know, but I promise: Top-shelf all the way, on me."

"Don't promise anything too quickly, man. It's not much to go on so far. And you probably won't believe this weird shit, anyway."

"Dude, everything I cover is 'weird,' remember?"

Derek's eyes flicked over to Regina again.

She smiled. "I'll keep an open mind."

Derek held back one more second. Then, shaking his head more and pointing back at the terminal as though he were telling them they should clear the area, he informed them, "Looks like everyone on board, every single person — the entire flight crew and a small number of passengers — were all slaughtered by some kind of animal. They're all dead. All of 'em."

Jason whispered, "God."

Regina did not quite gasp, but her intake of breath was still audible over the rain.

Derek nodded. "Yeah. I'm glad I didn't get too good a look. Don't need that shit in my head."

"But ... how the hell did the plane *land*, then? Was the flight crew—?"

"Auto-pilot did an emergency landing, apparently. I didn't know they could do that on their own. Guess they can."

"Yeah, but it was a rough landing," Jason told him. "And we saw the animal, when they first got the back of the plane open."

"Really?" Derek asked, his own curiosity slipping through. "Was it as big as they say?"

"Damn big. And fast. If it killed everyone on the plane, we're all lucky it didn't bother to kill anyone else on the ground, too."

"Fuck," Derek muttered. "And then it just took off? Just like that?"

"Yeah."

Derek shook his head. "Wild animal like that, fuckin' loose around here? Jesus."

Jason had so many questions, he didn't know where to start. "What was an animal doing loose on the plane in the first place?"

"We have no idea."

"What about where this plane might've had any stopovers? I'm guessing a plane that size didn't fly all the way here from Europe, right?"

"Can't help you there, either."

Jason glanced at Regina to see if she might have any speculation; she shook her head. He'd have to ask Trey about it later.

Then Derek muttered, "Shit. Gotta go. Now." He gave one final, forceful point away from the plane. "Talk later." He turned his back to them and strode away. Jason held his hands up in mock frustration before turning back to Regina.

She offered him an uncertain smile. "When I commented that our interview had gotten more interesting, I had no idea."

"Yeah. This has turned into one fu— one messed up night."

Regina laughed, though it sounded forced. "It's all right, Jason. You don't have to keep editing yourself. You can swear in front of me. In case you haven't noticed, I'm a big girl."

He smiled at that, but it felt no more natural than her laugh; the information from Derek weighed on them both. In retrospect, having seen the huge animal with their own eyes, they shouldn't have been so surprised. But for Jason, he had pictured the flight crew, at least, having barricaded themselves inside the cockpit, away from the beast. Or maybe the plane had been partitioned in some way, separating passengers from cargo bay? But to hear that *everyone* on board was dead — *slaughtered* — including Hellqvist...

They stood in silence for several long minutes, facing toward one another, but each pair of eyes gazing at the plane. Gurneys were eventually wheeled out of it, each with its own sealed body bag, one of which had lumps that did not appear to form an actual, complete human body.

"All right, that's enough, I don't need to see any more," Regina announced. "I have enough to start a story, even if it's not the story we expected. I can write about the deceased passengers and crew and the 'alleged' animal attack for now. If my editor wants a followup, that's on her."

Jason said, "Oh." He could understand wanting to turn away from this ghastly scene, but he couldn't help feeling disappointed that she was leaving.

"Don't worry," she added, perhaps misinterpreting his

expression, "I promise not to quote your deputy friend."

"Oh, sure, yeah, no, no worries, I trust you, otherwise ... um, yeah." He was rambling, so he closed his mouth.

She offered him her hand. "It was very nice meeting you, Jason. Even if the ending is darker than hoped, I enjoyed our time together."

Jason shook her hand and, before he could lose his nerve, asked, "Would it be all right if I call you sometime?"

She replied with a question of her own. "To compare notes?" Jason noted the twinkle in her eyes.

"That, too, sure, but I was hoping for a little ... more."

Her eyebrows shot up, and he half-expected her to retort with something to make him squirm in embarrassment. Instead, she let him off the hook and pulled out her phone. "What's your number?"

He told her, her thumbs flew over her screen, and his phone gave another *ping!*

"And now you have mine," she told him. "I look forward to hearing from you."

With that, she turned and followed the runway back toward the airport terminal. Even though she was every bit as drenched as he was, she still managed to look as though she were walking the red carpet at some movie premiere. He hoped he would get a chance to see that walk a lot more.

Don't get ahead of yourself, man.

Jason wasn't sure how much longer he wanted to stick around, either. Between the sickening sight of the bodies – covered or not — being unloaded from the plane, the miserable weather, and Regina's departure, he had also taken in about as much misery as he could stomach.

Then he saw one last thing that made him stick around a few more minutes.

On the heels of the final gurney, a large crate was taken from the plane. No, not a crate, more like a big metal box, maybe a steamer trunk — and heavy, by the looks of it. Then the authorities stood around it and got into some sort of debate.

Jason crept forward, keeping his advance slow and discreet. The rainfall had finally eased back to a drizzle, but he still could not hear anything the group was saying. Were they discussing jurisdiction? Why was this item of specific interest? In fact, why bother with this big trunk at all at a time like this? Surely the victims were a much higher priority — not to mention chasing down the animal that caused all of this.

Then one of the figures, another one of the sheriff deputies, saw him and scowled. He pointed a finger at Jason and raised his voice. "Hey! Get your ass back—!"

"Don't worry, sir," assured a familiar voice. "I got him." Derek advanced upon him. "You," he ordered, "come with me, right now."

Jason raised his hands in surrender and allowed Derek to escort him back toward the terminal.

Once they were a safe distance away, Jason asked in a low voice, "Dude, what's with the metal box?"

Derek scoffed. "Jesus, Jason ..."

"Dude, come on."

Derek shook his head, and used the motion to glance back over his shoulder. Jason looked as well, seeing that the group surrounding the trunk were no longer watching his escorted departure.

"Christ," Derek muttered, "I can't imagine what you'd be like if you worked for a real news site."

"Ouch."

"Whatever." But he sighed and continued, "I'll make this quick. But don't forget that you *already* owe me."

"I know, I know."

"And if you fuckin' quote me—"

"No quotes. Now give."

"All I can tell you is, except for the victims, there's no real sign of the animal having been on board. No piss on the walls, no shit on the floor, nothing ... except for that steamer trunk. God only knows why, but it looks like the damned thing tried to claw it open. Tried, but failed."

"Why the hell would it do that?"

"Can't help you there."

"Well, what the hell's *in* the trunk? Raw sides of beef?"

"Don't know. The animal didn't get into it, but now the lock is so mangled, we'll have to break into it ourselves just to find out if there's anything significant inside."

They were close enough to the terminal that Derek halted but pointed for Jason to keep going.

"That's all I got for now. We're not sure which organization is taking the trunk, and half of 'em think we shouldn't bother with it until we hunt down the thing that caused all this mess."

"Can't disagree there. I had the same thought myself."

"Yeah, me, too. Now do us both a favor, please, and keep back. Better yet, go home. I'll make sure you Watchdogs know about any official statements, but don't hold your breath waiting. This whole thing is FUBAR."

"Thanks, man."

Derek grunted and hurried off to rejoin the circle, leaving Jason to ponder alone.

This is gonna be a hell of a write-up: Anthropologist with "big news" chooses wrong plane. Big animal sneaks aboard, kills everyone, tries to open a steamer trunk, then runs off into the cold, rainy night.

What the hell is this all about?

Dinner Invitation

Away from the distractions of the scene of the actual crime, Jason discovered he was trembling as he made his way back, alone, to the parking garage — but this time, it had nothing to do with the cold. His eyes darted toward every shadow, his stomach rolled at every sudden sound. He didn't know why ... except he did know why.

Yeah, sure, the beast that killed all those people may have run off in the opposite direction, but that didn't temper his imagination. And he had never been a fan of horror movies.

In stark contrast with his usual affinity for wildlife, in retrospect, that blurred glimpse of the animal left Jason unnerved. Dangerous or not, this was a novel sensation for him to feel toward anything within Mother Nature's domain. Was it because he knew what it had done to Doctor Hellqvist and the others? It must be, right? Except this was hardly the first time a wild animal had killed humans, and *that* knowledge didn't appall him.

Yeah, except dogs or wolves or whatever the hell that thing was don't usually stow away on a fuckin' airplane to do their hunting!

True enough.

Once he was in his old Camry and actually driving, his adrenal glands chilled out a little. Surreal though the beast had been, he could not imagine its being able to get at him inside his vehicle.

Hell, if ol' Cujo couldn't break in, no *dog could.*

His nerves ticked back up a little when he pulled into the blacktop driveway of his small apartment complex. He parked in his designated spot, and as he climbed the stairs leading to his second-floor unit, he told himself over and over that the danger was miles away, miles and miles behind him — which might have made him feel better, if he hadn't seen how damned fast the thing was.

As he slipped his key into the door, a raised, angry male voice from the bigger apartment complex across the street gave him pause.

Come on, man, not tonight, I'm not in the mood to listen to this shit tonight.

Thankfully, there was no followup this time — no yelling, no screaming, and no sounds of slapping, or worse. That, at least, was one less thing to fray his nerves.

Once inside his humble abode, he stripped off his soaked clothes and took a nice, steaming hot shower. As the water gradually chased away the chill and jitters, he precomposed his article in his head, making sure to incorporate "a source close to the investigation" to protect Derek's anonymity. For that matter, he could imply that his source was someone within the airport staff; that should provide enough possible suspects to lead anywhere productive.

Once actually sitting at the kitchenette table in front of his laptop, the words flowed. He wondered if he would ever find out what the late Doctor Hellqvist wanted to impart to the world, but there was no question that the story had ended up a perfect fit for the niche focus of *Watchdogs of the Weird & Unusual*.

As he fired off his article to Trey, his stomach growled. He glanced down at the laptop's clock and blinked in surprise; no wonder he was hungry! Between getting to the airport and back, and the time spent standing around in the rain trying to get information about Hellqvist's plane, the hours had slipped away from him. The problem was, he wasn't sure what he had to eat here, but his cash was also running a little too low to go out. He was about to take stock of his refrigerator's meager offerings when a message appeared from his *Watchdogs* interface.

TREY ROMERO: LOOKS SOLID @ FIRST GLANCE. GOOD JOB. WILL POST AFTER EDITING.

Jason read the acknowledgment, but also noticed the little pinwheel spinning, which meant another message was coming his way. Picking up the stack of mail he had brought in from his box earlier that day, he flipped through the inevitable bills until — to his continuing surprise — the next message came through sooner rather than later. He was still getting used to how much faster Trey's messages had become over the past several months; he assumed his boss was using some form of speech-to-text software these days.

TREY ROMERO: DID YOU GET ANY PICTURES OF THE ANIMAL? I DON'T SEE THEM IN YOUR ATTACHMENTS.

JASON PHOTOG: NO, I WAS CAUGHT COMPLETELY OFF GUARD, SORRY. AND ALL I WOULD'VE GOTTEN WAS A DARK BLUR ANYWAY.

TREY ROMERO: THIS ANIMAL IS THE REAL WATCHDOGS STORY. WHAT WAS IT? WHERE DID IT GO? WILL IT KILL AGAIN? I WANT YOU TO STAY ON THIS.

That was interesting. Not that this sort of request *never* happened, but the Watchdogs were such a loose-knit group, it was often more of a first-come, first-serve sort of thing. Jason could only recall once before when Trey had requested that he, specifically, pursue a particular story. But Trey was the boss, and as always, Jason could use the extra money.

JASON PHOTOG: THANKS, TREY! I'M ON IT.

The question was, where did he go from here? He could rely on Derek, for the most part — so long as "the next round" was always on Jason. But at the airport, it had looked like jurisdiction was up in the air. So who would carry the ball on this? In the long run, deaths by wild animal wouldn't be construed as "murder," so this could all end up with Animal Services or, more likely, Animal Control for Wildlife. He just hoped the authorities impressed upon whoever took the reins just how big, fast, and dangerous the beast from the airplane—

His phone rang. Not a text, an actual phone call, from a new contact: REGINA FROM AIRPORT

For a moment, he panicked; like many people in this day and age, Jason was accustomed to using his phone for pretty much everything *except* actual phone calls. She was calling him? So soon? Didn't women have the same three-day rule that men tried to follow?

Yeah, and look how that's worked out for you. When was the last time you got laid?

Or did that even apply in this case, since they hadn't exactly been on a "date"?

Answer the damned phone, idiot!

He thumbed ACCEPT, tried to say a greeting, had to clear his throat when it came out like someone choking, then finally managed to get out a respectable, "Hello?"

An almost girlish titter came through, followed by, "Are you sure you didn't mean to say ..." She pitched her voice lower and somehow made the next word sound goofy. " ... 'tall'?"

Grateful she couldn't see him blush, he replied, "Yeah, I won't be living that one down anytime soon, will I?"

"No, you will not." Her breath played over her phone's microphone, which Jason took as more delightful laughing at his expense. "Am I disturbing you?"

"No. No, not at all. No."

"All right."

He could feel his blush deepening. "I, uh ... I just sent my article to my boss, Trey. He says he likes it, and it should get posted soon. After, you know, editing and stuff."

"Mmm. I've turned in my piece as well. But I have no idea if they'll actually run mine."

"Oh, I'm sure they will. Between us, *Watchdogs* and the *Register* will be ahead of everyone else."

"Yes, but remember, I was sent to interview an anthropologist who was making vague claims of grandeur, and I only ended up with that assignment because of how far down the food chain I am. Now that it's turned into 'real' news, I'm half-expecting that it'll be handed off and rewritten by someone more seasoned."

"Oh. That sucks."

"Yes."

"Jeez. I feel kinda bad saying this now, but ... um ..."

She chuckled, and the sound tickled his ear. "It's all right. Go ahead. You've already won a major award for your article, is that it? The Pulitzer?"

It was his turn to chuckle. "Nothing like that. Trey wants me to follow up on the animal that killed those people. But until someone actually locates the thing, I'm at a bit of a loss as to where to go with it. I mean, I'm into nature and all, but I'm Egyptian, not Native American; it's not like I have any idea how to *track* the thing. You know?"

The pause that followed sent his heart racing. Shit, had he just put his foot in his mouth? Did she think less of him because he made, like, a racial-stereotyping joke? Should he apologize? Or was he overthinking the whole—

Then she spoke up as though there had been no pause at all. "The reason I called is, I wanted to ask if you'd like to join me for a late-night drink? Perhaps a bite to eat?"

Now his heart raced for a different reason, and all concerns about his dwindling bank account flew right out of his head. "Yeah, yes. Yes. It's funny, I was just ... yes, I'd like that."

No giggle this time, though her breath played over the line again. "Good. You've been here longer than I have. Where do you suggest we meet?"

* * *

Jason chose a sports bar that he knew would still be serving food this late. That, plus it was one of the few that did not blast the various TV screens loud enough to kill casual conversation.

He drove pretty fast and expected to beat Regina there, but to his surprise, when he pulled into the parking lot, she was already standing by the entrance, waiting for him. He hustled out of the car and made a point of holding the bar door open for her; her smile of appreciation carried a tinge of amusement, but he was happy to err on the side of gallantry.

Inside, the bar itself was bustling with patrons — their collective attention on the various TV screens showing highlights from different games, most of them basketball recaps — but plenty of tables were available. An older woman standing behind the bar, her weathered face lined with wrinkles and her hair tied back in a messy bun — she wasn't the bartender; he was serving someone at the opposite end — waved them in and called out, "Sit wherever you like. I'll just be a minute." The smell of beer and fried food wafted through the air, together creating a comfortable atmosphere.

Jason allowed Regina to choose their table, and they made small, meaningless chit-chat about the rain's coming and going; it felt a little forced and awkward, so he was relieved when the woman from the bar arrived to hand over the menus. Regina ordered a steak; Jason — who fully intended to pay for the meal — kept himself from cringing at the prices as he ordered one of the same. They each added a beer, and the server wandered off.

"So ..." he began, then floundered. What should he talk about?

"So," she returned. Which wasn't exactly helpful, and he suspected she knew it. One thing he was learning about her: Her sense of humor was a bit wicked.

He forged ahead. "Okay, both our articles have been turned in. If we can put aside our journalist hats for a second, I'd like to ask you something."

She smiled. "All right."

He leaned forward. "Did seeing that big animal, and then hearing what it did to all those people ... seriously, did that freak you out as much as it did me?"

Her mouth twitched, and for a moment, he thought she was going to smile or maybe even laugh again. Instead, she answered in a serious tone, "I ... I don't think I know how I feel about it yet. Between learning what we did from your deputy friend and turning in my article — and don't worry, I remembered to keep my 'source' strictly confidential — I forced myself to adhere to nothing more than the dry facts; I *willed* myself not to picture what it must have been like, to be on that airplane when the animal struck. Since then..." She drew a deep breath and held it a second before letting it out. "Honestly, I don't know. I don't know what to think, about any of it. To witness such an undeniably powerful creature, primal and dangerous, one so fast that it was little more than an indistinct streak of darkness ..." She hesitated again, before finally locking eyes with him and offering a crooked grin. "I suppose that is a rather long-winded way of saying, *yes*, it did freak me out. And I'd be lying if I denied that's why I reached out to you so soon and asked for this." She gestured to him, to herself, and to the sports bar around them.

Jason was both heartened to learn that she had sought him for comfort and a little disappointed that it wasn't for something more amorous.

Still, he supposed that one did not necessarily preclude the other.

Easy there, pump the brakes. She's still way outta your league.

The server returned with their beers, dropping them off with little more than a knowing smirk that just might have agreed with Jason's own out-of-his-league assessment. They sipped their drinks, the cold liquid offering a welcome respite from the heaviness of their conversation.

As he set his glass back down, he met Regina's gaze once more. "I'm glad you reached out."

Regina smiled, her green eyes flashing. "Thank you for agreeing."

He scoffed at that. "No problem at all, believe me. Without such a pleasant distraction, I could end up with some pretty intense nightmares tonight." He chuckled. "My mother always thought that was the end-all consequence of unprocessed fright: 'You'll have *nightmares*!' But she might've been right on this one."

"Do you dream often?" she asked.

"Oh, yeah, every night. You?"

She shook her head. "I never remember my dreams. Sometimes I'm envious of people who do. Other times — like tonight — I wonder if I'm better off."

"Nightmares or no nightmares, I'd never want to give up my nocturnal adventures."

She leaned forward, resting her chin against her palm. "What do you dream about?"

Jason took another swallow of his beer before sharing, "Lots of different things, but more often than not, I dream about animals. No surprise there, I guess — 'cause, you know, the photography thing?"

She offered a subtle nod but said nothing, waiting for more.

"A few nights ago, I dreamed I was wandering through this lush, misty jungle when I came across an ambush of Sumatran tigers. At first I thought they might attack me, but they just stared at me with curiosity in their intelligent golden eyes — that was the entire rest of the dream, just me and those tigers, staring at each other." He chuckled. "A week or so ago, I dreamed I was way up high in the mountains, surrounded by a herd of these massive woolly mammoths, their tusks gleaming ivory and their shaggy fur blowing in the crisp mountain air. I reached out to touch one, and it made this rumbling noise — like an elephant's, but deeper. That sound echoed throughout the valley." He sat there a moment, relishing the dream-memory in all its glory. "Can't remember your dreams at all, huh?"

She shook her head.

Recognizing that the topic had run its course, he switched subjects. "So, how'd you end up in journalism? Did you always want to be a reporter?"

Her lips curled into a slight smile. "No, not at all. Sort of like you and your photography, journalism has been something of an accidental career for me. I wanted to be an actress; I thought my height would make me stand out from the crowd, literally. But it didn't work out that way — I towered over too many of my potential male co-stars. There was model work, but those jobs were *fixated* on my height, fetishizing it. I did take a few jobs for the money, but those were a bit ..." She paused to take a sip of her beer. "Anyway, to make a long story short, I ended up writing a brief article for a Men's website, just a silly topic about a woman's viewpoint on being taller than most of the men she meets. And very much to my surprise, I loved writing it.

"So when my last modeling gig ended and I came back around to California, I had new priorities. I pulled a few strings, called in a few favors, and ended up as an intern at the *Register*. I quickly learned that it's hardly as glamorous as the movies depict — long hours, tedious research for the reporters over me, writing pieces that just get rewritten, stuck sitting in city council meetings and other monotonous assignments. But even then, I liked the challenge of tracking down leads and uncovering information, even if it all ended up in other people's stories."

Jason nodded his understanding, but was reluctant to point out that, with a small organization like the Watchdogs, he had managed to skip over most of what she described. The last thing he wanted to do was rub that in her beautiful face.

After another sip of her beer, she confessed, "When I was younger, I'd've never had the patience for this kind of work—"

At that moment, two young frat boy-types entered the sports bar; rather than opening a single door and walking through one at a time, they yanked open both doors to strut in together, and a robust, chilly breeze gusted past Jason and Regina's table.

Jason made a show of shivering and said, "Damn. I know it doesn't bother you, but I can't wait until the classic California weather makes a comeback. I hate the cold."

She laughed her almost-giggle. "Your skin really has thinned since you left New Jersey."

"It really has. But that was so long ago, I guess I shouldn't be..." He blinked. "How'd you know I'm originally from Jersey?"

This prompted another chuckle from Regina. "You told me."

"I did?"

"Yes, when you told me about the red-tailed hawk that landed in your backyard. Your family had just moved to California from New Jersey."

"Right!" He shook his head, embarrassed that he had forgotten. "Right, right. Sorry."

"That's all right. Quite a *lot* has happened since that conversation."

He guffawed. "Man, that's true. It feels like that conversation was days ago, not hours."

Her expression grew somber, and she appeared to repress a shudder. "It does, doesn't it?"

As if on cue to break the heavier mood, their steaks arrived. At first, Jason tried not to tear into his too aggressively, but Regina was not so reluctant, digging into hers with gusto, demonstrating that she was every bit as hungry as he was. Pleased at the implied permission to behave a little like a pig himself, he chowed down.

When they each had little more than bones left, Jason sat back and finished off the rest of his beer. He considered ordering another, as she was still sipping hers, but their server was too busy at the bar for him to get her attention just yet. As the silence dragged on, he searched for something else to say — this awkward lull was the part of any first date (if that's even what this was?) that he hated the most.

Finally, he came up with, “What do you think might be up with that steamer trunk?”

“Hmm?”

“The steel trunk from Doctor Hellqvist’s plane? Any thoughts on that?”

She stared at him a moment, then shook her head. “I’m sorry, I don’t know what you mean.”

Then Jason all but slapped his forehead. “That’s right! You’d already left before they brought it out. Listen to this ...” He described what he had seen of the large steamer trunk and the authorities surrounding it on the tarmac. “... and to top it all off, Derek said that it looked like the animal from the plane tried to get *into* it.”

“Why would it do that? It’s an animal.”

“No idea. But according to Derek, it clawed the hell out of it, mangled the lock to the point that they — the investigators, I mean — will have to break into it to inspect the contents.”

“Nothing about it on the plane’s manifest?”

“Not that Derek mentioned.”

Regina mulled this over, then shrugged. “It doesn’t make any sense that an animal would care about cargo. Maybe, after killing all those poor people, it was so full of manic energy that it just lashed out at random?”

“Huh.” He couldn’t disregard that logic — why *would* a wild animal give a shit about the cargo on the plane? “But aren’t you curious now? About what might be in the trunk?”

She shrugged again. “Not really, not unless the authorities get it open and find something of interest inside. For now, we have no idea if that trunk is even related to Doctor Hellqvist or our original story. It could be nothing more than a red herring.”

“Huh,” he said again. She made good points — maybe the trunk was just a wild goose chase.

Then Regina leaned forward, her elbows on the table and her eyes sparkling. “Jason, I find your voracious curiosity endearing. It makes me wonder what other mysteries you might unveil, if you were to put your mind to it.”

Jason's pulse quickened at her sudden intensity; an energy swelled between them that hadn't been present a minute ago. He swallowed and tried to sound cool and aloof. "Oh yeah? Like what, exactly?"

Regina cocked her head to one side, that same enigmatic smile from the airport gracing her lips. "Well," she responded, her voice lower in both volume and pitch, "take *me* for example. *I'm* a bit of a mystery, aren't I? A strange woman shows up at the airport alone, a woman who just happens to be a journalist, like you, there to interview the very same anthropologist as you, who then invites you to dinner after the astonishing event we witnessed?" She arched an eyebrow. "I'm sure a clever man could unravel a few of my secrets."

Dear God, where did this *come from? Is this really happening? To* me*?*

She reached out, placing her hand on Jason's arm, and her voice dropped lower still. "You know ... in spite of the unsettling developments earlier ... I've really enjoyed our time together tonight — at the airport, and here. It's been wonderful getting to know you better."

Jason felt a spark of electricity from her touch. "I've loved spending time with you, too."

Regina's smile broadened, revealing a row of perfectly straight teeth. Her unblinking gaze locked onto his, ensnaring him, holding him captive in an exciting trap from which he could not escape even if he wanted — which he most decidedly did not.

Do I still have that condom in my wallet? Fuck, how old *is it? And where do we go? Her place or mine? No, no, my place is garbage, I can't take her there! It'll have to be—*

And then, just like that, the spell broke. Regina sat back, brought her hands together in a soft, feminine clap, and said, "It's getting late. After our remarkable evening, I'm sure you agree, Jason."

Jason felt as though he'd missed an entire reel in a movie. "Um? Uh, I, uh—"

But Regina had already turned in her chair and signaled their server with a classic "check, please" hand gesture. "I would like to pay for dinner. After all, I was the one who asked you to join me."

He struggled to regain his composure. "No, no, you don't— I,

I got it."

"Don't be silly. That's not necessary. And it's a bit sexist." She gave him a "dirty" look, but the glisten in her eyes told him she was just kidding. Again.

Hell, when isn't *she kidding? About anything? Fuck.* He felt that initial urge again, from back at the airport, to look around and see if this was being recorded at his expense.

In the end, they agreed to split the check. The server brought it over and Regina laid down crisp bills, but Jason was forced to use a credit card, and crossed his mental fingers that it wouldn't come back Declined. Fortunately, it did not.

She led the way through the exit, but then stopped under the awning. The rain was back, though it was again little more than a drizzle. They just stood there together for a beat, in silence. Jason sensed she was waiting for him to do or say something, but at this point, he had no idea where to go with this. Part of it was his wounded male ego, but even trying to be objective about it all, her behavior seemed strange to him.

Finally, she turned to face him full-on. "I do hope to see you again, Jason. Soon."

Before Jason could react to that one way or the other, Regina stepped forward, bent over, and kissed him. It wasn't a peck, either; it was warm and passionate — no tongue, but close enough. In spite of the bizarre back and forth inside the sports bar giving him emotional whiplash, he could not help but respond. He raised his arms to hold her, but hers were already wrapped around him, so he could only bend them from the elbow—

She twisted her head the other direction, and bit his bottom lip. Hard. Hard enough to draw blood.

Grunting, his impulse was to jerk away from the pain, but her hand clamped onto the back of his head and held him still as she kept kissing him. He was caught between pain and pleasure, and didn't know what to do.

After what felt like an eternity — good and bad — she released him and stepped away. All he could do was stare at her in bafflement. As with so many other things, this seemed to amuse her; she laughed, winked, and strode out into the rainy night. She didn't even go to a car, just traipsed out along the street and disappeared, all while he stood and gaped like an idiot at her retreating form.

He brought his hand up to his wounded lip, and flinched.

The fuck was that*?*

The door behind him opened, and when no one emerged, he looked over.

One of the frat boys from before gawked at him from the doorway, his eyes awash with admiration and awe. He glanced the way Regina had departed, then ogled back at Jason once more. “Dude,” he eventually said, “you are *so* fuckin’ lucky!”

Was he lucky, though? He wasn’t sure.

PRIMAL EMOTIONS

Jason drove home in a daze. By the time he got back to his apartment complex, his lip had stopped bleeding, but it continued to throb. Once parked, he shut off his engine and just sat there, taking a minute to collect himself.

The more he thought about it, the past several hours took on a surreal, almost hallucinatory quality. Driving to the airport earlier that evening? Normal. Hell, taking a nice, hot shower earlier? Normal, for the most part.

But meeting Regina, sneaking out onto the tarmac, standing around in the rain as a beast from hell burst from the plane, finding out Hellqvist (and everyone else onboard) was dead ... hell, even writing about all that now felt detached, like he had *read* about it rather than producing the work himself.

And the cherry on top: Regina at the sports bar.

Flirting, but not really flirting. Giving him the fuck-me eyes, then acting like she had somewhere else far more important to be. Kissing him — and biting the hell out of his lip — then almost literally disappearing into the night. It felt as though she were both inviting and rejecting him at the same time.

Jason did not consider himself "boring" exactly, but this was not his life. These sorts of things didn't happen, not to a guy like him. He reported about things that were weird and unusual, he didn't *live* them, goddamn it!

His throbbing lip argued otherwise.

He should get some sleep. In the morning, he would contact Derek again, see if he could beg any more details about the animal from the plane — massive dog, big wolf, long-limbed bear, *whatever* the hell it had been — and go from there.

His thoughts flitted to that steamer trunk again, but with less intrigue. Whether she was crazy or something else, Regina might have been right about its being nothing more than a "red herring," a distraction. Hell, if he were going to do any side research, maybe he should look into Regina herself.

It dawned on him that he did not know her last name. She had only offered her first name at the airport, and he never thought to examine her PRESS pass; he recalled her photo on it, nothing more.

He opened his car door and, as he turned to get out, he was treated to a charming, echoing, "Fuckin' *bitch*!" from across the street.

Jason deflated, his stomach churning in weary disgust as he sank back into his seat and almost closed the door behind him.

Something clattered in that same apartment. Had she thrown something at him? He might've been the thrower, but he was usually more of a—

There it was. A slap. No cry afterward, no more cursing. Just the hollow, too-loud *pop!* of hand against flesh.

He reached for his phone. Should he call the cops, again?

Another clatter, something else thrown. No slap in response this time, just silence.

Jason finally rose from his car, closed the door, and stood for a moment in the cold drizzle. If he wasn't going to call the cops, then he should probably just head upstairs and try to shut it out. But he felt an impulse — and not for the first time — to go over there and *do* something about it ... but what? What could he do? An out-of-shape photographer-turned-journalist? He had seen the guy before, he knew how big he was — an ugly, bitter white man who wanted so badly to be a member of the Latino gang community and, in that quest, had put on the muscle he thought might get him an audition in spite of his pale skin.

If Jason ever got mouthy with him, he would snap Jason in half without breaking a sweat.

So Jason turned his back, heading for the stairs and wondering when he had turned into such a skittish wimp.

He tried to tell himself that he wasn't a "wimp," he was smart, smart enough to recognize his limitations. But just because he couldn't offer direct interference, that didn't mean he would do nothing at all. He decided that, as soon as he got into his apartment, he *would* call the police after all — for the third time? No, the fourth — and report the domestic disturbance. Yes, she would probably deny everything and decline to press charges, just like all the other times, but at least Jason would know that—

Jason had just gripped the staircase rail and placed his foot on the first step when he halted, a chill running down his spine.

He was being watched.

Not normally given to feelings of a superstitious, "psychic" nature (again, weird and unusual were for reporting, not living), he was struck by the strength, the *certainty* of the belief. The sensation of eyes on him was so vivid, it was almost physical.

Heart pounding, hairs rising on the back of his neck, he kept his hand on the rail and, striving to appear casual, rotated back toward his car. *I'm worried I'm forgetting something,* he broadcast to the world. *I'm not suspicious of anything.*

The small complex's parking area wasn't well lit, but nor was it pitch dark. The streetlight a short way to the west, past the sizeable hedge that served as a "wall" to the property line, cast some light here, and the stretches of walkway between each unit boasted permanent light fixtures that automatically turned on with each sundown. So if anyone were sneaking up on him, Jason should be able to spot them ...

Nothing. Yet the feeling persisted.

He was tempted to call out, but if someone were creeping around, it wasn't as though they would respond. So what should he do? Stand here, getting wet while he cast about for what might be nothing more than his imagination? Or turn his back to mount the stairs and risk ... what? What was it he was really sensing here? It was ...

Menace. He felt menace. Part of him felt silly just thinking that, but his gut wasn't interested in skepticism on the subject.

Then another thought occurred to him, and it chilled him far more than the drizzle: The animal from the plane. Having dinner with, and getting bitten by, Regina had driven his earlier paranoia to the sidelines, but it returned now in abundance. Yes, the airport was miles away, and yes, the creature had run off in a different direction ... but it had been so damned *fast*!

He jolted when he caught movement in the corner of his eyes. There! Against the hedge, near the street: A shape, lurking within the shadows cast by the streetlight, too deep to be illuminated by the walkway lights ...

Jesus Christ, man, he thought with disgust, *you are* literally *jumping at shadows now!*

Okay, fine, assume it wasn't the animal from the airport — even though, in the murk, it appeared big enough. If not, then what was it? And what about his absolute conviction that he was being watched?

Then something else caught his attention, something different.

Jason's gaze shifted to the apartments across the street. There, up on the walkway of the second level, a small flame — a lighter — all the brighter for the complex's own gloom. Someone was lighting a cigarette.

Not just "someone." The cigarette ablaze, the smoker stepped forward into better visibility, and Jason saw that it was the very asshole who had been knocking around his girlfriend just minutes ago. Apparently taking a break from domestic violence, he sucked down a deep drag, leaned forward onto the metal railing, and stared down and across at Jason.

Again, Jason's peripheral vision caught movement, and he snapped his eyes back to the hedge wall.

The shadow was gone.

He looked back and forth, all along the hedge, around the other parked cars, and even cast a quick glance over his shoulder up the stairs.

Nothing. Whatever it had been, he couldn't find it now.

The cherry of the asshole's cigarette glowed again. Though Jason couldn't be sure, he thought he saw said asshole chuckling at his behavior. But that was probably his own embarrassment at play.

Had the shadow been there at all? Or was it just the asshole neighbor who triggered the certitude that he was being watched? Was that all it was?

His left brain latched onto that explanation with full

acceptance. His right brain remained skeptical.

Dude, that old left brain / right brain nonsense is just a myth, his left brain reminded him.

Oh, what do you *know?* grumbled his right brain.

Another glow from the asshole's cigarette, the tiny red-orange dot taunting him from across the street. Sir Asshole sure seemed to find Jason fascinating tonight.

His cheeks burning, Jason hurried up the stairs toward his apartment.

* * *

After the harrowing evening and night he had endured, Jason didn't take long to shrug out of his damp clothes and collapse onto his single bed. He welcomed the blissful darkness that enveloped him, taking him away from his troubles. And in short order, as he was accustomed, he began to dream ...

He was wandering — nude, funny enough; that was rare — through a dense, verdant forest; it reminded him, in many ways, of the jungle where he had encountered the Sumatran tigers. The setting sunlight filtered through the canopy overhead, dappling the ground in a chaotic yet pleasing pattern. He heard evening birds calling and the scurrying of small animals in the underbrush. It was all so peaceful, at first.

But as he strode through the forest, the sounds changed. The avian chirrups and hoots grew louder, restless, almost raucous. Other, stranger cries echoed through the trees. As he had experienced in the parking area of his apartment complex, he felt eyes studying him, assessing him, from the deepening shadows. And all that scurrying sounded brash now, confident, things crashing without a care through the undergrowth.

Jason spied what might be a clearing and headed toward it. He wanted to reach some open space before—

A pack of timber wolves emerged from the trees ahead of him, regarding him with radiant, amber eyes.

Jason froze.

The largest wolf, its deep black fur bristling, crept toward him, its teeth bared, while the other wolves fanned out.

Jason's heart pounded. He spun around, seeking an escape route but finding none; just like that, they had surrounded him.

The black wolf stalked ever closer, the coarse sound of its hot breath mingling with Jason's panicked gasps. Between its ebony fur and its size, it reminded Jason of the animal from the airport.

That beast was a wolf, too, *a part of him realized with new certainty*. It wasn't a big dog or a small bear, it was a hulking, black wolf. How could I've ever thought otherwise?

But he couldn't worry about that wolf right now. This *wolf was nearing striking distance.*

Jason's pulse thundered in his ears. What should he do? What should he do, *damn it?!*

The black wolf lunged.

Jason dodged its snapping jaws by a matter of inches, and he rushed past the animal, toward the gap it had created behind it, stumbling over knotted roots as he sought to flee the encircling pack.

They were wolves; they could have brought him down in seconds. Yet they allowed him to run. Why?

Thorns tore at his naked skin as he crashed without direction through the underbrush. The timber wolves began baying, and the sound came from all sides at once, reverberating between the dark trees with a strange, otherworldly quality.

Jason's lungs burned and his legs ached as he scrambled through the frightening cacophony.

Then the sun dropped all the way below the horizon, engulfing him in dreary gloom. Still he ran, ignoring the stitch in his side and the hot blood trickling down his arms and legs. The howls and snarls of the wolves were everywhere—

The ground fell away beneath him. He tumbled down a steep slope, the soil soft but for the occasional vegetation. The air rushed past him and the world spun in a blur, until he finally rolled to a stop. Struggling against dizziness and disorientation, he failed twice before he succeeded in regaining his feet. The trees had opened overhead, giving him a little more dusky light by which to see.

Then he saw why the trees had parted: He had fallen into a deep gully. The wolf pack ringed the edges, snarling down at him and blocking any chance of escape along the precipitous walls.

He was trapped.

A shuffling, scraping pattern sounded from behind him. He whirled to find the black wolf descending into the gully, its teeth bared in a mocking rictus of a smile.

Mocking him.

And much to his surprise, as the wolf reached level ground and prowled toward him, Jason's fear transformed into indignant fury. A primal rage, unlike anything he had ever felt, welled up within him. His hands clenched into fists, and a snarl — every bit as vicious as those coming from the wolves — rose from the back of his throat.

The black wolf hesitated, confusion entering its glistening eyes; the wolves above exchanged uneasy glances in an almost human fashion.

Good.

Jason threw back his head and howled; it resounded through the gully, raw and wild. When he looked up at the surrounding wolves again, it was as though his senses had sharpened; he felt he could see every hair on their bristling coats, could smell their musky scents. He roared at them, spreading his arms wide in defiance.

Then, whirling about before it could react, he sprang at the black wolf.

His muscles rippled as the two collided; they crashed to the gully floor in a mad tangle of snapping jaws and beating fists. When the wolf was about to twist free, Jason raked his fingernails across the animal's face and into its left eye, eliciting a yipe of pain.

During the struggle, a few of the pack had descended the slopes. These wolves moved in, nipping at Jason's legs, trying to assist their leader. Jason kicked out, scattering them with power that he had never before possessed but did not bother to question.

But the black wolf was relentless, clawing and biting in a frenzied counter-attack.

Jason wrestled the thrashing beast, using his newfound strength to pin it to the ground. With a sharp, guttural bark, he clamped his powerful hands around the wolf's neck in a crushing vice grip. The wolf's struggles grew weaker as his fingers bore deeper, cutting off its air.

With a mighty heave, he wrenched the wolf's head up and to the side, exposing its throat. His jaws opened wide and clamped down, hot blood gushing through its thick fur and into his mouth.

The wolf emitted one final, pitiful squeal of pain and fear, and then, with a sickening crunch!, *its throat collapsed.*

The black wolf fell limp, dead.

Jason rose to his feet, gore dripping from his maw, the wolf's body dangling from his arms. The pack gaped at him, their bright eyes filled with anxiety rather than bloodlust.

Heaving the body up and holding it over his head, its blood raining down upon him, Jason roared louder than ever, an ear-splitting thunder that reverberated throughout the gully and into the forest.

*Throwing the remains to one side, he took the whole pack in with one broad gesture and declared, "*Naetshai nitou asou ai!*"*

The timber wolves all lowered their heads in submission ...

... and Jason's eyes opened.

He sat up in bed, blinking and staring at nothing. The glow from the closed window blinds told him it was nearing dawn and allowed him to see his drab bedroom around him, but he didn't care about any of that. He was thinking about the forest, his flight from the pack, his victorious battle, and his words to the surviving timber wolves.

" 'Naetshai nitou asou ai,' " he whispered.

What the hell did *that* mean? He had no idea.

Fumbling for his phone on the nightstand, he thumbed around the screen until he located his Google Translate app. He tried repeating these words into the microphone, but the results were dubious. The app thought that the words *might* come from Greek, but it offered no real suggestions as to their meaning — its "translation" into English was just a barely different spelling pronounced phonetically like an American might say it.

Coupled with his fighting a wolf — and winning, in nasty fashion — it was one of the strangest dreams Jason had ever experienced.

At least my lip's stopped hurting.

Harsh Discovery

Jason eventually fell back asleep, and this time his slumber was dreamless. By the time he awoke again past Noon — unusual for him, to sleep so late — he had half-forgotten the details of the dream with the wolves and his triumphant declaration to them; for that matter, he had half-forgotten the strange words themselves. And what difference did it make, really? How significant could they be, a bizarre phrase that his psyche had probably regurgitated from some long-forgotten movie or whatever?

Hell, "night-sigh-whatever it was" probably had no more real-world significance than did "Klaatu barada nikto."

Once he was up and had eaten a breakfast of crispy bacon and a glass of orange juice, he moved to his laptop. It was time to get to work, following up on the huge black wolf — he no longer had any doubt that's what it was; that much of his dream still lingered. Given the circumstances, he fully expected to find an existing story about the wolf's capture, at which point he could compose an exclusive followup for the Watchdogs, highlighting his "I was there from the beginning" angle. Said research would also provide a distraction from dwelling over his weird "date" with Regina.

Nice idea, except Jason spent the next hour scouring the Internet for any mention of the wolf from the plane, but found nothing. No local news reports of surprise wolf sightings, no warnings from the police or wildlife authorities, not even any social media posts on the subject; he even checked out a few nature forums, and when he got really desperate, a cryptozoology site. As far as his search could determine, only his own story for *Watchdogs of the Weird & Unusual* reported on the animal at all — which, given his uncertainty at the time he wrote it, Jason had described only as a "large, fast, black-furred mammal."

He did locate several stories about the plane's alleged landing on autopilot and about purported casualties found aboard, but that was it.

Except for his *Watchdogs* story, it was as though the wolf had never existed.

Determined, he expanded his search, looking for any recent "unusual" animal sightings in the area — after all, not everyone would have reached his eventual conclusion that it was, in fact, a huge wolf.

Nothing.

Perplexed, Jason sat back in his chair, running both hands through his hair. How could an animal of that size escape detection in such a populated area? Even if it avoided human contact, wouldn't something like massive paw prints running through someone's backyard attract attention? Wouldn't its scent send dogs into a howling frenzy throughout the metro area? It didn't make sense.

If he were more "conspiracy"-minded, he would leap to the whole thing being a coverup, but a more level-headed explanation was that the authorities were simply trying to avoid a panic. He would be willing to bet that an atypically large number of Animal Control employees were making the rounds today.

Then something else struck him: If only his story for *Watchdogs* reported on the animal, what happened to Regina's story for the *Register*? Yes, she had told him she expected it to be "handed off and rewritten" by a senior reporter, but would they have completely excised all references to a wild animal aboard the plane?

Retracing his digital steps, he targeted the *Register*. Sure enough, their coverage echoed what he had already discovered overall — they reported about the plane's landing and speculated on "unconfirmed casualties" aboard. Nothing more. And Regina's name had, in fact, been removed from the byline.

Man, that's shitty. Thank God Trey never does anything like that.

Without thinking, Jason reached for his phone with the intention of contacting Regina, to express his sympathy, but then he hesitated. First, she had already told him that she was probably off the story; should he risk making her feel worse about that? Second ... well, his tongue could still feel the raised area where she had bitten his bottom lip; between that and her bewildering behavior, he had not yet decided if he wanted any further contact with her.

After several long seconds of internal debate, he left his phone where it lay.

Having struck such a sturdy brick wall in his search for the wolf, Jason decided to switch focus. If he couldn't learn anything new about the animal itself, what about its victims on the plane?

Over his next hour of searching, he made greater headway. By working backwards from the expected "names withheld pending notification of next-of-kin" toward chartering records and flight plans, he — eventually and indirectly — learned the names of the passengers. Several of them had been traveling with Doctor Hellqvist; he had to assume they were part of her team. He took copious notes, in case Trey changed his mind and asked him for a non-wolf-centric followup.

His greatest accomplishment during this second wave of searching came from finding the manifest report: If he was correct about some of the jargon and abbreviations, he concluded that the steamer trunk he had seen, the one the wolf attempted to claw open, *had* been registered to Doctor Hellqvist. But its exact contents were not listed; Hellqvist may have greased some palms to pull that off.

Again Jason sat back in his chair, summarizing in a mutter, "Doctor Hellqvist was my original story. Hellqvist was killed by a freakin' *wolf* that somehow got onto the plane. Same big-ass wolf tried, for some reason, to open a steamer trunk. Trunk belonged to Hellqvist."

He rubbed his eyes and sighed, trying to connect the dots.

Yeah, there's a thread here. For the life of me, I can't figure what *the thread is all about, but it's there.*

Phone back in hand, he texted a few of his police contacts, asking for any sort of off-the-record updates; none of them were as consistent or as reliable as Derek, but he was trying not to go back to that particular well again so soon. Unfortunately, even after he had taken a break to eat something for lunch and play some Solitaire on his laptop, he had not heard back from any of them except one, and that had been little more than the hemming-and-hawing equivalent of "No comment."

He waited a bit longer, holding out as best he could, but eventually he caved and reached out to Derek after all.

HEY! he texted. YOU AVAILABLE TO CHAT?

He sat back to wait again, but before too much time passed, he got a response: DEPENDS. YOU READY TO FINALLY MEET ME FOR TOP-SHELF DRINK(S) YOU OWE ME?

Jason thought about his wallet and his bank account, and replied: AFTER MY NEXT PAYCHECK, I PROMISE!

Derek took all of three seconds to send back a middle finger emoji.

Jason: COME ON, MAN. HOW LONG HAVE WE KNOWN EACH OTHER AT THIS POINT? YOU KNOW I'M GOOD FOR IT, EVENTUALLY.

Derek: YEAH, EVENTUALLY! Before Jason could compose an appropriate comeback to that, Derek followed up with: *SIGH* WHAT DO YOU WANT? NO, LET ME GUESS, ABOUT THE AIRPORT, RIGHT?

Jason: YOU KNOW ME SO WELL.

Derek replied to that with an eye-roll emoji, but Jason just waited.

Derek: NO 20 QUESTIONS, THIS IS ALL I GOT. ANIMAL (SOMEONE UP THE CHAIN DECIDED IT'S PROBABLY A BIG WOLF) STILL ON THE LOOSE. KEEPING QUIET = NO PANIC. (GOOD THING YOUR LITTLE WEBSITE IS SO LITTLE!) UPPER MANAGEMENT SHITTING BRICKS TO CATCH IT BEFORE IT EATS SOMEONE ELSE. SO FAR NO LUCK. LIKE THE DAMNED THING WENT POOF!

After patting himself on the back for his own conclusions proven correct — and ignoring Derek's "little" slight against *Watchdogs* — Jason replied: YEAH, I THOUGHT ANIMAL "RADIO SILENCE" WAS TO STOP PANIC. I DO HAVE ANOTHER QUESTION, THOUGH.

That earned him three eye-roll emojis in a row, but Jason pressed on.

Jason: DID THEY EVER MANAGE TO GET THAT STEAMER TRUNK OPEN?

Derek: SERIOUSLY? THAT ANIMAL/WOLF/WHATEVER IS LOOSE SOMEWHERE IN THE METRO AREA, AND YOU THINK BOSSES ARE WORRIED ABOUT SOME BIG METAL BOX? IT IS SO NOT A PRIORITY RIGHT NOW! NOT TO THEM, ANYWAY.

Jason: HEY, JUST ASKING! SO WHERE IS THE TRUNK NOW? AND WHAT DO YOU MEAN, "NOT TO THEM, ANYWAY"?

Derek: IT'S TECHNICALLY STILL PART OF THE CHAIN OF EVIDENCE, AT LEAST UNTIL THEY FIGURE OUT WHAT REALLY HAPPENED ON THAT F#CKING PLANE. SO THEY'RE COVERING THEIR @$$E$ AND LOCKED IT AWAY JUST IN CASE IT DOES TURN OUT TO BE SOMEHOW IMPORTANT.

Jason: SO WHERE IS IT?

Derek: SECURE PROPERTY WAREHOUSE, TEMPORARY HOLDING FOR THE EVIDENCE AND PROPERTY MANAGEMENT DIVISION. AND IN CASE YOU DON'T KNOW WHAT ALL THOSE CAPITAL LETTERS MEAN, DO NOT EVEN THINK ABOUT ASKING TO SEE IT. NO WAY I COULD GET YOU IN THERE, EVEN IF I WANTED TO. WHICH I DON'T.

Jason: *SIGH* UNDERSTOOD.

Derek: SERIOUSLY, DUDE, IT'S JUST A BIG METAL BOX. WHO KNOWS WHY THE ANIMAL CLAWED IT UP? GO REPORT ON SOMETHING ELSE.

Jason sent a final "THANK YOU" text, but Derek did not respond or acknowledge; it looked like they were done for now.

Setting his phone down, he stood and stretched. A glance at the clock hammered home the hours of the day having slipped through his fingers; he supposed that was what he deserved for sleeping in so late. Under normal circumstances, he might have fired off a message to Trey, updating him on his progress — but what progress, really? So far all he had been able to establish was that the wolf had gone "poof," as Derek put it, and his roundabout approach regarding the steamer trunk had run straight into a brick wall, courtesy of the Evidence and Property Management Division.

Maybe he should fly the coop for a bit, step out, get a real bite to eat somewhere ... or, considering his financial status, maybe just take a nice relaxing walk. Sure, why not?

The instant he opened his apartment door, the unseasonably cool weather smacked him in the face to remind him of its presence. He stood in his doorway, debating; in the end, he decided that, since the rain had stopped sometime overnight — the pavement outside no longer looked damp — the chill wasn't all that bad. Maybe "sunny California" was returning to form, finally? Zipping up his jacket, he locked up behind himself and headed for the staircase.

Once he reached the parking area's driveway and turned left on a whim, he decided that the cool, early-evening air really was fine once his blood got pumping. He spared a glance toward the apartment complex across the street, but there were no domestic disturbances in evidence; the only across-the-street neighbors he could see were some kids trying to coax a western gray squirrel out of a tree. He was tempted to call over that they would have better luck with fruits or nuts over the bologna they were offering, but opted to just let them have their fun; they didn't need some random grownup poking his nose into their business.

Then again, there is a gigantic black wolf on the loose ...

While that specific danger seemed unlikely to strike right here and now, the thought brought him back around to his flailing research. That, and to Regina. Without the distraction of diving through Google and nagging his sources (it sucked that only Derek had gotten back to him with anything even close to an update), he was no longer able to force her out of his mind.

Pausing at the next intersection, he pressed the button for the crosswalk and shifted his weight from foot to foot as he waited. The rumble of passing vehicles filled his ears, each one a blur of color, noise, and exhaust fumes rushing by as he thought about her. Based on his personal life experience up to this point, the whole scenario boggled his mind. On the surface, it was the stuff of sexual fantasy, something that — in the long gone days of yore — would have been ripe for *Penthouse Letters*: A super-tall, gorgeous woman strikes up a conversation at the airport, turns out to be in the same profession, is by his side to experience something extraordinary out on the tarmac, then calls and asks him to join her for dinner — and what a dinner it had been. Casual, then over-the-top flirting, then back to casual. Kissing him — with aggressive teeth, no less — and then calling it a night.

Yeah, at this point, his sex drive opted to take a backseat to caution. They say every man yearns to "stick his dick in crazy" at least once, but as far as Jason was concerned, "they" did not always know what the hell they were talking about.

The light changed, and Jason crossed the street on autopilot, enjoying the feeling of just wandering in both body and mind. His complex was in a far too suburban area to offer any view to speak of, unless he counted the odd Subway, Valvoline, or Starbucks; for that kind of walk, he would have to drive down to the beach, or maybe to one of the nature trails.

Ah, now *that* was where he would really like to be taking a stroll — if he hadn't gotten such a late start today, and if the weather hadn't been lousy of late. Instead of ambling along with his phone in pocket, he could be hiking along with camera in hand. Maybe he would come across a southern mule deer, or a cute little Virginia opossum carrying her young, or if he were feeling adventurous, a bobcat or coyote or ...

I need to get back to that. That's *how I wish I could make my living, damn it. If only it paid better; not that my* Watchdogs *stories are overflowing my pockets with cash of late. To just lose myself in nature with the coyotes or the mountain lions ...*

Or large, black wolves? prompted some smartass portion of his brain.

Yeah! he countered his dick-side. *At least I would know where I stand with a wolf. The same doesn't go for statuesque reporters with red hair and a tendency to play games. So fuck off.*

"Great," he mumbled under his breath as he passed by a department store parking lot. "Now I'm telling myself to fuck off. This walk isn't turning out as relaxing as I'd hoped."

Debating whether or not to just turn around and head back home, he halted his stride long enough to check out some European starlings that had made their nest atop one of the parking lot lights. He wondered how the local wildlife at large was reacting to the sudden presence of a large wolf in their midst. Sure, the wolf was evading *human* detection so far, but there was no way such a beast could hide from other animals.

A droplet of rain struck his upturned forehead, and that settled that. Turning on his heel, he headed back toward his complex.

So much for his nice relaxing walk. Besides, he was getting hungry again.

* * *

While the microwave hummed and whirred, transforming his frozen Stouffer's Salisbury Steak into something hot and edible, Jason opened his laptop to find a message from Trey.

TREY ROMERO: HEY, JASON. CHECKING ON YOUR PROGRESS WITH THE ANIMAL FROM THE AIRPORT. ANY UPDATES ON YOUR END? THE WATCHDOGS SEEM TO BE STANDING ALONE WITH OUR REPORTING OF IT.

JASON PHOTOG: NOT MUCH, SORRY. MOSTLY DEAD-ENDS, BUT A RELIABLE SOURCE TELLS ME THE LACK OF GENERAL INFO IS TO AVOID PANIC. BTW, THEY ARE NOW THINKING IT WAS A WOLF. AND I AGREE.

There was a pause, enough for Jason to retrieve his steaming meal.

TREY ROMERO: YOU DIDN'T CALL IT A WOLF IN YOUR STORY.

JASON PHOTOG: YEAH, SORRY, WHEN IT ALL HAPPENED LAST NIGHT, NO ONE KNEW WHAT IT WAS. WE JUST SAW A BIG, BLACK, FURRY BLUR, WHICH IS WHAT I THEN DESCRIBED IN MY PIECE.

Jason hesitated before typing the next bit. But then, if Trey of the Watchdogs wasn't open-minded, who was?

JASON PHOTOG: BUT LAST NIGHT I HAD A DREAM. I WON'T GO INTO ALL THE WEIRD DETAILS, BUT MY SUBCONSCIOUS MIND DECIDED THAT IT WAS LIKELY A WOLF. AND, LIKE I SAID, THE AUTHORITIES (SOME OF THEM, AT LEAST) SEEM TO AGREE. CANNOT BE 100% ON THIS UNTIL THEY CATCH IT, OF COURSE, BUT IT SOMEHOW FEELS RIGHT.

This bit was followed by another pause on Trey's end, so Jason dug into his food while he waited.

TREY ROMERO: IF YOU BELIEVE IT WAS A WOLF, I'LL TRUST

YOUR INSTINCTS. IF IT PROVES TO BE SOMETHING ELSE, WE'LL RUN A CORRECTION WITH ANY FOLLOWUP STORY. BUT WE CAN'T MOVE FORWARD ON ANY STORY WITHOUT MORE FACTS.

JASON PHOTOG: UNDERSTOOD. I'LL KEEP ON IT.

TREY ROMERO: GOOD. BY THE WAY, I NOTICED THAT THE REGISTER DID NOT INCLUDE THE ANIMAL/WOLF IN THEIR STORY? DIDN'T YOU SAY THE ONLY OTHER JOURNALIST WITH YOU AT THE AIRPORT LAST NIGHT WORKED FOR THE REGISTER?

That caught Jason off guard at first, until he remembered that he had texted Trey about Regina's presence while they were waiting around in the rain for any new developments.

JASON PHOTOG: YES, HER NAME WAS REGINA. BUT SHE'S JUST AN INTERN, AND THE REGISTER TOOK HER STORY AND GAVE IT TO ANOTHER, SEASONED REPORTER. WHO, CLEARLY, EITHER OPTED NOT TO REPORT ON THE WOLF, OR WAS INSTRUCTED NOT TO DO SO BY THE EDITOR.

TREY ROMERO: THIS SOUNDS LIKE MORE THAN A GUESS ON YOUR PART?

Jason hesitated again, his fingertips poised over the keyboard, then decided to plunge ahead. He was an adult; he could do whatever he wanted on his own time, right?

JASON PHOTOG: IT IS. REGINA AND I HAD DINNER LATE LAST NIGHT. SHE TOLD ME THEN.

TREY ROMERO: REGINA FROM THE REGISTER. LAST NAME?

JASON PHOTOG: I'M EMBARRASSED TO ADMIT IT, BUT I HAVEN'T FOUND OUT YET.

TREY ROMERO: "REGINA." WAS SHE ITALIAN? MAYBE ROMANIAN?

Jason shook his head in confusion, almost chuckled aloud. *What the hell is* this *all about?*

JASON PHOTOG: NO, I DON'T THINK SO. SHE'S FAIR-SKINNED WITH RED HAIR. AND VERY, VERY TALL. IF I WERE TO GUESS, I'D SAY MAYBE SCANDINAVIAN? ONLY A SLIGHT ACCENT, THOUGH, BARELY THERE AT ALL. I REALLY DON'T KNOW. WHY?

This time, Trey took so long to reply, Jason wondered if he had stepped away and forgotten to sign off. But, recalling the not-so-long-ago days when Trey was the slowest typist on the planet, he didn't want to prematurely disconnect. So he polished off his food, cleaned up, opened a Solitaire window on his laptop, and kept himself occupied while he waited.

Finally, after an almost concerning amount of time, Trey returned.

TREY ROMERO: SORRY ABOUT THAT. I SHOULD'VE SAID SOMETHING FIRST. GLAD YOU'RE STILL ONLINE.

JASON PHOTOG: NO PROBLEM. DID ANOTHER WATCHDOG PING YOU?

TREY ROMERO: NOT EXACTLY. I HAD NEW NEO CHECK SOMETHING FOR ME.

Jason's eyebrows rose. "New Neo" was a fellow Watchdog, but he didn't function as a reporter; he was the group's computer hacker. What in the world would Trey need to hack on the spur of the moment?

Then he found out.

TREY ROMERO: AS A GOOD FRIEND OF MINE WOULD SAY, SOMETHING DIDN'T SMELL RIGHT, BUT I WANTED TO BE SURE. YOU SAID THAT "REGINA" IS AN INTERN AT THE REGISTER, CORRECT?

Jason thought back. JASON PHOTOG: MAYBE NOT *LITERALLY* AN INTERN, NOT ANYMORE. I KNOW SHE STARTED AS AN INTERN, BUT AS OF LAST NIGHT'S ASSIGNMENT TO INTERVIEW DR. HELLQVIST, I THINK SHE ACTUALLY PUT IT AS "NOT MUCH MORE THAN AN INTERN" OR "ONE STEP UP FROM AN INTERN." OR SOMETHING TO THAT EFFECT. WHY?

This was followed by another brief pause, then, TREY ROMERO: REGINA WAS ALSO AT THE AIRPORT TO MEET DR. HELLQVIST?

JASON PHOTOG: YES, THAT COINCIDENCE WAS OUR WHOLE "BONDING MOMENT." WHY?

Yet another pause from Trey.

JASON PHOTOG: TREY, WHAT'S UP? THIS IS MY FOURTH TIME ASKING — WHY?

TREY ROMERO: JASON, I HATE TO TELL YOU THIS, BUT ACCORDING TO NEW NEO, THERE'S ONLY ONE WOMAN NAMED REGINA WORKING AT THE REGISTER RIGHT NOW, A MIDDLE-AGED BLACK WOMAN. HE CHECKED BOTH THEIR POSTED STAFF LISTINGS

AND THEIR EMPLOYEE RECORDS — NO OTHER REGINAS.

Jason stared at the screen, dumbfounded.

What ...? But then how ...?

He racked his brain, replaying every interaction with her — at the airport, on the phone, at the sports bar. There was no way he had misunderstood her. So what the hell did that mean?

JASON PHOTOG: TREY, THAT CAN'T BE RIGHT. SHE HAD A PRESS PASS AND EVERYTHING. ARE YOU SURE NEW NEO CHECKED EVERYTHING? THIS DOESN'T MAKE ANY SENSE.

TREY ROMERO: HE SWEARS ALL THEIR RECORDS ARE UP-TO-DATE. NO OTHER EMPLOYEE, INTERN, OR FREELANCE STRINGER NAMED REGINA. I EVEN HAD HIM CHECK PAST RECORDS GOING BACK TWO YEARS — ALL HE HAD TIME FOR ON THE SPUR OF THE MOMENT. HE FOUND NO ONE ELSE.

JASON PHOTOG: TREY, COME ON, MAN. MAYBE SHE USES A PSEUDONYM, LIKE WE DO? DID YOU THINK OF THAT?

TREY ROMERO: SORRY, BUT I TRUST NEW NEO'S WORK. AND THEY WOULDN'T PUT A PSEUDONYM ON A PAYCHECK OR INTERNAL RECORDS. NO - OTHER - REGINAS.

Jason's mind was spinning. If Regina didn't work for the *Register*, then who the hell was she? Was she, like, a spy or something? Lord knows, he wouldn't be the first Watchdog to express concerns about the government investigating them, but why would they do that to *him*? He wrote articles about weird stuff, that was all. He shied away from politics, which was the way Trey liked it. So ... why *him*? Of all the Watchdogs, why would they target a failed photographer who did not stand out in any other meaningful way?

Seriously, seriously, *what - the - fuck, man?*

Jason realized that he had been sitting there, just staring off into space, when another message came through.

TREY ROMERO: ARE YOU ALL RIGHT, JASON?

JASON PHOTOG: YEAH. NO. I DON'T KNOW. TREY, WHAT SHOULD I DO?

TREY ROMERO: WOULD YOU BE WILLING TO CONTINUE MEETING WITH HER? MAYBE TRY TO FIND OUT WHAT'S GOING ON?

Jason considered their dinner last night, her odd behavior, his still slightly swollen lip ...

JASON PHOTOG: HONESTLY, TREY, I THINK I'D RATHER NOT.

TREY ROMERO: I UNDERSTAND.

JASON PHOTOG: SORRY, I'M JUST NOT BUILT FOR THIS SORT OF THING. WHATEVER THE HELL THIS "THING" IS.

TREY ROMERO: I UNDERSTAND, NO PROBLEM. I'LL HAVE NEW NEO KEEP DIGGING, BUT OUTSIDE OF THE REGISTER, DO YOU HAVE ANYTHING ELSE WE CAN GO ON? DID YOU HAPPEN TO GET HER PHOTO?

JASON PHOTOG: SORRY, THAT NEVER OCCURRED TO ME. I'M NOT REALLY A "SELFIE" GUY, AND IT WOULD'VE BEEN WEIRD TO JUST, YOU KNOW, TAKE HER PICTURE. I GUESS THAT MEANS I KINDA FUCKED UP, GIVEN ALL ... THIS.

TREY ROMERO: JASON, REALLY, IT'S ALL RIGHT. I'LL HAVE SOME OTHER CONTACTS LOOK INTO IT.

JASON PHOTOG: ANOTHER WATCHDOG?

TREY ROMERO: SOMETHING LIKE THAT. WHY DON'T YOU CALL IT A NIGHT, GET SOME SLEEP? WE CAN CHAT MORE TOMORROW.

Jason did not feel like explaining how he had slept the entire morning away and probably wouldn't "get some sleep" anytime soon — especially not with his brain whirling around this delightful new development. And he didn't feel like talking about it any longer.

JASON PHOTOG: YEAH, THAT SOUNDS GOOD.

TREY ROMERO: AGAIN, I'M SORRY ABOUT THIS, JASON.

JASON PHOTOG: IT'S NOT YOUR DOING, MAN. BUT THANKS. I'D RATHER KNOW THAN NOT KNOW. HOPE REGINA — OR WHOEVER SHE IS — GOT A REAL GOOD LAUGH ABOUT IT. WE'LL CONNECT TOMORROW. GN.

And with that, he shut down his *Watchdogs* interface before Trey could express any more unwanted sympathy over the whole embarrassing situation. Disconnected, he returned to sitting and staring into space.

How could I have been so goddamn gullible?

Jason could not have cared less about whatever sick and/or twisted motive "Regina" had. Whether she was spying for some rival news source (*yeah, wouldn't that be fucking hilarious?*) or for some other, God-only-knows-what reason entirely. Right then, he didn't give a shit about any of that.

What was killing him was his own stupid, idiotic naïveté. To have thought that a woman like that — like *that*, like some wet-dream of a super-model — would have been interested in *him*? Sure, she'd played it well enough when he initially called her out on it back at the airport, spinning that "just in the mood for conversation" bullshit so that it flowed smooth as silk. But as soon as she called him for dinner, or when she started flirting — and don't even get started on that lip-biting kiss — as soon as that eclectic box of goodies was opened, he should have known:

Someone like Regina could *never* have been interested in someone like him.

So why the hell had he fallen for it? What was wrong with him? Was he really that desperate, that lonely? Sure, it had been a little while since he'd been with a woman (okay, it had been quite a while), but was that really an excuse for turning his brain off? He had known from the start that she could have had her pick of any man at the airport; with the idealized options of "tall, dark, and handsome," why would she settle for someone who offered only the "dark" part of that equation? The whole charade was so fucking obvious now, he felt like he should just—

Okay, part of him rallied, *that's enough. Let's not go overboard with the self-loathing, so stop it right there. Just* stop. *Yeah, this sucks. It's embarrassing, and it sucks big time. Yes, I'm out of shape. Yes, it's been a long time since any woman has shown interest. And yes, as I knew from the get-go, Regina is totally out of my weight class. And since there is no way she could not be aware of this, that means she was consciously* using *that to manipulate me.*

So let's remember who's the real villain in this scenario. Hint: It's not me.

Feeling somewhat mollified, Jason thought that maybe Trey had been right, maybe he should try to get some sleep. Yeah, it had been a pretty short day for him, but after hours of trawling the web for clues about the vanishing wolf, and now having this wonderful little bombshell dropped on his head, he felt strung out enough that he might be able to drift off sooner rather than later.

If nothing else, his dreams would offer a diverting escape from his woes.

But first, he needed to try to relax a little more ...

Jason stepped into the steaming shower, letting the hot water course over his body. As it cascaded down his back, he could feel the tension in his muscles loosen in stages. He took a deep breath, inhaling the muggy air into his lungs, and held it for several seconds before releasing. Closing his eyes, he attempted to empty his mind. He focused on the sound of the water striking his body, the walls, the shower floor, opening himself to the calm rhythm of that white noise.

For the time being, he forgot about Regina's duplicity and his wounded pride. There was nothing but the soothing shower and his own steady breathing.

After a good long time standing under the stream, he finally shut off the water and toweled himself dry with slow gentle strokes, clinging to this calm state of being. Stepping up to the fogged mirror, he used the same towel to wipe away the condensation, revealing his reflection.

Jason scooped up his hairbrush, but then paused and just studied himself in the mirror for a minute. It had been some time since he had last truly looked at himself, and ... well, he sort of liked what he was seeing — his dark hair disarrayed and damp, his brown eyes thoughtful, his features average, but not *un*attractive. Looking over the lines of his face, his neck, his throat, he reconsidered his harsh self-criticisms from earlier. So maybe he wasn't "model material," like Regina, but he liked his face; it was a *kind* face. Yes, his body was soft from lack of exercise, but as he ran his hands over his belly, he decided that maybe he was being too harsh there, too; he appeared to have lost a little weight since the last time he bothered to notice.

Jason took a deep breath, squared his shoulders, and placed his fists on his hips, striking what could only be described as a "Superman pose" ... which, in short order, served to crack himself up. He spent the next minute just standing in the bathroom, naked and laughing his ass off, and *that* made him feel better than he had all day.

Wrapping his towel around his waist, he stepped into the kitchenette long enough to grab his laptop and phone, then retired to his bedroom. Phone placed on night stand, he arranged his pillow so that he could sit up for a bit, reclined against the headboard, and placed his computer so that it lived up to its designated name.

Clicking through his folders, he brought up his collection of his favorite wildlife photographs; most of them had been snagged from different websites, a few of them he had taken with his own camera. And as he clicked through image after image of marvelous, breathtaking animals, Jason felt his last remaining stress oozing away.

A magnificent Serengeti lioness, her muscles tensed and ready to spring, hunting on the savannah at dusk ... an adorable baby brown-throated sloth, clinging to its mother high in a rainforest tree canopy ... a polar bear and her twin cubs frolicking in the arctic snow ...

Jason envied wildlife in their natural habitats, living their simple lives, in the moment, without artifice or pretense. During these calmest of down-times, when he was able to just chill out and click through photo after photo without distraction — like this one, that he had taken himself, of a pair of spotted skunks trotting along without an apparent care in the world — sometimes he could almost ... almost feel—

He jolted when his phone rang, his eyes snapping open and his computer nearly flying off his lap and onto the floor. Shaking his head to clear it — he had been so close to falling asleep! — he fumbled to pick up his phone, half-expecting it to be Trey with some sort of update.

REGINA FROM AIRPORT

He stared at the screen, the phone continuing to ring in his hand. Should he answer? Trey had asked if he would be willing to play dumb and string her along. And maybe, just maybe, if he confronted her, she might be able to offer a reasonable explanation?

You know what? No. *Nope, I'm out.*

He swiped down to decline the call. And then he took the extra step and blocked her number. He smiled at his phone before plopping it back onto the night stand, proud of himself, and glad to be free of the lying bitch.

So long, "Regina from Airport"!

And that was the end of that.

Dream Revelations

In a dream that he could only consider a "sequel," the forest floor, covered in a layer of damp leaves and twigs, crunched beneath Jason's bare feet as he led his pack of timber wolves through the deep shadows of night. His nude body was still marked with the scratches and bites from his dire combat with the black wolf, but they were scabbing over and healing. He did not know where he was leading his pack, but he dashed through the darkness with deliberate intent, and they followed.

As before, a part of him knew this was a dream, but he didn't care. He had never felt this free in his life! "Real world" problems like money or career choices or girlfriend-beating neighbors — or getting played by a certain tall-ass liar — melted into the farthest fringes of his mind.

This *is what mattered: Running with his wolves.*

Cresting a slope and slipping into a hollow between two trees, Jason slid to a halt. When he did so, he didn't need to make any sounds or gestures of command — his wolves stopped all around him, their bellies low to the ground as they nestled down to earth.

Through the darkness — his vision remained as enhanced as it was when he killed the black wolf — Jason spotted movement through the vegetation below and heard the ambulation of some large, ungainly animal, probably more than one. His pack was downwind, so he knew they had gone undetected.

He waited. His wolves waited, their noses twitching with eager anticipation.

Soon enough, a break in the trees exposed the invaders into their territory: Two Kamchatka brown bears, an adult female and a young male — presumably, Mama Bear and Baby Bear.

Jason's eyes scanned the vicinity. Any other bears around? Probably not. Kamchatka bears tended to be solitary; Mama Bear wouldn't even keep Baby Bear around for more than a few years. On the move in the dark like this, they must be hungry, foraging for food.

Which did not change the fact that the bears were trespassing.

The wolves on either side of him looked to Jason, awaiting his lead.

Jason considered. The cub would be easy enough, but Mama Bear would put up one hell of a fight. Worth it?

A threat — any threat — to what was his? He could not allow it— no, he would not *allow it.*

They - were - trespassing.

Again, Jason needed not bother with any sort of command, spoken or otherwise. The instant he leaped forward, his wolves launched alongside him.

The pack descended upon the bears with ferocious speed; silent until the last moment, and deadly. The cub was, indeed, easy prey — before the pair understood they were under attack, one wolf clamped his jaws onto the bear's throat while two others dragged it to the ground. But then Mama Bear reared up with a tremendous roar, swatting her giant paws and gnashing her teeth.

Before she could strike a crippling blow to any of his wolves, Jason leaped onto her back, clinging to her fur and scratching at her eyes and snout. The bear bucked and spun, trying to dislodge him, while his wolves darted in, biting and scratching at her limbs. One wolf yelped as her claws raked across its flank; another staggered away when she landed a heavy blow across its snout. But still they kept coming, harrying her from all sides.

With a desperate surge of strength, Mama Bear reared back, slamming Jason against a tree. His breath exploded from his lungs, and he lost his grip and tumbled to the ground, stunned. Mama Bear loomed over him, ready to crush his skull in her jaws. But then another of his wolves sank its teeth deep into her hind leg. She bellowed in pain and rounded on her newest attacker.

Grinding his teeth, Jason shook off his daze and, with the support of the tree, regained his feet and prepared to rejoin the fray.

The tree shuddered under an impact that had nothing to do with Jason or Mama Bear, and he could feel a heavy presence behind him. He turned, and looked up.

He had been wrong.

Another bear was *present — a male, and a* big *one, with an aggressive, ravenous look about him. To be roaming so nearby, he must have been stalking the other two bears, possibly intending to eat the cub and then mate with the female.*

But now his voracious eyes were locked onto Jason.

* * *

As the monstrous Kamchatka barked its rage and lifted a colossal paw to smite him from the world, Jason's eyes snapped open.

For the first few seconds, he panted and gawked at the ceiling above him, uncertain where he was and how the male bear had disappeared. Awareness crept back in sluggish stages, yet he found that the *feeling* of the forest — the sights, the sounds, and most of all, the smells — lingered, holding onto him with stubborn resolve.

Groaning, he rolled over and attempted to sit up on the side of his bed, but instead he slipped off the mattress and landed on one knee. He shook his head, but it refused to clear. Jesus, how much did he have to drink ...?

But no, that wasn't right. He had not been drinking alcohol that evening, at all. Was he high then? No, he couldn't remember the last time he had smoked pot with Roberto.

So what was wrong with him? Was he sick? Why did he feel this way, all thick and stupid and ... tingly? These symptoms meant nothing to him.

Struggling to his feet — which took much longer than it should have — Jason kept one hand against the wall for support as he inched his way toward the bathroom. As he moved along at a snail's pace, he was struck by another unpleasant surprise: His apartment stank. How had he never noticed before? His place brimmed with a musty odor, a mixture of old sweat, old food, unwashed laundry, and stale air. The combined fetor made his head spin worse than it already was. He really needed to air this place out! Not that he could deal with any of that right now ...

Stumbling into the bathroom, he didn't bother turning on the light. He leaned against the sink for balance, then shifted so that he was bent over the toilet. Was he going to vomit? He wasn't sure, wasn't sure what was wrong.

The toilet bowl tilted under his weight.

Great, fuck, did I break it?

Except it wasn't the toilet tilting, it was him. And before he could compensate, he had fallen over sideways onto the tiled floor. He made one feeble attempt to sit up, then collapsed onto his back.

His gasping breath slowed ... slowed ... and, not knowing if he were falling asleep, passing out, or outright dying, Jason closed his eyes ...

* * *

... and it was as though he had never left, as though no time at all had passed. His dream returned him to the forest, facing the raging male bear; if anything, the immense, monstrous Kamchatka was larger and fiercer than before, his hot breath blasting Jason's face as the bear reared up onto his hind legs.

The rest of the pack were occupied with Mama Bear.

This fight belonged to Jason, and Jason alone.

The male bear swiped a massive paw toward his head, deadly claws glinting in the checkered moonlight. Jason ducked and dove out of the way — those claws sliced through empty air where his face had just been, tearing into the bark of the tree.

Jason rolled onto his feet, his heart pounding yet feeling almost giddy with exhilaration. He feinted left, then right, barely avoiding another swipe of the bear's paws, then those snarling and snapping jaws. He knew he couldn't keep dodging forever. He had to fight back, had to tap into that primal side of himself that matched the bear's savagery, the concealed force that had allowed him to defeat the black wolf.

As the male bear lunged toward him once more, that

primordial core erupted again, a bold, bestial power surging up from deep within him. But this time, it was so much more than a driving tempest of the mind and soul: With wild pain that was both terrible and euphoric, Jason's limbs elongated, thick fur sprouted from his flesh, his jaws stretched into a long snout filled with razor-sharp teeth, and throughout he gained considerable muscle mass.

Jason was no longer just Jason; he had transformed into an enormous wolf-like beast, a creature of tooth and claw that also possessed human-deft hands and stood erect on his hind legs, a good match for the Kamchatka before him.

With an earth-shaking roar, Jason rushed forward to engage his great enemy.

The bear swiped his massive paws towards Jason, each dagger-like claw promising death. Jason dodged the attacks, moving with a nimbleness that belied his hulking new form; then he lunged forward, jaws open wide, and sank his new fangs deep into the bear's shoulder.

The bear howled in agony and rage, then displayed his own impressive agility as he thrashed his bulky body about with enough violence to dislodge Jason's teeth.

Pressing his advantage, the Kamchatka threw himself sideways, slamming into Jason. The two titans smashed into some younger, smaller trees, splintering bark and branches. Jason raked his sharp claws across the bear's hide, leaving deep, bleeding gashes. The bear bellowed and reared up, only to slash his paws right back down; Jason leaped out of the way as the impact cratered the earth.

The two beasts circled each other, panting clouds of steam into the cool night air. When the bear charged at Jason again, he was ready: He braced himself and met his opponent head on, grabbed hold of the bear's shoulders and — in spite of the ursine's greater mass — used the animal's own momentum to flip him over and onto his back. The disoriented bear writhed and flailed, slashing wildly with his claws, but Jason pinned him down with his powerful, transformed arms, his long nails gashing the bear's chest. Then, as he had done with the black wolf, Jason lunged forward to sink his fangs into the bear's exposed throat.

But the male bear had other ideas. The Kamchatka twisted his thick head around, blocking Jason's attack before it could find its mark. In a complete reversal, Jason found his face dangerously near the bear's snapping jaws; foamy saliva dripped from the bear's teeth as the maw stretched to lock onto his skull.

If that happened, he was dead.

In a rash maneuver, Jason seized the bear's lower jaw. Ignoring the pain as those sharp incisors pierced his padded palm, he closed his fist and, with all his strength, shoved away and down.

The bear's mandible creaked, then cracked, then — as the great beast cried out in agony — it snapped, one jagged shard of bone tearing through the furry flesh. Jason had failed to tear into the bear's throat before, but the animal bled aplenty now.

The bear still struggled, with enraged violence, agony, and desperation, but his movements weakened as blood poured from the awful trauma. Jason drew back his free hand and punched the bear in the temple as hard as he could — once, twice, and a third time.

And, with a final, guttural groan, the once-mighty Kamchatka bear fell silent and still.

Gasping for breath, Jason stepped away from the great bear. As his adrenaline faded, his monstrous wolf-like physique rippled and shifted back into human form. Turning away from his vanquished foe, he saw that his pack had also brought down Mama Bear. Regarding all the carcasses, he felt a tinge of regret; he bore no malice for these beautiful creatures, but an alpha must defend his territory, and his pack.

His timber wolves gathered around Jason and lowered themselves before him. If any of their canine minds had harbored desires to challenge him before, his defeat of the Kamchatka bear abolished them.

Looking around at them, he declared once more, "Naetshai nitou asou ai."

He smiled. And then he threw back his head and howled into the night ...

* * *

... and he was still howling when he opened his eyes again. He was also standing in the middle of his living room.

Jason blinked a few times, looking around. He knew that he had been dreaming about the bear — of course it had been a dream — but hadn't he been in the bathroom before? Lying on the floor? How—?

One of his neighbors pounded on the wall, and he had the feeling it wasn't for the first time. A muffled female voice shouted, "Keep it down, goddamn it!"

His first impulse was to call back with an apology, but one final thump against the wall drew a close to their discourse. Fine with him.

As he wakened further, he became aware that his "tighty-whitey" briefs, which were all he had worn to bed, were sagging around his hips. Looking down, he saw the elastic band had gotten stretched out to the point that the underwear threatened to fall off him altogether.

"What the *what* ...?" he whispered, but his voice felt louder somehow. In fact, he was hearing all kinds of little creaks and cracks and shuffling movement from the apartments all around his. The "stuffy" smell (a generous way to describe it) of his own place stood out stronger than ever, too.

And it didn't stop there. Even as he was reaching for the living room light switch, he realized that the dim glow from his microwave's display in the kitchenette and his Blu-ray player's clock were all he needed to make out the basics of his surroundings. When he turned the light on, he expected his darkness-adjusted eyes to be blinded by the sudden change; instead, they adapted in an instant.

Then he looked down again and, ignoring his warped underwear, really examined his nearly-nude body. His beer belly was not gone, nor were his muscles taut with power ... and yet, he could not deny that his gut was smaller, that his arms, legs, and chest looked firmer, as though it had been mere weeks, rather than years, since he last hit the gym.

Jason was on the verge of muttering another "What the what?" when a sharp pain shot through his mouth.

He grunted in discomfort, then again when the pain repeated, and finally cut loose with a full fledged "Ow!" when it struck once more. And that was when he realized that he suddenly had something inside his mouth, or maybe a few somethings. He spat whatever they were out into his hand, then just stared at the objects in confusion.

"The ... hell ...?"

On his palm lay three unknown items; two white-ish, one metallic. He gawked at them for a stretch before the realization finally struck: They were dental fillings.

The second that thought occurred, his tongue darted around his mouth as though it had a mind of its own, probing up, down, and side to side. But it found no suspicious holes or gaps in his teeth.

Returning to the bathroom, he turned on the light, placed the fillings on the side of the sink, opened his mouth wide, and craned his neck every which way as he stared at his reflection in the mirror. Given the oddity of the situation, he could not recall which of his teeth had been treated for cavities; evidence aside, he could not have sworn off-hand just how many fillings he even had.

Except he did know. The three fillings were the proof. The part that freaked him out was the fact that he could find no signs of their former homes in his mouth. It was as though his teeth had just ... what, regrown their enamel? Was that even possible? And even if it were, surely it would have been a slow process — not just, *pop!*, there ya go, fillings out, teeth whole!

Jason closed his mouth, backing away from the fillings and out of the bathroom. He huffed a few breaths, trying to calm down, but if anything, his heart pounded harder. His apartment was small, which had never bothered him before; in fact, he usually kind of liked it that way. But in this moment, this abode of his felt too confined, claustrophobic. He needed to get out of there — not in the morning, not in an hour, *now*.

Turning, he strode for the door, and had gotten as far as grabbing hold of the doorknob before he remembered that he wore nothing other than overextended briefs. His initial impulse was to just say "Fuck it!" and go outside anyway, but he managed to clamp down on that urge.

Resisting a full frenzy, he rushed back into his bedroom, allowed the briefs to fall from his legs, then grabbed the basics — new underwear; socks; jeans; T-shirt; sneakers — and he could not have cared less if anything matched. He dressed as he returned to the front door, hopping as needed to keep moving. He wanted, needed to get out of there!

Finally yanking the door open, he stepped out onto the walkway, grasped the safety rail, and focused on breathing the cold night air. He had no idea what time it was, all he knew was that it was night, damp and chilly, and he was no longer surrounded by four stifling walls.

While he had escaped the stuffy, domestic stink of his dwelling, he discovered a bewildering new olfactory hodgepodge outside: Recently cut grass; flowers attempting to bloom in the persistent cool weather; cigarette and marijuana smoke; the lingering aroma of food from nearby restaurants; car exhaust — all of it creating a unique, suburban brew. And topping it off, a hint of rain in the distance, promising another wet start come morning.

A sharp gust of wind blew past him, and he came to another awareness: He should be miserable in this cold. Given the dark hour, it was chillier outside than it had been when he had been at the airport — dryer, true, but colder. And yet it didn't bother him at all; in fact, he found it refreshing.

What's happening to me?

The darkness shifted, and he looked up. The cloud cover had parted just enough to allow the half-moon to peek through. With the way his eyes were reacting, it was as though someone had turned up a great dimmer switch, making the outdoor environment a good twenty percent brighter.

Christ, what is happening *to me?*

Setting aside his inexplicable new tolerance to the temperature, he did feel better being outside, but he found he had trouble standing still. He paced a few steps back and forth, but didn't want to disturb his neighbors by pounding his heels on the walkway. Maybe he should go for another walk, and stick with it this time?

Yeah, that sounded good. And he tried to avoid dwelling on the fact that he had zero need to return to his apartment for his jacket.

He crept to the staircase and was halfway down when his nose caught another scent, something familiar; he slowed to a halt as he identified it, and peered over the railing.

No fucking way.

She stood in the middle of the parking area, smiling up at him.

Regina.

CHALLENGING ENCOUNTER

Jason gripped the railing of the stairs, his knuckles blanching, as he stared down at Regina for a solid minute; he wanted it to be an intense "glare," but his bewilderment at everything going on left him too off balance to sell it.

Regina just stood there, her smile unwavering. The silence did not faze her in the least.

Growing frustrated at the standoff, Jason descended the final steps and marched toward her, stopping a good ten feet away. Not knowing how else to begin, he spat, "You followed me home?"

This amused her. "No need, Jason. I already knew where you lived."

He so, so wanted to have some confident, bad-ass/smart-ass, snappy comeback to that, but nothing leaped to mind. The "weird and unusual" had finally come home to roost, and he wasn't ready for it. All he could think to do was try glaring again, but the effort was even less effective than before, and only amused Regina further — which irked Jason even more.

Then the night breeze shifted, and he smelled her again ... and she smelled good, really good, *intoxicating*. The scent he had detected from the staircase paled before the potency of how she smelled as she stood before him. Like most Westernized men, Jason had always been drawn in by a woman's perfume, but Regina's natural musk was on an entirely different level from anything that might come from a bottle. His body responded in a way it hadn't since his teen years.

Regina noticed, glancing down at the engorgement in his pants and unfettering one of her almost-giggles.

Jason's *body* might be stimulated, but his *mind* was not the least bit interested anymore. Not since learning that she had lied to him, not since her flirting games, not since she bit the hell out of his lip.

Unsolicited, his tongue reacted to that thought and darted forward to probe his lip once again.

Nothing. No discomfort, no swelling at all. It was fully healed.

"You've done something to me," he stated, the words slipping out without forethought. "I want to know what."

"All I've done," she told him, that smug smile still on her face, "is guide you toward your natural—"

His hands clenched into fists. "Cut the shit, 'Regina' — or whoever the fuck you are. What have you *done* to me?"

"This is your awakening, Jason Bakari Samir. Or ..." She lolled her head to one side, as if considering a new possibility. "... or maybe you're still *dreaming*. Are you, Jason? Are you dreaming? Is *this* just a dream, right now?"

That notion appealed to Jason; he couldn't deny it. If this were all some bizarre extension to his dream of turning into a kind of wolfman and fighting a Kamchatka bear to the death—

But no, no. As much as he wanted to buy into her suggestion, to accept a dreamland fantasy as an alternative to his body changing, his senses expanding ... he couldn't. His dreams might seem quite real while he was *in* them, but upon awakening, there was no true comparison between the two — in contrast, dream sounds were never quite right, dream environments didn't make sense, people and things came and went without explanation ...

No, unfortunately, he knew he was awake — as outlandish as this whole situation was, it was his reality, now. He would not allow her to manipulate him that way.

But what Regina did next shattered his aplomb.

He had paid little attention to her clothing — form-fitting but all black, lost amidst the poor lighting — until she kicked off her shoes and started removing her pants. His eyes bulged and he whirled about, checking to see if any of his neighbors might be watching. They were not; it was, after all, the dead of night.

Turning back to her, he lowered his voice to demand, "The fuck are you *doing*?"

Regina behaved as though she were standing in the privacy of her own bedroom. This was not a "striptease" — in spite of her on-again/off-again flirtations, this did not appear to be an effort to seduce him. She was simply disrobing, as though she had grown tired of this outfit and wanted to wear something else.

Goddamn it, he could not help but notice as her shirt came off, *she even has fucking chiseled six-pack abs. Because* of course *she does. And oh, sure, no underwear, either, so now I know the carpet matches the drapes. Fuck.*

When she stood completely nude before him — black clothes hanging over her arm and shoes in hand — she offered the casual suggestion, "You'll want to take off your clothes and leave them behind. Otherwise, they'll get ruined." Her tone was as nonchalant as if she had said, *Don't forget an umbrella, otherwise you'll get rained on.*

She turned around and — as Jason willed himself not to ogle her fantastic ass — crossed to the far side of the parking area, placing her clothes in a neat pile at the foot of the hedge wall. She then strode back toward him on her long, toned legs, raising eyebrows that asked, *What are you waiting for?*

"Uh-uh," he said, maintaining rigid eye-contact, "no, I'm done. You're not going to explain what's happening to me? Fine. I'll figure it out on my own. So you can take your little ..." He gestured up and down her naked body. "... whatever it is you're trying to do here — because you're not *that* hot, lady — and shove it right ... up..."

His words trailed off as he caught sight of the large shadow emerging from between two parked cars. Even when the moon peeked from behind the clouds once more, the beast's appearance remained obscured, courtesy of its black fur.

Jason's eyes felt as though they might pop from his head. He tried to scream, "Holy fucking shit!", but it came out as little more than a breathy whisper. He pointed a shaking hand at the approaching wolf as he stumbled back, almost tripping over his own feet; had his bladder been full, he surely would have voided it. "Reg—" he choked, then tried again, rasping out, "Regina ... *behind you ...*"

The huge black wolf sauntered up to Regina's side, its ebony fur glossy under the moonlight, and stopped. It just stood there, waiting, gazing at Jason as though appraising how he might taste. Regina reached down and touched its head, keeping her hand there; she didn't "pet it," exactly, but it was definitely a contact of familiarity, if not affection.

Jason gaped at the wolf, then up at her, then back at the wolf. As the silence stretched on and the surrealism of *all* of it — the dreams; the changes to his body; the wolf; Regina, standing like a nude goddess before him — threatened to overwhelm him, his fear sort of shorted out, and he found himself evaluating the wolf with a photographer's eye ... and damned if it wasn't a gorgeous beast. With its sleek fur and powerful build, standing tall and proud, the animal was undeniably stunning, its eyes glistening like amber jewels in the low lighting. And while its scent was nowhere near as enticing as Regina's, it did possess its own allure.

That didn't mean that he wanted to let it *eat* him.

For the first time, he became aware that his arms were up in a classic defensive posture, as if to ward off the wolf or woman or both. Knowing how foolish and ineffective it must look on pretty much every level, he forced himself to lower them.

Swallowing hard, he asked, "So ... what's happening, exactly? You obviously, uh, know our big 'friend' here, whatever the hell that means. And I'm gettin' a lot of mixed signals ..." His eyes flitted up to her magnificent breasts — he couldn't help it — then back down to the wolf once more. "I honestly can't tell if you're planning to fuck me, or have me mauled to death. You clearly have the upper hand, so what's your play?"

Regina smirked. "I did suggest you take off your clothes."

Jason's jaw dropped. He had been (mostly) joking about the "planning to fuck" comment. "*Seriously?*"

She laughed. It was kind of loud, here in the parking area in the wee hours, but by this point, if any of his neighbors poked their heads out, the sound of laughter would swiftly become the last thing on their minds.

A car drove past the apartment complex; for a split-second, its headlights spilled across them. Neither the wolf nor the completely bare Regina paid it any mind.

"We have a lot to teach you, Jason," she told him, "but only if you're as strong as we hope you are. So why don't we make this into a little game, hmm?" Her hand shifted on the wolf's head, mussing its thick fur. "My 'friend' here will run. You'll chase him. If you catch him, then I'll refrain from having you 'mauled to death.' How does that sound?"

"Uh, sure. Just, um, let me grab my car keys—"

Regina made a face. "Don't be obtuse, Jason. I didn't say you would 'drive after him,' I said you would chase him."

Jason snorted in brief laughter, though nothing about this was remotely funny. "How the hell could I catch a wolf *on foot*, Regina?" He studied the canine again. "It's huge, but I know it can still—"

"Not 'it,' Jason. *He*."

"Fine, *he* is huge, and *he* appears to be a black-coated grey wolf. Average grey wolves can run over thirty miles-per-hour, and, at the airport, we both saw how fast *this* bastard can move." He huffed in disbelief as a thought struck him. "Fuck, you *knew* he was on that plane all along, didn't you? Did you arrange for him to kill all those people, including Doctor—?"

"Stay on topic, Jason. Doctor Hellqvist—" She said the name with some disdain. "—should be the last thing on your mind right now." She smirked again; he was getting tired of that smug little smile. "You have a wolf to catch."

"Regina, how am I—?"

"You know how."

"Goddamn it, Regina, I have no—"

The wolf lunged. Jason had seen no warning signs, heard no snarls, no barks — hell, the whole time he and Regina had been talking about him, the wolf could've been nothing more than a detailed statue. One instant he was stock-still, the next he was leaping for Jason's throat!

Jason yelped, throwing his left forearm up to take the bite and drawing back his right arm in preparation for some kind of counter-attack—

—except that the wolf did not collide with him. His "leap" had been a feint; he had shot up onto his hind legs, which was quite the sight, given his size, but that was all. He was already back down on all fours, having come barely any closer.

Meanwhile, Jason's heart felt as though it were trying to burst straight through his rib cage. He panted, "What ...? What was ...?" but could not get out anything more than that.

"Look at your hand, Jason."

He blinked at his left hand, still held out before him to block the—

She rolled her eyes. "Your *other* hand, Jason."

He blinked some more, feeling stupid, and then did as he was told.

When he had drawn back his right arm, he had planned — as much as he had "planned" anything in that flash of terror — to ball his hand into a fist and maybe punch the black wolf in the snout or something. Instead, his fingers were splayed and curled inward at the tips as if to slash, as though he sported claws rather than stumpy little fingernails ...

Except his hand wasn't just a "hand" anymore. And it did sport claws, big ones.

Jason's jaw dropped. Between sharp claws, budding pads, and a lot more hair than normal sprouted up past his wrist ... he still had fingers, but otherwise, his hand looked like it was halfway to becoming a *paw* — just as they had been when he shapeshifted to fight the Kamchatka bear in his dream. But since he knew he was awake this time ...

He wanted to both laugh and cry at the same time. *Okay, there you go. I'm officially losing my mind.*

"No," Regina told him. "You aren't."

He tore his gaze from his hand-paw. "You ... you read minds?" Because sure, why the hell not? With everything else going on, how much more could telepathy hurt?

But she shook her head. "No. But I've been where you are." She drew a breath, considering. "How do you get in the pool, Jason?"

"... what?"

"When you go swimming, how do you get in the pool? Are you

one of those who eases their way in, getting used to the cold water a bit at a time? Or do you jump right in?"

Jason worked his jaw, trying to answer her baffling non sequitur, until finally he had to settle for a confused shrug.

"For this, I suggest you jump right in." She pointed at him, her finger aimed at his chest. "Strip."

Jason looked at her, then at the wolf, then back at his right hand; it better resembled a human one again, but not enough to convince himself that the change had been a hallucination. He felt numb, shell-shocked, and that was probably why he asked no more questions before doing as instructed; he started taking off his clothes, right there in the middle of his apartment complex's parking area.

As the clothing peeled away, mystified though he was, his growing nudity in front of Regina gave him some pause. Sure, he had looked better in the bathroom mirror, but his body still couldn't hold a candle to hers, not even close. A half-memory danced through the back of his head: While making one of those CGI/motion-capture films from several years ago, the male cast members had been joking together about how silly they all looked in their unflattering "pajamas" with the symbols and dots on them, but when the film's starlet arrived, she had looked so damned good in her own form-fitting attire, that's when they all became truly self-conscious of their every sag and lump.

Undressing in front of Regina, Jason could relate to how they must have felt.

Thank God I don't feel so cold *now,* he thought, giving thanks for small favors.

When he was finished and stood exposed before her, holding his loose clothing a little below waist-level, she told him, "Go put them in a pile next to mine, then come back."

She sounded as though she were explaining this to a small child for the umpteenth time. He resented her tone, but he did as she said.

Once he returned, still attempting some level of modesty, Regina patted the huge wolf on the rump. The wolf glanced back at her, and Jason could've sworn that he saw indignation in the animal's eyes, but then the beast leaned forward, his furry shoulders hunching before bolting out into the night, almost as fast as he had back at the airport.

"God almighty ..." Jason whispered, staring after the black streak as it disappeared around the hedge wall.

"All right, Jason," Regina said. "Change, and go after him."

"Ch-change?" But he knew what she meant. His right hand looked normal again, but that did not erase the memory of its belonging to a wolfman.

She held her patience, though her face betrayed some slippage. "Change, Jason. Now."

"I ... I don't know how."

A low growl rumbled through the night air, but the black wolf had not returned — it was coming from Regina. Her green eyes seemed almost luminescent, and when she next spoke, her teeth seemed larger, sharper. "Now, Jason. *Now!*"

Not knowing what else to do, he closed his eyes and focused. He thought about his dream, thought about his right hand, thought about what failure would mean, and he *pushed.*

A hot spasm shot up Jason's spine. In the dream, the change had been painful enough, but reality was proving even more torturous — fiery spikes came and went with each snap and crack as his bones shifted and reshaped themselves. Dark brown fur sprouted all over his skin, itching and prickling as it emerged, and he was forced to stifle a cry of agony when his lower face elongated into a snout, his teeth distorting his gums and grinding against one another as they lengthened, sharpened, and expanded.

Regina watched with an impassive air, offering no comfort as he collapsed onto his hands and knees. But then, halfway through his hellish metamorphosis, her own body also began to change. Fur — red, much like her human hair, but darker — spread across her pale skin, and her limbs twisted into new proportions. Faster than he could have believed possible (had he been able to believe *any* of this insanity), she stood before him as another giant wolf — not as husky as the black wolf, but rangier, taller at the shoulder — towering over him in his half-transformed body.

Biting down against one final, guttural cry, Jason found himself standing on four legs, his hands and feet now paws. He panted in heaving relief as the pain receded, his long tongue lolling from his new muzzle. He had no mirrors down here to consult, but he knew what he had become: A third wolf, sleek and powerful in all the ways he had always loved about the glorious animals.

Part of him exalted in the feeling, the pure strength pulsing through his limbs, while the rest of him reeled from it all, and he thought he might pass out.

wolves do not faint.

Jason's wedge-shaped head jerked up. What? Where had—?

wolves are strong, always strong. you can be strong as a wolf, and more.

It was not a voice inside his head, not like the telepathy he had considered before. And yet it was like no communication he had ever experienced — part smell, part sound, part something else, something unfamiliar.

He regarded the red wolf. With his transmutation complete, she was no longer quite so much taller than him, and her scent—God! His previous experience could not compete with how she smelled to him as a fellow wolf. Her essence combined the sharp tang of fresh pine needles, wildflowers and honey, earthy moss, and some undertones of a basic, raw fragrance that simply screamed "wild animal!" It overwhelmed him, drawing him in like a moth to a flame. All he could think about was mating with her, right here and now.

Easing forward on his four legs — how natural it already felt — he angled around to sniff at her hind quarters, but she twisted and nipped his ear.

not now. not yet, she "said" to him.

when? he demanded. Or did he? Was he doing it right? Had she "heard" him?

Apparently, yes, she had. later. after. after you catch the

black wolf.

He looked to where the black wolf had disappeared. Nostrils flaring, he caught its scent lingering beneath hers, and knew he could follow it.

He would show her, show her that he was fit to be her mate.

He glanced her direction, did his best to smile around his new maw and lips, and then he turned, ducked his great head, and bounded forward, his wolf eyes seeing with less color but sharper clarity even in the darkness. Inhaling once more, he locked onto the scent of the black wolf, allowing it to drive his instincts.

But Regina did not let him rush off alone.

And so it was *two* wolves who gave chase under the half-moon light, one brown and one red.

Challenging Endeavor

Free. Jason had never felt so *free*! If this was what it felt like to run as a wolf, he had no desire to be human ever again.

Exhilaration coursed through his lupine veins as he raced through the night. The wind rushed past his muzzle — wind of his own creation, so fast was he moving — as he sprinted with effortless grace. Part of his exaltation stemmed from how much more *fluid* his thoughts were in this form; he still possessed his human memories and knowledge, but as a wolf, his anxieties—such as concern over the "impossibility" of this entire shapeshifting affair — could no longer take root as he experienced what it meant to truly live in the moment.

Ahead, the stealthy black wolf kept clear of the few humans out and about, evaded the equally few cars on the surface streets, avoided the freeways and their too many lights like the plague, and stayed deep within the shadows at every opportunity. And Jason did the same.

good, "said" the red wolf near his side, you are learning.

Jason angled his eyes toward her. I was promised a good reward.

Regina angled her green eyes toward him in return. I promise nothing more than what you earn.

He chuffed, and ran faster still.

Once more, he lost himself in the sensation of running on four legs, and marveled at the heightened agility that came with this form — and the *speed*; he had no way of measuring for certain, but he felt pretty damned sure he was running a lot faster than thirty miles per hour! Yes, he still pursued the black wolf, locked onto its unique scent, but that was almost incidental. He rejoiced at the high-contrast sight of the nighttime world around him; the occasional whiff of a domesticated animal or intoxicated human added to the experience. Hell, he even snatched an unfortunate moth from the air and relished its taste — just an hour ago, the notion would have made him gag.

Then Regina broke his reverie by edging ahead of him. *follow*, she commanded.

but the black wolf—?

follow, she repeated, and arced to the left, away from the black wolf's trail.

Growling his confusion and disappointment — what would this mean, regarding his reward? — he followed after her.

Up to this point, the human side of Jason's mind had been able to track, more or less, where their pursuit was taking them; when Regina veered off in another direction, this changed. He considered himself reasonably familiar with Southern California, and Los Angeles County and Orange County in particular. But the red wolf was leading him into less recognizable territory, the smells of human habitation lessening as a more industrial bouquet grew stronger, as did the salty aroma of the ocean — add to that the considerable stink of abiding jet fuel, and he presumed they were not too far from LAX.

When the red wolf finally slowed, easing to an eventual halt in the shadows between streetlights, Jason took in their surroundings, seeing lots of large buildings, which his nose told him served as warehouses of varied purpose. But Regina focused on a specific three- or four-story structure, a bland-looking, mostly concrete box of an edifice that, to Jason, screamed, "government property."

is that where we're going? he asked. He lifted a front paw, ready to keep moving forward.

wait, she warned.

Impatience chafed him, but a few seconds later, his new hearing informed him why she hesitated: Footsteps, and less than thirty seconds after that, a guard appeared around the far side of the square-ish building, marching along in their direction with his flashlight at the ready. He didn't amble along like some rent-a-cop security guard; he carried himself with fair discipline — *bored* discipline, perhaps, but he still seemed to take his job seriously.

Even with his enhanced night vision, Jason could not discern the particulars of the guard's uniform, but if he were to guess, he would say this was a *real* cop, working for the city, county, or state. The only upside — especially given that Jason had no idea what their intentions were — was that the guard was alone.

Regina kept waiting, and so did he. She chuffed, a quiet sound, and cocked her snout upward, above the small front entrance; Jason took a few seconds, but then he spotted the two security cameras, each covering both the entrance doors and different angles of the few parking spaces.

The guard made his way to the near corner of the building, then patrolled past the front entrance and along the wall in a counter-clockwise pattern until he finally disappeared from sight again.

now, she commanded as she hustled forward. *swing wide, avoid cameras.*

As before, Jason followed her lead, but confusion gnawed at him. *why are we here?*

follow.

In no time, the wolves stood at the base of the building, along the side where the guard had first appeared; they had been fast as ever, but Jason wondered how long they had before the guard's route brought him back around.

why are we here? he repeated. He looked left, right, and up. He saw no windows or doors or any other means of ingress, so what was the point of their standing here?

Regina did not respond, but nor did she remain where they were: She crouched, all limbs coiled to spring, then leaped halfway up the wall, her left paw somehow clutching onto a slender pipe while her right and both hind paws dug their claws into the structure's concrete.

Jason cocked his head in awe. How in the world had she—?

The answer, when it struck home, was obvious: Regina was no longer fully wolf; she had shifted mid-leap. Her limbs were a bit longer and straighter, and her paws — especially her front paws —

had returned to something closer to the human shape. It was enough to give her *hands*, which is how she had grabbed hold of the pipe.

She looked back down to him, and he saw her face had shifted as well — she was less a wolf and more a "wolfwoman," enough of a change so that she was able to (or perhaps forced to?) use actual words as she said in a low growl, "Follow."

how? he tried to ask. how do you stop the change partway?

If she "heard" him at all in her current form, she chose to ignore him. She scampered the rest of the way up the wall, using the pipe as her guide until she disappeared over the top and onto the roof. She did not look back to see if he were following as instructed.

And now he could again hear the guard's footsteps drawing closer from the rear of the building.

Great, he growled inside. *Thanks for the trial-by-fire, Regina.*

Jason closed his eyes, flattened his ears, and held his breath against the myriad of distracting smells all around him. He had managed this before, back at his apartment complex — without even trying! — transforming his hand halfway. If he could do it then, he could do it now.

The guard's footsteps drew closer on his left; hell, the man was near enough that, as the wind shifted and the air swirled, Jason could smell the nicotine gum he was chewing. And to make matters that much more stressful, he heard the building's front door open around to his right, alerting him to even *more* potential danger.

No choice.

He opened his eyes, judged the distance to the slender pipe, and leaped.

As he vaulted upward, he reached out with his left fore-paw just as Regina had. But it was still a paw, damn it, still a paw, he was going to collide with the wall and tumble down at least fifteen feet, probably landing on his back or head and then the guards would find him and assume *he* was the wolf from the airport because they were cops and cops would know about that and they would unload their guns into him and he didn't even know if they needed to use—

Jason's furry left hand closed around the pipe, and his

claw/fingernails on his right hand dug well into the concrete — judging from the previous little holes, they struck almost exactly where Regina's had. His feet scraped and scrambled for a second, then they, too, held firm.

Trying not to pant his anxiety, the wolfman hustled up toward the roof.

Regina reappeared, still a wolfwoman, and reached down to offer assistance.

"Gee, thanks," he grumbled under his breath, in a voice much deeper than usual. His sarcasm, however, did not prevent him from accepting her aid.

Jason cleared the roof edge in the nick of time. As they lay prone on the graveled surface, the first guard, the one rounding the corner from the back of the building, called out a simple, "Yo."

"'s up?" came the equally nonchalant reply from the other end. "Anything?"

"Nah. Quiet as a mouse fart."

"Big surprise."

The voices were coming together almost directly beneath where Jason and Regina were sprawled on their bellies.

The first guard asked, "Really think you need Louie?"

"Probably not. But since that big-ass heist at the money storage facility, brass still wants it all stepped up, ya know?"

Jason had just enough time to wonder who "Louie" was and how long their chitchat would go on when he caught a new scent, one that even his human-self would recognize.

As if it had been waiting for that very cue, a tremendous barking erupted from below. The police K-9, a predictable German shepherd, was going ballistic, its woofing and yapping and whine-growling all directed straight up to the roof. And Jason did not need to ask Regina what had pissed off the dog.

"Jesus, Louie! What the hell?! Knock it off!"

"What set him off?"

"Oh, who the fuck knows? Louie! *Quiet*, right now!"

Louie settled down, but Jason could hear the dog's nails scraping against the pavement as it paced back and forth.

The first guard spoke again, and based on the change in his

vocal quality, Jason was pretty sure the man was peering upward. "Sure it's nothin' to be worried about?"

The second guard's voice was also directed toward the roof, but his attitude was more lackadaisical. "Fuck, man, he probably just smells a cat or a squirrel or somethin', who the hell knows with him sometimes. Louie, sit. *Sit*, damn it."

"You sure? 'Cause that's the whole reason we have, you know, police dogs. Should we just ignore 'im? He seems pretty upset."

"Man, you *just* told me you got nothin' to report — 'quiet as a mouse fart,' right?"

"Yeah. But—"

"You got any reason to think someone climbed up onto the roof — without a ladder in sight — in the time it took you to walk 'round the building?"

"No. But still ..."

The second guard sighed. "Fine. You wanna sound the alarm?"

A respectable pause dragged on before the first guard finally admitted, "Nah. Nah, I don't want to hear about it if we're wrong."

"You could always blame Louie."

"Nah, you're right. Just ... radio and let me know if Louie gets upset like that again, okay? If he does, we go up there and take a look around. Cool?"

"Sure, man, whatever. Go on inside and warm your ass up."

"I hear that. See you in an hour?"

"Yeah. Come on, Louie." Two footsteps, then, "Come *on*, Louie. Oh, now you wanna keep sittin'? There's nothin' up there, ya dumbass. *Heel*. Now."

"I'm serious, let me know if he—"

"Yeah, yeah, yeah, I got it. Go get warm."

And with that, the guards parted ways, though Jason could still hear poor Louie whining a bit as he was dragged along in a now clockwise pattern.

Jason looked to Regina, who shook her head with an expression of distaste — a strange sight on her wolfen face. "Our cousins' cousins," she whispered in her gruff wolfwoman voice. "They always know. But the humans almost never listen."

He whispered back, "So ... why *are* we here?"

She rose onto her hind legs, her back still hunched to stay low. "Follow."

"That's starting to piss me off," he groused, but he obeyed.

Careful to crunch upon the gravel as little as possible, they moved to the center of the roof. The building had a rooftop access, but it was not an upright structure; a simple metal cover lay flush with the roof's surface. Jason glanced around and was surprised by the absence of security cameras up here — the cops must have felt confident that nothing short of a firetruck ladder could reach this high.

Regina halted over the cover, inspected it for a few seconds, then wedged a single fingernail-claw into the gap opposite the hinges. She maneuvered her claw a bit, sliding it back and forth in what he could only presume was an effort to find, open, or break whatever locked it in place. Given that she had no room for twisting her claw, the effort struck him as futile; of course, if he had any idea *why* they were here in the first place ...

Grunting in casual frustration, she withdrew her single claw and moved to one edge of the cover. She jutted her furry chin across from her and rumbled, "Take that side."

He moved into place, but rumbled back, "We're not going to be able to open it. No leverage."

This appeared to amuse her, though he was still learning to read her wolfen expressions. "Do as I say. But pull carefully; we don't want to make too much noise."

"And if I refuse to help, refuse to go any further until you tell me what the fuck we're doing here?"

Regina just stared at him, her eyes flat yet impatient.

An intangible energy passed between them, far more than a "staring contest" between regular humans; it both frustrated and stimulated Jason. And, after several strained seconds, he buckled and lowered his gaze.

Muttering, he angled his hands so that he could dig eight of his ten fingernail-claws into the tight gap — an effort, as his wrists were not quite as flexible in this form. Across from him, Regina did the same.

No one counted to three, but they both exerted force at the

same instant. Something metallic groaned and then snapped on the front opposite the hinges, and the cover jolted open. He had followed her order of caution, however, so the metal lid offered minimal squeaks as they raised it until it locked at about an eighty degree angle from the rooftop.

"Follow," she growled as she took to the short ladder within.

Jason was really beginning to hate that.

They found themselves inside a shallow attic, little more than a cramped, unkempt crawlspace, filled with darkness, dust, and the musty smell of neglect; the web-encrusted overhead hung so low, they were forced to proceed on all fours toward a second ladder. Only two rungs were visible above another lid, this one made of cheap plywood lined with foam edges, and unlocked.

Regina cocked her head, her left ear shifting toward the lid, and held herself as still as a statue; he did the same. Muffled voices drifted from somewhere below, but none of them were close enough to cause concern. The wolfwoman reached out and eased the cover upward barely an inch, her nostrils quivering as she sniffed multiple times; again, he mimicked her.

Their ears and snouts informed them that the coast was clear; it would be safe to proceed, with discretion.

Regina opened the lid far enough to slip through and indicated with a nod that Jason should hold on to it. Foregoing the ladder, she dropped through to the tiled floor below; her landing on her padded feet made almost no noise, even to his enhanced hearing. Crouching, she checked the hallway in both directions, then gestured for him to join her.

Taking the ladder to avoid any "bang" if he were to just let go of the access cover, he hurried down the rungs to stoop next to her and whispered, "Now what?"

Regina held up her hand, then she shifted back into full-wolf form and sniffed the air with more intensity, her head waving back and forth; it reminded Jason of a charmed Indian cobra. He looked around, taking in the empty, bland hallway they occupied, and found it as predictably industrial as the building's exterior. One side of the hall sported a series of windows, lined up one after the other, long rectangles of wired glass panes that were still yellowed by—

his nose told him — age-old cigarette smoke, from back when such a pastime was tolerated indoors. Since Regina was occupied with her cryptic olfactory venture, he crept toward the nearest window and peeked over the sill with one eye.

Below them lay a vast, crowded warehouse, the metallic sheen of tall shelving units — stuffed to capacity with a variety of cardboard boxes — reflecting the bright fluorescent lights. Railed along the floor, the storage shelves could be adjusted to vary the aisle space; even as he watched, a stout worker navigated her way down one of the claustrophobic aisles to slide a box into an open space. This was why he'd had difficulty judging how many floors this place had from the outside; the "ground floor" was more than twice as tall as that of most buildings. In addition to the worker, he spotted three more people, two of them in police uniforms — he imagined the day shift was made up of a larger staff, but he couldn't discount the possibility of others hidden from his vantage point, not to mention at least one more cop and his K-9 unit patrolling outside.

Behind him, the red wolf chuffed and headed down the hallway to his left.

"Wait, there're several people down there," he rumbled, "and too much light. We won't be able to move around without being seen."

She paused just long enough to stare back at him, then continued on her way.

All her dismissals grated on his nerves; he strongly considered returning to the ladder, the crawlspace, the roof, and away. Instead, he also shifted back into a full wolf — pleased to note that, each time he changed, it not only grew easier to initiate, it caused him less and less pain — and followed after her, again.

As she led him through the non-windowed and equally-dull corridors beyond, his nose caught the slightest trace of something that smelled dry and earthy, with the barest hint of incense or spices or maybe resin ... and very, very old — *ancient* was probably the better word. He did not know what it was, as he had never smelled anything quite like it in his life; were he not in full-wolf form, he suspected he would never have detected it.

He found the scent unsettling. And as he followed after Regina, who kept sniffing along with intensity, the smell grew stronger.

The apparent trail guided them to a nondescript door marked with a simple "Evidence Room C-7" sign. Rising up onto her hindlegs and shifting again into a wolfwoman, Regina reached for the doorknob and displayed zero surprise when she found it locked. Jason saw no evidence of a keypad or card-reader; it must have worked on a simple, good ol' fashioned key — quaint, but effective. Were they going to break it down and risk drawing attention? And why did they want into this particular room, with whatever the hell was giving off that disquieting smell?

She readjusted her grip, taking firm hold of the doorknob, tensed her muscles ... then hesitated. Looking over her shoulder, she told him, "Take half-form. You'll need hands." She then stepped away from the door.

He shifted, but before clutching the knob, he asked, "Why do you want me to do it?"

She smiled — at least, he thought so. That half-wolf face ... "You've explored speed, and the true scents of the world. You've chased, you've leaped, you've climbed. Now enjoy the power of your new *strength*."

In spite of himself, Jason liked the sound of that. Who wouldn't? First, he tested the doorknob, much as she had; it would only rotate a fraction of an inch before bumping against whatever mechanism prevented it from a full turn. So he gripped the knob tighter and twisted it with more force, his forearm flexing as—

Something *snapped!* inside, and the knob both wobbled and turned, hanging a little loose when he released it; he could not help but smile at this successful feat. Then the door drifted open a crack, and even his half-wolf nose could detect that hoary aroma once more.

Regina nodded in approval, then nudged past him and into Evidence Room C-7. She turned on the fluorescent light, reached back to pull him inside, then pushed the door against the jamb; it did not stay in its exact place, but so long as no one came along and took too close of a look, the fluorescents out in the hallway would camouflage any light bleeding from this room.

C-7 appeared to be some sort of transitory holding station, with relatively few bags of evidence placed upon smaller, uncrowded versions of the gigantic shelving units in the warehouse below, and no boxes in sight.

Or rather, no cardboard boxes.

On the floor against the wall opposite the door rested a large, and familiar, steel steamer trunk.

"Waaaait," Jason growled — and this time it wasn't just due to the limitations of his wolfman's throat. "Hellqvist's trunk? *That's* why we're here? I thought you weren't interested in it. You said it was a red—"

"I hadn't decided if you were worthy yet." Rather than meeting his irritated gaze, her eyes were scanning the room.

"If I was '*worthy*'? Are you fucking serious? What, did Hellqvist keep Mjölnir in there?"

Regina did not deign to respond. Instead, she padded over to a particular shelving unit and removed a digital pad from its charging dock. She held it in her left hand while her right shifted into an even more human-like condition, and then she began tapping and swiping at the screen. Her brow furrowed, and Jason guessed she might be facing a sign-in screen, but at this point he was too irked to feel any sympathy.

Creeping closer to the steamer trunk, he padded back down onto all fours and became a full wolf once more. What *was* that smell, coming from the trunk owned by an anthropologist with some big discovery to reveal to the world? He could only imagine how potent it would be if the trunk were opened, but the longer he breathed it in, the less it bothered him — no *appeal* to it, uh-uh, not at all, but it was raising his hackles less.

Then he stopped sniffing and used his eyes: In addition to the visibly mangled lock on the front of the trunk, some heavy-linked chains and a shiny, solid-looking padlock had been added — no simple name-brand lock, this one. Why would the police do that? Derek mentioned that the trunk was part of the "chain of evidence," but since they couldn't open the damn thing because the built-in lock was damaged, what was the point of making it *harder* to get into? And the weight of those links smacked of overkill.

Then his nose kicked back to the forefront: He had almost

missed it, but now he detected something else, another odor. Neither as distinct nor as robust, it was less about how it tickled his nostrils as the way it left an unpleasant metallic taste upon his tongue. Was it also coming from inside the trunk? No, he didn't think so. It wasn't the chains; he could distinguish them easily enough. He thought that it might be coming from that custom-looking lock that bound the heavy chains together. But why? Why didn't the lock just smell like the steel wafting up from the chains, and even from the steamer trunk itself? Was it some kind of tailor-made alloy? Why would anyone go to such an effort for something as simple as a padlock?

Stepping closer, Jason pushed his snout right up to the gleaming lock, his curiosity over this strange enigma serving up a nice distraction from his confusion over why they were here in the first place—

"*No!*" Regina barked from behind him.

Too late.

The instant the rubbery tissue of his nose touched the lock, searing agony crackled through his muzzle and radiated deep into his skull. Jason howled as he recoiled, eyes watering, pawing at his snout in frantic desperation with both forepaws, anything to rid himself of this awful torment. It was a sharp, sweet pain, different and worse than his transformation earlier this night, when his bones had twisted and reshaped themselves in unnatural contortions; this was an insidious pain that both burned and chilled. He staggered away from the trunk, his lupine features contorted, shaking his great shaggy head to clear away the ugly sting.

Regina crouched at his side, her hand upon his flank. Her expression, such as it was, hinted at sympathy, but her tone straddled that fence as she snarled, "Idiot. That lock is made of *silver*." She spat that last word out as though it were a foul curse.

Her touch served to ground Jason, and he was able to ease back into his wolfman form. Better able to reach with more human-shaped arms, he raised a gentle clawed hand to his abbreviated muzzle, probing the tender flesh at the tip of his nose. The initial agony was already dulling to a persistent throb, but the memory of this pain — and the knowledge of his own vulnerability, in spite of his new power — would linger far longer. He smelled intense heat, something actually burning, and feared that the flesh of his nose had been scorched by the damned metal.

Then their ears perked up as voices were raised all over the building; Jason could even hear the K-9 outside losing his damned mind.

"Oh, shit," he moaned. "My howl ..."

"Yes," Regina growled in return. "Damn. We go, now. Follow."

This time, Jason took no issue with her command. They shifted into full wolves and raced through the hallways. Had they remained two-footed — or worse, simply human — he doubted they would have made it out soon enough; the echoes of doors slamming open and boots pounding on tile told him they were no longer alone on this upper floor.

But as wolves with preternatural speed, they outdistanced their would-be captors and reached the ladder with time to spare. Back to half-human, they climbed the rungs, scampered through the crawlspace, and burst out onto the rooftop — all while closing the lids behind them to cover their tracks. Regina gestured for him to pause a moment, listened, then conducted him to the side of the building they first scaled. Down the familiar pipe, and the final drop was nothing to them. Then, again avoiding the cameras, they absconded into the night.

After several miles of the same avoid-lights/cars/people tactics, Regina slowed and guided him into the deep shadows between two closed businesses, one dark sign including the word "...Emporium," the other "Gallery ..." — their arrival scared the shit out of a pair of Persian cats, their fur matted with grime, that had been circling one another to either fight or mate; the cats bolted in opposite directions. She shifted back into a wolfwoman, and he matched her on the assumption that she wanted to talk with him; instead, she paced back and forth on her padded feet, her wolfen expression tense as she stewed in silence.

Jason took the time to rub at his snout again, the throbbing having lessened a great deal but still present; if nothing else, he did not feel any signs of literal burning. It would have been nice if she had advised him that the legendary werewolf's aversion to silver was true ... but really, even with that foreknowledge, how could he have anticipated that someone would have gone to the trouble and expense of making a *padlock* out of it? Or that it would have any distinctive smell? His human nose of old had never detected any particular odor from silver, unless it was the cheap, plated stuff.

"*Silver*," Regina grumbled at last, still pacing, her eyes scanning the cluttered pavement as though searching for something in the shadows. "Heavy chains, and a lock made out of fucking *silver*."

"I am well aware, *now*," Jason growled under his breath, knowing she could hear him.

She did not take the bait, but kept pacing. "They *knew*. They knew we would come for it." She barked her frustration. "*Of course* they'd know. They sent you to the airport, that was already a sign."

"The Watchdogs?"

She stopped and glared at him. She seemed about to say something else, but settled for, "... yes, the 'Watchdogs.' And do you know who guides the Watchdogs?"

"You mean my boss, Trey?"

She scoffed. "Yes, I mean Trey. But do you know who Trey really is?"

His first instinct was to pop off with an annoyed, *Of course! ...* but then he paused, and scowled. "Not really, I guess, no," he admitted. "But I've known that 'Trey Romero' is just a pseudonym. We all use them. For security."

"Security against what?"

"The Watchdogs generally steer clear of political crap, but there're still people out there who might not be happy about the stuff we share with the public. It protects our identities from backlash or retribution." Then something occurred to him for the first time. "And like an idiot, I told you who I was at the airport."

She waved that away. "I already knew who you were when we met. I would have smelled it on you in a heartbeat."

"Yeah, but ..."

Indeed: *Yeah, but ...*

This little exchange was reminding Jason that, no matter how enticing her personal scent, no matter that Regina was a werewolf and had known that he was at least a potential werewolf, apparently ... he still didn't really know who the hell *she* was. And now she was giving him "they" this and "they" that, hinting that there was, what, another faction of werewolves out there or something? An enemy, who was in some way behind *Watchdogs of the Weird & Unusual* — a news website that had been little more than a glorified blog not so long ago? And that *Trey* was somehow involved in all this?

Sure, he might not know who Trey "really" was, but the same could be said of "Regina from Airport," couldn't it — fellow werewolf or not?

As though sensing the shift in his thoughts, she pried her harsh gaze from him and looked toward the sky above, her nose twitching a bit as she sampled the air. She then declared, "Our unexpected delay might have been for the best. The sun will rise too soon."

He grunted. "And just like that, now you don't mind getting turned away by 'unexpected' silver, is that it?"

She ignored his question and its implied jab. "You're too new to this, Jason. You're not prepared to handle the intensity of the full moon and all it entails, and you *do* require the night, at least for the time being. The sun will diminish your gifts too far."

"What's inside that steamer trunk, Regina?"

She tried to wave him off again. "We can discuss that later—"

"No. Not 'later.' Now."

She turned on him again, her eyes afire as though daring him to challenge her.

He held his ground. "You went to a lot of trouble for this, pretending I was supposed to catch the black wolf, then bringing me here and locating that trunk — the trunk you pretended to blow off before because you didn't know if I were 'worthy,' whatever the fuck *that* was supposed to mean. But then we got turned away because 'they' got to it first and wrapped it up with a nice silver bow. So, again: What - the - *fuck* is inside that trunk, Regina?!"

He never saw her move. One instant, she stood looming over him, looking displeased but otherwise calm; the next, Jason heard a loud *smack!* and then found himself laid out by the alley wall with his left cheek burning, his jaw hurting, and his left ear ringing.

Glaring down at him, she lowered her slapping hand and stated, "That was a fair enough question, Jason." She flashed her wolfwoman fangs. "But I didn't care for *how* you asked it."

Jason gathered himself, flexed his wolfman muscles, then attempted a kip-up flip onto his feet — he'd seen the move in multiple martial arts movies, and figured it might be doable with his new strength and ability. But with his head still spinning from her power-slap, his execution was, at best, sloppy; he managed to regain his footing, but ended up slumping sideways against the wall to save himself from falling back down onto his ass.

Regina placed her hands upon her hips and watched, perhaps waiting to see whether or not he would take a swing at her in return. While he did consider doing just that, Jason was forced to accept her superior experience with these powers and forms, and settled for righting himself and holding his head high.

Satisfied, some of her tension eased as she told him, "The answer to your question, Jason, is that we're not certain what, exactly, is inside that trunk."

He rolled his eyes. "For fuck's sake, if you still don't want to tell me, just say so."

"This is not an evasion: We don't know what Hellqvist brought back with her. But we're concerned that it could be a potential threat to our community."

"Wow, that's helpful: 'Could be.' 'Potential.' And by 'community,' you mean your lycanthrope club?"

"*Our* club, and yes."

"Fine. How many of *us* are there?"

Her brow furrowed, and her voice dropped as she responded, "Not enough." She gave a little shake of her head and continued, "We tracked Hellqvist through her travels in Europe and the Middle East as best we could. She then spent a great deal of time in Egypt—"

He perked up. "I'm Egyptian."

"Yes, we know, Jason" she snarled, irked by the interruption. "And before you ask: We do not know for a fact if there's any direct connection to you or your heritage, or if it's just happenstance.

From what we can tell, she found *something* in Egypt that excited her, but she faced skepticism and even suspicion with any educational institutions or news organizations she approached for her 'grand unveiling.' For all we know, Hellqvist might have been exactly what those groups decided she was: A well-to-do crackpot with too much time, money, imagination, and possibly narcotics on her hands. All our efforts to find out what, *exactly*, she possessed have been frustratingly thwarted; there are simply too few of us to cast a tight enough net." She drew an irritated breath and spat, "Iyare was *supposed* to settle this matter on that plane, but his primal hunger clouded his judgment of Hellqvist's condition — he overestimated her initial injuries — and while he was indulging himself, Hellqvist took action to protect her steamer trunk. Iyare was then unable to open it before the plane landed."

"And 'Iyare' is the black wolf?"

"Yes. Afterward, all he could share with me was a description of the smell coming from the trunk. You've smelled it for yourself."

"Yeah. Pretty distinct. But you still don't know what it is?"

She shook her head. "Only that it smells very, very old."

"*Hrm.* I got that much, too." He thought for a moment. "And no one has posted *any* of the details on any scientific websites, or even social media about it? Not Hellqvist herself, not her team, not the various organizations she approached — even if just to mock her?"

"No. She spoke only in broad strokes — 'earth-shattering' and the like. Her stance was essentially 'seeing would be believing,' but she also wanted to keep her personal stake in the matter, so she kept the details private while seeking guarantees for full credit. But she, and all of her team, died on the plane. They appear to be the only ones who knew for certain what she found. If she told *anyone* else, we haven't uncovered it."

"Sounds like some sloppy work on Iyare's part."

Regina's eyes flared again, but she nodded her agreement. "I've dealt with Iyare over his 'sloppy work.' The matter is closed. I suggest you don't say anything about it to him."

Then another notion struck Jason. "You said before that you don't know if her trip to Egypt is in any way related to my being

Egyptian ..."

"Your point?"

"My point is that you had an answer ready for me — before I could ask, remember? Which means you're either a smooth liar, or— oh, wait, how silly of me, I *know* that you're a smooth liar."

She held her head high. "I'm not going to apologize for my subterfuge when we first met, Jason. But after showing you *this* ..." She gestured down her own body, then across to his. "... I would hope you can see we've moved beyond deceptions."

"Okay, *that* is an extremely flawed argument, but let's set that aside. *If* you're not lying to me anymore, then that means you and Iyare and whoever else makes up this 'community' of yours—"

"Of *ours*."

"—took the time to consider the *possibility* that Hellqvist's trip to Egypt was, somehow, related to me or my 'heritage.' Am I right?"

Regina neither confirmed nor denied his suggestion.

"Not tryin' to sound egotistical here — this was your presumption, not mine — but your group considered it at least feasible that this Swedish anthropologist went on some mysterious, globe-trotting hunt that led her to my proverbial homeland, and that she either found something in Egypt related to me or she followed a trail *to* Egypt because of something to do with me. Does that about cover it?"

Regina remained still another beat, then she offered a stiff nod.

Jason had been kind of hoping for a rebuttal. "Okay. Okay. So, then ... why *me*? I mean, yeah, apparently I'm a werewolf— which itself is a mind fuck I haven't had time to deal with yet, thank you very much. But so are you, and Iyare, and at least a few others out there. So ..." He raised and dropped his clawed hands in confusion and exasperation. "If there's a whole *pack* of us running around, what the hell would make *me* so special? Why would Hellqvist zero in on me and not you, or Iyare, or anyone who was *already* sprouting fur under the moon?"

Regina opened her mouth, closed it, drew a deep breath, and opened it again; Jason realized that this was the first time he had seen her unsure of herself. "I must stress, again, that we - do - not -

know if her hunt had anything to do with you."

Jason rolled his eyes. "Fine. Next topic: 'They' are responsible for the silver padlock, 'they' knew we would come for the trunk, 'they' are somehow associated with the Watchdogs. Stop playing the goddamn pronoun game, Regina. Who the hell are 'they'?"

Heat flickered through her eyes once more; Jason thought it might have been spawned of anger, or fear, or both. But when she spoke, her voice was level and smooth. " 'They' are an opposing force who—"

The sound of a metal gate being rolled up startled both of them. The noise came from the downwind side of the building she had knocked Jason against, and neither of them had heard anything to forewarn the sudden activity. Though it was still dark out, without any hint that Jason could perceive of the rising sun, the business that operated out of that building — the one with the "Emporium" sign — was already preparing to open for business.

As the echo of wheels rolling across a concrete floor drew closer, Regina whispered, "Follow. Now." She barely got the words out before assuming full-wolf form and bolting, and Jason needed no further encouragement to accompany her.

It didn't take long for Jason to realize she was leading him back to his apartment. He couldn't check the time on his phone, obviously, but he still could not see any lightening of the sky — everything appeared just as gloomy as before. However, he did notice some small variance in the *smell* of the night. How did that work? He decided he was likely picking up on shifts in temperature and humidity from the easterly wind.

He should ask Regina about it sometime, once she finished doling out the important information; getting anything useful from her was like pulling teeth!

By the time they reached his complex, he could no longer deny that the eastern sky looked more grey than black; soon it would take on a bluish tinge, or if there were more of those lingering winter clouds, then bronze, red, and yellow would follow. What might that look like through his wolf eyes? He suspected he would not have time to find out because, as Regina had cautioned, he was feeling a strange ... not quite an "ache" in his limbs, back, and elongated snout, but that wasn't too far off. He believed his body was yearning to return to its human form.

Once they reached his complex's parking area, they followed along the hedge until they were certain none of his neighbors were lurking about. In the clear, she and then he shifted back into their half-wolf forms.

"Collect your clothing," she told him as she did the same. "I suggest you stay home today. I'll see you later, and we'll talk further."

Jason nodded. He started to point out that she had implied that sex would be on the agenda before they parted ways once more, but to his surprise, he wasn't really interested anymore. As the sky brightened — the "ache" to become human had lessened once he shifted into a wolfman, but it wasn't gone — his mind was growing hazy and soft; at this point, he wanted to sleep more than he wanted to get laid, even by a statuesque former model.

So he indulged his body and returned to human form, gathered up his clothes, and, still naked, headed for the stairs. Should he say "goodnight" to her? That felt too trite, somehow, after the astonishing, mind-blowing experience they had just shared.

As he placed his free hand on the railing and his bare foot on the first step, she called, "Jason."

He looked over his shoulder, finding her also human and fully dressed save for her own bare feet. "Yeah?"

Her voice stern, she told him, "Unblock my number on your damned phone." But he thought he saw a little twinkle in her eyes, which took the edge off her command.

He offered a half-smile in return. "Sure."

She nodded in satisfaction, then, shoes still in one hand, she broke into an easy jog toward the street. As she rounded the hedge wall and disappeared from sight, he thought he might have seen another figure, a man, emerge from the shadows and join her, but he was so groggy at this point, he couldn't be sure.

After fishing his keys from his jeans, Jason entered his apartment and dropped his clothes into a careless pile on the floor. Back in familiar territory, it was tempting to believe that all of that had never actually happened, that he had somehow dreamed it while meandering around his parking lot or the nearby streets ... but no, his eyes, hearing, and especially his nose were still far more sensitive than they had ever been.

It had happened. It was real.

He was a werewolf. A fucking *werewolf.*

"I am truly," he mumbled aloud, "a prime subject for *Watchdogs of the Weird & Unusual*."

He never saw that coming.

Before collapsing onto his bed, he took the extra few seconds, as ordered, to unblock Regina on his phone. He didn't expect to hear from her right away, but before he could drift off to sleep, he got a *ping!* Groaning, he rolled over and checked his phone again, fully intending to mute it next ...

It was a text from Regina, all right. But at least she was short and to the point:

"THEY" ARE CALLED THE TRIUMVIRATE.

Escalating Circumstances

Upon waking, Jason lay on his bed and stared up at the ceiling for some time. Most of those lost minutes (hours?), his mind floated — not quite blank, but never settling on any single thought long enough to qualify as "thinking."

If there were a central theme to his drifting stream of consciousness, it would be described as: *I'm a werewolf.*

At last, that motif flowed through with a little too much clarity, too firm of substance, and he burst his own hazy bubble by saying aloud, "No way. Bullshit. All bullshit. She must've drugged me or hypnotized me or ... um ..."

But his denial died in its infancy. He wouldn't escape that way. Much like he had entertained, then rejected, Regina's suggestion that he was still dreaming as he faced her in the parking area, he could not pretend that the events of the previous night had not occurred.

Don't be insane, you gullible idiot! screamed a part of him, a desperate part. *Do you actually believe that you experienced something weird with your nose and ears and all your fillings fell out, then you went outside, found a super-tall goddess waiting for you, she got naked, a black wolf showed up, you got naked, then she turned into a fucking wolf, then* you *turned into a fucking wolf, and you both chased the black wolf for miles and miles before sneaking into a police-operated warehouse of criminal evidence, only to sting your "snout" on a padlock made from actual silver ... and then you just came home and went beddy-bye-bo-bo? Does that pretty much sum up what you think happened last night? Huh? And you believe all of* that *is somehow* more *plausible than her drugging and/or brainwashing you?* Huh*?!*

God, it was so tempting to embrace that, to accept the unreality of his situation *as* unreality, and to therefore dismiss it as "obviously" impossible. Contact Trey, tell him that Regina was more insidious than they feared. Or maybe just reject Regina's part in any of this, and seek a therapist who dealt with full-sense delusions, or better yet, check himself into a mental health facility somewhere so that he could be watched around the clock ...

No, no. While that would be a wonderful way out, sort of, he couldn't buy it. Did last night's events seem more "plausible"? Unfortunately, yes. Because even now, as he lifted his right arm so that his hand appeared before his face, he could feel it. Regina had been correct that the light of day was blocking his ability to shift — something which she hinted was temporary; that he needed the night "for the time being." But even though he couldn't change, couldn't make his hand grow pads or fur, he could still *feel* that side of him, the wolf, lurking within, like tiny ants crawling just beneath his skin — part tickle, part ache, all *potential*, just waiting for the return of night.

Could he be *that* crazy? Crazy enough to imagine phantom sensations under his flesh with such clarity? He supposed that might be the case, but he didn't believe it.

What was he supposed to do now? It struck him that Regina and he had made no arrangements, no specific agreements about getting together again at any particular time or place. But he had unblocked her on his phone, so maybe that didn't matter. He had no doubt that she would be in touch.

So ... what next, then?

For one thing, he needed to get his ass up. Lying here would no longer be a numb comfort now that he had allowed these thoughts to come into focus. He would only drive himself crazy.

Best to *try* not to think about his new "physical condition" for a while.

Ha. That's gonna be easier said than done, since I can hear the neighbors all around me better than the thin walls can explain. Hell, I can smell exactly what each of the dudes below me had for breakfast this morning.

Dragging himself up from the bed, he pulled on his underwear and nothing else. And when he stepped into the bathroom to brush his teeth, he caught his reflection in the mirror.

"Jeez," he commented, turning one way, then the other. If there were a silver lining to this madness, it was that his body was really toning up. He hadn't been in this kind of shape since ... well, honestly he had never been in this kind of shape. He repeated the same "Superman pose," and this time he was too amazed to laugh; before he knew it, he was going to end up with honest-to-God six-pack abs.

Like Regina's.

"Yeah," he confirmed without rancor. "Like Regina's. Wonder if I'll gain height, too?"

Probably not. But at this point, he wasn't prepared to dismiss anything. Seriously, once you start shapeshifting, where was the limit? *Was* there a limit?

Leaving his appealing reflection behind, he moved over to the toilet to relieve his bladder. When he was finished and leaned forward to flush, it both intrigued and grossed him out that the odor held a new appeal for his heightened olfactory sense; he was tempted to bend down and "check the quality" of his own urine, just like his family dogs used to do after hiking a leg.

Then he shook his head. "Nope, uh-uh. I've gotta set *some* limits on this thing." And so he flushed the toilet with more vigor than necessary.

Stepping out of the bathroom, he wondered again about what, exactly, was next. What's a brand new werewolf supposed to do with his time? After a few seconds, he collected his laptop. He was a journalist, after all; maybe it was time to flex those muscles instead. He was feeling a little confused about his allegiances these days, so he would tackle what he could head-on.

Logging onto his *Watchdogs* interface, he saw that Trey appeared to be online (though he knew this status notification was as shaky here as it would have been on social media). Without giving himself a chance for second thoughts, he typed:

JASON PHOTOG: GOOD MORNING, TREY. SORRY, MAKE THAT "GOOD AFTERNOON." I HAVE A QUESTION FOR YOU: AS THE GUY WHO OVERSEES THE WATCHDOGS, HAVE YOU COME ACROSS ANY

GROUP OR ORGANIZATION — OR MAYBE JUST THREE INDIVIDUALS, I GUESS — WHO GO BY THE NAME "THE TRIUMVIRATE"?

He sat back to wait. He was hoping his ostensible boss would come back with ... well, he didn't know exactly what he was hoping for here. At this point, he would be happy for something that either shattered the foundation of Regina's accusations *or* any sort of confession from Trey; either of those would help him better understand where he stood. Of course, Trey might reply, "You mean, like, the form of government or something?" Or hell, he could just respond with, "No. Why?"

Eventually, enough time passed that Jason knew Trey was either away from his computer or was avoiding his "simple" question. If the latter, was this, in itself, a confession? He had no way of knowing.

Great, so much for that idea. So what else could he do, right here, right now?

After he had verbally cornered her, Regina admitted that she and her furry comrade "Iyare" reckoned it was *feasible* that Hellqvist had ended up in Egypt because of Jason, or his family line, in some way. Was there anywhere he could go with that? Should he call his parents, ask about their lineage? But which parent's side? Neither of them had actually grown up in Egypt. His mom's family had been here, in the United States, long enough that it was a minor miracle that she was full-blooded Egyptian. On his dad's side, it was Jason's grandparents who had made the trek with their child, his dad's older brother, in tow; his grandmother had not even known she was pregnant with his dad at the time. Both of those grandparents were deceased now, and Jason's dad was their only living child — Jason's uncle, Amon, had been killed in a car accident when he was twenty years old. Jason never met him, and his dad seldom spoke of him; in fact, his dad rarely talked at all about any of his family history, just having shared that his grandfather in particular had been happy to move his family away from such a volatile part of the world.

With that in mind, Jason doubted his dad would be able to help much; he would not be able to offer any family history from before they immigrated to the States. The same would go for his mom, even more so given how Americanized her side of the family tree was.

Damn it. Square One again.

Okay, what about this: Trey wasn't the only fellow Watchdog he could contact.

Jason pulled up the list for the other *Watchdogs* contributors; there weren't all that many, but they had added another half-dozen since breaking the Arach-mageddon story. He scrolled through the names, considering who might be able to help him dig deeper into this mysterious Triumvirate ...

One name jumped out at him: Shelley_O, the self-proclaimed "Occult Detective." If anyone on the Watchdogs team would have insight into some secret cabal, it would be her — for a website that steered clear of traditional conspiracy theories, Shelley_O was the one Watchdog Jason could easily imagine having a corkboard in her bedroom with thumbtacked photos and red string threaded over it like a spider's web. He had always been a bit skeptical of Shelley_O's areas of so-called "expertise," often dismissing her skill set as closer to tabloid fodder than Trey typically allowed. But ... desperate times, et cetera.

Unfortunately, the interface showed her as being offline, but he could still send her a message.

JASON PHOTOG: HEY, SHELLEY. I'M WORKING ON A STORY, AND I COULD USE YOUR HELP WITH SOMETHING: MIGHT YOU KNOW ANYTHING ABOUT A GROUP CALLED "THE TRIUMVIRATE"? THIS HYPOTHETICAL GROUP — AND I STRESS THE WORD "HYPOTHETICAL" — MIGHT HAVE SOMETHING TO DO WITH PEOPLE WHO BELIEVE IN LYCANTHROPY. YEAH, YEAH, I KNOW, NOT MY USUAL BEAT — I PROMISE, I'M NOT TRYING TO HORN IN ON YOUR TERRITORY! BUT THIS COULD BE RELATED TO THAT INCIDENT AT THE AIRPORT (YOU WOULD NOT BELIEVE THE RUMORS RUNNING AROUND ABOUT THAT, OR MAYBE YOU WOULD?). IF "THE TRIUMVIRATE" RINGS ANY BELLS FOR YOU, I'D APPRECIATE ANY INSIGHT YOU COULD OFFER. THX

Jason sent the message, then perused the contact list again ...

The next hour proved quite frustrating. As he reached out to each of the Watchdogs who were indicated as being online, he grew suspicious of how many of them were also, apparently, "away from their desk." One of them, Deeper Throat (Jason always rolled his eyes at that one; sure, he got the historical Watergate reference, but come on!), sent a simple "Hi!" in response to Jason's, but as soon as Jason typed out his request for any information about the Triumvirate, all he got was:

DEEPER THROAT: SORRY, JASON. GOTTA GO. TTYL

And then his online indicator went dark.

While that exchange with Deeper Throat was the most blatant example of avoidance, they all seemed to be ducking him. Why in the world would they do that? It would be one thing if he had been asking something volatile, like, "Any suggestions on how to put together a homemade explosive?" But he was just asking about a *word*, for fuck's sake!

Except with most of them, he never got that far, never got to "trigger" them with the term "Triumvirate," because the assholes weren't bothering to respond to his initial greetings.

Come on, now. Don't get paranoid. These people have lives, you know. Hell, you're barely *scraping by with your stipends from* Watchdogs*; you can bet most of them have to work another job. And how many times have you forgotten to log out properly? They probably aren't even on the interface right now.*

Fine. He tried not to make too much of this "colleague snobbery." Still ...

Jason rose from his chair, intending to engage in some energy-burning pacing, when he got a pleasant surprise.

SHELLEY_O: BONJOUR, JASON! ARE YOU STILL THERE?

Jason plopped his butt back into his seat so hard, his chair rocked to the side.

JASON PHOTOG: SHELLEY! YES, HI, I'M STILL HERE. HOW'VE YOU BEEN?

SHELLEY_O: I'VE BEEN GREAT! SO, YOU WANNA KNOW ABOUT A WEREWOLF GROUP CALLED THE TRIUMVIRATE? BOY, YOU WEREN'T KIDDING — THIS IS NOT YOUR USUAL WHEELHOUSE, IS IT? LOL BY THE WAY, I LOVED YOUR PIECE ABOUT THOSE WEIRD, SCARY "ROARS" PEOPLE WERE HEARING A FEW MONTHS AGO! I WAS PROUD THAT A FELLOW WATCHDOGGY FIGURED OUT IT WAS

JUST COMING FROM THE LOCAL DAM! LOL

Jason almost corrected her assumption about "werewolf group" and "the Triumvirate" automatically going hand-in-hand. Instead, he wrote:

JASON PHOTOG: THANKS! SO DOES "THE TRIUMVIRATE" MEAN ANYTHING TO YOU? APART FROM THE METHOD OF GOVERNMENT, OF COURSE.

SHELLEY_O: OF COURSE! AND YES, IT SURE DOES.

Jason's heartbeat quickened.

SHELLEY_O: BUT SERIOUSLY, WHY THE SUDDEN INTEREST IN THIS? THIS IS USUALLY MY THING, AND YES, I'M WELL AWARE OF WHAT MOST OF THE OTHER, MORE "GROUNDED" WATCHDOGS THINK ABOUT ME. I JUST DON'T CARE! LOL

Frustrated that she had changed the subject again, Jason considered his answer. Rather than outright lie to her, he decided to stick as close to the truth as he dared; it also occurred to him that Trey probably had the ability to see everything they were writing to one another.

JASON PHOTOG: TREY HAS ME FOLLOWING UP ON THAT CRAZY INCIDENT AT THE AIRPORT. I'M TRYING TO TRACK THAT HUGE ANIMAL FROM THE AIRPLANE, AND AMONG OTHER RUMORS, I'VE COME ACROSS ONE THAT IT WAS A "WEREWOLF" (SMH, NO OFFENSE). AS I'VE LOOKED INTO THAT — JUST TO COVER MY BASES — I'VE COME ACROSS THIS WORD, "TRIUMVIRATE," A COUPLE OF TIMES. I'M TRYING TO RUN DOWN WHO THEY MIGHT BE, AND WHY THEY MIGHT THINK THE ANIMAL WAS A WEREWOLF. WHAT CAN YOU TELL ME?

SHELLEY_O: JEEZ, JUICY STUFF! WHERE DO I START?! LOL

SHELLEY_O: OK, HERE'S SOME OF WHAT I'VE HEARD THROUGH MY SOURCES IN THE OCCULT COMMUNITY. KEEP IN MIND, THIS IS ALL JUST RUMOR AND SPECULATION. SERIOUSLY, EVEN *I* TAKE THIS STUFF WITH A GRAIN OF SALT, AND YOU KNOW HOW I AM! BUT WHERE THERE'S SMOKE, THERE'S OFTEN HELLFIRE, IF YOU KNOW WHAT I MEAN. ;-)

SHELLEY_O: "THE TRIUMVIRATE" ARE SUPPOSEDLY THIS TRIO OF UBER-POWERFUL SUPERNATURAL CREATURES. SOME THINK THEY'RE KIND OF THE ILLUMINATI OF THE MONSTER WORLD. THESE

BIG THREE AREN'T JUST WEREWOLVES, EITHER! THEY'RE SAID TO BE MADE UP OF ONE WEREWOLF, ONE VAMPIRE, AND (GET THIS!) ONE ZOMBIE! CAN YOU IMAGINE? TALK ABOUT A MOTLEY CREW. :-D

Jason's eyes both widened and rolled. *What the hell is she—?*

SHELLEY_O: FROM WHAT I'VE BEEN ABLE TO GATHER, THIS TRIUMVIRATE POLICES AND CONTROLS THE ACTIVITIES OF ALL THE OTHER MONSTERS, KEEPING THEM IN LINE SO THEY DON'T EXPOSE THEIR EXISTENCE TO THE HUMAN WORLD. THEY'RE REALLY HARDCORE ABOUT SECRECY, AND WILL RUTHLESSLY ELIMINATE ANY CREATURE THAT THREATENS TO BLOW THE LID OFF THE SUPERNATURAL. WOULD THAT MEAN US HUMANS, TOO? I DON'T KNOW.

SHELLEY_O: THE WEREWOLF IS RUMORED TO BE THE APEX ALPHA, STRONGER AND FASTER THAN ANY OTHER LYCANTHROPES OUT THERE, PRESUMABLY INCLUDING YOUR WOLFIE FRIEND FROM THE AIRPORT. THE VAMPIRE MEMBER IS SUPPOSEDLY A NOSFERATU, ONE OF THE ANCIENT ONES WHO HAS INCREDIBLE MIND CONTROL ABILITIES. AND THE ZOMBIE? WELL, NO ONE KNOWS WHAT TO MAKE OF THAT. A SENTIENT ZOMBIE WITH FREE WILL? COME ON! IT BOGGLES THE MIND: A WEREWOLF, A VAMPIRE, AND A ZOMBIE (SOUNDS LIKE THE SETUP FOR A "WALKS INTO A BAR" JOKE!), SOMEHOW WORKING TOGETHER? IT MAKES EVEN THE MOST DEVOUT MONSTER AFICIONADOS QUESTION IF THEY EXIST AT ALL, OR IF THEY'RE ALL JUST A "BOOGEYMAN STORY" MONSTERS TELL EACH OTHER TO KEEP THEMSELVES IN LINE.

Jason sat back from his laptop, his mind reeling from the avalanche of fantastical information Shelley_O had unleashed upon him. A werewolf, a *vampire*, and a fucking *zombie*, secretly controlling the monster world from the shadows? It sounded utterly ludicrous!

... and yet, a day ago he would have felt equally skeptical about the werewolf part, too.

He raised his arm and again felt that wriggling tickle beneath his skin when he tried to make it change; it remained the same in appearance, but the sensation, the potential, was undeniable.

Yeah, but there are limits, for God's sake! he thought, shaking his head. *Supernatural bloodsuckers and undead cannibals? At*

least "werewolves" are, like, an amped-up version of something real, *of actual living, breathing animals. The others are just ...* impossible*!*

But then he regarded his arm once more. Here he was again: After last night, could he discount *anything* out of hand? He would ask Regina about all of this, really push her about it, since she had proven herself, at best, inconsistent with the flow of information.

In the meantime, Shelley_O was still going:

SHELLEY_O: OOOOOH, WHAT I WOULDN'T GIVE TO ACTUALLY MEET THESE THREE AND GET THEIR STORY! THAT WOULD BE THE INTERVIEW OF A LIFETIME, NOT TO MENTION PROVE TO EVERYONE THAT I'M NOT TOTALLY NUTSO AFTER ALL! BUT I IMAGINE I'D PROBABLY END UP WITH MY THROAT TORN OUT WITHIN ONE MINUTE. LOL

SHELLEY_O: ANYWAY, YEAH, THAT'S THE GIST OF WHAT I'VE HEARD ABOUT THIS MYSTERIOUS MONSTER "TRIUMVIRATE." PRETTY CRAZY, HUH? OH, I'D LOVE TO KNOW IF THEY'RE ACTUALLY INVOLVED WITH THIS AIRPORT "WEREWOLF" SITUATION. KEEP ME POSTED ON WHATEVER YOU FIND OUT, OK? PROMISE?

JASON PHOTOG: OF COURSE! I APPRECIATE YOUR HELP WITH THIS, SHELLEY. IF THREE SUPERNATURAL BEINGS KNOCK ON MY DOOR TONIGHT AFTER SUNSET, YOU'LL BE THE FIRST PERSON I TELL ... UNLESS IT'S JUST A WITCH, A TROLL, AND A SASQUATCH, IN WHICH CASE I'M SURE YOU WOULDN'T BE INTERESTED. ;-)

SHELLEY_O: LOL YEAH, WHO WOULD WANT TO INTERVIEW LOSERS LIKE THAT?! :-P

Jason was trying to think of a polite way to end the conversation when she added something that recaptured his attention.

SHELLEY_O: SERIOUSLY, THOUGH, FORGET SCORING AN ACTUAL INTERVIEW (AS MUCH AS I WOULD LOVE IT!). IF I COULD EVER FIND SOMETHING, ANYTHING THAT COULD PROVE A THING LIKE THIS TRIUMVIRATE REALLY EXISTED, THAT WEREWOLVES AND VAMPIRES AND ZOMBIES WERE NOT ONLY ACTUAL, REAL THINGS, BUT THAT THREE OF THESE BADDIES WERE OUT THERE, WORKING TOGETHER, MAYBE TREY WOULD SHOW MORE INTEREST NEXT TIME, AMIRIGHT?

Jason froze, then hit Backspace until the "talk to you later" message he had been composing disappeared.

JASON PHOTOG: WHAT DO YOU MEAN "NEXT TIME"?

SHELLEY_O: WELL, WE ALL KNOW THAT TREY DOESN'T LIKE TO MOVE FORWARD ON A STORY WITHOUT SOMETHING AKIN TO HARD EVIDENCE. THAT'S WHY THE WATCHDOGS WEBSITE DIDN'T REALLY GET ON THE MAP UNTIL ARACH-MAGEDDON (WHICH IS ALSO WHY ALMOST ALL OF US ARE LOCATED AROUND AND ABOUT SOCAL, CAUSE WE WERE HERE FOR IT!). BUT NOW THAT WE ARE ON THE MAP, I THOUGHT WE MIGHT BE ABLE TO STRETCH OUT A LITTLE? LET'S FACE IT: MOST OF OUR REGULAR READERS ARE PRETTY "FRINGE," BUT THAT DOESN'T MEAN THAT THEY (WE) ARE ALL CRAZY!

SHELLEY_O: I'VE BEEN INTO THIS STUFF MY WHOLE LIFE (BIG SURPRISE I'VE ENDED UP A WATCHDOG, AMIRIGHT?), BUT I'VE REALLY BEEN HEARING INTERESTING RUMBLINGS FOR THE PAST FEW YEARS, STUFF LIKE A SUPER-WEIRD SLEW OF MURDERS (REALLY BLOODY, TOTAL MASSACRES!) IN OKLAHOMA, WITH THE SUSPECTS DISAPPEARING INTO THIN AIR (NOT LITERALLY... OR WAS IT?!); CORPSES TURNING UP IN MAJOR CITIES WITH THEIR THROATS MANGLED BUT NOT NEARLY ENOUGH BLOOD ON THE SCENE; RUMORS ABOUT WEREWOLVES UP IN ALASKA LAST SUMMER; CADAVERS UP AND VANISHING FROM MORGUES; HOMELESS PEOPLE BEING EATEN! TERRIBLE BUT INTRIGUING STUFF LIKE THAT.

SHELLEY_O: WHILE ARACH-MAGEDDON WAS STILL THE HOTTEST TOPIC IN TOWN, I THOUGHT I COULD FINALLY PUT TOGETHER A REAL STORY, MAYBE START A WHOLE SERIES, BEGINNING WITH: A FEW NEIGHBORS OF THAT AWARD-WINNING FILMMAKER WHO WENT MISSING, FRANCIS MORSE, SWORE ON A STACK OF BIBLES THAT SOME REALLY WEIRD SHIT WAS GOING DOWN AROUND HIS HOUSE IN THE WEEKS LEADING UP TO ARACH-MAGEDDON. THESE PEOPLE SWEAR ON THEIR MOTHERS' GRAVES THAT MONSTERS WERE AFOOT!

SHELLEY_O: ONE OF THEM WENT ON ABOUT HUMAN-SIZED SPIDERS (WHICH I HAD TO TAKE WITH EVEN MORE GRAINS OF SALT, GIVEN HOW SPIDER-FREAKED EVERYONE WAS AT THE TIME), BUT A THROUPLE WHO LIVED DIRECTLY ACROSS THE STREET FROM

MORSE TALKED ABOUT NOISES THAT WILL GIVE THEM NIGHTMARES FOREVER AND A DAY. *AND*, THE NIGHT EVERYTHING EXPLODED AND ANGELENOS' ATTENTION WAS PULLED IN EVERY DIRECTION, THEY CLAIM THEY SAW THREE MEN LEAVING MORSE'S PLACE AND SNEAKING OFF INTO THE DARKNESS, AND THEY WERE ALL TORN UP TO THE POINT WHERE NORMAL PEOPLE WOULD'VE BEEN CALLING FOR MEDICAL AID!

SHELLEY_O: NOW ... WERE THOSE "THREE MEN" THE EVER-ELUSIVE "TRIUMVIRATE"? I'M NOT READY TO DRAW THAT CONCLUSION. NOT YET. BUT I DID THINK THAT I COULD RIDE THE COATTAILS OF ARACH-MAGEDDON FAR ENOUGH TO WRITE AN EDITORIAL ABOUT IT, YOU KNOW?

Shelley_O paused there, and Jason realized that was his cue for some sort of affirmation.

JASON PHOTOG: YEAH, SURE. WHY NOT? PERFECT TIMING—EVERYONE WAS PANICKED ABOUT SPIDERS LOSING THEIR COLLECTIVE MINDS, SO MAYBE THEY'D BE OPEN FOR SOMETHING EVEN WEIRDER THAN OUR USUAL TURF, RIGHT?

SHELLEY_O: EXACTLY! BUT WHEN I PITCHED IT TO TREY, HE SHUT ME DOWN, HARD. I DON'T MEAN THAT HE WAS RUDE ... WELL, ACTUALLY, YEAH, I KIND OF THOUGHT HE WAS RUDE, BUT SINCE YOU CAN'T HEAR SOMEONE'S TONE OF VOICE OVER A MESSAGE BOARD, I TRY NEVER TO PROJECT MY OWN FEELINGS, YOU KNOW?

SHELLEY_O: ANYWAY, BOTTOM LINE IS: TREY TOLD ME THAT HE WASN'T INTERESTED IN ANY "TRIUMVIRATE" EDITORIALS. I MEAN, HE WAS A LITTLE MORE ELOQUENT THAN THAT (WHICH ITSELF WAS KIND OF SURPRISING, CONSIDERING HOW SLOOOOOOOW HE USED TO TYPE AND THE SIMPLE VOCAB HE USED TO USE; WHEN DID THAT CHANGE?!), BUT THAT WAS MORE OR LESS THE MESSAGE.

SHELLEY_O: WELL, SPEAK OF THE DEVIL! HANG ON, JASON. BELIEVE IT OR NOT, I'VE GOT TREY PINGIN' ME. BRB!

Trey, back online and pinging Shelley_O *right now*? Was that a coincidence? He could only wait and see.

While he bided his time, Jason stewed over this newest info: Trey shut down Shelley_O's story about the Triumvirate. Then something more occurred to him, and he tabbed over to his message thread with Trey; the little green circle indicated that his question to Trey about the Triumvirate had been read, but Trey had chosen not to reply to it.

What did all of this tell him? Anything? He couldn't be certain yet, but it didn't give him a good feeling. Not at all.

He tabbed back over to his conversation with Shelley_O and waited. Another minute passed, then two. She was still showing as online, but that little indicator had not served him well today—

The little dots started dancing; she was typing something. He leaned forward in his chair, more anxious about receiving an online message than he had been in quite some time. Finally, it came through:

SHELLEY_O: HEY, JASON. SORRY, I'M AFRAID I HAVE TO GO. :-(

He wanted to reply with, "What? Why?" But he had a feeling he already knew why — not that he understood what the hell this was all about.

Unless Regina was telling the truth. About Trey, and about this so-called Triumvirate.

He saw no sense in making Shelley_O feel bad about it, so he settled for:

JASON PHOTOG: OKAY.

He could see that she had already been typing, so her reply appeared right on the heels of his.

SHELLEY_O: I CAN'T SAY MUCH, BUT I WILL SAY THIS: I AM LOGGING OFF UNDER PROTEST!!!

JASON PHOTOG: THAT'S ALL RIGHT, SHELLEY. WE'RE COOL, OKAY?

SHELLEY_O: OK. YOU TAKE CARE OF YOURSELF, JASON. STAY SAFE. WE'LL CATCH UP SOMETIME. PROMISE. GB

He wanted to write something more, but Shelley_O was already offline.

Growling in anger — and not at all conscious of how animalistic it came out — Jason snatched up his phone, fully intending to text Trey with some equivalent of "What the fuck is your problem, man?!" But then he thought better of it and tossed the phone aside; it skipped across the table and fell to the carpet.

Instead, he resumed his intense pacing around his living room.

Okay, what do I have here? Regina implied that Trey, via the Watchdogs, was using me somehow, and that it involved some enemy faction called the Triumvirate. So I asked Trey about it, all innocent-like, and now Trey's ignoring me, and the other Watchdogs are ignoring me, except for Shelley_O — until she got pulled aside, Internet-style, by Trey, after which she logged off "under protest."

Except, now that I think about it, my chronology is off: Even online, there's no way Trey could have spread the word so quickly after I asked him about the Triumvirate, which means he had already told *the others not to talk to me — except for Shelley_O, who must not have gotten the memo soon enough.*

How could Trey have been prepared for this ahead of time, unless he somehow knows what happened to me last night, which would mean he's been spying *on me?*

He halted his stride, took a deep breath, and held it until his lungs burned. Okay, getting paranoid was not going to help his mental stability. If Trey were spying on him, if he *knew* Jason had become a werewolf, he wouldn't ignore him or scare the other Watchdogs away — Jason would become Story Number One, something to blow away Arach-mageddon as the biggest break yet for *Watchdogs of the Weird & Unusual.*

Except he shut down Shelley_O's story about the Triumvirate.

Okay, fair counterpoint. But the difference (if he were to play devil's advocate on Trey's behalf) was that Shelley_O's story would have still been based on rumors and hearsay; Shelley_O herself had admitted as much — "take with a grain of salt" and all that. But Jason's being able to *literally* turn into a large wolf? Photos could be faked, as could video these days, but he would have expected Trey to beg him for a tell-all interview. First stop, live-streaming on *Watchdogs*; next stop, live primetime television event.

Unless, as Regina hinted, Trey is involved with *this Triumvirate, in which case breaking stories about us would not be his primary goal.*

Jason moaned, running his fingers through his hair. Damn, paranoia was a slippery slope! Who was he to believe? Regina or

Trey? Or rather, Regina *against* Trey, since Trey had not actually done anything, except ask him to follow up on the wolf-at-the-airport story.

That, plus seeming to have told the other Watchdogs not to talk to him.

"Christ, there I go again," he muttered.

He continued pacing, but it wasn't enough. Like the night before, his apartment confined him; he wanted to move, he wanted *out*.

Fine. At least this time he could be reasonably sure that he would not find Regina waiting for him outside — and even if she were out there, he doubted she would pull another striptease in the middle of the afternoon. He also remembered to get dressed before reaching for the door.

Outside, he leaned against the railing and drew a deep breath. All the same odors, both pleasant and putrid, remained present, but they had changed in the light of day; the warmth of the afternoon sun intensified some smells while diminishing others. He also discovered that he was better able to filter them, to choose which ones came to the forefront while he pushed back the rest.

That'll come in handy the next time I have to drive past a backed-up sewer.

Descending the stairs — he took them two at a time, with no habitual fear of tripping flat on his face — he headed toward the road. Last time he went left, so he decided to go right this time, simply for a change of scenery. Neither direction mattered much, so long as he was burning energy. Unfortunately, before he had even left his complex, frustration built over how *slow* it felt to walk on two legs; after last night's exhilarating escapade, he was already spoiled by the sheer speed of—

"Fuckin' puta!"

Jason's head snapped forward. The yell was not as loud as other times he'd had the misfortune to listen to it, but with his new hearing, Sir Asshole might as well have had his apartment door wide open. And his delightful salutation was followed by a sound even pre-enhanced Jason could have heard: *Slap!*

Jason reached back for his phone ... then stopped. The tension, the anger that had arisen within him prompted a whole-body flex, and fur or no fur, he could feel his taut new muscles, feel their strength yearning for release.

Yeah, this would burn more energy than any walk. And calling the cops never helped, anyway.

Another slap came, this one less dynamic, but he could still hear the sobbing that the second blow provoked.

Jason crossed the street. The city had no traffic light here, but he wouldn't have had the patience to wait for the right-of-way. Someone hit their brakes, shouted at him with her window still up; he ignored her. The same kids he had seen playing around with the western gray squirrel stood from some sort of card game so they could gawk at Jason; he ignored them, too.

He hit the stairs on the left, climbed to the second floor, and marched toward the offender's apartment; he knew it well from watching the police's futile visits in the past. Clenching his fist, he pounded hard enough for the door to rattle in its frame, bringing an instantaneous pause to the domestic "squabble" inside — Sir Asshole and his Stockholm-Syndromed girlfriend probably thought it was the cops, again.

"Yeah?!" Sir Asshole called, his voice cagey as he approached to answer.

Jason placed his right hand over the peephole and pounded on the door again with his left. And he realized that his pulse was pounding in his temples just as hard; all of his confusion and frustration over Regina-versus-Trey percolated to the top in the form of righteous fury, and he was more than happy to have found a deserving target for it.

He heard Sir Asshole grumble "Goddamn it ..." under his breath from the other side, then he raised his voice, "Who the fuck is it?!"

Jason said nothing, his lips curling back into a half-smile, half-snarl, as he banged some more.

Figuring the cops would not play this game, Sir Asshole's temper got the best of him (big surprise) and he started unlocking the door. "Aw right, fuck-head, I'm gonna mess—!"

The instant the doorknob turned, Jason stepped back and

kicked the door inward as hard as he could — to Jason's disappointment, it slammed into Sir Asshole's muscular chest as much as his face. But it still knocked the white guy back; he caught his thigh on the arm of an imitation La-Z-Boy, sending him sprawling to the floor.

As Jason moved into the apartment, a flurry of panicked Spanish flew his way. He glanced toward a hallway to see a scantily-clad, young-ish Latina, whose expression fell somewhere between fear and anger — the latter did not surprise him; this was the same woman who never pressed charges when the police showed up. Nor was he surprised by the redness of her left cheek and the swelling under her left eye.

When Jason looked back, Sir Asshole was scrambling to his feet, blood visible in his right eyebrow. The impact from the door had discombobulated him, but he tried not to let it show. "The fuck are *you*?!" he demanded. "Wait, I know you! You live across—!"

Jason wasn't here to exchange words with Sir Asshole. He drove his fist into the guy's gut.

But, new muscles or not, Jason was not an experienced fighter, and Sir Asshole was; the bigger man turned his torso just enough that Jason's fist caught him more in the ribs than the solar plexus. He retaliated with a thick left forearm that caught Jason across the jaw.

Days ago, such a blow would have flattened Jason, the fight already over. But that was the old Jason; he was someone else now.

The gangster-wannabe attempted to follow this with a vicious right hook to Jason's face. Jason pulled his neck back to avoid the punch, then jerked forward, head-butting his opponent — their height difference allowed Jason a perfect forehead-to-nose impact, and he felt the satisfying crunch of bone as Sir Asshole's schnoz burst like a ripe tomato. Blood gushing down his lips and chin as he toppled over backward, Sir Asshole still managed a kick that caught Jason in his right shin just below his knee.

Sir Asshole was slower to recover this time, which allowed Jason to reach down and rub his painful tibia. He didn't have time for more than a brief massage — a blur in his peripheral vision forced him to duck farther as a glass ashtray whirled past his head.

He twisted toward the new threat ...

The Latina girlfriend picked up the next item she could lay her hands on — this time, laughably, a thick magazine — and hurled it toward Jason as she scurried down beside her abusive man, her hands hovering over his bloody face in uncertainty. "Mi amor," she wailed, "¿estás bien?!" Her top was so skimpy that the move had exposed her left breast, but under the circumstances, Jason found the sight more depressing than lewd.

Voices drifted in from the open front door. None of Sir Asshole's neighbors had appeared yet, but they were creeping closer.

This was stupid. I didn't think this through. If I wanted to go all vigilante on this loser, I should've gone about it better. Too many witnesses!

But Sir Asshole had already stated that he recognized Jason. What the hell should he do now? Should he contact Derek, confess what happened but stress the *why* of it, see if maybe he could get some law enforcement ass-covering that way? If he called Regina, he imagined she wouldn't be too happy about the unwanted attention this would bring.

Then it occurred to him: *Or could this actually be my way out? I can't help Regina with the steamer trunk* or *this Triumvirate if I'm locked up for assault.*

Tempting notion, in theory. But did he really want to spend time in jail over *this* prick?

Speaking of, Sir Asshole was using the wall to pull himself back to his feet. His eyes were blinking a lot and a bit unfocused, but he looked more angry than in pain; he glared at Jason, though the effect was lost somewhat because of the crimson streaming down his face.

"You piece of shit," he snarled, spitting blood. "You're fuckin' dead, you hear me? Fucking. *Dead.*"

His girlfriend clung to his arm even as she belatedly realized that her top was revealing too much and rolled her shoulder to fix it. "Déjalo, mi amor!" she pleaded with him. "¡No vale la pena!"

But Sir Asshole shook her off with a rough snap of his arm; for a second, it looked as though he might slap her again, and if he did,

Jason wouldn't be able to refrain from diving into the fight anew. Instead, Sir Asshole settled for hissing at her, "Shut up, puta."

The girlfriend dropped her eyes to the floor and shrank back.

Sir Asshole took an unsteady step toward Jason, fists clenched at his sides. "I'm gonna make you regret the day you were born, cabrón. No one fucks with me and gets away with it. You understand, you piece of shit?"

Except Jason met his furious gaze without the slightest flinch. "You *sure* you wanna pursue this?" Jason asked; in spite of the sunlight drifting in from behind him, his voice came out so close to a literal growl, it surprised even him. "I promise, it will not end well for you." He advanced with measured ease, bringing him right back into Sir Asshole's personal space.

Jason was reasonably certain that he did not shapeshift at all; that he was, as Regina had warned, still limited by the daytime. But *something* in Jason's eyes made Sir Asshole hesitate — maybe it was a feral gleam, a hint of animal savagery lurking beneath the surface; or maybe it was Jason's utter lack of fear, the confident resolve of a predator who knows he can, and will, tear his prey to shreds. Whatever it was, it gave the ugly white man pause.

"Mi amor, por favor," the girlfriend whispered, daring to get close enough to touch him again, to tug at his blood-soaked shirt. "No sigas con esto."

Sir Asshole's eyes darted between Jason and his girlfriend, indecision warring across his battered features. The voices outside grew louder; Jason needed to get out of here.

Finally, with a disgusted snort, Sir Asshole backed down. "Whatever, fuckhead," he muttered, wiping at his bloody face with the back of his hand. "Fuck off outta here before I change my mind. But remember: *I know where you live*."

Given Jason's presence in *his* home, that final threat was absurd, but it set him up for Jason's comeback. "And I know where *you* live, obviously. If I *ever* hear you raise your voice at her — or *hit* her — ever again, I will come back for you. Do you understand me?"

Sir Asshole made quite the face at that, trying for amusement, disgust, and dismissive spite, but he couldn't quite sell it with his eyes refusing to meet Jason's.

Jason slapped him. Not hard; in fact, the casualness of it added greater insult than injury. The guy flinched away, his eyes blinking rapidly again, heavy with surprise — and shame, when he did nothing in return.

Jason bared his teeth. "Do - you - understand - me?"

Sir Asshole tried sneering, but settled for blinking some more and lowering his gaze again. "Yeah," he spat in frustration. "I understand."

"Good. Because I'll be *listening*."

Sir Asshole shrugged, still desperate to save some pride but too flustered to achieve it.

Keeping a wary eye on him just in case, Jason backed out of the apartment. Once out on the walkway that wasn't much different from the one at his own complex, he sauntered toward the stairs, doing his best to ignore the gawkers, as well as keeping his face turned downward and away from the many cell phones that were recording his exit. His heart pounded with adrenaline, and with something else: The thrill of dominance, of putting that abusive bastard in his place.

As he descended the stairs and crossed the street (this time waiting for an opening in traffic), he couldn't help feeling a rush of savage satisfaction.

In short, the wolf inside him howled with approval, and that brought a smile to his face.

* * *

Jason's lycanthropic (and testosterone-fueled) high lasted as far as his return home.

Standing in his own living room, away from Sir Asshole's defeated posture, Jason's confidence evaporated. Had he scared the guy? Yeah, he thought so; he had kicked a fair amount of ass, and the only up-front cost was a sore jaw and bruised shin (and both were recovering faster than his pre-changed self would've expected). But how long would Sir Asshole stew in the juices of his embarrassment, his disgrace over losing a fight to someone smaller than him and his gym muscles, before he decided that he must do something to redeem his honor?

If he were still too skittish to take Jason on again one-to-one, he might ask a handful of friends to help jump Jason when he least expected it. Or hell, he had told Jason, point blank, that he was "fucking dead." Maybe he would work himself up into something *more* than a returned ass-kicking? Jason had learned the hard way that lycanthropy and silver were an awful mix, but what would happen if Sir Asshole shot him with a regular bullet? And what if it was a gunshot to the *head*? Would his new abilities allow him to walk away from something like that? What were his limits?

Only one person could answer these questions: Regina.

Pulling out his phone, he hesitated. Texting her, texting Trey; every damn move felt risky, given his uncertain allegiances. At what point would he become dependent enough on Regina that he would be committed to her "side" by default?

But how else was he supposed to get answers? For God only knew what reason, Trey seemed to have cut him off from Shelley_O and the other Watchdogs. And Jason had no desire to fall down the rabbit hole that would be a Google search on "rules for werewolves;" he could only imagine—

Jason jolted when his phone *pinged!* in his hand. Given the timing, he fully expected it to be Regina, maybe even texting him along the lines of, "Why would you do something stupid like that?!" After all, he suspected that Trey might be spying on him, but he knew for a fact that Regina had already done so.

But instead, he found the text was coming from an Unknown Number. On the one hand, that did not eliminate Regina as a possible sender; on the other hand, if she were going to change phones, why insist that he unblock her original number?

Could it be her furry partner, Iyare? With the exception of scaring the shit out of Jason in the parking area, there had been no direct interactions between them, but that didn't mean it would stay that way.

Or I could just read the damned text and stop wondering about it.

True enough. So far as he knew, he might be getting worked up over Spam.

But upon opening the text, the mystery deepened:

J, THIS IS D (THINK ABOUT WHO YOU OWE THE MOST DRINKS). WE NEED TO MEET. NOT THE USUAL PLACE. YOU KNOW ANDY'S OFF HARBOR?

It took Jason no time to reason out who "D" was — Derek, whom he did in fact owe more drinks than anyone else.

But why the mystery? Why the Unknown Number? Why just "J" and "D" for names?

Still, he did the courtesy of not writing "Is this Derek?" in his reply.

SURE, I KNOW ANDY'S. NEW PHONE?

Derek's reply was almost immediate.

BURNER PHONE. SEE YOU IN A FEW.

That was it. No "Are you busy right now?" or "Can you come right away?" Just the clear expectation that Jason would drop everything and run off to meet him at a bar. But why? Whatever the reason, he didn't care for being "summoned" like this.

Still, he couldn't exactly snub Derek. Even if he didn't end up needing Derek's help with Sir Asshole, he couldn't afford to piss off one of his best police sources. Plus, he didn't want to blow off a friend.

So, Jason was going to Andy's.

Turn of Events

Jason spotted Derek as soon as the creaky door closed behind him. No surprise, given how small the place was — Andy's was no sports bar like where he ate with Regina; its cramped quarters fell more into the "hole in the wall" category. Jason spotted only a few other customers; Derek, out of uniform, sat at a table tucked away in the farthest corner, hunched over a beer bottle and a glass of something stronger.

"Get ya somethin'?" the bartender asked with minimal enthusiasm and no eye contact.

Jason opened his mouth to order his own beer, but found that it didn't really sound appealing. "Not yet, thanks. I'm just joining my friend over there."

But the bartender had tuned him out as soon as the words "Not yet" left his mouth, so Jason made his way over to Derek.

On the drive here, Jason had deduced that the only news Derek might have to share with him would be some development regarding the black wolf from the airport. Since Jason was far more up to date than Derek could imagine — hell, he even knew the (were)wolf's *name*! — he was prepared to fake enthusiasm and appreciation for the update.

But as he drew closer, the angry scowl on Derek's face caught him off guard.

"Derek," he said by way of greeting, trying to keep his expression neutral under the heat of that glare.

Derek's only reply was a sharp, "Sit down."

"Oooookay," Jason said, trying to lighten the mood as he complied. "Sorry if I took too—"

Derek cut him off. "Did you tell anyone what I told you about the steamer trunk?"

As far as Jason's theories had gone, that had been pretty far down the list. "Um ... what?"

"The anthropologist's fuckin' trunk. The one you kept askin' about. Did you tell anyone about where it was being kept?" He leaned forward, the agitation in his demeanor building. "Or did you decide to do a little 'investigative journalism' last night?"

Jason played dumb, which wasn't hard; even if Derek could have somehow known he was there, he and Regina had been furry the whole time — nothing that could have prompted the "investigative journalism" remark. "Dude, seriously: What the fuck are you talking about?"

His performance must have passed muster, because Derek eased off a little, but he was still tense. "When you texted about the trunk, I told you they were stowin' it in a secure property warehouse, remember?"

"Yeah, I guess. But, I mean, you didn't say *where* that was ..."

Derek backed down further, his eyes drifting until he was staring over Jason's shoulder. He picked up his stronger drink — which Jason's nose told him was brandy of some type — and finished what was left in a single gulp. He embraced that warmth for a few seconds, then admitted, "No, I guess I didn't, did I?"

"Derek, what's this about? Why'd you text me from a burner phone? Why're we meeting here, instead of our usual spot? What the hell's goin' on, man?"

Derek stared into his empty brandy glass for a bit, then admitted, "Shit, man, I got ahead of myself. Way ahead of myself. Sorry. Really. It's just ... the *timing* was so ..." He sighed. "Because of the timing, I thought maybe you might have somethin' to do with this bizarre shit, and then I got worried about the texts we'd already shared, so I didn't want anythin' else to be traceable back to me, so I got all paranoid, I admit it, and I wasn't sure what else ..." He stopped rambling and fell quiet again, then shook his head and said, "Fuck it. Can I talk to you, Jason? *Off* the record, just as a friend?"

"Sure. Yeah, of course."

"I mean, I'm not stupid. I know I'm just a 'source' to you—"

"That's not true. Yeah, you help me out when weird stuff is

afoot and I need to turn in a story. But that doesn't mean we're not *also* friends."

Derek looked a little skeptical at that, but let it go. "Whatever, man. I just need to vent, ya know? To bend the ear of someone who doesn't wear a badge."

Jason realized that Derek was a little intoxicated — something he probably would have already smelled, if it weren't for their alcohol-rich environment. "Sure, man. Go right ahead."

"*Off* the record?"

"Off the record."

"You fuckin' swear, man?"

"I swear. If anything ends up on the *Watchdogs* website, I *swear* it won't come from you."

Derek nodded and took a sip of his beer.

"So ..." Jason prompted, "what're we talkin' about here?"

"That fuckin' plane, that fuckin' anthropologist, that fuckin' wolf, that fuckin' steamer trunk. Take your pick. But it was the goddamn trunk that got me textin' you on the down-low."

"Okay, then. Let's start there, with the trunk. Why did you ask me if I told—?"

"There was a break-in last night. It's ... weird. Really weird." He smirked. "You'll love it."

"I'm guessing you mean a break-in at this secure property—?"

"At the secure property warehouse, yeah." He took another swallow of beer. "Okay, first, most of what I'm about to tell you is ... I guess they'd call it 'hearsay' in court, because except for the plane, I didn't personally witness any of this shit. I mean, I'm pretty far down the food chain, but this shit has all of us on alert."

"Got it."

"Just the guys talkin', ya know? Shootin' the shit? Because believe me, we're *all* talkin' about this weird-ass case. If it *is* a case, and not somethin' that should've been turned over to Animal Control for Wildlife as soon as that thing charged right outta the fuckin' plane."

Jason was dying to know what the cops were making of all this, but he held onto his casual façade. "Okay, we'll call it 'workplace gossip.' Understood. So what happened at the warehouse?"

"Someone broke in. How many perps? No idea. Guards saw nothin', cameras saw nothin'. Where'd it happen? Up on the top fuckin' floor — looks like the perps broke in through the roof. What'd they steal? Nothin', so far as we can tell, but the one and *only* room they broke into — word is, they twisted the locked doorknob 'til it fuckin' snapped inside, without leavin' any usable fingerprints — is where they're keepin' Hellqvist's trunk. But since the perps got past all the guards and cameras, *what*, you may ask, tipped 'em off that there was trouble? I shit you not, everyone workin' last night swears to God they heard a fuckin' *wolf* howl! Like that thing from the airport, right? So they run upstairs, find nothin', almost chilled out about it as just a freaky mystery, until someone noticed the broken doorknob."

Jason bit the inside of his cheek and kept acting his "innocent" ass off. "Wow. I mean, yeah, man, you weren't kiddin', that's pretty weird—"

But Derek waved his hand to shut him up.

"Fuck, man, it gets *weirder*. Lemme back up. Again, this's just hearsay — 'workplace gossip,' as you put it. It's another reason I flew off the handle and wondered about you. Sorry again about that."

It was Jason's turn to wave his hand, dismissing the repeated apology as unnecessary.

"Anyway," Derek continued, "they figured the perps must've gotten *stymied*, because the steamer trunk got locked up. And I don't just mean in the warehouse itself, I mean someone added *extra* security to it, but not us — like, not the local police."

Jason allowed himself to lean forward in interest, but kept his face only a little more curious. He was glad that Derek didn't have newly-enhanced hearing like his own; otherwise, he would have heard Jason's heart rate pick up. "What does that mean?"

"A few hours earlier, not too long after dark I guess, these three dudes showed up. They had FBI credentials, and they claimed to have an interest in the Hellqvist case, and they wanted to see the trunk. Well, this surprised no one — the Feds've been in the loop since we found out what happened in that plane. Showin' up that late seemed a little hinky, but whatever — everyone with a badge knows this ain't no regular-hours job, right?

"But the way I hear it, the dudes themselves were odd. First off, there were three of them, and the Feds usually travel in twos, ya know? These were two white guys and a Black guy, and I'm told the Black guy was huge — like, pro-football lineman huge, barely fit into his suit — and one of the two white guys spoke with what sounded like an Irish accent. That wasn't enough to deny their request or anythin' — just raised some eyebrows after-the-fact — so they got escorted upstairs.

"Now listen to this: They went up there and took a look at the steamer trunk. Our guys had tried to warn 'em about the messed-up lock, tell 'em they wouldn't be able to open it without some tools or whatever. But they didn't seem to care. Instead, they opened this canvas sack they brought along and pulled out some heavy-ass chains, which they apparently wrapped all around the trunk — that metal fucker was heavy, but I guess the lineman dude was able to handle it, no problem.

"But get this: The chains on, the Black Fed pulled out this pretty, shiny padlock, and — I shit you not — the two cops who escorted them upstairs insist that the two white Feds actually took a step back, like the fuckin' thing was radioactive or some shit.

"So the trunk's sealed up tight — tighter than seemed necessary, what with its broken lock and all, right? The Feds leave, and later that night, our guys hear that eerie animal howl. They run upstairs, yada yada, find the door broken, look around the room, nothin' appears taken, but *then* ..."

Derek paused, and Jason knew that was his rapt-listener's cue. "Then what?"

"Then they noticed that pretty, shiny padlock, the one the Feds put on the chains? It's all fucked up — like, it's *melted* or some shit."

Jason blinked and leaned back a little, his sincere surprise thankfully natural at this point in Derek's tale. He remembered all too well the searing pain when his nose touched the silver. But he had been so distracted, so focused on his anguish that he hadn't given the padlock another look, though he did recall the stench of something burning and fearing it was his skin. "'Melted'? *How*?"

"They have *no idea*, man. None whatsoever. But it brought back concerns over *why* the two white guys backed off — like, radiation fears, all over again. It's the damnedest thing in a whole situation that makes up the damnedest thing. I hear the chains're still intact, padlock's still there, but it looks like someone took a blowtorch to it or something. Only there's no other scorch marks or signs of fire — just the lock itself, all fucked up."

The silver, Jason realized, must have reacted to his touch, the contact releasing some kind of heat or energy. So *he* had somehow melted the lock. He struggled to keep his expression neutral as his turmoil grew. Did Regina know about this part? She must, right? "Dude, that's ... that's wild."

"Oh, it gets wilder still: This morning, the higher-ups contacted the FBI — on top of everything else, they wanted to, ya know, ask WTF about their special little padlock ... and it turns out those credentials were *fake*. Whoever the hell those three guys were, they *weren't* FBI."

That was when it finally struck Jason: Three men, pretending to be Feds and locking up the trunk with chains and *silver*.

Regina's Triumvirate? They *had* to be!

Derek misconstrued his silence, but not by much. "I know, stunnin' turn of events, right?"

Jason replied with a truthful, "I don't know what to say, man." Then he forced a playful expression onto his face. "I also don't know if I should be insulted or flattered that you thought *I* might have anything to do with all this."

Derek hung his head in shame, but by this point it was mostly in fun. "I know, I know." Then he looked up, his expression somber once more. "Okay, you're the expert — *Watchdogs of the Weird & Unusual* and all that. What do you make of all this?"

Jason sat back in his chair, pretending to contemplate the story; in actuality, he was only half-pretending, but he mainly wanted to find a way to extract himself from the scene and text Regina. "Can you tell me anything else about the fake Feds?"

Derek held up both hands in a helpless gesture before letting them flop back onto the table. "Like I said, I wasn't actually there. Two white guys, one possibly Irish, and a huge brother. The chains would be too awkward to fingerprint, the lock is too fucked up, and between its journey on the plane and gettin' it to storage, there's no tellin' how many people handled that trunk. The cameras out front are under scrutiny, too, because they somehow only caught *two* of the three of 'em comin' and goin'. And those two had their heads down both ways."

Only caught two *of the three ...* For obvious reasons, Jason's skepticism about werewolves had taken a major hit over the past few days, but now Shelley_O's story about a vampire being part of the Triumvirate came back to him. Christ Almighty.

Jason began making his exit, "How about this: I can't help you with the mysterious 'wolf howl' or melted padlock, but let me do some digging about these three fake Feds. I wish you had more for me to go on — and if you do hear anything more, text from your burner phone — but I can at least see if there've been any other, similar impersonations going on recently. Though I really can't fathom what they would've been after, locking up that steamer trunk without opening it or trying to take it away. I ... I'll just see what I can come up with, all right?"

Derek nodded, his head bobbing enough to remind Jason that he was tipsy. "Sure, sure. And yeah, let's keep the burner going — if *you* come up with anything, text me there. I'll keep it as long as it feels safe. Yeah?"

"Yeah, sounds good."

"Cool. And, uh, thanks for listenin', man."

"Anytime. Seriously, you're not 'just a source' to me, okay?"

"Okay."

But as Jason rose from his chair, Derek cocked his head to one side, his eyes narrowing in something like suspicion.

Now what?

Derek opened his mouth, hesitated, tilted his head the other direction, then asked, "Dude ... have you been workin' out?"

Jason glanced down at himself, realizing how much tighter his clothing fit in some ways, how much looser in others. He was grateful that the last time they had seen one another, he had been huddling in his jacket against the drizzle coming down over the airport. "Yeah, some. Glad to hear that it's showing."

"Yeah. Lookin' pretty good there, Jason. Keep it up."

Jason smiled and nodded. "Will do."

Again, he attempted to make his exit, but then Derek perked up as he had a new thought. "Hey, what about that tall babe with the red hair? She's kinda involved in all this, I guess, since the two of you were the only reporters who saw what went down at the airport. Remember to keep *me* out of it, but do ya think she might be able to help you figure out these three dudes? Maybe you could reach out to her."

Jason couldn't help but smile again. "You know, I just might do that."

New Developments

Before starting his car, Jason texted Regina:

HAVE NEW & INTERESTING INFO ON THAT SILVER PADLOCK, AND MAYBE YOUR TRIUMVIRATE. CAN WE MEET?

After hitting Send, he realized that updating her like this brought him one step closer to her "side" in this conflict of hers. But with the way Trey was handling things on his hypothetical team, what choice did he have?

By the time he drove back to his apartment complex, Regina had not yet replied. He found himself wondering what she did with her time. Out investigating the opposition? Catching up on sleep after overnight ventures? She had been clear that *he* was limited by daylight, but that suggested she was not; was she out somewhere, right now, as her red-furred wolf? Where in the greater Los Angeles area could she pull that off without raising all sorts of alarms — especially with the authorities already looking for a large wild animal?

As he climbed the stairs to his floor, Jason just barely heard, over the sounds of light traffic and other domestic noises, a muttered curse, "Pendejo."

Pausing, he turned that direction, his eyes locking onto the apartments across the street ... and there he was, Sir Asshole, out enjoying a cigarette in his usual spot. No shadows this time; the sun was getting lower, but was still bright enough to expose the gangster-wannabe.

Jason stared at him, and even from this far away, Sir Asshole was clearly startled — he would have considered it impossible to have been overheard by the standards of the "real world," but Jason's zeroing in on him so specifically must have been quite unnerving.

For a few seconds, Sir Asshole tried to glare back, but he faltered and looked away, grinding the remains of his cigarette under his toe and stomping off, back up the walkway toward home and his easier-to-intimidate girlfriend.

Jason smirked. He thought about shouting something in the neighborhood of "Yeah, run along home, little boy!" but decided that they were too far apart for that to come across as anything but lame.

Closing the apartment door behind him and standing in his living room, again assailed by the stink of his own domicile (he really needed to clean up!), he was unprepared for a sudden chill to wash over him. The cause mystified him, until he realized that it was his own viewpoint — that Sir Asshole would not entertain being overheard by Jason, because of "the standards of 'the real world.' "

Referring to normal life as the "real world" — in quotes — meaning that he, Jason, was no longer a part of that world.

He raised his hand, a move that was growing familiar, and attempted to change it, to alter its shape in some way to prove to himself that this whole business of his becoming a werewolf was not some wild psychotic break on his part. He felt it, as before, that potential to change lurking within, but he still wasn't able to thicken his palm flesh or grow a single strand of fur.

That "potential" could be nothing more than my imagination.

For one terrible moment, the chill grew into a heat that threatened to erupt into full-blown panic. Had he, in fact, lost his mind? Wouldn't that make more sense than all of this incredible, impossible lunacy that has swept through his life since that night at the airport — hell, *including* that night at the airport?

He closed his eyes, clenched his fists, and got hold of himself.

No, he thought. *I'm not going down this road any further. Unless I'm willing to accept that* everything *around me is part of a deranged psychosis, I'm not going to keep questioning my reality like this. I smell things I couldn't before, I heard Sir Asshole mumble a curse at me from about a hundred yards away, and Derek even commented on my new physique.* And *I knew things that happened inside that secure property warehouse* before *Derek told me — about the rooftop break-in, about the doorknob, about the steamer trunk and chains and padlock, all except the part about the padlock melting. Even if I somehow "hallucinated" the wolf parts, all the rest of it is* proof *that something extraordinary has happened.* Then he chuckled aloud before adding, *Something, dare I say, weird and unusual?*

His heart and breathing slowed, and soon he was copacetic again — well, copacetic relative to all the unsettled issues looming over him: He needed to cement his positions regarding his attractive-but-dangerous, would-be-ally turning him into a werewolf without consent, his employer cutting him off from his coworkers without explanation, and that same employer possibly being part of some "Triumvirate" of newfound enemies.

Yeah, he still had reason to be a little tense. But speaking of the aforementioned employer ...

Jason checked his *Watchdogs* interface, and was disappointed but not shocked to find that his message to Trey remained unanswered.

What to do next?

If — and this was an increasingly big "if" — the situation with Trey and the other Watchdogs turned out to be some huge misunderstanding, that Regina was wrong and something else, something unrelated, was behind this odd communications blackout ... well, officially, he was still supposed to be working on a followup story about the wolf at the airport. Maybe he should do some writing, to stall for time?

Of course, he would have to make it all up from scratch, unless he wanted to lead with:

> "THE MYSTERIOUS ANIMAL, WHICH ESCAPED THE PLANE CARRYING THE LATE DOCTOR AIMÉE HELLQVIST, AMONGST ITS OTHER VICTIMS, HAS TURNED OUT TO BE A WEREWOLF WHO GOES BY THE NAME OF 'IYARE' (EXACT SPELLING UNCONFIRMED). RATHER THAN BEING LITTLE MORE THAN A SIMPLEMINDED BEAST, THIS REPORTER — WHO STOOD FACE-TO-FACE WITH SAID BEAST IN HIS OWN

APARTMENT COMPLEX PARKING AREA — HAS PERSONALLY UPGRADED SAID WEREWOLF'S STATUS FROM SIMPLY 'EVIL' TO POSSIBLY 'CHAOTIC HENCHMAN.' BUT FINAL EVALUATION REMAINS ONGOING, PENDING A FULL EXPLANATION FOR THE SLAUGHTER OF ALL THE PLANE'S OCCUPANTS ..."

Yeah, *Watchdog* readers would love that. Trey, not so much.

"Heh," he grunted. "Maybe Shelley and I should quit and start our own website-for-weirdos."

But even after he got serious, little time passed before Jason realized that he was too keyed up and distracted to get any writing done, let alone creative fiction that sounded like actual investigative reporting. He kept glancing toward the window, gauging how much longer the sun would be up, how much longer before he could change shape again. He also kept checking his phone to see if he had missed any texts or calls from Regina — which was ridiculous, given that his phone was right next to him.

Closing his blank document, he found himself doing what he so frequently did when yearning to mellow out: Browsing wildlife photos. At first, he clicked through his favorite websites at random, but he was not at all surprised to find himself soon gravitating toward images of wolves.

And boy, did he run the gamut: Arctic wolves, Red wolves, Ethiopian wolves, Himalayan, Eastern, Indian, Mexican, Northwestern, Tundra ... Jason considered himself something of an "amateur expert" on wildlife, but he was discovering that there were more different breeds of wolves than he had ever realized. Italian wolves, Eurasian wolves, Iberian, Mongolian, the list went on. They were often separated by images of good old grey wolves — many of the others were considered subsets of the grey wolf, especially the bigger breeds.

But none of those were as big as Iyare's black wolf form. Hell, Regina was nearly as big, and while he'd had no opportunity to take stock of his own size, Jason suspected his own full-wolf form was up there, too.

Fun fact, kids: Werewolves aren't just supernatural

shapeshifters, they're the biggest *fucking wolves you've ever seen!*

He found himself staring at a female Red wolf. Not as red as Regina's full-wolf form, it was a sleek, beautiful creature. The tall ears, glossy muzzle, the slender legs ...

When Jason realized how his body was reacting to the image of this captivating animal, he jolted upright in his seat.

No. No, no, no. Just as he had refused a closer inspection of his urine in the toilet bowl, he slammed the brakes on this, this feeling. The same as sniffing his own piss, he was drawing a line in the sand here. Whatever the hell he was now, following the mental flow from this lovely animal to Regina's equivalent form to sex — it was too much.

"Nope," he stated aloud, and changed the Internet tab from wildlife to pornography. "There, you freak. You wanna fantasize to something? Fantasize to a *real* woman, pervert."

But the lingering "ick" factor kept him from getting too invested in it. His attempts to masturbate floundered, and more than anything else, he kept checking the level of daylight shining through the window.

Giving up (something that would have sooo offended his teenage self), he went back to browsing wildlife photography, but he stuck to *other* animals so as to avoid reigniting his frustrations all over again. A snowy albatross, a Yukon moose, a silverback gorilla, an argali sheep, a Kodiak bear, a green iguana, Muscovy duck; they were all so beautiful in their own ways, especially when the photographer knew what he was doing. Jason had always had a soft spot for the big cats, probably going back to his experience with that mountain lion, and soon he was scrolling through photos of lions. Like wolves, lions came in a remarkable variety of breeds, from the smaller West African lion on up to the massive Barbary lion.

Leaning back in his chair and stretching his arms above his head, Jason checked the daylight once more. Not much longer now...

He clicked through the next batch of lions, spent time on a few different breeds before settling back on the Barbary lion, the (disputed) largest lion ever documented. Unfortunately, all of the photographs were quite old, as the Barbary was believed to have been extinct in the wild for some time. That did not stop people from posting colorized versions of some of the black & white pics, or creating digital and/or A.I.-augmented images that looked pretty true to life, even to his photographer's eye.

Jason studied the latest Barbary image. So different from a wolf, yet so impressive. A testament to why lions were so often described as "majestic" ...

His eyes rolled toward the window. Getting late, the shaft of sunlight coming through thinning, paling. He had been looking forward to this all day, so he was surprised that, on the cusp of nightfall, he felt this languid. Not "sleepy" really, more relaxed, like he was meditating — or rather, how he had always imagined meditation. This was a nice feeling, much better than his horny frustration earlier.

Jason slow-blinked, and suddenly his living room was even gloomier than before. He furrowed his brow in confusion and looked toward the window once again — it was noticeably darker outside. Was it night yet? Maybe dusk — sun below the horizon, but the sky still aglow with remnants of its inhibiting rays? Of course, he could just get his lazy ass up and go take a peek, or even check the time on his phone or online, but that seemed like a lot of work just to confirm the inevitable: He would be able to change very soon.

In fact, was it already dark enough to do so? How far past the horizon did the sun have to go before he could turn into a wolf again? And what about a wolfman? Was that doable? A surge of latent excitement swelled within him; why not give it a try?

Indulging in his growing tried-and-true test, he raised his right hand — a sluggish move this time, but he got it up there eventually. Jeez, why was he so lethargic? Hell, *how* was he so lethargic, when he felt this expanding tingle, like raw energy, spreading all over his body? He imagined it must feel like being on weed and cocaine — or *any* strong upper and downer — at the same time.

Staring at his hand, he focused his willpower and — after several long, impatient seconds — the tingling intensified, starting in his fingertips and rippling up his forearm, and a triumphant smile spread across his face as his hand began to shift.

Yes! he celebrated. *I knew it was real, I* knew *it!*

Then again, he was feeling so funky right now, could this be a dream?

Shut up and enjoy this, he chastised himself as his bones shifted and fur sprouted across his body. There was almost no pain at all this time, and what few spikes there were felt different somehow, affecting different parts of his body. He could foresee a time when there would be zero discomfort as he changed forms.

His chair, however, grew uncomfortable enough for him to slip out of it and onto all fours on the floor, and by the time he remembered that he was still dressed, it was too late — like Lou Ferrigno on *The Incredible Hulk*, his clothing stretched and ripped away from his body as it not only changed shape but expanded.

The transformation settled and, looking around his apartment, he noticed more differences: While his sense of smell did not seem to have increased quite as much (maybe because he was getting adjusted to his already-heightened olfactory in his human form?), his night vision was as sharp as ever. And his hearing sure hadn't missed a beat: Conversations all around him, televisions and computer playing, someone using a bong, cars driving by outside ... he heard everything; it helped that he could control and angle his ears if he wanted to single out any one target.

As he paced around on his four paws, he realized that his body felt different somehow, more spry, more agile, than the night before; he also found himself more conscious of his tail. He hadn't really stopped to think about it much last time, being far more distracted by his new senses and the sheer speed of his wolf form, but he had known it was there. When he attempted to wag it now, he felt it writhe about behind him; he wasn't sure what he would ever do with that, but it was yet another novel sensation among so many.

Out, he thought. *I want out.*

But he didn't just want outside, he wanted to run. No, not just run, he wanted to *prowl*, he wanted to *hunt*. These urges had been present before, but they were stronger this time.

Which led him to another, uncomfortable thought: As he

evolved into being a full-on werewolf (whatever that meant), just how much would his animal side control him? When Regina explained about his being limited by daylight, she had also mentioned that he was not prepared for the "intensity of the full moon," or something to that effect. What had she meant by that? She had not bothered to warn him about the dangers of silver; what other dangers had she failed to disclose? If he was noticing this many little differences and urges on his *second night* of shapeshifting, where would it end? What would happen under the full moon? Would he lose control?

Then again, he barely felt in control *now*. He didn't want to hurt anyone, and yet the urge to hunt was growing stronger even as he paced. What could he do? Find some neighborhood pet, maybe a dog loose in its backyard so that he could chase it around a little, give it a good, harmless scare? Or even head up into the local hills and find something more challenging to bring down?

No! I don't want to hurt any animals, either. How do I clamp this down? Maybe if I just run as far and as fast as I can until I'm exhausted—

But he was getting way ahead of himself. It wasn't the middle of the night this time; the sun had barely set. People were out and about — more cars, more pedestrians, more neighbors smoking out on the walkway. Hell, he'd have to change back to his wolfman form just to open his damned door, let alone sneak past all those potential witnesses.

But he did know firsthand just how fast he could move. When he had seen the black wolf burst from the airplane ...

Come on, man. Even with that speed, you can't just go out the front door.

He could always revert to his human self, get dressed, and drive off somewhere ... but after waiting all damned day, the idea of shifting back to his boring original form almost angered him — he didn't want to drive, he wanted to *run*!

Someone dropped something metal and heavy, probably a cast-iron skillet, in the apartment beneath him; he heard it with his sensitive ears, felt it through his paws. At least his complex only had the two floors, so he didn't have to listen to feet clomping around over his head. As it was, he could hear some birds hopping around up on the roof—

The roof.

Jason eyed the ceiling; without awareness, his ears twitched and his nostrils flared as well. He never before had any reason to think about the roof of his apartment complex, but there must be a way up there, right?

No, that's stupid. I mean, yeah, there's gotta be a way up — for maintenance or whatever — but that's probably through the manager's office or something, right?

Except the manager's office was on the ground floor. And way back, when he first moved in, hadn't—?

Jason bolted for his bedroom. His closet door stood open; the only time he bothered closing it was when he had a woman over and was hoping things might move into a more intimate setting.

There! The darkness did not prevent him from making out a short, thick, cobweb-encrusted pull-chain, dangling from one end of a plain square that differed from the rest of his dated "popcorn" ceiling. He barely recalled the manager mentioning it the day he moved in — the old fart had tossed an apathetic gesture up at it as he pre-scolded Jason against ever opening it, while also commenting that the maintenance staff might require access to it from time to time. But in the years that Jason had lived here, this had never once come up, so Jason had more or less forgotten about it.

Now it was just what he needed.

Standing on his hind legs brought him much closer to the ceiling than he could have reached in his shorter human form, but he would still need fingers, not a paw, to grab the chain and pull.

Keeping his eyes on the pull-chain, he braced himself against the wall with his left forepaw as he eased his right arm upward, willing it to shift halfway back to human form. He felt its internal structure altering again, and by the time his right hand came into view, he did indeed have fingers once more.

Yet when he reached farther to seize the chain, he hesitated, his focus drifting from the roof access to study his hand. Were his fingernails even longer than when he was a wolfman last night?

And more curved, too? And was his fur lighter in color? Yes, he had outstanding night vision, but judging different hues of brown was still a stretch in the deep shadows of his closet.

Why would his fur change color? God, he had so many more questions for Regina.

Mentally shrugging it away for the time being, he snagged the chain and tugged. He had kind of expected it to deploy a noisy, folding spring-ladder like his parents had leading into their attic, but had he stopped to think about the dimensions of his closet, he would have realized it could not have fit. Instead, the smooth panel snapped downward, depositing clumps of crusty dust onto Jason's upturned face and revealing another, metal surface a few inches above it — he experienced deja vu, as the "lid" reminded him of the roof access at the property warehouse.

Jason growled — wow, even his growl sounded different, deeper — and shook the dust from his face, then reached as high up as he could and shoved the metal barrier. It flopped up and over, the screech of rusted hinges and *clang!* of it striking the rooftop much louder than he would have preferred.

But through the open hatch, he could see the night sky above, and even as he willed his hand to rejoin the rest of his body in full-animal form, he tensed his hind legs and leaped.

Overall, his jump was a success, but it further added to his feelings of change, of difference: As he cleared the opening, he felt the fur along the sides of his head brush the edges, which made no sense, as his shoulders passed without contact; he also felt far more agile than when he had made the leap up the wall of the property warehouse — granted, this was a lesser distance in terms of height, but as he sailed up in a smooth arc onto the roof ...

Though it was nighttime at last, the rooftop was far better lit than the interior of his apartment, and especially his closet; the light pollution alone was more than enough for his new vision. As such, when he alighted onto all four paws in a perfect landing, he could not help but see the changes in his forepaws. They were bigger, stronger, and unquestionably a lighter color of fur than the last time he was a wolf; more than that, the fur itself—

A door slammed, hard, somewhere behind him, coming from

across the street and spiking above the cacophony of other neighborhood dissonance. And while Jason had heard nothing leading up to it, no shouts or cries of any kind, he caught the familiar voice that followed the wooden impact; it was spoken quieter than usual, but his ears were more than up to the task.

"Maldita perra estúpida," Sir Asshole griped. Then, in a lower voice that even Jason could barely make out, he added, "I oughta *kill* that goddamn bitch."

Based on their pattern to date, Sir Asshole probably didn't mean it — not literally, at least; it was likely just pompous grousing, the musings of an abusive macho-braggart. Then again, lots of abusers grew in intensity over time, their violence building toward a crescendo until, one day, they crossed the line from assault to manslaughter, or maybe straight-up murder. And especially with the humiliation Jason had dished out to him earlier ...

Turning around, the mystery of his fur and paws forgotten, Jason spotted Sir Asshole, lurking in the shadows, preparing to light up his cigarette.

That fucker, he thought, as simple as that. *That mother*fucker.

In that moment, fears of and repulsion toward hurting anyone hailed from a far distant part of Jason's mind.

And then he stopped thinking altogether. Instead, he ran.

And he leaped.

* * *

Carlos Blanco — whose real name was actually "Charles White," but he had never used it since moving to Southern California, except to cash his uncle's support checks — cursed some more under his breath; he was so out of sorts that, through half of it, he forgot to stick with his preferred Spanish. Carlos (Charles) had been having another bad day of colossal proportions, and if he hadn't walked out on Esperanza and her incessant carping just now, he might have done something that they would both regret.

And see, *that*! *That* right there. That was what had turned his bad day into a worse evening. Why the fuck should *he* regret shit about putting that irritating bitch in her place? Because that Indian or Middle-Eastern or whatever-the-fuck-he-was motherfucker had threatened him? In a fair fight, Carlos knew he could break that little shit in half!

Except you didn't, nagged a voice that sounded so close to Esperanza's mother that he wanted to spit — and did. *You didn't break him in half, he owned you, you worthless* perdedor. *And that's why you walked out just now. Because you are* asustado, *you are a* cobarde — *a* coward — *and you know it.*

Fuck that, that was bullshit! Carlos Blanco feared no man! And if the local BST gang could just *see* that—

Cobarde ... Esperanza's mother whispered, full of spite.

"Shut the fuck *up*, perra fea!" he barked, louder than he had intended, but he refused to flinch about it, refused to acknowledge any fear of being overheard by that nosy little shit across the street.

Grumbling further under his breath in both English and Spanish, he lit another cigarette and inhaled a deep drag.

While all of this inner conflict was going on, Carlos remained oblivious to his surroundings (aside from the occasional furtive glance toward the neighboring complex). He had not registered a set of brakes squealing, nor one of those bratty kids downstairs blurting out, "Whoa! Did you see *that*?!" With all the cars and people about, those two incidents were far beneath Carlos' fuming notice. The sound of some heavy, gravelly impact and scrunchy sliding noise from the units across the courtyard from where he stood came closer to seizing his focus, but they had occurred at the exact instant he barked at Esperanza's absent mother, and so he had missed that, too.

But when Carlos took a second long drag from his smoke, someone along the back walkway bellowed, "Holy *shit*!" loud enough to finally get his attention. More irritated than curious, he ambled around to see what that little pussy from apartment ... number ...

Carlos' initial reaction was to laugh aloud in disbelief. The sight before him was so ridiculous, so impossible, that he knew it had to be a joke, somehow. As his laughter faded, he choked out, "Okay, who's fuckin' with me?!"

Except the handful of witnesses to this astounding event did not laugh. They were either far enough away to pull out their phones and start recording, or close enough to curse and run for their individual apartments, slamming and locking their doors.

Stalking along the walkway toward Carlos was the biggest goddamn lion he had ever seen in his life. Not that he had seen all that many lions — just whatever happened to be lounging around their exhibits at the zoo — but he had no doubt that this motherfucker *had* to be some kind of record-breaker.

A low, deep rumble of a growl oozed from the lion's throat as it approached closer. Carlos could feel that growl in his guts, in his bones.

And suddenly, nothing about this was funny.

Carlos' heart thundered in his chest as he stumbled backwards, almost tripping over his own feet in his haste to flee — he had no idea where he could go to escape this massive son of a bitch, but all he could think was to get away! Floundering around, he attempted to run—

In two great, effortless bounds, the lion pounced on him. Over 900 pounds of apex predator crashed into Carlos' retreating back, knocking him face-first onto the walkway. Razor-sharp claws dug into him as the lion's immense weight trapped and crushed him.

As those claws ripped at his flesh, a blood-curdling scream ripped from Carlos' throat, but his shriek was cut off as fangs as long as steak knives clamped onto the back of his neck. Hot breath washed over him; vertebrae ground together under the pressure. The coppery scent of his own blood filled Carlos' nostrils.

Then the lion removed its paws and shook its great head from side to side. Carlos' limbs flailed about like a marionette with its strings cut; his vision tunneled to black as the sheer agony overwhelmed him.

Then, with an awful, sickening, shredding sound, the lion rived a chunk of flesh and sinew from Carlos' neck and shoulder.

Distantly, as if from deep underwater, Carlos heard shrieks of horror and more slamming doors. He gurgled a weak cry for help, blood bubbling and frothing from his lips, as his bladder and bowels released.

The lion lifted its gore-streaked muzzle and roared, a bestial declaration of pure, terrifying bloodlust. Then the massive feline pawed Carlos over onto his bloody back, lowered its head, and — with a vicious twist — ripped Carlos' throat out in a spray of vibrant crimson.

Carlos Blanco — a.k.a. Charles White, gangster-wannabe, and abuser of Esperanza and many other women — was no more, just a broken, grisly mess on the apartment walkway.

For nearly a minute, the Barbary lion crouched over its kill, its sides heaving, blood dripping from its jaws and staining its magnificent mane. Then, in a motion almost too fast for the witnesses peeking through windows and around doorjambs to follow — the videos many were taking with their phones would register little more than a tawny streak — it gathered its haunches and leapt, propelling the big cat up and over the second floor railing in a breathtaking feat of strength, agility, and speed.

Screams rang out and more car brakes screeched as the huge lion bounded away into the crowded night with preternatural velocity and grace, its smooth course taking it well away from the home of one Jason Samir.

AfTermaTH

The harsh racket of his phone's buzzing on the table dragged Jason up from the depths of his slumber. When had he switched his phone to vibrate? And what was the point of the vibrate option when the damned thing's resonance was so damned loud?

Then he remembered that it was probably his improved hearing, which he possessed because he was now a werewolf.

Then he remembered transforming into something other than a wolf last night.

And then he remembered what he had done.

Jason bolted upright from where he had apparently slept curled up on his living room floor. He had been using his forearm as a pillow, and his skin wanted to stick on both sides because of all the dried blood. A flood of guilt and horror swelled from within his gut, and he almost did not make it to the bathroom before vomiting. Except he didn't really vomit, just dry-heaved, because—

Because I didn't eat *Sir Asshole. I just murdered him.*

He retched more, then eventually moved to look at himself in the mirror — and recoiled.

Yes, his mouth and chest were a gory mess, but that wasn't why he shrank away from his reflection. For a split-second, his eyes weren't his usual dark brown — they were the rich amber of a lion's. When he blinked several times, they appeared normal.

He was fairly certain it had *not* been his imagination.

Out in the living room, his phone buzzed again. Someone was texting.

That would have to wait, as Jason refused to do anything else before he scoured his face and body clean in the shower.

The process took far longer than he wished.

Even after the water coursing off his body transitioned from rusty to red, to pink, and finally to clear, Jason remained where he stood, the hot flow cascading off his scalp. He did his best to clamp down the tumult of anxiety and shame that clutched at his chest, and attempted to recall the events of the previous night — or was "previous" even the correct word? Thinking about it, he realized that when his phone had awakened him, his living room had still been pretty dark. Either he had slept through an entire day, or it was still the same night.

Over the low roar of his shower, his ears picked up his phone, still in the living room, vibrating with another incoming text.

Okay, okay, stop worrying about your phone, focus.

He remembered the strange, lethargic haze that swelled over him as the sun finally set, his transformation into what he had initially *thought* was his full-wolf form, his urges to run and hunt, his escaping his apartment through the rooftop access in his closet...

... and that's where things had gotten hazier still. He remembered the slow realization that his body was different, not a wolf this time, more cat-like? A huge cat? Maybe a tiger or a lion or something?

"Christ," he muttered into the water streaming past his mouth. "I thought I was supposed to be a were*wolf*, not—"

Not *what*, exactly? His list of questions — demands, at this point — for Regina grew ever longer.

What had triggered the muddled loss of control up on the roof? He had finally absorbed just how different his hands (paws) were, the differences in his fur, and then ...

... and then he had heard a door slam, heard Sir Asshole muttering intended violence, zeroed in on the perfect target for his predatory compulsions, leaped from his rooftop — *all the way across the street* — onto the neighboring apartments' rooftop! Then he found his way down, stalked Sir Asshole, and ... and he tore into him.

He gagged when he thought about the rush of the man's blood into his mouth.

"Keep it together," he choked through clenched teeth.

After Sir Asshole was dead, Jason fled the scene — though

"fled" didn't really apply, as he had felt more elation than concern or fear. And then he ...

All he could remember was running, running fast, streaks of lights flashing by and cars honking and people screaming as he sprinted past them, but to the best of his ability, he could not remember hurting anyone else (that brought him some relief; at least his sole victim had been someone of less than stellar character). Beyond that, it was all running and running, and then he was awakened by his phone. He had zero memory of how he got back home, but thank God he did.

Why did I maintain control of myself as a wolf, but then lose my shit when I turned into some kind of cat?

Grow, list of questions, grow.

When he finally emerged from the shower, he did not bother to get dressed — after all, he still had an ugly blood stain to clean out of his living room carpet (*Oh, how I'm so looking forward to that!*), and what would be the point of messing up fresh clothes? At least he could use the torn shreds of yesterday's clothing for cleaning rags.

The first thing he did, however, was check the rooftop access in his closet — it was closed. Next, he retrieved his phone, hoping the texts were from Regina.

They weren't. The three texts lined up with his contact listed as "C.S." for "confidential source" — he hadn't been sure how else to label Derek's burner phone, since he wanted to honor his friend's privacy just in case his own phone was hacked, stolen, or subpoenaed.

The first text: YOU STILL LIVE IN THE SAME PLACE?

Second text: FIRST A WOLF AT AIRPORT, NOW A FUCKIN LION IN YOUR NECK OF THE WOODS? MAN, WTF IS GOING ON??? SRSLY, TEXT ME IF YOU HAVE A CLUE!

Third: YOU GOTTA TELL ME IF YOU KNOW ANYTHING ABOUT ALL THIS, MAN. I AM LITERALLY LOSIN SLEEP OVER THIS SHIT.

Jason resisted a chill as he dropped his phone back on the table. Not that he'd had any true doubts before, but this was confirmation that his latest experience was not a dream or hallucination; Derek talking about a lion was not a "coincidence" he could accept.

He started to open his apartment door, until he remembered that he was stark naked. Instead, he moved to his bedroom window, leaning to the left side of the frame to maximize his view to the right, and peeked through the blinds.

Based on the sky, it was barely past dawn, so all the police lights coming from across the street painted the cars and hedge in the parking area below with strobes of red and blue. He unlocked his window and pushed it upward just an inch, which was enough for his ears to focus past the chatter from a dozen different conversations and hone in on the professional, projected voices of multiple field reporters spreading the news for their early-morning viewers.

"... the unfortunate victim was mauled to death by what neighbors ..."

"... several videos of the attack have gone viral, in spite of ..."

"... bring to mind a recent incident at an airport located ..."

"... have described it as 'enormous' and 'gigantic' ..."

"... so far, no zoos have reported any escaped ..."

"... witnesses all over the city and county ..."

"... was allegedly a large *lion* ..."

"... that an escaped *lion* ..."

"... a *lion* ..."

Jason closed the window and stepped away; he stood still in the center of his bedroom, attempting to process everything that had changed about his life in such a short amount of time.

Well, he found himself thinking with an acerbic smile, *now* everyone *will probably be running the story about the wolf at the airport, but* Watchdogs *broke it first. It's Arach-mageddon all over again. Trey will be so pleased. Go, team.*

He slumped forward, hands on his knees, controlling his breathing and trying to figure out what in the world his next step should be ... then jolted as though with electricity when he heard a knock at his apartment door.

Shit. Shit shit shit*!*

Had someone traced the lion to his complex? Were the police going door to door already? No one would believe that *he* was the lion, but how would he explain the bloodstain on the carpet if they came inside? His hair was still dripping wet, so he'd have to—

The knock repeated, a faster tempo that suggested urgency.

Not knowing what else to do, Jason threw on the first pair of jeans he laid his hands on and hustled back to his living room, attempting to assume a mask of sleepy innocence, with a dash of confused irritation.

He could have looked through the peephole, but he was so certain that it had to be the police canvassing all of Sir Asshole's neighbors, it did not occur to him to do so.

Jason opened the door to find Regina standing before him, her hand raised to knock a third time. She was more "dressed down" than he had ever seen her — plain, beige button-up shirt; worn jeans; worn sneakers; a baseball cap with her red hair tucked (mostly) within; at this point, her conspicuous height was the only quality that would have made her stand out in a crowd. Her gaze had been down-turned in that first instant, but when she lifted her head to look at him, he saw that the left side of her face was purple and black, her eye swollen and her lip split. All told, it was one hell of a humbling from her typical presentation and poise, and it threw him as much for a loop as did her sudden presence.

Behind Regina stood an older Black man whom Jason did not recognize, at first. Very dark-skinned and nearly as tall as Regina, his clothing was as casual as hers. He, too, appeared to have been in some sort of fight — though the man was doing his best to keep it hidden with the carriage of his right arm, blood had seeped through his yellow pullover shirt along his flank. His knuckles on that hand were also bruised deeply enough to show up even against his onyx pigmentation.

When Jason finally inhaled to speak, though he had never before seen the man in this form, his nose identified him: Iyare, the black wolf.

Then his eyes darted back to Regina as she asked around her injured lip, "Jason, may we please—?"

"Yeah, come in, come in," he blurted, stepping back to allow them entrance. As soon as they crossed the threshold, he closed the door against all those flashing red and blue lights.

Jason guessed that his visitors could probably see in the dark as well as he, if not better from experience, but he flipped the living room light on out of social habit. Regina removed her baseball cap, which exposed a raw stretch of scalp along the right side of her head; it appeared as though a handful of her beautiful hair had been ripped out.

As many pressing questions as he had for her, he could not help but ask, "Jesus, Regina, what happened to you?"

But it was Iyare who answered in a thick, unfamiliar accent, "The Triumvirate happened."

Jason looked to Regina for confirmation. "You guys met the Triumvirate? Face to face?"

She nodded, but again, Iyare answered, "We *fought* them."

Regina continued nodding, adding, "And we lost."

"The two of you tried to take on the three of them—?"

Once more, Iyare spoke, "There were seven of us. The Triumvirate killed all the others."

Jason was getting a little annoyed at Iyare's speaking for Regina, but he let that go for the time being. "Regina," he said, taking her hand, "what *happened*?"

She squeezed his hand in hers. "Since the Triumvirate anticipated our attempt to inspect Hellqvist's steamer trunk, Iyare and I thought we could turn the tables on them. We gathered five more of our strongest wolves and took a pair of rooms at a cheap motel not far from LAX airport. We then spent the entire day texting one another, calling one another on our cell phones, chatting on supposedly private websites, discussing how we were going to take the police's property warehouse by force, how we would slaughter any and all opposition we encountered, the exposure be damned." She smirked, then winced a little at how it pulled at her injured lip. "We did everything we could short of buying a billboard saying: 'We will be there tonight.' After recent events, we suspected that the Triumvirate has means of spying on us, so we thought we could use that to our advantage."

Jason studied her bruised face again. "And they took the bait?"

Iyare snorted. "That, or they knew it was a trap from the beginning. The *bastards*."

Jason looked again at the man's bloody shirt. "You need

something for that? A towel, or bandages?"

The man shook his head.

Jason turned back to Regina, gestured at her eye. "You want some ice?"

She also declined. "If this had been inflicted by a normal human, it would have healed already. Injuries from other supernatural beings are slower to recover."

Jason was curious as to the "Why?" of that, but set it aside. "So you moved ahead with your feint for the trunk ..."

"Yes, we gathered at dusk on a rooftop near the property warehouse, pretending to watch the guards — there are more guards now, as I'm sure you can imagine."

Jason nodded. "My sheriff friend, Derek, says all hell has broken loose."

"After nightfall, we shifted into our half-forms, grunted, growled, tensed. We thought we might have to go through our 'warmup' a few times, maybe over and over all night. But the Triumvirate had outmaneuvered us, again."

"They were already there," Iyare snarled. "Not on that exact rooftop, but somewhere very nearby. Probably the only reason they waited for nightfall at all was so their vampire could join them."

"So it's true, then?" Jason asked. "The Triumvirate are a werewolf, a vampire, and a zombie? Is that right?"

Regina and Iyare looked at one another in surprise. Regina asked, "How did you—?"

Jason shrugged. "I've been doing research on my own since you named them. In fact, I texted you to say that I had some info on them, asked if we could meet."

"I'm sorry. I saw that you'd texted, but with everything going on ..."

Jason waved it off. "We'll come back to that. What happened with—?"

But Iyare cut in, again. "They trashed us. They *massacred* our pack! Regina and I were the only ones to get away. And it took us over an hour to lose their werewolf's pursuit."

Anger boiled off the man, though Jason was (reasonably) certain it was not aimed at him. He said, "I'm sorry to hear that."

Iyare dismissed his sympathy with a harsh swat, as though waving an annoying insect away from his ear. Then he muttered under his breath, “K’éma rˋbˋn ní sˊ...”

Jason could not help but cock his head. “Those words, your accent. Where—?”

“I am Nigerian,” Iyare snapped. “What of it?”

Jason held up both hands in a placating gesture. “Nothing. Just curious.” Then he offered, “I, uh, I’m Egyptian, by heritage.”

“Yes,” Iyare responded, and there was something odd in his voice. “We know.”

“Jason,” Regina said in a guarded tone he had not come to expect of her, “what happened at the apartments across the street? Do you know?”

The vicarious tension Jason experienced upon hearing of their deadly confrontation gave way as his prior revulsion and remorse resurged. “Yeah,” he admitted. “I do know.”

Regina and Iyare glanced at one another again, this time with less surprise and more caution. Iyare pushed, “... and?”

Jason sighed, and it came out in a tremble. “I changed last night and I, uh ... I lost control. I killed someone.”

Regina nodded in sympathy. “The sensations of the wolf can be overwhelm—”

Jason pounced. “That’s just it. I didn’t turn into a *wolf* this time. I think I— I mean, I know that I turned into a *lion*.”

Iyare gasped. For the first time since appearing at Jason’s door, his air of vague disdain gave way to something else. Jason thought it might have been ... awe?

Regina, for her part, looked excited, her eyes widening and her lips parting as she drew a measured breath. “A *lion*? Are you sure?”

“As sure as I can be, I guess. It didn’t sink in at first — the difference, I mean, between the one animal and the other — and by the time it did, my mind gave way to those overwhelming ‘sensations’ you just mentioned. That, and bloodlust. I ... I kind of already hated the guy I killed. Still makes me feel like shit, though.”

Regina opened her mouth to say more, but Jason’s persistent confusion and frustration swelled to the forefront.

“Why the hell didn’t you tell me that could happen?” he

demanded. "I thought you told me I was a were*wolf*, and suddenly I'm a were*lion*, too? What else have you been holding back? You did this whole thing to me without asking, you dragged me along on your first little 'raid' at the police warehouse, you didn't warn me about silver until I'd burned my fucking nose on it — which, by the way, was apparently so intense it *melted* the goddamned lock, so thanks for that heads up. Then you drop the word 'Triumvirate' in my lap, but ghost me when ... I ..."

Jason trailed off when he absorbed the expressions of pure shock on both Regina and Iyare's faces. Regina tried to speak, failed, then cleared her throat and licked her swollen lip before trying again.

"What do you mean? About 'melting' the padlock?"

Thrown for a loop, Jason shrugged. "The silver padlock. According to my sheriff friend, it melted. He heard it was like a blowtorch had been taken to it or something. Why? Is that not ... how ...?"

When his words fell away this time, it was not because of any new expressions on the faces of his guests.

To Jason's absolute bewilderment and stupefaction, Regina and Iyare each dropped to one knee ... and bowed before him.

NEW REVELATIONS

Jason blinked several times before finding his voice. "Um ... wh-what's happening?"

Regina said nothing at first. With her head down, he could only judge from her body language that she was in the midst of an enormous, emotional moment.

Still bowing his own head, Iyare whispered, "I ... didn't believe. Not truly. Aro. I didn't believe you could be *real*. Mogban ... Aro ... Aro ..."

Regina reached out to Iyare, taking his hand without lifting her gaze. "Iyare, it's all right. We've all had doubts."

Iyare nodded as she spoke, but the instant her words ended, he switched to shaking his head. "Aro ... Aro ..." He stole a brief glance at Jason, before dropping his chin again. "I-I beg forgiveness."

Jason felt many conflicting things during all this, but as it dragged on, embarrassment swelled to the forefront. "Guys. Seriously. What— What *is* this? What's going on?"

At last, Regina looked up at him, her green eyes glistening with tears. "Jason Samir. You have no idea how long we've looked for you. And now, here you are."

"Regina, we met *days* ago, and you didn't 'bend the knee' then." Jason found this unexpected shift in their power dynamic perplexing, to say the least. He huffed and made a broad, repeated "get up" gesture with both hands. "Christ, please, stop this. Stand up. You're freakin' me out. Stand *up*."

Regina finally rose to her feet and pulled Iyare along with her. They both kept their eyes downcast, and Jason was fairly certain they were also slouching a bit, as though now unwilling to showcase their greater height.

"Okay," he said, trying to keep his voice both calm and calming, "let's take this one step at a time. Why in the world did you just *bow* to me?"

Regina cleared her throat again. "As I said, we've been looking for you, Jason. For a long time. You're ... you are *special*."

"Why? Because I'm a—" He almost said "werewolf," but after turning into a lion, he wasn't so sure that label still fit. Instead, he settled for: "Because I'm a shapeshifter? We're all shapeshifters, all three of us. I don't see you bowing to each other."

"Oh, Jason ..." Regina breathed, the tears building in her eyes once more, "Jason, you're so much *more* than we are. Yes, we — Iyare and I — are shapeshifters. We're werewolves. But you?" She reached out to touch his arm, then held back from actual contact. "Jason, you are a *panwere*."

After a pregnant pause, Jason quipped, "I'm guessing that's not a type of cookware."

Regina actually chuckled at that, but only for one brief outburst. Then she was back to being serious — though he was pleased to see that her expression held less angst. "No, not at all. A panwere has only been a theory, until now. It's a lycanthrope who is not bound to any one single animal."

"So ... I can turn into anything? Any animal?"

Iyare nodded, his eyes still wide as he stared at Jason. In a shaky voice, he answered, "As a panwere, any animal you can picture in your mind."

Regina picked up the thread. "The theory is that a panwere would be able to do *more* than meld with the wolf within themselves — and go beyond our enslavement to the cold cycle of the moon. A panwere could tap into the greater pulse of the Earth, the warm collective life force of the world all around us.

"Jason, your changing into multiple animals was already a *huge* step toward proving our hypothesis right. But what you said about the silver padlock ..." She shook her head in amazement. "Silver is our truest weakness, even more than fire. And I'm sorry that contact with the padlock hurt you, but for the reaction to have *melted* it!" She shook her head again. "That pain, that *power*, thrown back at its source — and on your very first night as a wolf? Jason, I wouldn't be surprised if silver eventually stops affecting you at all."

Jason struggled to keep up with all this. He'd already had a heap of questions for Regina, but half of those just flew out the window. When would this whirlwind of supernatural chaos slow down? Less than a week ago, his biggest issues had been how out of shape he was and writing enough *Watchdog* articles to keep Trey happy and a roof over his head. Now he stood here, shirtless and barefoot in front of a gorgeous, fit woman (the fact of which just occurred to him), sporting his own six-pack abs and being told that he could transform into any—

Iyare interrupted his thoughts. "Could you please show us?"

"What?"

"Please," Iyare requested in a beseeching voice, so different from the arrogance he had borne when he first arrived, "could you show us a transformation? Into something other than a wolf?" Then he held up his palms together as though in prayer. "It's not as though we disbelieve you, but to see it with our own eyes ..."

The begging in Iyare's tone still did not sit well with Jason. "I ... I'd be willing to, sure, but ..." He pointed toward the brightening blinds of his living room window. "It'll have to wait for nightfall, I guess. Right?"

Regina exhaled through her nose in good humor. "Jason, you turned into a lion last night. I doubt that the sunlight will limit you any longer."

"But you said—"

"Someone who is 'just' a werewolf would require more time, yes. But I doubt the sunlight will limit *you* any longer."

"Um ... okay, yeah. Sure, then."

Regina and Iyare perked up, expectant.

A mischievous idea flashed through Jason's mind to change into the most exotic animal he could think of, to give them a show for the ages! But, dialing it back to reality (or what passed for "reality" these days), he reminded himself that his transformation into a lion had been completely unintentional, sparked — he assumed — on a subconscious level by his greying out while scrolling through wildlife photos of lions. His nebulous, suggestible state of mind had, evidently, allowed him to tap into this "pulse of the Earth" thing. But doing it on command?

Something small, something straightforward, one step at a time.

Repeating his newfound ritual of raising his right hand before his face, he gazed at his open palm and focused.

After only a few seconds, his familiar potential rushed to the surface, and his hand shifted into that of his wolfman. Okay, easy enough. So he pushed further.

Again, the bones transfigured, and both Regina and Iyare sucked in a breath as his fingernail-claws altered and his fur's quality and color morphed into the more feline tawny-brown he had seen last night.

One more, he urged himself as his own excitement swelled. *Try for one more!*

Jason closed his eyes and let his mind cast about. When they said "any animal," how literal was that? He presumed they couldn't mean, like, nightcrawler earthworms or Caribbean microtityus scorpions, but was he limited to mammals? He supposed he could ask, but he didn't want to disrupt their awestruck spirit.

Let's split the difference. Nothing totally freaky, but something a little more striking.

Jason's eyelids rose to half-mast. He concentrated on his lionman's paw, and *pushed.*

At first, nothing happened. Then, just as he was about to give up:

Again, the bones shifted around, while his fur receded into his skin, revealing small, tight scales underneath. His fingernail-claws curved farther, darkened ...

Regina's eyes widened; Iyare's mouth dropped open.

Heh, Jason thought. *Turns out reptiles are on the menu, too.*

Jason, whose arm remained more or less human to his wrist, held his new hand above his head, rotating it from side to side. "Lady and gentleman," he declared with a proud, ear-to-ear grin, "I present the hand of the great Komodo dragon."

His grandstanding, however, was sullied when his Komodo hand convulsed with an abrupt chill, and his forearm cramped. He winced, bringing his arm down and grasping his wrist with his other, human hand. Some nascent instinct kicked in, and his appendage shifted back to that of the more familiar wolfman; within seconds, the cold discomfort passed.

Then Regina was holding his padded, clawed hand in both of hers. "It's all right," she told him. "That alone was more than enough. You *are* our panwere."

Still, after his big bravado, Jason felt a little embarrassed even as he reverted back to all-parts-human. "I think it might've been having a reptilian hand but a mammalian arm. Maybe my blood tried to go cold and warm at the same time?"

"You'll adjust," she assured him with confidence. "You'll adapt. And you will be powerful, *unstoppable*."

"So powerful," Iyare echoed, "even those Triumvirate tyrants won't be able to stand against you."

"What's the story with them," Jason asked, "the Triumvirate? Why do they want the steamer trunk?" He looked back to Regina. "For that matter, why do *you* want the trunk so badly? Am I finally deep enough in your 'inner circle' to get some honest answers?"

Regina had the decency to blush a little. "Of course you are. Now that we *know* you are our panwere, the panwere we've waited for, we'll tell you everything you want."

He gestured for her to continue. "Have at it, please."

"First, you must understand that our world is at something of a tipping point. Almost all of the supernatural elements we know of have cropped up over the past two to three years. Those that are heaviest with power were established somewhere ... else."

"What does that mean? Like, another planet or something?"

Jason had meant it as a joke, and was surprised when Regina started to shake her head, then hesitated. Instead, she said, "In a way. None of us truly understands how it works, but the majority of the werewolves, vampires, and other mythical archetypes originated in some sort of alternate dimension. A parallel world where the supernatural was almost as common as the natural, with legendary beings operating in near-open normalcy."

Jason huffed out a breath and held up his hands for her to pause. "Okay, okay, hold on a second."

Regina cocked her head to one side. "Are you—?"

"I'm fine, I'm fine, I just need to take a second and breathe."

Which he did, for the better part of a minute, while the other two waited with patience. He hunched up his shoulders, relaxed them, did it again, then tilted his head in every direction until his neck had cracked multiple times.

Regina asked, "Are you all right, Jason?"

He sighed. "Yeah. I will be, yeah." Then he released a short laugh that betrayed some skepticism against his own assurance. "It's just ... I've already been juggling all these thoughts, trying to balance out what I used to think of as 'real' against all the undeniable changes you've brought into my life. And now you're throwing *alternate dimensions* at me?" He laughed again, and this time it came out longer and more at ease. "Okay, sure, whatever. An alternate dimension. Why the hell not, right?"

"We don't know for certain that's what it actually is," she stressed. "As I said, we don't really understand how any of it works. But the Triumvirate, for example: None of us had ever heard of them prior to a couple of years ago, and yet, several counter-groups — especially among the older vampire community — now seem to have this long-standing knowledge of the Triumvirate, animosity toward them, and even grudging, fearful respect *for* them."

Iyare grunted at that, his eyes downcast. "After last night, we understand why."

"But back to your question regarding Hellqvist's steamer trunk, and the fact that I said *almost* all of the supernatural elements in our world came from somewhere else:

"At some point in her career as an anthropologist, Doctor Hellqvist discovered historical evidence of the supernatural. As I shared with you before, we don't know the details as to her findings, but we know it sent her on a focused quest. The hunt became an obsession for her, costing her a great deal in terms of her family finances and her professional reputation — the latter of which was mitigated somewhat by her secrecy. Her trail ultimately led her to Egypt, and from what little we were able to discern then and since, we think she may have discovered some sort of *proof* of the supernatural in ancient times. Proof *of* us, and possibly something that could protect humanity *from* us — in other words, a threat *to* us.

"But what *is* this supposed proof of hers? Some of us speculated that it could explain the ancient Egyptians' fixation on gods who were part human, part animal, but that's all it was — speculation. The Egyptian gods, after all, were depicted as sharing many different animal qualities — cats, pigs, cobras, vultures, crocodiles, the list goes on. But all we have seen with our own eyes or even heard of is were*wolves*." She took a moment to smile at him. "Until now, that is.

"Whatever Hellqvist found, it must be inside her steamer trunk — you smelled it, too, at the warehouse, smelled that sheer *age*.

"Our original interest was little more than an idle, supernatural twist of anyone's curiosity into their family lineage. But all our attempts to approach Hellqvist were rebuffed, which elevated our inquisitiveness into concern. We tried to woo her, we tried to bribe her, and we went too far, stoking her paranoia with our persistence. Frustrated, we wanted to secure the trunk — to determine what the hell she actually had, and whether or not it was truly any sort of threat — before it either became too famous an item for us to steal away into the quiet night, or before someone *else*, perhaps an elder vampire wealthier and more powerful than Hellqvist's family, stole it for their own collection."

"Or," Iyare piped in, "before someone in the government — *any* government — decided it was too controversial and made it disappear, like the Ark of the Covenant in that Indiana Jones film."

Regina continued, "That's why we maneuvered Iyare onto the flight crew of Hellqvist's chartered plane as a last-minute substitute. He was to incapacitate everyone on board, discover the actual contents of the steamer trunk, and escape upon landing in California. I was only going to be there to monitor the fallout. It should have been very simple, but ...

"Two things we did not expect: The passengers and flight crew resisted with greater strength than anticipated, which sent Iyare into a bloodlust fury and distracted him from Hellqvist at a key moment."

Though Regina kept her voice level and her eyes on Jason,

Iyare lowered his head in disgrace.

"And we learned that *you* were going to be there, at the airport that same night — and to interview Hellqvist, no less! That split my focus, and it was too late to summon any of the others to pitch in." She shrugged. "Our goal of assessing the steamer trunk was thwarted when Hellqvist jammed the steel trunk's lock, but I, at least, was placed in a position to observe you more closely."

"So ..." Jason confirmed. "... you *did* already know about me, before we met at the airport."

Regina blinked in confusion. "Well ... yes. I told you as much after our first incident at the security warehouse — in the alley, remember?"

"Oh, I remember. No offense, but I'm still catching up on what you've told me that was or was not a lie."

Regina lowered her gaze until she was peering down at his chest. "I'm sorry about that."

Jason started to dismiss it, then held back, deciding to let her feel at least some shame for all the mind games. Instead, he asked, "Was I the only one you were spying on?"

She shook her head. "No, not the only one. We've had our eyes on three others over the past year or so. But you were the most promising, which is the other reason I was positioned in California."

He asked, "How did you know?"

She met his eyes again. "We didn't, at first. We couldn't be sure. That's why I had to get to know—"

"No, I mean, how did you know about me, or the other three, at all? Know that this panwere-thing was even real? You said you've been looking for me for a 'long time' — which I'm guessing means this search precedes you and Iyare?"

They both nodded.

"If panweres are so rare—"

"More than rare," Iyare interjected in a soft, respectful voice. "Virtually unknown. A theory."

"Right, that. If we're 'virtually unknown,' how did your 'theory' get started? How did you know to start looking in the first place?"

Regina and Iyare glanced at one another, then she smiled again and said, "Some of us only did it out of vague hope, hope for a powerful ally against the vampire community, and against the humans who know about us and would exterminate us. But for myself? I *knew*."

"You 'knew' doesn't seem like much ... of ... a ..." Jason's eyes widened, and he unleashed a heavy sigh. "Regina, please, *please* don't tell me that this was all some sort of *prophecy*. That I'm, like, the 'chosen one' or some other bullshit—"

But Regina was already shaking her head. "No, no, Jason, nothing like that. Did our search require *some* faith? Sure, because anything that takes a lot of time also takes a little faith not to give up. But prophecy? Not at all. Our theory was based on genetics and probabilities—"

"Wait, 'genetics'?"

She nodded. "Lycanthropy can be spread by infection, such as when I triggered your potential by biting your lip — sorry about that — but it can also be inherited. If rumors can be trusted, the Triumvirate's own werewolf was born like us, having received his gift from one of his parents, probably his father. That's how it almost always goes for those born with it: One parent carries it, usually the father — males are more susceptible to the potency of the full moon as well.

"But what if *both* parents carried the potential? Even if they themselves weren't active werewolves, what if two people — people whose grandparents, or great-grandparents, and so on — passed their double-potential on to their child? What would that mean?"

Jason shrugged. "The obvious answer would seem to be someone who's much more likely to become a werewolf."

"Yes. And *that's* why the search has gone on for so long. Most of the time, it just meant another werewolf in the fold. But our studies into lycanthropy and genetics suggested there was another possibility. Are you familiar with stem cells?"

Jason's face scrunched up for a second. "Not really. Just what I've picked up from the news. Aren't they related to babies? Something that made stem cells controversial?"

"Stem cells can be found in both babies and adults. They're unspecialized cells that can adapt themselves to match other cell types. Embryonic stem cells are the significantly more versatile of the two, hence your controversy.

"Now, keep in mind that some of this is rather metaphorical — we've been trying to apply science to the supernatural, so there are a lot of grey areas in this. But an extension of our theory has been that lycanthropy affects the body in a way that turns almost *all* of its carrier's cells into latent stem cells. That's why werewolves can shapeshift; their cells adapt and change to an extreme — both in form and speed — that no normal human could ever hope to match, could ever *dream* of matching. And that's with your 'average' werewolf. But if a person were born with the right combination of genes, with a level of these 'supernatural stem cells' above and beyond all other lycanthropes, and if those receptive cells could successfully tap into the biological energy that is the pulse of the Earth to a degree that the ancient Egyptian 'gods' were able to achieve ..." She shook her head in wonder. "That's where our theory of the hypothetical panwere was born."

Iyare raised his hands before him, an up-sweeping gesture toward Jason. "And now ... here you stand." His eyes glistened with such reverence that it made Jason uncomfortable all over again.

Looking back to Regina, Jason drew a careful breath. "So. You're saying both of my parents ...?"

"Yes," she said, "that's how you first came under our scrutiny — assisted in no small part by modern web services such as Ancestry.com, MyHeritage.com, and all the rest. Both of your parents share full Egyptian heritage, each of their family trees hailing specifically from the biodiverse Sinai Peninsula of Egypt, and the people of that region have an exceptionally high profile of lycanthropy in their genes — the reason for *that* remains unclear."

"Unless," Iyare put in, "there were some truth to the ancient Egyptians and their animal-gods."

Regina nodded again. "And at some point, Doctor Hellqvist

stumbled upon some part of this, or all of it, and Hellqvist's interest in Egypt accelerated our own. For all we know, she might have even figured out that modern-day 'animal gods' — as she would likely have viewed werewolves through her new lens — were still alive and active in the world. And did that knowledge motivate her to seek some protection from, or weapon against, us? And if she did, is it just more silver? Or something *else*? " She grunted. "Yet another reason why we need to find out what the hell the good doctor found, what she brought home inside that damned steel steamer trunk."

Jason asked, "If Doctor Hellqvist was so private with all her information, her discoveries, how do you know there's any threat at all?"

"Fair point. A good deal of this *is* supposition on our part, collected over many months of circumstantial evidence and dogged attempts to ascertain why she—"

All three of them flinched when a knock sounded from Jason's apartment door.

"Oh, great," Jason muttered. "The cops have arrived after all."

Regina's eyes widened. "You were expecting—?"

"Not 'expecting,' but with all the police activity across the street and all the witnesses yammering about the lion they saw, I worried ..."

Jason's words trailed off when Iyare perked up, his entire body tensing as he sniffed at the air.

A second later, Regina followed suit. "Oh," she whispered. "Oh, no."

Jason looked at them and started to ask what was wrong, but then he finally picked up on it, the personal scent of his visitor seeping around the doorframe.

Jason didn't have as much experience as the other two, but he was pretty sure his visitor was another werewolf.

The knocking came again, each rap spaced further apart but landing a little harder than before.

Iyare looked to Regina. "What do we do?"

Before she could respond, the doorknob turned. In his surprise over Regina and Iyare's arrival, Jason had forgotten to lock the door. It swung open to reveal a handsome, casually-dressed, middle-aged white man. He was grinning in a friendly way, his impressive muscles bulging through his T-shirt in a nonchalant display of strength.

Then he said in an Irish accent, "Hello there! Fancy meetin' ye two again so soon."

Uninvited Guest

Jason put it together after a few seconds. Between Regina and Iyare's obvious anxiety and what Derek had mentioned about one of the fake Feds having an Irish accent, he deduced this was a member of the infamous Triumvirate.

And it made sense: Beyond his strong werewolf aroma, the newcomer exuded power on a level that Jason probably could not have detected when he was just human; that, or at best it would have been relegated to a simple "gut feeling" that he would have been unable to articulate beyond, *Don't mess with this guy!*

"Jason," Regina said, her voice tight, "back away from him."

"Now, now," the Irishman chided as he crossed the threshold by a single step even before Jason realized that he had, in fact, followed her command and backed away, "if I meant ye any immediate harm, would I've knocked?" He leaned against Jason's open doorframe, his arms folded, his demeanor completely at ease.

"I think," Iyare growled, "your vampire is down for the day, and your zombie can't be walking around in broad daylight, so perhaps you're stalling for time."

The Irishman shrugged, an affected "aw-shucks" gesture. "Then why announce myself at all? I could've just watched ye from afar, and ye'd never've known I was here." He smiled his friendly smile again. "Besides, ye're right about Alistaire, but Trey passes far better than ye might expect these days. Ye wouldn't know that, 'cause ye only saw him at night."

Jason's heart thundered. "*Trey ...?*" he whispered.

He hadn't meant to say it aloud, but the Irishman's gaze shifting from Iyare to him revealed the slip. The Irishman considered him as though just truly recognizing his presence, then he took a long sniff, his nose directed first at Jason himself, then around the apartment in general. “Interestin’. She called ye ‘Jason,’ I believe?”

“If you’re seeking some sort of parley,” Regina snapped, a good deal of bite returning to her voice, “speak with us. Leave him out of it.”

But the Irishman kept his attention on Jason, to whom he said, “I was just followin’ their scents; I dinna expect to meet ye just yet, Mister Samir. But I have to say, ye smell a bit ... *different* than I expected.”

Oh, shit, Jason thought. *“Just yet”? “Mister Samir”? Christ, they know who I am. And* Trey! *Regina was right about him — Trey works for the Triumvirate. But what did he mean by Trey “passes better”?*

Then he put the next pieces together.

Oh, my God. Holy shit! Trey? No, no way. Trey *is ... their zombie? No fucking way. I’ve chatted with him online, so many times! And what kind of zombie sends* texts, *for God’s sake?*

During this reflection, the Irishman was looking him up and down and giving him another round of sniffs without moving from his repose against the doorframe. “A word of advice, Jason — if I may call ye ‘Jason’? Ye might want to reconsider the company ye keep.” He lifted a finger from his muscular arm to point at Regina and Iyare. “These people are a bad influence.”

Iyare spat a guffaw at that, a hostile bark of a laugh. “We? *We* are the bad influence? That’s quite an accusation, coming from a terrorist who persecutes his own kind!”

While Iyare’s laughter had been harsh and humorless, the Irishman’s responding mirth was pleasant, almost cheerful. “Did ye— ... did ye honestly just call *me* a ‘terrorist’?” He shook his head with a bright grin. “God, that’s rich! I’ll be sure to share that one with my friends. Usually we find it’s the vampires who’re the biggest hypocrites, but I guess they don’t hold the exclusive rights to it.” He thumbed back over his shoulder, toward the apartments across the street. “Part-time abstainers that ye are, which, by the way, is the *only* reason we let ye go last night—”

Iyare demanded, "You 'let' us go—?!"

"Damned straight. I can tell the stink of those who indulge their wicked selves from those who at least *try* to hold back. But yer group is the big game in town right now, so're ye gonna try'n tell me *that's*—" He jabbed his thumb toward the neighboring apartment complex again, harder this time. "—not the handiwork of one of yer pack?"

Iyare stole a brief glance toward Jason, but Regina stepped forward to keep the Irishman's attention. "It is not."

The Irishman rolled his eyes. "Oh, really? A civilian got mauled to death by some *random* wolf, then?"

Regina sniffed in derision. "Maybe your hearing is not as acute as ours. Apparently, that civilian was mauled to death by some random *lion*."

The Irishman stared at her for a moment before laughing again. He shook his head in disbelief and muttered, "Mar dhea."

"Listen for yourself," she insisted. "I'm sure everyone over there is still talking about it. Go ahead. *Listen*."

The Irishman shook his head again, but his eyes lost focus as he shifted attention to his ears. Several seconds later, the smile slipped from his face and his brow knitted a little, and shortly thereafter, he muttered, "I'll be damned."

After eavesdropping a bit longer, he looked back at Regina, started to say something, then paused. Instead of expressing whatever thought had initially come to his mind, his gaze moved from her to Jason, and his brow knitted further.

Before any speculation on his part could come to fruition, Regina raised her voice. "Now that *that's* settled ..." She growled, literally; while she remained mostly human, her eyes changed and her fingernails grew longer. "What - do - you - *want*?"

The Irishman studied Jason for another beat, then held up his hands in a placating gesture, his relaxed, we're-all-friends-here smile returning. "Easy, lass. As I pointed out, I'm not here lookin' for another fight. Quite the opposite, actually." He stepped all the way into Jason's apartment and closed the door behind him with a gentle click.

Something about that act, the presumptiveness of it, bugged

Jason. For the first time since his visitor arrived, he felt something less like caution or fear, something a little closer to indignation.

Meanwhile, the Irishman clasped his hands before him and settled back against the door. "The way I see it," he mused, "yer lot wants the good doctor's trunk somethin' fierce, while my friends and I aim to keep it safe and sound. I suppose we could call this a stalemate, 'cept I think we demonstrated last night that the odds're a bit more in our favor, don't ye agree?"

Regina snarled, and Iyare matched her previous growl as he, too, edged toward a more feral state.

The Irishman's amiable grin faded a bit. "If ye're thinkin' that yer two — or three? — against my one puts those momentary odds back in yer favor, I'd beg ye to think on recent history, and reconsider. I'm not the one still sportin' visible wounds, now am I? So ..." His grin dropped further and his eyes glistened toward a more lupine hue. "... do ye *really* want to take us there?"

Regina and Iyare exchanged meaningful glances — probably, Jason imagined, remembering their five dead friends — before settling down and reverting back into their fully-human forms.

The Irishman chilled out as well, and his smile regained its full, previous warmth. "That's better. Now, yer side 'n mine could keep dancin' around each other, playin' this game of cat and mouse — or triad and pack, if ye prefer. But what's the point of that, really? More bloodshed, more loss of life, and let's not forget the risk of exposure to the general public if we don't clean up after ourselves properly — not to mention our spat gettin' recorded by the public's many, many camera phones. I think we can all agree that would be undesirable, aye?

"Here's what we propose: What's left of yer pack, ye walk away. Now. Leave the steamer trunk be, stop tryin' to get around us. Walk away, and we'll let bygones be bygones — for the minute, anyway. No more skirmishes in the night, no more throats gettin' ripped out, no more bloodletting."

Then, for the first time, his expression grew quite serious.

"I hope ye appreciate the generosity of this offer," he said in a heavier tone, "especially after what ye did to Doctor Hellqvist and her associates, not to mention the innocent bystanders on the plane."

"Why?" Regina countered; her tone was defiant, but Jason thought he detected a note of honest curiosity buried within. "Who was Hellqvist to you? Why would—?"

"Settin' aside the aforementioned *innocent* lives," the Irishman snapped, "Doctor Hellqvist and Alistaire had become correspondents in recent months. That's one of the reasons she was comin' here, rather than continuin' her pursuit for media coverage in London or New York. Alistaire had convinced her to have a sit-down with him — we even helped her charter that cargo plane. We've had a growin' concern about certain knowledge spreading too far, too quickly, and as I'm sure ye can imagine, Alistaire can be quite persuasive.

"Had we not been otherwise detained on unrelated business, Alistaire and I would've been at the airport when she landed. 'Course, as we all know, we would've been too late to save the doctor, but I assure ye, a certain black-furred butcher would *not* have slipped away into the rainy night."

Iyare snarled at this, but it only prompted an eye-roll of dismissal from the Irishman.

"So that's it. Ye go yer way, we go ours. We're offerin' ye a chance to cut yer losses and move on with yer lives." He paused, fixing Regina with an acute stare, his eyes piercing right through her as they again became not quite human. "But make no mistake, lass: If ye persist in meddlin' in our affairs, things'll get ugly right quick. Cross us again, and we won't be extendin' this courtesy a second time." He let that settle for a beat. "So ... do we have an understandin'?"

The air in Jason's apartment crackled with tension as the Irishman waited for Regina's response. Waves of precarious aggression emanated from Iyare, but Regina stood lost in deep thought, her brow creased as she considered the Irishman's proposal.

After a long, significant pause, she spoke, her voice low and controlled, "What guarantee do we have that you'll keep your end of this little bargain? The Triumvirate's treatment — *your* treatment — of our kind is renowned."

The Irishman shrugged. "None, I suppose. Ye'll just have to trust us. A gentleman's agreement, if ye will — or a gentle*woman's*, in yer case." His grin returned, but there was less warmth in it.

Regina held his gaze a few heartbeats longer, then gave a single, sharp nod. "Agreed."

Aghast, Iyare snapped his head toward her. "Regina!" he blurted.

Regina offered him no words; her forceful glower shut him up.

For his part, the Irishman also appeared surprised. "Well, that's good to hear. I'd hate to make a mess of Jason's apartment." He glanced down at the bloodstain on the carpet where Jason had awakened. "More of a mess, anyway."

He paused, perhaps waiting for any of them to offer some explanation. When none of them spoke up, he continued.

"I must confess, I dinna expect ye to comply so readily. But I am glad we could reach an armistice."

Iyare turned his back, grumbling so low even Jason's enhanced hearing didn't catch the words. The Nigerian opened and closed his fists and his muscles flexed, but he remained fully human.

The Irishman pushed off from the door, spreading his hands in a magnanimous gesture. "Ye've made the right choice, so there's no need for any more unpleasantness between us. But I do think it's best if ye leave California straightaway — wouldn't want any *misunderstandings* to arise, would we? I could say the two of ye have 'til nightfall, or somethin' equally dramatic, but I think it's only fair to give ye a bit of time to gather any remaining pack members and tie up any loose ends before leavin' the West Coast behind. Shall we say ... forty-eight hours? That should be enough time for ye to settle yer affairs and be on yer merry way." He raised an eyebrow in a questioning manner.

Regina gave another curt nod. "Understood. Forty-eight hours. We'll be gone."

Iyare whipped back around; he growled at Regina, then at the Triumvirate's representative. Again, the Irishman ignored him.

"Grand!" Sean then returned his attention to Jason. "Lad, we've not been properly introduced, have we?"

Jason did his best to maintain a poker face. "I guess not.

Mister...?"

"Mallory's the last name, but please, call me Sean." He extended a hand, the gesture again coming across as nothing but sincere.

After a brief hesitation, Jason reached out and accepted it, noting the impressive strength in Sean's grip before letting go.

"Now, Jason," Sean said, his tone light and conversational, "I get the feelin' ye and I should have a chat sometime, just the two of us. Get to know each other a bit, yeah? I think we might have some things in common. Not the least of which: An acquaintance with an affinity for those 'of the Dead' movies?"

Jason swallowed, his mouth dry. He had no idea what Sean wanted with him or what the hell he meant by that random-ass movie reference—

Then it hit: "Of the Dead," as in *Night of the Living Dead*, as in director George Romero.

As in *Trey* Romero, his boss' pseudonym.

Jason wanted to ask about Trey, about what it all meant and what the real purpose of the Watchdogs might be and why Trey had been jerking him around lately. But the simple fact was, since revealing herself as a werewolf, Regina — for all her prior duplicity — had been more embracing of him than Trey, who had cut him off without a word of explanation the minute he asked about the Triumvirate. *Was* there an explanation? Maybe. But at this point, standing here in his living room with three werewolves and still expecting the cops to maybe show up ... well, he didn't know if he wanted anything to do with Trey, or Sean, or their Triumvirate — not to mention whether or not Trey was some weird kind of zombie!

Still, antagonizing this Irishman seemed unwise, so Jason forced a noncommittal shrug and replied, "Yeah, uh, maybe sometime. Soon."

Sean's grin sharpened, his eyes glinting with amusement and something deeper, possibly darker, possibly *predatory*. "I'll hold ye to that, lad." He nodded — to Jason or himself? Jason wasn't sure — and turned to face them all. Clapping his palms together, he declared, "I believe my business here is concluded. Regina, I trust ye'll be on yer way soon. Remember, ye have forty-eight hours — mornin' after next, ye're gone. And Jason ..." He winked, as if they were old pals just kidding around. "I'll be seein' ye, lad."

With that, Sean turned on his heel and opened the door, stepping toward the morning-lit walkway beyond. At the last second, he paused on the threshold, looking back over his shoulder. "Oh, and Regina?" He jerked his chin toward Iyare. "Ye might wanna keep yer dog on a tighter leash."

Jason thought Iyare was going to go full-wolf then and there, but Regina clamped a firm hand on his shoulder.

Sean chuckled and closed the door with a courteous, gentle *click.*

Choosing Sides

The instant the door closed, Iyare whirled on Regina and hissed under his breath, "I should fucking kill you."

Regina glared right back at him; though heat filled her eyes, her whispered voice was ice cold. "Watch your mouth, Iyare, or you'll be forced to try."

At first, Jason wondered how they could be having such a hostile exchange without raising their voices. Then, as he caught Mallory's footsteps on the stairs outside, he remembered that the Irishman's werewolf ears would still be able to hear them if they spoke at normal volume.

Iyare did not back down, spitting, "We should have taken him together, not *kowtowed* before him."

"I'm not prepared for another fight," she returned, "and you're in worse shape than I am. And we couldn't risk Jason, either — he's not yet ready for *any* supernatural fight, especially not against one of the goddamned Triumvirate."

Iyare began pacing and sing-songed in an affected, mock-Irish accent, "'Mallory's the last name, but please, call me Sean.'" Then he spat, literally this time, on Jason's carpet.

Rather than take issue with Iyare's disrespectful sputum, Jason added to the conversation — keeping his voice low as well. "I don't pretend to know anything about your supernatural politics, but I didn't care for his holier-than-thou undertone. I mean, he tried to come across all charming and friendly, but how hypocritical is that when he's threatening your lives?" Then another thought occurred to him. "What'd he mean about 'abstainers'?"

Iyare stopped pacing and faced Jason. "What?" Some of his anger at Regina remained evident, but that one word demonstrated that his reverence for Jason held steady.

"He called you 'part-time abstainers,' and claimed that's why he let you escape. What's that mean?"

Regina answered him, which allowed Iyare to return to his pacing and stewing. "Contrary to legend and pop-culture, not all werewolves are savage, unrestrained beasts. Females are not as beholden to the full moon as males, and some males — like Iyare — do their best to govern themselves the rest of the month. But even for females, it can be difficult sometimes, especially when the blood-fury runs high — like what happened between you and your neighbor last night. Iyare and I *try* not to give in to our untamed sides out of hand." Her eyes drifted toward the door, and the departed Irishman. "To use Mallory's word, we do our best to abstain from the arbitrary killing of innocent people. We don't view ourselves as the 'top of the food chain,' we don't view humans as our 'natural prey' or any of the other sick shit the vampires like to spout.

"Have we killed? Will we kill? Oh, yes. I won't lie to you about that. But we strive to make it the exception rather than the rule."

"Then why go after you at all? I mean, isn't the Triumvirate all about keeping the supernatural a secret from the public? That tracks with some of what he said about Hellqvist's trunk, but if you don't—"

"Who told you that?" she cut in.

"What?"

"Who told you the Triumvirate were all about keeping the supernatural a secret?"

"Oh. Um, that's something I dug up while I was on my own. A fellow Watchdog said they're, like, the Illuminati of the monster world, and squash anyone who blows the secret?"

Regina shook her head. "That's not quite accurate. The Triumvirate stand *against* other supernatural beings, and fancy themselves the self-appointed guardians of humanity."

Jason took a moment to process that, while Iyare grunted as he continued his pacing; when the latter spoke, it was at a normal volume for the first time since Mallory left. "They're more than happy to smite any of our kind. They *murder* us, endlessly, without consideration, without *mercy*."

Jason's brow furrowed at this proclamation. "Except ... he said they let you go last night *because* you abstain, mostly. *And* he's giving you a chance to walk away from all this. Wouldn't that count as 'mercy'?"

Iyare did not reply in words, but Jason noticed a hitch in his stride, after which his pacing slowed a bit as his countenance appeared less enraged, more thoughtful.

"I admit," Regina said, "that I hadn't expected that offer from them, because Iyare's point that the Triumvirate are not known for clemency *is* accurate. Maybe there's more to them than the rest of us think? I don't know, but what concerns me more right now is their fixation on Hellqvist and her steamer trunk. What don't they want us, or the public, to know?"

The three fell silent as they contemplated this. All of this started — for Jason, at least — with his prospective interview with Doctor Hellqvist about her "earth-shattering" discovery, and it felt as though things were coming full circle.

After a minute or so had passed, Iyare asked Jason — again, in a deferential tone, "Did you understand his movie reference?"

"I'm sorry?"

"When he spoke to you, Mallory made some comment about acquaintances and 'Dead' movies?" Iyare shrugged his ignorance. "I am sorry, I may know *Raiders of the Lost Ark*, but in general, I am not a 'movie buff.' Did *you* understand what he was talking about?"

Jason's first impulse was to lie, to plead ignorance, to keep that little exchange private and secret ... but why? Yes, Sean had been far more gracious toward him than the other two, and yes, this seemed to solidify the notion that Trey was not only involved with the Triumvirate, but was actually a member — and, don't forget, some kind of *zombie*. If this big, scary, powerhouse trio of the supernatural world were inclined to be amicable toward him, wouldn't his smartest move be to roll with that?

Then again, Regina already knew about Trey and the Watchdogs' connection to the Triumvirate. And Iyare's and her reaction to his being a panwere? That was more than his ego ever asked for, but ...

"Yeah," he finally answered, concerned that his hesitation had gone on long enough to be obvious. "I'm pretty sure he was making a reference to George Romero." He looked to Regina, reminding her, " 'Romero' is the last name Trey uses for his *Watchdogs* pseudonym."

Iyare simply said, "Ah." Regina, however, nodded in a slow, knowing way, and — wherever his allegiances would eventually solidify— Jason knew he had made the right call by being honest.

He was on the cusp of asking what the hell their next step was, especially since Regina and Iyare were under a ticking clock, but before he could speak, his phone *buzzed.*

Damn; he realized that he had yet to respond to Derek's texts. Sure, it was early, earlier than he would normally be up, but given the severity of the situation ...

Jason picked up his phone, fully expecting to see another message from "C.S.", but his heart skipped a beat when he saw the name of the actual sender, a true "speak of the devil" moment.

I UNDERSTAND YOU'VE MET MY IRISH FRIEND (AND THAT YOU'RE KEEPING QUESTIONABLE COMPANY). YOU AND I SHOULD MEET, FACE TO FACE. NAME ANY PLACE WITHIN AN HOUR OF WHERE YOU LIVE, AND I'LL BE THERE. AND I PROMISE, I WILL EXPLAIN *EVERYTHING*. BUT PLEASE, JASON: COME ALONE. GET AWAY FROM THEM AS SOON AS YOU CAN.

Jason stared at the screen, a chill running down his spine. A week ago, he would have been intrigued by the idea of finally meeting Trey in person, but after everything he had learned about Trey's affiliation with the Triumvirate, the prospect of facing him — alone, no less — felt like walking into the belly of the beast.

Regina asked, "Jason?"

He looked up to find the others watching him with curiosity and concern, especially Regina. He told them, "It's Trey. He wants to get together with me. Alone."

Iyare blurted, "A trap! It *must* be."

Scowling, Regina returned, "That, or a recruitment drive. You saw how Mallory was with him."

"What should I do?" Jason asked them. "Knowing what I

know, seeing your injuries and witnessing Sean's threats, the idea of meeting Trey scares the hell out of me. But he's been my boss, and my friend ... well, online friend. Do I owe it to him to hear what he has to say?"

Iyare shook his head with vehemence and snarled, "You owe him *nothing*. He deceived you all through that 'friendship.' He works to destroy our kind!"

"I suppose ..." was Jason's half-hearted agreement. He stared at his phone again.

"We can't tell you what to do," Regina said; Iyare's hot gaze snapped toward her at those words, but she ignored him. "We can only advise you. And while it's tempting to have you go along with it, to try to get more information, to learn their true motives surrounding Hellqvist's trunk ... I ..."

Jason looked up once more, and was surprised to see her expression of uncertainty, even timidity, and damn, were those *tears* swelling in her eyes? This was not the Regina he had come to know, who exhibited an armor of unerring, supreme confidence at almost all times.

She continued, "I'm afraid. For you, for all of us. While knowledge can be power, I don't *want* you to go."

Jason shifted his attention to Iyare (no question where he stood), back to Regina, then down to his phone. He deliberated a few more seconds, then typed out his response:

OKAY, SOUNDS GOOD. BUT I NEED TO WRAP SOME STUFF UP FIRST, PUT SOME THINGS TO REST. MAYBE IN A FEW HOURS? LET ME GET BACK TO YOU.

He hit Send before he could second-guess himself.

Trey's reply was immediate: LOOKING FORWARD TO IT.

Jason let out a breath and told them, "I bought us some time, but whatever we're going to do, we need to do it soon."

There. He had chosen his side.

For better or worse, the die was cast.

It should have been one of those "cinematic" moments, a significant shift in his life going forward — maybe Regina would take his hand, or kiss him; maybe she and Iyare would bow before him again; hell, maybe one of them would give him a comradely punch on the arm before they all turned and left his apartment, possibly forever ...

Instead, Jason sighed in exasperation when his phone *buzzed* again in his hand. Was Trey going to suggest a location of his own? Then he looked at the screen, absorbed what he was seeing, and said, "Oh, shit."

This latest text was not a follow-up from Trey. It was the one he had expected beforehand, from Derek's "C.S." phone:

DUDE, DID U HAVE SOME KINDA ALTERCATION WITH THAT GUY WHO GOT KILLED BY THE LION LAST NIGHT? LIKE, JUST A *FEW HOURS* BEFORE THE ATTACK? NO ONE THINKS U GOT A PET LION IN YR CLOSET OR ANYTHING, BUT IT'S NOT A GOOD LOOK — *HORRIBLE* TIMING! U GONNA NEED A LAWYER? I SURE HOPE NOT, BUT MIGHT NOT BE THE WORST IDEA.

Jason was still reading as another text came through.

RU EVEN HOME RIGHT NOW? CAUSE I'M GIVIN U A FRIENDLY HEADS-UP — COMPANY'S COMIN YR WAY. TREAD CAREFULLY, AND DON'T BE AFRAID TO LAWYER UP!

DELETE THIS TEXT THREAD, MAN.

Jason perked up his new super-ears and detected footsteps down in the parking area approaching the stairs. Did they belong to police officers? Forget his "altercation" with Sir Asshole — how could he explain Regina and Iyare's battered state, let alone the conspicuous *bloodstain* on his carpet?

"That was Derek," he told Regina in a rush. "The cops are coming. We have to go, *now.*"

New Plan

"How?" Regina asked. "In an apartment like this, I assume there's no back door?"

Jason thought about it for all of two seconds. "Follow me."

Jason paused only long enough to grab things like his wallet and keys, and to throw on a complete set of clothing and toss the biggest shirt he owned to Iyare, to cover his dried blood. Even with two of them injured, leaping to pull themselves up onto the roof was simple; the challenge was its being broad daylight, and the relative ease with which the uppermost neighbors from across the street might see them emerging.

Keeping as low as possible — especially Regina, with her towering height — they closed up behind themselves and hustled away from the main street side of the building on their proverbial tiptoes. As they neared the back of the property and were judging the best way to get down, Jason overheard a loud knocking, followed shortly thereafter by a proclamation of "Police!"; he gave himself exactly one guess as to which apartment was being addressed.

Wow, he thought. *From wannabe-photographer/struggling-reporter to werewolf, to panwere, to fugitive-from-the-law in less than a week. My parents will be so proud.*

His silent attempt at wry humor prompted a surge of almost blinding panic. Was he really doing this? Running from the police? Throwing in with a woman who had lied to him and her overeager compatriot, all because they had inflated his ego by bowing to him?

It's not that simple and you know it, he scolded himself. *Deal with these emotions later, when the cops aren't hot on your heels, when the Triumvirate isn't looming behind them.*

The three human-form werewolves were more than athletic enough to descend to ground-level in short order and without witnesses; they slipped through the back of the neighborhood to put some distance between themselves and Jason's apartment complex.

"I don't suppose," Jason asked Regina as they headed south along the sidewalk, "you have a car around?"

Regina sighed. "Yes. Parked back at your apartment."

Jason grumbled, "Awesome. If your appearance wouldn't've prompted too many questions, you could've walked right down the stairs, past the cops, and driven around back to meet Iyare and me."

"I think," Iyare commented, "the police would have seen which apartment she emerged from and stopped her either way."

Jason grunted. "Good point." He pulled his phone from his pocket. "I can call for an Uber or Lyft, get us out of the area. If they just found out about my fight with my neighbor, it should take them a little time to get a warrant or whatever for my records. After that, though, they could ... trace ..."

Jason's stride slowed as he stared at his phone. His companions looked at one another, then at him with expectation; he ignored this while he thought about electronic devices, and about the Watchdogs' hacker, New Neo.

After a few more seconds of contemplation, he said, "*I* may have some time, but I think we need to get rid of your phones right away. You said the Triumvirate were able to tap in or whatever, to know about your supposed group-attempt on the warehouse, right? They knew all the whens and the wheres?"

Regina nodded. "Yes. That's actually what we counted on before, but now ..." She looked to Iyare. "Mallory might not have 'tracked' us to Jason's apartment after all — not with his wolf senses, anyway."

Iyare growled his low opinion of Mallory's arrogant bluff.

Regina pulled hers out. "We can remove the SIM cards, then—"

"Wait," Jason said, "wait, don't do that. I have an idea."

* * *

Jason had only been to this bus station once before, so he had zero idea how many security guards were afoot, let alone where all the security cameras might be — to play it safe, his beaten-and-bruised company were waiting at a McDonald's about a mile away. He knew he would only be able to pull this sort of thing once or twice; if the police started looking for him in earnest, he would have to avoid places like this.

The station itself, which also catered to train services, was big and impressive to the eye, but he could have done without the smells; it wasn't too crowded this morning, but he could still detect larger numbers of past clientele in a variety of hygienic states. Purchasing his ticket online allowed him to interact with fewer people as he made his way to a service kiosk.

He entered his confirmation number and collected his ticket to Greensboro, North Carolina — the hope was that the bus ticket, purchased with his credit card, would throw the police off his trail. He had also gotten lucky that a couple of early departure times had been available, so he didn't have to wait around too long.

Soon enough, the gruff, lethargic bus driver was scanning his ticket, and he was among the first passengers to take a seat. As boarding continued, a pair of police officers meandered past his window, but they appeared more bored than observant; besides, he reminded himself as he experienced a twinge of anxiety, it was far too soon for any sort of APB to have gone out for him — as Derek pointed out, no one could realistically connect him to a lion-mauling.

As the minutes ticked by and departure time drew near, Jason reached into his jacket pocket, retrieved Regina's and Iyare's phones, made sure they were both on — Iyare's charge was low, but there was nothing he could do about that — and tucked them down between his seat and the side of the bus beneath the window. He put on a perfunctory show of checking his other pockets, then standing and checking around his chair; this little display was probably unnecessary — the other passengers' visages ranged from sleepy to bored, and overall apathetic — but he did it just in case anyone was asked later.

Finally, he stepped back into the aisle and hustled toward the open door.

"Gotta schedule t' keep," the bus driver warned without looking up from his tablet.

"I know," Jason replied, "I understand. If I'm not back in time, just leave without me."

He expected the driver to inquire as to how long he might take, or whether or not he had any luggage stowed below, or why he was disembarking, or *something*. But the driver just flipped his hand up in the air, as if to say, *Of course I will, idiot.*

Jason stood there a second longer, wondering if he should say anything more, then decided to cut his losses and leave.

By the time the bus departed, he was no longer in the station.

* * *

The alluring aroma of greasy fast food, especially the breakfast bouquet of pancakes and syrup, biscuits, crispy bacon, and well-done sausage, wafted through the restaurant, mingling with the fragrance of fresh coffee from nearby tables. All these smells would have enticed him before his change; now, they really made his stomach rumble, especially the meats — he hadn't realized how hungry he was.

Jason found Regina and Iyare sitting opposite one another in a corner booth. They both had breakfast meals in front of them, but neither had eaten much. The morning light caught Regina at the right angle for him to notice the improvement in her bruises and swelling — injuries from supernatural enemies might be slower to heal, but their recovery rate was still superior to normal humans; even her traumatized scalp, what little he could see under her hat, appeared to be growing back her hair.

He smirked at himself, thinking about "normal" humans in such an offhanded manner, as if all of this weren't so new to him.

"How did it go?" Regina asked as he slid into the booth next to her.

Holding up a finger, first for her to wait then moving it to his lips, he pulled out his own phone and removed its battery. Placing them on the table together, he answered, "Without a hitch. Your phones are heading east. With luck, they'll get all the way to North Carolina before anyone finds them."

She nodded, while Iyare asked them both, "What next?" Like Regina, the man looked better, but he also appeared restless, his agitation palpable.

Before answering, Jason caught himself staring at Regina's unfinished breakfast. "Are you going to eat that?"

Regina responded by sliding her plastic tray over in front of him. He dug in.

As he wolfed down (pun intended) the rest of Regina's food, Jason did his best to enunciate as he told them in a lower voice, "I've been thinking about my deputy sheriff friend, Derek. Regina's met him. He was at the airport when Iyare made his dynamic appearance, and he's the one who told me the story about the Triumvirate adding the chains and silver padlock to Hellqvist's steamer trunk. He's also the one who gave us enough forewarning to duck the police at my apartment earlier, though I doubt evasion is quite what he had in mind."

Regina asked, "How might Derek help us?"

"He knows just enough to be freaked out by everything that's going on. A wolf killing people on a plane, fake Federal agents securing a piece of evidence by unusual means, and now a *lion* killing someone? He'd already asked me to take a crack at this, as a journalist, and to keep him updated because it's really bothering him. I hate to say this about my friend, but ... I'm wondering if we could use that to our benefit."

Iyare grimaced. "A human lawman, getting mixed up in *our* world? That rarely ends well."

Jason shook his head, and said in an even lower voice. "This isn't a recruitment drive. I don't want to get Derek any more involved than he has to be. I don't want him to know that he's dealing with a *were*wolf or a *were*lion, and I sure don't want to put him on the Triumvirate's radar. But all of this centers around Hellqvist and her damned trunk, and right now Derek is the closest thing we have to an 'inside man.' Otherwise ..." He lifted his hands in defeat. "... I don't know what else we could do but take the Triumvirate's offer and leave town."

A slight smile played across Regina's lips. "'We'?"

Jason returned her expression along with a casual shrug. "Dodging the police, lying to stall Trey, not to mention that I really am responsible for my neighbor's death, deserved or not. I'd say I'm pretty committed now, aren't I?"

She blinked her beautiful green eyes at him. "Are those the *only* reasons?"

"Maybe not."

They did not exactly clasp hands, but Regina moved so that their forearms were touching, and Jason did not pull away. For his part, Iyare appeared lost in some vague place between vicarious joy and discomfort.

Then the moment passed, and consternation returned to Regina's eyes. "As much as I hate to involve your friend, we're running out of options. I believe you're right; we either ask for Derek's help, or we retreat." She glanced at Iyare. "And I don't want to retreat."

Iyare nodded his agreement.

"Okay," Jason said. "I'll reach out to Derek, but I'll keep it vague — we have to assume that Trey could be monitoring my phone by now, too. At least Derek and I already have a discreet place we can meet. Regina, you're already a familiar face; we can sell the idea of this being a shared journalistic pursuit on our parts — hell, he actually recommended that when I saw him yesterday." He shook his head as he muttered in disbelief, "Jesus, was that only *yesterday*? Damn." Then he continued as before. "Iyare, your presence might cause him to lock up on me. Is there some safe place you can lie low for a bit while we meet with him?"

Iyare nodded. "We have a few bolt-holes scattered around the area, places our pack secured before it all went to hell. I can take the nearest one."

"Good." Jason let out a long breath, releasing some of the tension that had taken up residence between his shoulder blades. Then he snapped the battery back into his phone and opened his "C.S" thread.

* * *

Limited to texting back and forth — Jason presumed Derek would not want to accept a phone call on his burner — it took some time and effort to cajole him into meeting in person right away; Derek was on duty and reluctant to show up in uniform. Jason, ever mindful of New Neo's potentially hacking his texts, felt as though he used up half a thesaurus talking around anything critical, and he was relieved when Derek finally acquiesced.

This time, Jason arrived at Andy's first; after stopping at the bar for a couple of beers, he led Regina to a spot in the dimmest corner — the better to disguise her lingering bruises. The small, old, well-worn tables weren't built to entertain three patrons at once, but he moved the two chairs around and snagged a third to make it work.

Next, he once again removed the battery from his phone and pocketed each separately. Then they settled in to wait for Derek.

The door opened and closed, patrons came and went, time passed. Jason drummed his fingers on his thigh.

Under her breath, Regina quipped, "You could try turning into some animal that's renowned for its patience."

He offered a crooked smile. "Did you know that Siberian tigers will stalk their prey for up to thirty minutes?"

She released a single, soft chuckle. "I did not."

"Yeah, I'm full of trivia like that." He shook his head. "You know, your people are lucky I turned out to be your panwere — with my fascination with wildlife, I'm like a walking animal-encyclopedia."

"You don't really think that's a coincidence, do you?" When he raised his eyebrows in question, she added, "Why do you think you've always been so taken with wildlife?"

His burden of responding to that was relieved when the door opened again and revealed Derek's silhouette. He breathed, "Showtime."

The clientele at Andy's was sparse at that hour, and the few patrons tensed up upon seeing a sheriff's deputy, in uniform, step inside. Derek took off his sunglasses and nodded to the bartender, who nodded back (which put most of the other customers at ease), as he made his way straight toward them.

When he reached the table, he did not sit. Looming over them, he asked Jason, in a tone that was not the friendliest, "Did you evade the authorities at your apartment this morning?"

"Not at all," Jason lied. "I appreciate your heads-up, but I wasn't home this morning, or last night."

"Uh-huh. Then where were you?"

"Dude, c'mon. Really?" Jason inclined his head toward Regina, who did a passable job of pretending to blush as she flashed a demure smile and blinked down at her clasped hands.

The innuendo succeeded; Derek shuffled his feet in an awkward dance for a second, then removed his uniform cap and mumbled, "Oh, uh ... sorry, I just, uh ... sorry, ma'am." After one more excruciating beat, he pulled out the third chair and sat across from them.

"You want a beer?" Jason asked as an olive branch. "I'm buying this time."

"No, no, I'm on duty," Derek replied with a cursory fingernail tap against his badge. "Next time, for sure." Then he rallied and put some authority back into his voice. "So what's this about you getting into a fight with your across-the-street neighbor, before a fuckin' *lion* killed him?"

Jason shrugged and sipped at his beer. "It really wasn't much of a 'fight.' More of an argument."

"That's not what the people around his complex are saying."

"Derek, I met with you — right here — less than an hour afterward. Did I look like I'd been in a fight?"

Derek considered this. "Not so much."

Jason spread his hands as though to say "there you have it."

"What'd you two fight about?"

"Well, Sir Asshole was abu—"

"Who?"

"Sorry. The guy I argued with. I didn't know his actual name, so I always thought of him as 'Sir Asshole.' And the reason for that is, he was always abusing his girlfriend, and he was doing it again yesterday. If you check, I'm sure you'll see a number of domestic dispute calls to their place — several of them from me. I told him I was tired of it, and that I was going to start calling the cops every single time I heard them going at it. Seriously, that's pretty much it. And I hope you'll share that with your colleagues."

Derek's expression was inscrutable. While it would be wonderful if Jason didn't have to worry about the cops looking for him, he wanted to get off the subject sooner rather than later, so he opted to switch gears.

Grinning, he asked, "So ... what's all this horseshit about a lion killing the guy? I mean, seriously, a *lion*?"

Derek's entire demeanor deflated. "Just that. Your 'Sir Asshole' was killed last night. By a goddamned lion."

Jason allowed his smile to fade and exchanged it for a look of disbelief (trying not to overdo it) with Regina. "You are serious."

"Absolutely."

"And it was a *lion*, not that other one? The black wolf from the airport?"

"We've got dozens of witnesses, plus phone videos, of the world's biggest and fastest lion — L - I - O - N — tearing the guy apart, then running off. It was spotted a hundred times after that, runnin' through the streets, until the fucker somehow vanished — just like the wolf from the airport."

Jason acted as though he were taking this all in for the first time. "Holy shit."

"Yeah." Derek scrubbed a hand over his face, after which he looked exhausted. "Every uniform is burnin' it at both ends tryin' to stay on top of this shit. I don't know what the hell's goin' on, man. The world's goin' fuckin' crazy or somethin'."

That was their cue. "That's part of why I reached out to you."

Derek eyed Jason with less than enthusiasm. "Figured we'd get around to that. You two intrepid reporters learn *anything* about all this weird-ass shit?"

Regina sat forward and spoke up. "We're working on it, together." A twinkle appeared in Derek's eye; Jason half-expected some comment or insinuation, but before that could happen, Regina added, "And we're hoping you might be able to help."

The deputy sighed and looked tired all over again. "So long as everything I say is kept off the record, sure, why the hell not?"

Regina assured him, "Of course. All confidential."

Jason nodded. "To start with, do you have anything new on your end? Anything at all? About the plane investigation, about the wolf, about the steamer trunk?" To embellish his supposed ignorance, he tacked on, "Or even about this *lion*?"

Derek pursed his lips and squinted at the wall over Jason's head, betraying one final layer of reluctance, but it didn't last more than a few seconds. "The lion's too new. Everyone's reeling from that one, and there hasn't been enough time for any rumors or gossip to trickle out through the grapevine. But the trunk, and those fake Feds? Yeah, I've been hearing more about that shit. Honestly, if you hadn't reached out to me — and if that lion hadn't pulled so much focus — I probably would've texted you myself about it."

"So spill it."

Derek leaned back in his chair, ran a hand over his head, then sat forward again, frustration etched into every line of his face. "Nothin' new about the wolf, it's still MIA, but those fake Feds? That shit was a head-scratcher from the start, but it's gone from strange to downright bizarre. Get this: Yesterday, those imposters were big news. But sometime last night? The higher-ups decided to drop the investigation. No explanation, no reasoning, nothing. Like they just completely lost all interest."

Jason hadn't known what to expect, but it wasn't that. "They just ... *dropped* it? That doesn't make any sense."

Derek nodded his agreement, which evolved into his shaking his head. "None at all. I mean, who the hell were those guys? And what was so goddamn important about that steamer trunk that they felt the need to chain it up — with a *custom silver padlock*, of all fuckin' things?" He hesitated, then reached across the table and stole a swig of Jason's beer — propriety be damned. Setting the pint glass down with a clunk, he continued, "And believe it or not, that's not even the weirdest part. Word is, they're moving the trunk after dark tonight. Shipping it off to Washington."

"*Washington*?" Regina interjected. "As in Washington *D.C.*?"

"That's what I'm hearin'."

"But ... why there?"

Derek responded with a brief, angry chuckle. "Hell if I know, lady. You'd think they'd just turn it over to the local FBI or something, especially after those federal imposters? Nope! Apparently it's gettin' an express ticket straight to the goddamned capital. And why wait to move it outta the property warehouse at *night*? Why not just get rid of it ASAP? No idea." He leaned back again, rocking his chair onto its rear legs while crossing his arms over his chest. "I'm tellin' you, real fuckin' freaky shit's been goin' on lately. Last year it was crazy spiders, now we got huge wolves and lions rampaging through the streets, mysterious goons posin' as federal agents, and physical evidence bein' whisked away to Washington with no explanation?" He shook his head. "It's like somethin' outta a goddamn conspiracy thriller, or maybe a straight-up horror story." He fell silent for a long moment, his gaze drifting up over Jason's head again. Then he leaned forward and fixed Jason with a pointed look. "You said you're lookin' into all this, and I wanna know whatever you find, but I'm also tellin' you: Watch yourself, man. There's some seriously shady shit goin' down, and I don't want to see you *or* your lady friend here gettin' yourselves in too deep, you hear me?"

Jason could not help but think, *Jesus, if only he knew ...*

Derek stood, his abrupt movement scraping his chair's legs on the floor. "That's everything I got, and I gotta get back on patrol. But keep me posted, and *watch your ass*. I got a bad feelin' about *all* of this." He hesitated again, then added, "If I can figure out a nonchalant way — without it smellin' too 'off' — I'll put in a word with your city locals, tell 'em I bumped into you at random and that you had an alibi during the attack. Though honestly, I'd love to see how they were gonna try to pin a wild animal attack on you."

"Thanks, man," Jason said, and meant it; one less thing to sweat about, at least.

Derek donned his cap, gave them a curt nod, and turned as though to stride out of the bar ... but then he paused. He stood in profile to them, seemingly lost in thought.

Jason asked, "Derek? You good?"

Derek turned his head toward them, his eyes unreadable cop's eyes once more. "Just so we're clear: I know you two know more than you're letting on. I'm not mad, but I want you to understand that I'm not an idiot."

Jason glanced at Regina. “Um ... I don’t—”

“Coupla minutes ago, I mentioned that those fake Feds used a custom padlock made out of silver — *silver*. I hadn’t told you that before — hell, I didn’t even know about it until about an hour ago, and only because I’ve got my own man on the inside, so to speak. But neither of you batted an eye at that little detail ... which tells me you already knew about it. Which means you’re privy to information that only people in uniform should know.”

Jason’s jaw dropped as he struggled to figure out what to say.

Derek looked straight ahead again, once more giving them his profile. “But ... since this conversation never took place, I guess I can’t really do much with that knowledge. Not yet, anyway. Just remember what I said: Watch - your - ass, Jason.”

And with that, Derek finally marched away from their table and out of the bar.

Jason and Regina looked at one another, and Jason said, “Oops. I guess I wasn’t being as clever as I thought, huh?”

“Do you think ...?”

“I think if Derek were going to act on this, he would’ve done so right here and now.”

“Then I suppose we should get back to business.” She turned in her chair to better face him. “I think Washington D.C. is a misdirection. And I’d be willing to bet that the Triumvirate’s vampire is behind last night’s sudden, inexplicable loss of interest in the ‘fake Feds’ case.”

“You mean he can—?”

“Yes, older vampires are able to sway weaker minds.”

Jason couldn’t help but grin as he commented, “Like a Jedi?”

Regina shrugged. “If you wish. Their vampire must also be the reason they’re waiting until nighttime to move the trunk. Maybe they’re setting out one last round of bait, maybe they want it for themselves, or maybe they just want it to disappear. But wherever the trunk is officially going, I’m telling you, it won’t reach its destination.”

Jason shook his head. “We can’t let that trunk slip through our fingers, Regina. Whatever Hellqvist discovered, the answers are locked inside.”

Regina responded with a slow nod.

"Okay." He paused, thinking it over. Pulling out his phone and battery, he reconnected them as he went on. "Derek specifically said they would be moving it out of the property warehouse tonight, so at least we know it's still there."

"Assuming his scuttlebutt is accurate."

"True. But—"

His phone *pinged!*, startling both of them. Exchanging a look, he checked the text.

HEY, JASON. IT'S BEEN 'A FEW HOURS,' SO I'M FOLLOWING UP WITH YOU. HOPE YOU TOOK MY ADVICE, AND THAT YOU AREN'T HEADING EAST RIGHT NOW. LOOKING FORWARD TO MEETING WITH YOU.

Jason sniffed. "That answers that."

"What?"

Jason angled his phone so that she could better see it; he couldn't help but notice that she leaned until their shoulders were touching. "Trey hopes I'm not 'heading east.' They're definitely tracking your phones."

"But not yours?"

He thought about that. "Maybe not. Or that could be another deliberate mislead." He sighed. "Not that we have much choice but to keep it as long as we can. In the modern age, we're going to have a hell of a time getting around without a phone — we can't exactly change form and run around on foot. I mean, I guess I could shift into a dog, but you, and especially Iyare, would stand out too much. If only we'd been able to get one of our cars."

Regina took her turn thinking things over. "If we assume that, even with Derek trying to 'clear your name,' a conversation with the police would take too long, what if we made our way back toward your complex so that I could retrieve the car Iyare and I were using? Your neighbors won't know me. And look ...." She scooted back and turned her face from side to side. "I think I've healed enough to not stand out too much. Derek didn't even comment on it. What do you think?"

Jason studied her beautiful face a few seconds longer than

strictly necessary, and smiled. "I think that I have an idea, too."

She smiled in return, and he couldn't deny that it was a touch sultry. "And what might that be?"

"I got ahead of myself," he confessed. "I should've said: I have the *beginning* of an idea. Once we've got your car and don't have to Uber everywhere, it'll involve stopping at a boating store."

That caught Regina off guard. "A *boating* store?"

Jason smiled again, and this time it was quite mischievous.

EYE ON THE BALL

"This won't work." Iyare held up his hand to shade the setting sun from his left side. He squinted, not because of the sunlight, but in an effort to make out their target in detail. "We can't see anything from here."

"It'll work," Jason assured him. "Trust me."

Iyare opened his mouth to argue, considered to whom he was speaking, and kept it to himself, his body remaining tense. Regina said nothing aloud, but when she was sure Iyare was focused northward, she looked to Jason and raised an inquisitive eyebrow.

Jason responded to that by showing crossed fingers on both hands.

Regina offered a grin in return, then moved closer to Iyare.

Jason was grateful when their mutual attention was directed away from him. While he had been somewhat more honest with Regina, even that had been a quasi-humorous attempt to deflect from how uncertain he actually felt about this scenario.

Following Jason's lead, Regina and Iyare again found themselves standing on a rooftop in what could be loosely described as the "vicinity" of the secure property warehouse where the authorities were keeping Hellqvist's steamer trunk. This time, however, they were not across the street, or one street over, or even two streets over. They were standing atop a much taller business building two miles south.

Jason glanced toward the sun. He felt the urge to check the time, but he no longer had his phone. After texting Trey a couple of hours ago — saying that he still had some "research to do," but he would be in touch about their getting together "as soon as he was finished" — he had left his phone wedged between two random books at the Los Angeles Public Library. If the Triumvirate were tracking his phone, too ... well, that was no longer a concern.

God, I hope this works, Jason thought. He was by far the most inexperienced of their little trio at this sort of thing — whatever "this sort of thing" was, exactly; and hell, even calling himself "inexperienced" glorified matters. He was winging this solely based on concepts he had seen in movies or read in books, coupled with a growing but still gut-based grasp of who, and what, he truly was. Regina suggested he had been drawn to observing animals his whole life because of his nascent potential as a panwere, and now he was counting on his accumulated knowledge to push his newfound abilities to their fullest.

The sun touched the edge of the western horizon. They were minutes from go-time.

That was assuming, of course, that the trunk was moved as soon as the sunlight faded. What if they waited an hour, or two, or more?

Doesn't matter, he told himself. *If we have to wait, we wait. But if I were a vampire, limited to nighttime-only, I would want to maximize my useful hours. I'm betting the Triumvirate's vampire feels the same.*

"Jason!" Regina barked, pointing. "I see movement. A large truck, I think."

He glanced at the still-visible sun again. *Well, fuck my well-thought-out, keenly-analytical timetable, I guess.*

Iyare squinted until his face screwed itself into a knot, then swung his fist through the defenseless air before him. "Damn it, we cannot *see* this far away, Jason!"

Jason strode forward, almost to the edge of the building. "Okay, give me a second. I'm going to shift."

Iyare shook his head in frustration. "No, Jason, that won't help! Wolves have no better distance-vision than humans."

Regina placed a hand on Iyare's shoulder, a slight smile gracing her lips. "You forget, Iyare."

"I 'forget'?! I—? Oh!" Iyare sagged in shameful embarrassment.

Jason closed his eyes. Focusing, concentrating, feeling for that potential, seizing it, willing it to obey his command ...

He sensed his skin altering, tingling and tightening, but no fur grew — no *fur*, but something else sprouted from thickened follicles. His bones shifted, but rather than gaining mass, they thinned. His shirt and jeans felt tighter, as though he had been crammed into them with care, while his arms elongated and his legs shortened. His face — his eyes, his nose, his mouth — altered in new, unfamiliar ways; his hearing felt as though it remained the same, but he still caught Iyare's soft moan of surprise and rapture.

Jason tottered, unsteady on his feet — and not just because his sneakers were now the entirely wrong shape for him. He spread his arms and legs as he battled waves of dizziness.

Iyare mumbled something in his native language, while Regina asked in concern, "Jason? Are you all right?"

He nodded, drew a deep breath through his nose (wow, did *that* feel different!), released it, opened his eyes ... and gasped in awe.

Jason gawked around himself, taking in beauty such as he had never before seen. It was as though his human vision had been a VHS videotape all these years, and now for the first time, he was viewing the world in Ultra-High Definition. The city of Los Angeles was no longer just a city, it was a breathtaking masterpiece, the setting sun gleaming and glittering off the glass and steel structures, which rose in majestic elegance against the backdrop of the bright orange and red sky; even the mundane concrete and asphalt shimmered in ways that brought literal tears to his eyes — his large, oversized eyes.

He peered down at his hands. Gorgeous brown feathers covered the backs of them, and his fingernails were long, black, and curved, but overall, they were still more like human hands than talons; he could see every vein, every wrinkle, even his warped fingerprints were sharp and clear to him. Additional feathers ran along the underside of each arm until they disappeared into his overstuffed shirt, but they were still arms, not wings.

"Yes," he finally answered Regina — the words slurred as his nose and upper lips had joined to form a shortened beak, and his voice was a lot raspier than usual. "Yes, I'm all right. After that uncomfortable mixing of the Komodo dragon hand with my human arm, I decided against trying for just Bald Eagle eyes or a Bald Eagle's head, so I went for something like an 'eagleman.'" He tried to smile, but his new mouth couldn't quite pull that off. "I guess it worked."

"Jason," Iyare said, almost whispering in his veneration. He pointed northward. "The warehouse ...?"

Shaking off the reins of his latest, amazing experience, Jason turned his acute vision toward the warehouse two miles away. The evening shadows lengthened as the sun dipped farther below the horizon, but to his sharp new raptor's gaze, it might as well have been midday. Despite the distance, every detail stood out to him in crisp clarity.

As Regina had surmised, an armored truck had backed up to an open loading dock, which had been sealed tight the night of his and Regina's nocturnal visit. Several police officers and a couple of men in suits gathered around, overseeing the loading of a blocky wooden crate. Jason studied the suited men, but neither appeared to be Sean Mallory. One of them, an older white guy, was signing a bunch of forms, while the other — Hispanic, so far as Jason could tell — adhered labels to the sides of the crate.

Even Jason's new avian-vision could not read the labels from this distance, but his gut told him what they almost certainly boiled down to: "Hellqvist's Secret Steamer Trunk."

And yet ...

"I see some activity," he hedged to the others. But why hedge? It's what they had been waiting for, so why was this bugging him? "They're loading up a wooden crate, handling it with care, lots of paperwork. It ... the crate looks big enough to hold Hellqvist's trunk."

Regina and Iyare leaned forward, straining to see better, but their eyesight just wasn't up to the challenge. They would have to rely on his play-by-play.

Jason watched as the men maneuvered the heavy crate up the ramp and into the truck, which evidently had no liftgate to assist them. Once the crate was presumably secured — he could not see inside the truck from this angle — they closed the heavy, reinforced door, exchanged a few more words amongst both groups, then one uniformed cop and one suited man got into a black sedan that Jason had not paid attention to until now, while one more of each climbed into the cab of the armored truck. With a rumble of its smoky, clunky diesel engine, the truck pulled away from the loading dock, with the sedan following close behind.

"The truck's leaving," he narrated. "Heading west. Probably to LAX."

"Then we need to hurry," Regina proclaimed. "We can't let Hellqvist's trunk get on a plane. Let's go."

Iyare nodded his relieved agreement, and the two headed toward the roof access.

But Jason held up a feathered hand. "Wait."

The others halted, and this time Regina's agitation was as obvious as Iyare's. "Jason, we have to—"

Jason cut her off. "Something about this doesn't feel right. It's too ... too obvious, too neat, all wrapped up for us like a Christmas present." He glanced toward the western horizon; the sun had slipped down out of sight, but the sky was still glowing. "And too early for the Triumvirate's vampire to participate in its transfer." He shook his inhuman head. "We should wait, keep watching."

Regina looked like she wanted to argue — and Iyare appeared about to explode — but instead she drew a deep, calming breath and nodded her assent. "All right, Jason. If that's what your instincts tell you, we'll wait."

She had delivered that last bit to Iyare, whose jaw muscles flexed as he ground his teeth together but said nothing.

So they waited. The sky darkened, true night falling over the city. The bright lights of Los Angeles came to full life, creating a dazzling display — an alluring spectacle for his new eyes, but Jason remained focused on the warehouse.

Minutes passed, then more, until nearly an hour had ticked by. Jason ignored the impatient rustling of first Iyare, then Regina behind him. He felt plenty of his own anxiety, but as Regina had put it, his instincts told him to wait.

So he did. He made himself, *forced* himself, to wait. And just when his doubts were growing insurmountable, he saw it:

Another vehicle, another truck, this time a nondescript, plain, white box truck. The new vehicle pulled to a stop alongside the warehouse, then backed toward the loading dock.

Jason pointed a taloned finger. "Another truck just arrived."

Regina and Iyare perked up, peering as best they could into the darkness. Regina asked, "What're they doing?"

As Jason watched, the new truck kept rolling until its back door was kissing distance from the dock. Unlike the previous occurrence, where the crate had been loaded in plain view with more personnel gathered than were actually needed, this transfer looked like it was going to entertain a lot less "pomp and circumstance." The driver of the box truck opened the door and got out, but his back was turned so that Jason couldn't get a look at him; all he could see was that the man was wearing casual clothing. The man slipped around the end of the truck and disappeared into the warehouse.

"Jason," Regina asked, her voice strained, "please tell us what's happening."

"Nothing yet," he told her as he kept watch. He described the box truck and the more casual activity around it.

Iyare snorted, and not in amusement. "It sounds like nothing more than a simple delivery."

"This isn't a place of business," Jason returned, almost snapping at the Nigerian, "it's a police facility. If it's a 'delivery' for this place, it should arrive by some type of police transport. It would *not* be dropped off by a civilian driving a commercial truck. That wouldn't— Wait."

The box truck shook, then shook again, rocking on its axles as something heavy moved around inside it. Another long moment passed, then the driver reappeared. Was that Sean Mallory? He thought it might be, but he couldn't be sure — as amazing as his eagle-vision was, he wasn't Superman.

Mallory or not, the driver returned to the truck cab, started the engine, and pulled away from the warehouse.

"The truck's leaving. Heading east, away from the airport."

"Do we follow *this* one?" Iyare demanded. "Or do we continue to wait?"

The secure property warehouse loading dock closed.

Jason was already shifting form as he said, "We follow."

* * *

The three tore down the stairs in their respective wolfman and wolfwoman forms. The many offices had been near closing when they arrived, and through their hasty departure, they detected no more than the occasional working janitor or lazing security guard — easily avoidable, though one such guard almost literally shit his pants when three detailed blurs tore past him in the stairwell, the darkest one barking loud enough to prompt the near rectal disaster.

At the street, they reverted to fully human form as they burst from the building and piled into their car, Regina taking the driver's seat. "Which way?" she prompted.

"Head straight for the warehouse, but turn right one street short," Jason told her. "We'll need to run some red lights and blow through the stop signs until we get that truck back in sight, and I don't want to tempt fate by speeding past a police facility."

She nodded, the car already in motion.

The next few minutes were tense as they attempted to locate the truck. It could have made any number of turns after departing, but just when all three of them began cursing under their collective breaths, Iyare spotted it.

"There!" he cried from the backseat. "Turn right again at the next intersection."

Regina did so, and soon they were trailing several cars behind a white box truck.

"Jason," she asked, "is that the right truck?"

"I think so," he said aloud, while keeping *I hope so!* to himself. "I can't be sure without getting a look at the driver, but if it's one of the Triumvirate — and I *think* it might've been Mallory — I don't know if we can risk that."

After a few seconds of silence, Iyare suggested, "What if you turned into a Bald Eagle again, but fully this time? You could fly past them, get a look at the driver, then return?"

Jason considered that, and the mere notion filled his guts with butterflies. "I don't know if I'm ready to try, you know, actually *flying*. Not without practice first."

"Wouldn't your animal instincts take over?" Regina countered. "Many animals are born with an innate understanding of their nature."

"Yeah, but others have to be taught by their parents," he returned. "How to hunt, how to feed, all sorts of stuff. If I try flying for the first time ever, right out the car window, and I screw up ..."

She nodded. "All right. Let's assume that's the right truck. What else can we do?"

What else, indeed.

The truck continued eastward for several miles, bypassing various freeways as it drove along the surface streets at a casual pace. Either they had no idea they were being followed or they didn't care, but Regina always kept a vehicle or three between them. The only time she dared to get any closer was to avoid missing a traffic light, but she always faded back afterward.

From the backseat, Iyare muttered, "How far do we go? How long before you spring your 'surprise' on them?"

Jason considered the bustling city around them — typical Los Angeles traffic, rows of cars puttering along with the occasional honk of impatience at other drivers; pedestrians strolling along the sidewalks, weaving between the shadows of towering buildings; a good number of businesses still open, their neon or digital signs flickering in the settling dusk and casting colorful reflections on the asphalt. Yet it didn't seem like enough for his idea to work, not the way he hoped; as crowded as it was, it somehow still felt too *confined* for his plan to unfold. They needed more, needed things to be bigger, broader, something—

"I think they're getting on the next freeway."

Jason whirled back to the front. Sure enough, the truck had drifted over into the entrance lane, which prompted a grin from him. "They're taking the Santa Ana Freeway."

Not a local, Regina peered up at the signs. "That's the ...?"

"The Five," Jason clarified, pointing at the I-5 symbol. "He's taking the Five south."

She noticed his smirk. "Is that good?"

"That could be *very* good. It depends on how far south they go.

Fingers crossed."

The truck pulled onto the freeway and merged into the customarily dense Los Angeles traffic, and Regina followed. She looked around at all those brake lights, then at her speedometer, before commenting with a dry, "At least we know they can't outrun us now."

"Just make sure you don't get stuck in an exit lane. If you're not careful, you could find yourself trapped switching over to a different freeway. Stay in whatever lane they do."

Regina grunted her acknowledgment.

After that, their pursuit slipped into a peculiar limbo of tension and monotony. The traffic puttered along at a sluggish crawl while they followed the truck. Rinse and repeat, an annoying loop of acceleration and braking. Thankfully, no one needed to use the restroom, but they all eventually snacked on beef jerky and water. And followed the truck. And followed some more.

Finally, at last, traffic thinned a little; the box truck continued along its way south, and Jason's grin returned. He said nothing, but reached forward into a shopping bag on the floorboard between his feet. Retrieving the three objects they had prepped earlier, he passed one to each of his companions before pulling aside his shirt and clipping his own to his belt.

Iyare looked it over. "I'm still not sure about this."

"Iyare," Regina glared into the rearview mirror, "your cynicism is getting tedious."

Iyare did not back down. "Forgive me if the deaths of our friends still weigh upon me. I should be so lucky to shake it off with your ease."

Regina snarled at that, whipping her head around to snap at him.

Jason spoke up. "Eyes on the road, Regina. This is going well, people, so stay focused."

Regina faced forward again, and Iyare remained silent.

The truck rolled on, gaining more speed as the freeway added additional lanes.

"All right," Jason proclaimed, "this'll do. Start catching up to them."

Regina looked around. "There are fewer cars than before. How is this better—?"

"Fewer cars on the road itself, but do you know where we are?" She shook her head, so he pointed to a huge billboard as they passed it. "The Triumvirate wants to keep things quiet, right? Not letting the general public learn things — 'certain knowledge spreading too far, too quickly' and all that? Well, what's more public than an amusement park?"

Regina looked at him, then smiled. "You're right. This *will* do, will do much better."

"If an amusement park works well," Iyare asked, "why don't we keep going? Isn't Disneyland coming up in a few more miles?"

"We don't know if they'll keep going that far," Jason told him. "For what I have in mind, Knott's Berry Farm will do just fine."

As she sped up, pulling into the lane to the right of the truck's, Regina commented, "This stunt will get plenty of attention on its own."

"Yeah. It'll happen pretty fast, but if some of them turn into looky-loos who follow us, so much the better." He unbuckled his seatbelt. "Pull up alongside them as soon as you can. Iyare, roll down your left window, then scoot over. I'm comin' back.

Iyare complied, Regina closed the gap, and Jason climbed over the seats.

"Remember!" Regina called over her shoulder, raising her voice over the increased noise. "The Triumvirate has no idea you're a panwere! Tap *only* into your wolf side, unless you have no other choice!"

"Got it!"

As he stuck his head out the window, with the wind roaring in his ears and blowing his hair every which way and the surface of the interstate racing past, the reality of what he was about to try struck home. His heart hammered, his stomach flipped over, his mouth dried, and he struggled not to hyperventilate.

What if his newfound agility wasn't up to the task? What if the glass did not break as he hoped? What if the truck suddenly slowed or changed lanes?

A lot of What Ifs, which he forced out of his mind. If he

allowed them to fester, they would lock him into immobility. He didn't have time for that.

"Here it comes!" Regina shouted.

The vehicles ahead of them parted and their car surged forward, while the white box truck kept going at its same steady pace. Three car-lengths away, two car-lengths, one—

Just as their front bumper aligned with the truck's rear end, a motorcycle blasted between them, the rider taking full advantage of California's lenient lane-splitting laws. Regina grunted as she jerked the car to the right before correcting their course. Another vehicle somewhere behind them honked.

Jason held his breath, waiting to see if the driver of the box truck noticed. *If* he had been at all aware of being followed and glanced in his side mirror right now ...

The truck continued on its way, business as usual.

"Now, Regina!" he yelled, his voice deepening as he edged toward his wolfman form. "Do it now!"

Within seconds, they began easing past the truck. He drew back a clenched fist, tensed every muscle, and ...

Jason leaped, exploding from their car straight at the truck's passenger side window. And as his body closed the distance, he swung his fist around with all his might.

That split second when he hung suspended in open space, with nothing but the road rushing beneath him at seventy miles per hour, lasted a brief eternity. His life didn't quite flash before his eyes, but he was engulfed by a detached euphoria that everything he had ever done — every choice, every moment — had built toward this one act, wherein he would either succeed or die. The sensation was terrifying and exhilarating, horrifying and glorious in equal measure.

Then his knuckles connected with the window, the safety glass shattered into a thousand granular cubes, and he sailed into the truck. Had the confines of the cabin been as tight as the car he had just exited, he would have ended up in Mallory's lap; instead, he was able to scramble upright so that he sat in the passenger seat facing the driver, as though nothing extraordinary had occurred.

Mallory, for his part, had flinched but not panicked, not even swerving in his lane. He had raised his right hand across his chest, prepared to backhand whoever, or whatever, just smashed into his truck cab. But then he recognized Jason as the Egyptian shifted back into fully-human mode, and Mallory paused.

"Ah," Mallory commented, his tone conversational as he relaxed his arm, "as I live and breathe, it's Jason Samir. Hello, again." He made a show of glancing past Jason before turning his eyes back to the road. "Might have to ask ye to pitch in for the damages. This's a rental."

A deep voice sounded from the box body of the truck, muffled by the metal barrier and turbulent wind from the broken window but still audible to each of their werewolf hearing. "Sean?! What was that?!"

Mallory called back, "It's all right, it's just Jason!" He flicked a glance to Jason himself. "We were a bit worried ye might try somethin' like this, though my money was on ye waitin' to see where we're goin'."

This wasn't playing out quite how Jason imagined, but if this wasn't going to turn into a fight while driving down the freeway, he was content not to look this gift horse in the mouth. "The Beach Boulevard exit is coming up soon. Take it."

"Ah. And what happens if I don't comply? I'm not sayin' I won't, mind ye, I'm just curious as to what exactly ye're threatenin' me with."

Jason reached for the item clipped to his belt — and experienced a micro-heart attack when he didn't find it, only to discover a second later that it had shifted farther back while he had been aiming for his Stunt Man of the Year award. He held it up for Mallory to see, his finger on the trigger.

Mallory nodded at the bright red object. "Ye'll shoot me with that funny-lookin' gun?"

"It's not a regular gun."

"Oh, I know what it is, Jason. I'm not as old as Alistaire, but I've seen a few summers. Soooo, ye're thinkin' that a flare gun'll hurt me more, 'cause it'll burn me instead o' puttin' a hole in me? Credit where it's due, that's not a bad idea. Wish I'd thought of it. Not that I—"

Mallory cut himself off when Jason pointed the gun toward the open window.

"I'm not going to shoot you, Sean," Jason informed him. "I'm going to fire it outside, where a shitload of drivers can't help but see it, maybe even a cop or two."

Mallory pondered over that for a few seconds. "And that's supposed to make me comply because ...?"

"Because you made it clear at my apartment this morning that you and Trey and your vampire want to avoid publicity. And can you imagine the response if I fire off a flare from this truck while driving down the Five freeway?"

Mallory scowled a bit. "Ye didn't exactly keep a low profile when ye jumped through my window. Eyes're already on us. How much more—?"

"Until now, the drivers around us don't know what to think. My jump went by so fast, a lot of them wouldn't've had time to register that it even happened — let alone the fact that I was furry when I pulled it off. But I'm guessing we've still got a dozen phones aimed at us right now, waiting to see what'll happen next. So far, they could *maybe* chalk it up to some YouTube idiot risking their neck for their fifteen minutes of Internet fame — that, or the most bizarre instance of road rage they've ever heard of. But if *flares* start going off ..."

Mallory deliberated over their situation again. "If memory serves, those flare guns only hold one shot at a time. That'll go by pretty fast, too fast—"

"I have two more rounds in my pocket. And even if you stop me from reloading, my friends each have their own flare gun — they can turn this strip of the freeway into the Fourth of July, if you make them. They're pacing alongside us right now."

Mallory glanced past Jason at the side mirror. "Aye, I can see that."

"Good. So, you either take the Beach Boulevard exit and drive where I tell you, or we get so many eyes on us, there's no way you'll be able to avoid a mountain of unwanted attention. And if I absolutely have to, I'd be happy to turn furry and wave at anyone and everyone who's looking."

Mallory gave a slow, unhappy nod. "Ye've thought this out pretty well. Congratulations. I have to admit — sittin' here, right here 'n now — I canna think of a way around ye're little trap. Not a lot of our opponents have managed that."

"Thanks, I guess."

"Don't take it too much to heart. I'm not typically the brains of our outfit. That'd be Alistaire."

"Your vampire."

"Aye. 'Our vampire,' as ye put it."

"Can't wait to meet him."

"Careful what ye wish for, son."

That last bit sounded like a threat, but Mallory put on his blinker to move toward the Beach Boulevard exit, and since that had been Jason's goal, he didn't bother trying for a witty retort.

What's in the Box?

Jason directed Mallory to the parking garage nearest the amusement park; he would've preferred it be right across the street, but those ideal locations were all open parking lots rather than structures. As they entered and drove upward from level to level, he was a little worried that Mallory might slam on the brakes while they were more or less out of sight from the general public, but he kept his flare gun aimed toward the garage's outside open view at every opportunity, and Mallory opted not to pull any fast ones.

"How far in are we goin'?" Mallory asked.

"All the way to the top."

Mallory grunted as though that were no surprise.

They reached the uncovered uppermost level, and Mallory drove the truck to the farthest spot available, as far from the other parked cars as he could get — he clearly wanted to distance them from as many potential witnesses as possible.

Jason let him have that one.

Once Mallory shifted the gear into Park, he unbuckled his seatbelt and rested his left hand on the door handle. "I'm guessin' we're headed 'round back?"

"You guess correctly."

Mallory sighed. "Ye know, this might not go the way yer hopin'."

"Honestly, we're not really 'hoping' for anything more than finding out what the hell this has been all about. We want to know what Hellqvist thought was such a big deal, what *you* three think is such a big deal. Then we can go our separate ways."

"I already gave yer 'friends' their chance to walk away. Ye were there."

"Yeah, I was there — for the threats and everything."

Mallory sighed again, and this time it sounded sadder. "Ye know ... this mornin', when I first met ye at yer apartment, I was fairly sure I smelled blood on yer breath. Human blood. Oh, I tried to convince myself, and my partners, that I might o' been mistaken, that it was the blood on yer carpet or maybe comin' off the other two. Now I'm not so sure."

Oh, no. Oh, shit! Does he suspect that I'm *responsible for Sir Asshole? Even though he heard for himself that a* lion *killed the guy?*

Does the Triumvirate suspect I'm a panwere after all?

Setting aside that gut-punch of doubt, the heartfelt regret in the Irishman's voice also threw Jason off-kilter. "I'm ... I'm not looking to hurt anyone."

"Do ye mean 'hurt anyone *else*'?"

Jason swallowed. "I'll just say that I never expected any of this, and I've never aspired to be a hero, but I have *no* interest in being a monster, either. From what I gather, you and your partners choose a different path, right? You choose not to be monsters — at least, from a human point of view? That means *I* can, too."

"That's good to hear, lad. Truly, it is. But sadly, it isn't that simple. It falls into that mean little cliché of 'easier said than done.'" He looked Jason square in the eyes. "We can help ye with that, ye know."

"Thanks, but I'm not a real fan of how you seem to do things. I'll take my chances with my friends."

Mallory snorted his derision. "Yer 'friends.' I tried to warn ye about them. So did Trey."

Jason shrugged, but it didn't come across as nonchalant as he had hoped. "Hey, you were the one who called them 'part-time abstainers.' "

"The key there is 'part-time,' lad."

Jason nodded, thinking about that. He also thought back to how it felt when he turned into a wolf for the first time, and especially when he turned into a lion and greyed out before taking off after Sir Asshole. He held Mallory's gaze and asked, "You gonna tell me that *you* never slipped, that you've *never* killed anyone when the beast came out?"

Mallory didn't look away, but something behind his eyes flinched. "No, lad. I canna tell ye that."

"So *none* of us are perfect. Good to know." He smirked. "But I get the feeling this little debate could go on all night and then some, and I'm pretty sure my friends — and probably yours — are getting antsy. Shall we get this over with?"

Mallory nodded. "Aye."

They each kept the other in watchful view as they opened their respective doors and slid out onto the pavement. Then, without looking away, Jason called out, "Regina?!"

Her voice came from somewhere beyond the back of the truck. She didn't shout, which reminded Jason that almost everyone present possessed enhanced hearing. "We're here, Jason."

"Are you able to see Mallory from where you are?"

"Iyare can."

"Good. We're coming back."

Iyare spoke up. "Wait. Another car has come up onto our level. It's driving this way."

"That'll be Alistaire," Mallory told Jason through the open truck cabin. "He was following us, and I'm sure he's been bidin' his time since yer little *Fury Road* stunt."

Shit, Jason thought; he had presumed that both the vampire and Trey were in the back of the truck with Hellqvist's steamer trunk. Then he asked Mallory, "Why didn't he try anything?"

Mallory shrugged. "He trusts me. If the truck'd started swervin' all over the road, I'm sure he would've taken action."

"Jason?" Regina called.

"It's all right for now," he told her, and saw Mallory nod. "Just keep those flare guns ready."

Jason was still unnerved by letting Mallory out of his sight, but he and the Triumvirate's werewolf made their way to the back of the truck without incident.

As the new vehicle pulled up alongside the truck — Regina had parked several spots back — Mallory looked around at the three of them, then asked Jason, "What's next?"

Trying to keep the vampire's car in his peripheral vision, he told Mallory, "Open the back."

Rather than taking any action to do that himself, Mallory pounded his fist against the truck twice, paused, then thumped it once more in softer fashion. The back door rolled up, revealing the chained-up trunk and a massive, casually-dressed Black man.

Jason had never seen Trey. He had exchanged texts with him, chatted with him online, and heard Derek's second-hand account of the man, but Jason had never before *seen* Trey with his own eyes; it turned out that describing him as a "pro-football lineman" was pretty spot-on. Trey looked down at him — he would have "looked down" at Jason even if they had stood on even ground; adding the height of the truck made him all the more intimidating.

"Hi, Jason." Trey stepped off the lip of the truck, landing on the parking structure pavement with an impressive *thud!* "I'm sorry we've never had a chance to meet before under better circumstances."

"Yeah," Jason told him, and meant it. "Me, too."

This would be the part where, normally, the two men would shake hands, if not hug. That wasn't going to happen tonight.

Trey looked over at Regina and Iyare, his expression more or less neutral. Jason was still wrapping his head around the notion that Trey was some sort of "zombie," and this was his first evidence: Something wasn't right about Trey's eyes — they were too matte, sort of hazy, what Jason might have otherwise expected to notice in a blind man, except that Trey could obviously see. That, plus his smell was *off*, somehow; kind of sour, like beef that had started to go bad.

Trey looked back at Jason, then down at the flare gun. "What's happening here, Sean?"

Mallory offered a slight shrug. "Our friend here has decided to force our hand. He and his compatriots are quite insistent on seein' what's inside Hellqvist's trunk."

"*Are they now?*"

The new voice seized Jason's attention, while Regina and Iyare each took a step back.

A white man had emerged from the Triumvirate's car. Slender, with striking blue eyes, dark hair, and finer clothing than the T-shirt-and-jeans of the other two, the newcomer appeared to almost glide as he strode around the vehicle to stand on the other side of Mallory. Even with his new hearing, Jason barely detected his footsteps.

Jason resisted the urge to lick his dry lips as he said, "I'm guessing you're Alistaire."

The man tilted his head forward in a regal nod. "*And you would be Jason Bakari Samir.*"

With Trey, his eyes had been the giveaway that he wasn't normal. With Alistaire, it was the voice; it bore a strange tonal quality that Jason could not quite define, free of any particular accent (and pretty dry on emotion), yet not sounding local, either. Plus, like Trey, his body odor was a little nasty, at least to Jason's nose. Was that how all vampires smelled?

Jesus, how can Mallory stand to be around both of those two? Like, all the time?

And those blue eyes of Alistaire's were all the more dazzling up close, too. They were ... were kind of ...

"Jason," Regina snapped under her breath.

Jason shook his head. Had the vampire just tried to mesmerize him? Maybe, maybe not, but either way, he dragged his gaze away from those eyes.

In the meantime, Alistaire was also speaking in a low voice, seemingly to Mallory. "*He does not smell like the other two. He does not smell like any werewolf I have ever encountered.*"

Sean nodded. "Aye."

Jason did his absolute best not to react in any way to their remarks, keeping his focus on Trey. "We just want some answers. We're not looking to expose you or anyone else — not unless you force us. You sent me to interview Doctor Hellqvist at the airport. Maybe *you* had other plans for that night, maybe I was never meant to actually talk to the woman after all—"

"That's not true," Trey interjected in his deep voice. "We—"

Jason interrupted him right back. "Hellqvist wanted to reveal some earth-shattering discovery to the world. We want to know what that discovery was. After that, we'll leave, and you three can do whatever you want with her steamer trunk. We just want to *know*."

Behind him, Iyare made a sound in his throat, as though he were desperate to add something but was biting his tongue. But they had covered this all before, when they had put together this outrageous plan, so Jason ignored him.

"It's not that simple, Jason," Trey responded. "Knowledge is knowledge. Even without physical evidence, the information—"

As if they had practiced the move, Jason, Regina, and Iyare all raised their flare guns so that they were pointed skyward once more.

"One way or another," Jason stated, "we are going to see what's in that trunk."

Regina added, "Think of all those people visiting the amusement park — at any moment, any number of them could return to those parked cars behind us. And we're almost certainly surrounded by security cameras right now. The longer this takes, the sooner some security guard or police officer will come up here to find out what's going on." Jason couldn't see her, but he could hear the grin in her voice. "Make up your minds, Triumvirate. Now. Or we'll put on a fireworks display for the ages."

Trey regarded Jason and his friends for a long, thoughtful moment, then looked to Mallory and the vampire. Some tacit communication passed between them, because without their saying a word, Trey turned back and said, "All right." Then he climbed back into the box truck.

Jason exchanged his own glances with Regina and Iyare, hardly able to believe their plan was actually working ... unless it wasn't? Were the Triumvirate up to something here? This was not the time to relax.

Jason expected a long scraping sound as Trey pushed or heaved the chained steamer trunk toward the truck's open rear, but instead the large man hefted it in his long arms, setting it down close to the edge. From here, even though they were outside, Jason again noted that air of tremendous *age* coming from the trunk.

Trey stared down at the steel box, his expression of one lost in thought. After a few seconds, he commented, "We haven't been able to figure out why the police melted the silver padlock — none of the officers on duty this evening had any clue. Was it because of your attempted theft? If so, that's an odd solution."

Jason maintained a straight face, but it wasn't easy. Were the Triumvirate honestly ignorant of how that happened, or was Trey fishing for some sort of confirmation? If they truly didn't know about his little "feedback loop" with the silver, if they still didn't suspect that he was a panwere — though Jason recalled Mallory's seeming to imply a connection between Jason and Sir Asshole's death — if they had *only* been keeping their own eyes on him because they thought he was just another potential werewolf... if *all that* held together, maybe Jason and his friends had a decent chance of actually walking away from this after all.

Trey bent over the trunk and gave the heavy chains some experimental tugs, glanced up at everyone, including his own partners, then returned to his inspection. "All of you might want to step back a little. When I break these chains, fragments of that melted silver mess could go flying. If that happens, I'm the only one here who won't be harmed."

Everyone complied with Trey's suggestion, even the vampire. Trey took one of the chains in both hands and pulled in opposite directions; the sturdy links resisted. Tendons standing out in his arms and neck, he pulled harder, and harder still. And just when it looked as though they might need a backup plan, the chain finally snapped with a sharp *clang!* The link that gave up was the only one to break, so Trey's concerns about flying silver shrapnel proved unfounded. Still, once the chain's tension faltered, the husk of melted silver twisted free, swinging down on one loose end so that it clattered onto the floor of the truck. Trey stooped and picked it up, staring at it for a second before tossing it deeper into the truck.

After pushing and shoving the loosened chains aside and off the trunk's lid, Trey rested his hands on his knees and considered the built-in lock. "I might need assistance with this part."

Although he was almost certainly speaking to his Triumvirate partners, Jason surprised himself by stepping forward. "I'll help with that."

Renewed tension slithered its way through both groups; Jason's team certainly had not accounted for this impulse of his. Trey glanced toward Mallory and Alistaire again; the werewolf lifted and dropped his shoulders in an uncertain shrug, while the vampire merely raised one eyebrow, Spock-style.

"I'd just like to be a part of this," Jason clarified, and meant it. "I promise I won't upend the trunk or anything else sneaky."

When neither of his Triumvirate partners offered any objections, Trey looked back to Jason and made a little "Come on, then" gesture with his hand.

Having reached this agreement, Jason felt more nervous than less. Before he could lose his nerve, he bent his knees and leaped up into the back of the truck.

Once he stood across from Trey — damn, this guy was big! — his Watchdogs boss pointed at the trunk and commented, "This won't be easy. Hellqvist's key was broken off inside even before the whole thing got damaged."

Jason really, really did not want to put his flare gun down, but he wasn't sure how else to go about this; he clipped it to his belt, trusting Regina and Iyare to hold their ground. He then hunkered down to examine the trunk's built-in lock. Everyone was right; Iyare had torn the hell out of it.

Trey squatted next to him — it was such a casual move, Jason didn't even go to Red Alert from his proximity; it was as though they were a couple of old friends working on a problem together. "Forcing it by pulling on the lid might work," Trey suggested, "but it'll be hard to hold onto that slick metal. You said you wouldn't upend it, but that might happen by accident if we go that route."

"What if we just dig in around the whole lock casing itself?" Jason suggested. "Aren't these things usually just, like, brass or nickel? Not too strong?"

Trey thumped the top of the trunk. "Hellqvist spent good money on this, top-dollar. I think the entire thing is solid steel. She wasn't taking any chances."

Jason smirked as he poked at the damaged lock. "So I'm guessing we're not going to get it open just to find it's nothing more than her great-grandmother's crusty old lingerie."

Trey chuckled in the back of his throat. "Probably not."

It was a nice moment, the kind of easy exchange that Jason — under different circumstances, before his world turned upside-down

— would have expected, or at least hoped for, upon meeting Trey offline. But his world *had* turned upside-down, and even as he strove to hold onto that comfortable calm, he could not help but ask, in a soft undertone, "So, you're, uh ... you're a zombie?"

Trey paused before finally answering in an equally low voice, " 'Fraid so."

"So you're technically *dead*?"

"Yeah. But the alternative would be to be *dead*-dead, so ..."

"Yeah, but you don't ..." For a second, Jason stopped even pretending he was evaluating the lock, and looked straight at Trey. "Do you eat brains and all that?"

Trey chuckled a little louder this time, but kept his eyes on their work. "Don't get me started on the whole 'brains' thing. It's not about *brains*, at all. Never has been."

"So ... so what do you—?"

"I used to make do with raw beef, but that stopped working. More recently, I've been feeding on sexual predators and the like."

In spite of everything that he had seen and experienced over the past several days, Jason's jaw still dropped at that. "You ... you do *eat people*?"

Trey's gaze shifted to meet his, and those hazy eyes were more unnerving than ever. "Mainly child molesters. But, yeah."

The pleasant mood burst like a balloon. Trey, his nominal boss at *Watchdogs of the Weird & Unusual*, was a fucking *cannibal*! Or did "cannibal" even apply when talking about a zombie, which was no longer strictly human? And the goddamned Triumvirate had threatened Regina and Iyare because they were *only* "part-time" abstainers? He almost looked over his shoulder to stare some daggers at Mallory.

Then he pictured Sir Asshole's face, both when glaring at Jason after his beating in his apartment and when Jason later stalked him in the form of a lion. And he remembered his own words to Mallory, just a few minutes ago: *None of us are perfect* ... which made him feel like something of a hypocrite for his indignation.

But this was a superb example of "Neither the time nor the place," and he wrestled his turmoil into submission.

Aloud, Jason stated, "Let's get this over with." And his sharp tone told Trey their friendly conversation was done.

Trey's expression betrayed no open reaction of his feelings on the matter; yet, for just a split-second, Jason thought he might have seen something akin to sadness flash behind those dead eyes. Then Trey blinked, and the impression was gone.

Without saying a word, Trey straightened his hips so that he could reach into his front jeans pocket. Jason tensed, his own hand drifting toward the flare gun at his belt, but then Trey pulled out something that looked kind of like a Swiss Army Knife.

"It's a multitool," Trey explained as he turned it over and around, considering his options. "I use it when I tinker with my computer — something I've only recently been capable of doing."

Thoughts of Trey's much-improved typing speed shot through Jason's mind; had it struck him thirty seconds ago, he might have asked Trey about it, but that window had closed.

Trey selected the largest flathead screwdriver the tool offered. As Jason watched, he wrestled with it until he had wedged the tip of the screwdriver into a narrow fracture in the seam where the locking mechanism was welded into the trunk's body. Despite his thick fingers — and bein' a freakin' *dead man* — the big guy worked with deft precision, wriggling the screwdriver until he had created the slightest gap. Back and forth, back and forth, he rocked his tool, widening that gap tiny bit by tiny bit.

Finally yanking his tool free, Trey nodded toward the slim opening he had created. "Do your best to get your fingers in there while I work the other side."

Jason saw where Trey was going with this, but he also recognized it was a good way to inhibit his response time if the Triumvirate made a move. He glanced back at Regina and Iyare, who remained vigilant, their flare guns still pointed skyward. Regina gave him an almost imperceptible nod. He returned his attention to the trunk and tried to wedge his fingertips into the slight gap Trey had created.

Trey labored for a good minute before he managed to jam the screwdriver into the opposite edge, then he said, "Let's give it a try. On three: One ... two ... three."

In spite of the horrible leverage, Jason wrenched at it as best he could, while Trey struggled to force the screwdriver in deeper, hammering the butt of his tool with the palm of his hand. The metal creaked in protest, but held firm.

Trey grumbled, "Hang on a second." Jason eased off while the big man hammered the multitool a few more times. "Okay, again."

"Wait, wait a second." Jason concentrated, pushing his hand toward wolfman status; his fingernails shifted into claws, which dug farther underneath his side of the lock and increased his purchase. "Okay."

"All right: One, two, *three*."

Together, they again pried at the damaged lock, Jason straining until the veins in his forearm bulged. The metal groaned. He felt as though his claws were in danger of tearing from his fingertips, and he was pretty sure Trey's screwdriver was bending. Something inside shifted, slightly, but overall the stubborn mechanism refused to budge.

"Almost there," Trey grunted, bracing his other hand against the top of the trunk and applying more pressure. "Keep at it."

Jason was seconds away from giving up when the lock casing warped and the welding began vibrating as small steel screws popped free one by one with sharp *pings!* that echoed in the truck's interior. Then three things happened at virtually the same instant: Trey's multitool's screwdriver bent almost ninety degrees, the claw on Jason's ring finger cracked and split, and the lock Iyare had fucked up so badly surrendered, squealing in resounding torment as it twisted around until it was hanging loose from one lone welding point.

Jason felt triumphant, but he also couldn't resist sticking his stinging fingertip in his mouth and sucking at the blood. Trey, for his part, stared at his ruined multitool and grunted.

After that, a long moment of silence hung over them all.

Jason's heart pounded faster. The large steamer trunk was, at last, accessible, the ancient smell leaking from within stronger than ever. All that remained was to open the lid and peer inside, but how to go about it?

Jason looked up at Trey, then out at the others. Regina and Alistaire stared at the trunk—Regina with an expression of hunger, the vampire with detached curiosity. Iyare and Mallory were glaring at one another in mutual loathing — between those two, violence appeared imminent.

Jason turned to Trey. “Before we open it, let’s lower the trunk to the ground.”

Trey surveyed the expansive parking level; the two groups remained alone, but for how long? “I’d rather not invite curiosity. As your friend pointed out, people might return to their cars at any—”

“I don’t think bringing everyone up here — into the truck, together — would be a good idea.” He inclined his head toward Iyare, then Mallory. Trey looked where he indicated, and understood. “Our motivations have been different, but all of us have gone to great lengths to learn what’s inside this thing. It seems fair enough we should all find out together.”

Trey considered this, and nodded. “All right. I’ll hop down, you push the trunk to me, and I’ll lower it to the ground.” He then looked to his people. “No one make any moves against anyone else. I’m calling a sincere truce for this. Agreed?”

Alistaire nodded right away; a few seconds later, Sean followed.

Trey then looked at Jason in expectation, so Jason told him, “You don’t have to worry about duplicity on our part; no attacks from you, no flares from us. Like I’ve said all evening, we just want to *know*.”

Trey again considered this, and again nodded. Without another word, he stepped over and out of the truck, while Jason further cleared the loose chains.

Easing the steamer trunk to the ground was a bit awkward, given its size, but soon enough, it rested before the truck’s rear bumper, the six of them standing in a half-circle around it — Jason and his friends on the right, the Triumvirate on the left.

“So,” Mallory said, his tone light, “who gets the actual honors, then?”

Jason expected each side to stake a claim, but much to his surprise, all five of them looked at him. Regina and Iyare made sense, but the others?

Trey shrugged. "As they say, this is your show." He gestured with a casual toss of his hand. "Open it, Jason."

Jason swallowed, his heart going even faster than before. He knelt, unsnapped the clasps on either side of the loose lock ... and, holding his breath in anticipation, Jason opened Doctor Hellqvist's steamer trunk.

As the lid creaked back, a strong wave of that hoary redolence flooded outward, so potent that Jason recoiled. It was like nothing he had ever experienced, as a human or otherwise — a complex aroma of oxidized metal, heavy dust from forgotten vaults, and something else, something primal that repelled yet resonated with the animal parts of his being.

The first thing visible was a layer of thick, well-worn canvas cloth, tucked with care over whatever lay beneath. After a brief glance at the others, Jason reached inside and, gripping the canvas with gentle fingers, pulled it out and laid it onto the underside of the lid, revealing a second layer of canvas, a small metal canister, several leather-bound journals stacked to one side, and a tablet computer.

Trey leaned forward, hands on his knees, murmuring, "Hellqvist's field notes." A presumption on his part, Jason thought, but a logical one.

Jason picked up the topmost journal. Given the feeling, the *mood* surrounding the contents of the trunk, he half-expected it to be cracked and worn, itself nearly as old as the smell that permeated it and the rest, but the journal was in good shape. He opened it and flipped through a few random pages, finding them filled with a woman's meticulous handwriting, blocks of dense text in multiple languages, including English. He handed it over to Regina for further inspection, with no objection from the Triumvirate.

Next, he took out the tablet; clicking the Power button, he was a bit surprised to find that it still had juice, though the battery icon showed it was running low. Luckily, it did not ask for any sort of password, but he did not recognize its operating software; neither Android nor iPadOS, the text appeared to be Swedish, which made sense. Between that and his desire to appear as "fair" as possible, he handed the tablet to Trey — his fellow Watchdog knew computers, and maybe Trey's vampire partner could read Swedish (hell, for all he knew, *Trey* might know Swedish).

As Regina inspected the journal, holding it against her sternum and fumbling page after page while keeping the flare gun secure in her opposite hand, she stated, "There are dates written in here that span decades, all in the same handwriting. I'm seeing references to Romania, Mongolia, Ethiopia ... they're notations from the nineteen-seventies, the sixties, fifties ... here's one that's circled a few times from the nineteen-forties ..."

Trey, who was indeed tilting the tablet's screen toward Alistaire (though the vampire's knitted brow suggested some difficulty on his part, too), commented, "Doctor Hellqvist wasn't nearly that old. She was referencing the work of others before her, building on it."

Jason returned his attention to the trunk's contents, this time focusing on the metal canister. Surprised by how light it was as he plucked it out, he rotated it around until he found a label. "Huh."

Iyare asked, "What is it?"

" 'Nitrogen gas,' apparently. Why would Hellqvist include something like this?"

Without looking away from the tablet, the vampire answered in his strange, dispassionate voice, "*Nitrogen has many uses, but in this instance, I believe it was to help preserve the steamer trunk's cargo by displacing oxygen.*"

Jason inspected the nozzle, which he found had been left the slightest bit open. Not knowing what else to do, he shook the canister. "I think it's empty."

Mallory, glowering at Iyare from the corner of his eyes, said, "Hellqvist didn't know it would have to last this long."

Iyare sniffed at that, but offered no rebuttal.

Ignoring the remaining journals for the time being, Jason moved the second canvas layer over to the lid, which exposed yet another layer of cloth that covered two-thirds of the box's space, alongside a small collection of artifacts: A timeworn terracotta slab inscribed with unfamiliar pictographs; a small, lidless wooden box, plastic film stretched across its top, that contained what appeared to be ... fossilized teeth? ... with little slips of modern paper tucked between and around them; several golden tubes, the purpose of which he could only guess; and a partitioned Lucite container holding a collection of small stone figurines of what appeared to be various animals — though it was difficult to be certain, given their age-old smoothing from the elements.

"Begad," Mallory mumbled under his breath in surprise. "These things must all be worth a fortune. Hellqvist must've been collectin' 'em over her entire little quest."

Curious as he was about this eclectic assortment of items, Jason focused on that next layer of canvas; as engaging as all of those items were, both his nose and his gut told him that the real treasure rested below, just out of sight.

Until now, the top floor of the parking garage had been enshrouded by a blanket of general noise. The six of them were alone up here, but the traffic just a few levels below — engines revving, horns honking, music playing from car speakers, hundreds of tires upon the asphalt — the buzz of the bright, antiquated lights, and the rides and screams coming from the nearby amusement park carried to all their sensitive ears (and to Trey's? Did zombies have enhanced hearing?) ... *all* of that dropped away as Jason reached for that sheet of canvas, with only his pulse still thudding in his ears. He took the canvas in his fingers and lifted it up and over, adding it to the growing pile on the steamer trunk's open lid.

Jason could not understand what he was seeing at first. The entire left side of the trunk — the same two-thirds of its width, plus all of its remaining length and depth — was filled by another, much larger Lucite container; he presumed it was meant to be air-tight, but the thick aroma suggested a crack, split, or other imperfection somewhere out of sight. He tilted his head to one side, trying to make sense of it.

Inside the Lucite, nestled within a bed of protective foam padding, lay something that resembled ... a petrified tree root?

No, Jason, you idiot. That's not a tree root, not even close. Stop fucking around and look *at it.*

Jason blinked, and in that instant, it all fell into place.

The Lucite encased a human skeleton — at least, he *thought* it was a human skeleton, or most of one, anyway. The skeleton lay on its side, curled into itself like a fetus in the womb. He could make out an intact spine with ribs attached, though the vertebrae themselves looked not quite right to his amateur eye. The bones were a color like amber, stained by the great passage of time, yet still reasonably well preserved. But where he would have expected to see its arms and legs — or rather "leg," as the left one, the one against the foam, was missing at the hip — he looked upon limbs that did not appear to belong to Homo Sapiens.

The arms appeared more or less human below the shoulder, but starting at the elbow, the proportions fell out of whack; the radius and ulnae of the forearms looked too short, the carpal bones of the wrists appeared too long. The fingers of the left hand were mostly missing, but on the right hand they were too thick, and foreshortened — especially the thumb; Jason had never seen an x-ray of a household cat's paw and dewclaw, but he guessed it might look something like this. The right leg had similar discrepancies, the bones elongated and the knee bending the wrong direction, though the foot looked like a regular, homegrown human foot.

Coiled underneath the lone leg, therefore partially obstructed from view, was what appeared to be a tail. Too long to be a dog or cat tail; if he had to take a wild guess, he would have said it belonged to a crocodile.

Regina whispered, "My God ..."

This break in the silence prompted Jason to ask, "What *is* it? Some kind of prehistoric creature?"

No one answered, but even as he spoke the words, he knew that wasn't right. No dinosaur skeleton he had ever seen or heard about had as haphazard a structure as this, certainly nothing so near-human.

Trey shook himself, dragging his attention away from the specimen and back to Hellqvist's tablet; Alistaire must have succeeded in getting him over the language barrier of the Home screen, as he began tapping and scrolling with confidence.

Jason looked back to the skeleton, this time letting his eyes explore upward from the torso. In its proper place atop the spine was a normal neck and the majority of a skull, which, at first glance, he again took for a normal human head. But like its limbs, the longer he stared at it, the more the discrepancies piled up.

The forehead looked normal except for where part of it was missing — the portion that disappeared from view into the padding bore a symmetrical hole; whether the individual in question was alive or dead when that hole was created, Jason could not say. But the eye sockets swelled a little too wide, the cheekbones protruded a little too far, and the jaw jutted outward to accommodate enlarged teeth. Despite their oversize, most of those teeth (a few were missing) retained normal human shape, except for the premolars on the bottom opposite the eye teeth — those two bottom teeth, hooked to wicked sharpness, belonged more to a payara fish than any human being.

Mallory mumbled aloud, "Not a werewolf."

"*No,*" the vampire responded. "*The bones share both human and lupine traits, but the other disparities cannot be ignored.*"

"Aye," Mallory agreed. "That, plus werewolves revert to human form upon death. This thing sure didn't."

"*Typically, yes. But remember our experience in Alaska.*"

"Aye ..."

Jason didn't know what the reference to Alaska meant (though, for a fleeting moment, thoughts of Shelley_O danced through the back of his mind), and he did not bother to ask. Seeking to look at the specimen from another angle, he shifted his position to the right, and the parking garage lights glinted off something he had missed before.

He bent closer. There, along the underside of the skeleton, just an inch or so above the padding — a spike of some kind, or maybe an arrow given how narrow it was, emerged from between two of the front-torso ribs; had the skeleton not lain on its side with its right limb in the way, he could not have missed it. He didn't know if the spike/arrow had pierced where a human heart would sit, but it looked pretty damned close to him. Whatever it was glistened like silver, though given the age of the specimen, the lack of oxidation suggested it must be some other metal; silver would have tarnished long ago, while this thing looked shiny as ever, with a bit of a bluish tinge.

"Got it," Trey announced. "Thankfully, this part's in English. Okay, so ..." He spread his finger and thumb apart against the screen, magnifying what he was reading. "According to her notes, Doctor Hellqvist discovered these remains — a female in early adulthood — within the mountains of the Sinai Peninsula of Egypt. To date, the oldest Egyptian mummy found was estimated at forty-three hundred years old; preliminary tests suggested this specimen could be much older, at least five thousand years, maybe more. Hellqvist mentions growing tensions amongst her team, angry debates about whether or not this was all some bizarre hoax ..."

Trey scrolled some more, while the others stared at the ancient wonder in the steamer trunk.

"Sounds like Hellqvist placated her team, but not before coercing them into signing more Non-Disclosure Agreements — something they weren't happy about, since they'd already signed a bunch of NDAs before traveling with her ..."

Trey scrolled some more.

"More debates, but Hellqvist stood her ground: She believed this specimen represented proof of the origins of supernatural folklore, in particular the lycanthrope ..."

Both Mallory and Iyare grunted at the same time, which prompted each to frown at the other.

Trey continued, "She compared and contrasted these findings with a bunch of others, some of which are included here ..." He waved a hand toward the other items in the trunk without taking his eyes off the screen. "... and ... wow, she's, uh ... she drew some pretty wild conclusions, even considering the nature of all of us standing here ..."

Trey descended back into his reading, the tablet inching closer to his face as his matte eyes scanned back and forth.

Eventually, Regina huffed. "And ...?"

Trey jolted, and actually offered her an embarrassed smile. "Yeah, sorry, uh ... Okay, keep in mind that I'm just reading the doctor's notes; these are *her* thoughts, not mine."

Mallory rolled his eyes. "Just get *on* with it, would ye? I'm curious 'bout my 'cousin' here."

Trey proceeded. "First, according to Hellqvist, these are not the remains of any ordinary lycanthrope. This skeleton belongs to what she called a 'panwere.' "

"A *panwere*?" Mallory repeated.

Jason, Regina, and Iyare all went still. Jason swallowed, and willed his heart to slow down — or at least *quiet* down. But he couldn't help his eyes widening as he gaped at the skeleton; another panwere, but from millennia ago!

He half-expected the Triumvirate to turn on him at once, and was relieved when the Irishman instead pivoted to face their resident vampire.

"Alistaire, could panweres've been real after all?"

"*The doctor thought so.*"

"Wait, did ye *know* about this? Did she tell ye?"

Alistaire shook his head. "*Not in any detail, no. It was clear from our correspondence that she was onto something well within our realm, but she did not elaborate — certainly not this far.*"

Mallory also shook his head, but for him, it was an expression of wonder. "All these years, we've never encountered anythin' but were*wolves*. I thought the legends of so-called 'panweres' was just a great pile of shite." Mallory thought for a moment, then posed, "Remember the stories we heard about those weretigers in India? Maybe they weren't were*tigers* at all, maybe they were panweres?"

"*Let us not jump to conclusions,*" Alistaire warned. "*We never confirmed the existence of those alleged weretigers at all, let alone making the leap to panweres. I admit* that—" He indicated the figure in Lucite. "*—is an intriguing find, but that does not mean Doctor Hellqvist's theory was correct.*"

The vampire's words were all about caution and healthy skepticism ... yet after he stopped speaking, his blue eyes drifted from the steamer trunk to Jason, and lingered.

Be cool, man, Jason chided himself. *You can be a little tense, given the circumstances, but if you start freaking out while the vampire's watching ...*

Fortunately, Trey spoke up again, which reclaimed Alistaire's attention.

"Guys," the big man was saying, "Hellqvist's theory goes way beyond that skeleton belonging to a panwere. Just, uh, just listen to this:

"Between her studies, explorations, and all the finds in this trunk, the doctor came to believe that the ancient Egyptian 'gods' were *real*, but that they were, in fact, lycanthropes of different 'persuasions.' Sean, you mentioned weretigers? Well, Hellqvist believed the whole Egyptian pantheon was comprised of actual werefalcons, werecats, werebulls, werecrocodiles, werewolves, and more, a lot more. She even has a side-note which suggests that — for whatever genetic reasons — only the werewolves were able to successfully interbreed with humans." He looked up at Mallory. "If that's true, Sean, it could explain werewolves like you, who *inherit* their lycanthropy without getting bitten by another werewolf."

"So I'm part 'god' am I?" He smirked in a playful way, one of the lightest moments of this strained evening. "Aye, that explains a few things."

Alistaire, on the other hand, looked as though he had bitten into a lemon. "*If anything, it simply proves that the Egyptian* netjeru *were no 'gods' at all, but lycanthropes who manipulated the Egyptian population into* believing *they were gods.*" His shoulders straightened in something like pride. "*As always, there is only* one *G-God.*"

It was Jason's turn to raise an eyebrow; he would have expected a vampire to avoid speaking the name of God at all — as suggested by that odd stutter. And why would a vampire give a shit about any of that, anyway?

Still sounding just short of irritated, Alistaire prodded, "*Is that everything, Trey?*"

"Yes and no. She goes on a bit about potential genetic tests and other methods of 'proving' that these remains do come, not only from a lycanthrope, but from a panwere. But she also claims to have evidence and documentation from the burial site — there're memory cards tucked inside there somewhere, with photo and video files — detailing why the panwere was put to death.

"Hellqvist believed this young woman, the only panwere known at the time — or since, based on all her research — was feared by the Egyptian 'gods.' They worried she might stage some sort of coup with the locals, demonstrating her superior *heka* —

which sounds like it meant 'magic' — and threatening their reign; they feared she would attempt to replace them or, at the very least, introduce doubt into the Egyptians' entire religious system. They would've lost all their devotees, a whole population of willing serfs and vassals and such."

"In other words," Mallory grumbled, "their slaves."

Trey nodded. "Pretty much, yeah. So the top worshipped lycanthropes — the big ones who presented themselves as Ra and Osiris and Anubis and so on — acted like they wanted the panwere to join them, then murdered her and buried her remains far away from the Nile. The hieroglyphs recorded within the panwere's tomb were nothing like all the famous ones, about pharaohs going into the afterlife or whatever; they were meant to forewarn and forearm future lycanthropes, if another panwere should ever arise. But it looks like one never did, and the rest of the 'gods' died off or moved on to other places, so no one laid eyes on *any* of this until Hellqvist and her team located the burial vault. All they had were rumors and hearsay from within the supernatural community itself — which Hellqvist clearly knew existed, though she doesn't explain how or why here, at least not that I've seen so far.

"So not only does all of this turn Egyptian mythology on its head, but since Hellqvist considered it irrefutable proof that the supernatural *truly* exists — or, at the very least, existed a few thousand years ago — she was going to use it to demonstrate she was not just some quack who could be ridiculed or ignored any longer."

"And think, Alistaire," Mallory marveled in a low voice. "All of this ... it isn't from *our* world, it's from *this* world."

Alistaire nodded. "*Indeed. This world's supernatural roots go deeper than we ever suspected. And with the surprising variations we've been witnessing ...*" This time when he shook his head, his expression leaned toward concern.

Jason wondered if their usage of "our" world and "this" world pertained to what Regina and Iyare had told him about alternate dimensions, but so long as the topic hovered around panweres, he didn't want to ask for clarification — especially since Alistaire's gaze had again drifted in his direction.

Then Regina asked, "How did they kill this panwere? With silver?" She pointed at the spike or arrow Jason had noticed earlier. "If so, how could the other lycanthropes endure exposing themselves to it?"

"Hang on ..." Trey scrolled forward, then back. "I saw something— yes, here it is:

"First, once inside the burial tomb, Hellqvist's team found a standard stone sarcophagus encircled in large chains with flattened links, the metal of which apparently wasn't much more tarnished than that metal shaft in the skeleton's chest. They assumed it was meant to keep others out, but once they made their discoveries and later paid for metallurgical tests on the links, Hellqvist adjusted her theory to propose that it was meant to keep the panwere trapped inside, just in case her execution somehow didn't work. On top of the chains, they found two shafts embedded in the specimen: One we see there, which punctured her heart, the other had impaled her skull where there's just the hole now — I don't see any mention of what happened to the one from her head, but maybe they used it for more tests. It's probably down in the trunk somewhere.

"To answer your question, Regina: No, it's not silver — not *pure* silver, anyway. The metal shafts and the sarcophagus chains were forged from an alloy that mixed silver with three other metals. Seems like pure silver didn't affect the panwere like it did all the other lycanthropes, but they were persistent and motivated, and worked until they had identified something that they believed would."

Shit, Jason thought. *Regina and Iyare thought I'd eventually be able to shrug off silver, but here's evidence of my own special Kryptonite. Thanks, Hellqvist.*

And Alistaire was still staring at him. Didn't the bastard ever blink?

Trey kept reading. "I guess even though the alloy does contain a good amount of silver, the impurities helped the lycanthropes to handle it with bearable effects. Hellqvist was hoping to run further, more extensive metallurgical tests, once she found someone else willing to foot the bill, but based on what they managed to learn from the tests in Cairo, the chain links and shafts ..." He peered closer to the screen. "Okay, looks like they were composed of—"

Without warning, Regina dropped the journal she had been holding into the steamer trunk; once free, her hand shot out and snatched the tablet away from Trey, and she hurled that inside, too — and with enough force to shatter the screen. She then fired her flare gun into the trunk, setting everything within ablaze at nearly three-thousand degrees Fahrenheit.

As Mallory and the vampire moved to retaliate, Iyare fired his own flare gun — not toward the sky or into the trunk, but at the Triumvirate's werewolf. The burning projectile struck Mallory below his left collarbone, suggesting Iyare had been aiming for his heart.

The Irishman screamed, "Bloody *fuck*!" and fell, rolling away and swatting at the tiny inferno.

Playing catch-up, Jason jerked his own flare gun from his belt and—

Trey's large hand locked onto his wrist; Jason pulled the trigger on reflex, and the flare shot underneath the box truck, setting its underside aglow. Trey then kicked the trunk closed, the lid slamming shut with a harsh metallic *clang!*

The big man dragged Jason forward, bringing their faces together. His lips curled back from his teeth, but instead of biting, he rumbled, "I didn't want this, Jason."

"Neither did I." Jason attempted to yank his hand free from Trey's grasp, without success.

"Stand down, *right now*," the big man demanded, "and I might be able to convince—!"

Jason shifted into wolfman form, hopped up so that his sneakers connected with Trey's muscular chest, and pulled again — this time adding the strength of his legs to the effort. His now-furry wrist finally slipped loose, sending him into a wild backflip that he wrestled into enough control to land upright. He then hustled backward, putting space between himself and the zombie.

Glad as he was to be free, at some point during their struggle, he had lost his grip on his flare gun. That left his extra cartridges useless, and without the threat of a bright display to draw attention from all corners, all that remained was an outright brawl between his side and the Triumvirate.

He feared the odds were not in their favor.

All-Out War

Retreating as Trey advanced, Jason attempted to check on his companions, but even as he turned his head, the biggest wolf he had ever seen — and that included Iyare back at the airport — plowed into him. They rolled over twice, with the massive brown beast ending up mostly on top.

The wolf — Mallory — shoved against Jason's forehead with one paw as his jaws opened wide, exposing Jason's throat while those enormous fangs thrust toward his Adam's apple. Another inch, maybe two, and they would gouge into his throat length-wise.

Weird technique, dude, he wanted to taunt, but he couldn't spare the energy as he struggled to shove Mallory back. When it became clear that Mallory was going to win this contest of strength, Jason changed the rules.

All at once, he stopped pushing against Mallory's big shaggy head, clasped onto his upright ears, and *pulled* to the right, twisting his body the same direction. Rather than sinking his teeth into Jason's flesh, Mallory's snout punched into the concrete. Jason then jammed his clawed thumb into the burn near Mallory's collarbone — still smoking and smouldering from Iyare's flare — and when Mallory yiped in pain from that, he pushed with his legs until Mallory was no longer on top of him.

Then he got really dirty: With all his supernatural might, he kneed Mallory in his big, furry wolf balls.

Werewolf or not, Mallory was still male — he howl-coughed and rolled away from Jason, which helped him avoid Jason's second assault but offered no real relief for his genital pain; he shifted back toward his own wolfman form so that he could cup his scrotum and moan.

But Jason didn't have a chance to savor his little victory. He scrambled upright just in time to spot Trey barreling toward him like a freight train, long arms spread low and wide to prevent Jason from dodging out of the way. So Jason again used his legs, not for another cheap-shot to the gonads but to propel himself straight up into the air. And as Trey thundered beneath him, he slammed his feet into the zombie's shoulders with brutal force and launched himself again, this time forward, earning the separation from his enemies he sought before.

More than a dozen yards away, Regina and Iyare — in their wolfwoman and wolfman forms — stood on either side of the vampire. Alistaire looked distinctly less human now; his fingers had lengthened with nails closer to talons, his face displayed aspects of the demonic, and his eyes were glowing white.

Even as Jason hustled in their direction, Iyare lunged low, with precision that should have hamstrung the bastard, slicing the vampire's tendons clean through. Except, at the last instant, the vampire *dissolved into an eerie, ivory mist* and Iyare's claws passed right through it, his meticulous attack rendered useless.

Holy shit*! I should've asked Regina what vampires are actually able to—*

Jason's thoughts screeched to a halt as Iyare, overbalancing when his attack hit nothing solid, stumbled forward, and the mist resolidified into the vampire — except now Alistaire stood with his left arm around the back of Iyare's neck and his right, taloned hand poised over his chest.

Alistaire's voice carried shades of sincere regret as he met Iyare's gaze and said, "*Gott vergebe dir.*"

The vampire tightened his hold on the African's neck and — with a horrifying, sickening wet *crunch!* that Jason would never, ever forget — flesh and bone yielded in grotesque harmony as he drove his hand straight through Iyare's ribcage. Iyare's eyes shot wide in shock, and he convulsed as Alistaire, in a move both effortless and savage, wrenched his heart from his chest.

Regina howled in anguish, but Jason could only stare in disbelief.

Iyare looked at his own heart, then at Regina, then finally at

Jason himself. The wolfman's lupine face reflected equal parts disbelief and devotion ... and then Iyare dropped dead, his body already easing back toward his human form.

Regina howled again, but this time it betrayed less sorrow and more rage. She surged forward, both clawed hands reaching toward the vampire—

Dropping Iyare's heart and clenching his bloody hand into a fist, Alistaire swung his arm around with blinding speed, a blur even to Jason's eyes. He backhanded Regina with so much ferocious power that she tumbled away from him, rolling until she collided with a parked car in a jarring *crash!* of dented metal and bruised bone.

The car's alarm went off, but Jason barely heard it.

Backing toward Regina, who slumped to the pavement and did not move, Jason kept his eyes and ears on the Triumvirate — Alistaire and Trey approached him with some caution, and Mallory, looking pissed off, shifted into full-wolf again as he rose onto his four shaky paws.

What do I do? What do I do*?!*

"Daddy, *look*! What's *that*?!"

Jason and the Triumvirate turned as one.

Led by a boy some four years old, a tired Hispanic family of five emerged from the parking garage elevator some fifty yards away; if the lift had sounded any bell to announce its arrival, the supernatural opponents all missed it. The young boy who had spoken was pointing at Sean, but his older siblings and parents spread their attention across all of them — the mother wheezed in alarm, while the slack-jawed father simply stopped in his tracks; the older kids, a boy and girl, took the predictable action of any modern youths and pulled out their phones, pointing them toward this viral-worthy spectacle.

Perfect! Jason thought with a wolfen grin. *The flares didn't work out, but here's the attention the Triumvirate wanted to avoid. This is my chance to grab Regina and get the hell out of here!*

But in the next moment, Jason hated himself for thinking that. Just how determined were the Triumvirate to keep their existence a secret? Were they hellbent enough to actually *kill* this innocent, merch-clad family to cover their tracks? How long would it really take Mallory or the vampire to dash over there, break all their necks, and return to finish off the wayward lycanthropes?

The Triumvirate had made no such move, yet, but Jason decided he couldn't take the chance. Shredding the last of his clothing as he shifted into his own full-wolf form, he planted his four paws against the pavement, raised his thick muzzle skyward, and roared at the top of his lungs, an intense, sustained howl that echoed off the cars, the parking structure walls, and the taller buildings all around them.

Thankfully, that sent the family into a panic. The mother screamed and snatched up the youngest child while the father cursed and herded their other kids, without resistance, back into the elevator so that, to Jason's relief, they all disappeared from sight.

But now the clock was really ticking; more witnesses were sure to follow, and soon. The Triumvirate would have to take him down fast.

Their audience gone, the three turned back to him. The werewolf padded forward to Trey's left with the vampire taking position on Trey's right, a symbolic line of death as they resumed their march toward him. He half-expected them, probably Trey, to call out something like, "Last chance to give up, Jason!", but no such offer was extended.

He glanced back at Regina, who was beginning to stir but was in no condition to help him fight *or* run, not even close.

It was all up to Jason. And he saw no choice but to play his last ace — and hope against hope that, under these arduous circumstances, he possessed the focus necessary to delve into that ethereal pulse of the Earth when he most needed it.

Still in full-wolf form, Jason growled and snarled, pawing at the pavement like a pissed off bull before moving forward to meet them, trying to project the impression that he had decided to go out in a blaze of glory. He aimed dead center, straight at Trey.

In response, the Triumvirate's vampire and werewolf fanned out, allowing the zombie to spread his arms as before; his fingers splayed as well, giving Jason the distinct impression that Trey was planning to seize his muzzle.

Which was *perfect.*

The distance between them vanished as Jason bolted into a full-legged sprint, leaped ... and — in a breathtaking, midair shift — transformed into a silverback gorilla.

Trey's eyes widened in disbelief, Mallory barked in alarm, and even Alistaire hissed in incredulity as Jason crashed into the zombie. The *thud!* of their impact resounded with another echo; as with all his animal forms, Jason didn't just become a silverback, he became an enormous *behemoth* of a silverback. Weighing nearly half a ton, he drove Trey off his feet and crushed him flat onto his back, then raised both mighty arms and brought them down like twin sledgehammers onto the zombie's torso. Everyone heard the disturbing *crack!* as something inside Trey's chest gave way, and while the undead man didn't crumple as any normal human would, the blow was devastating. Trey struggled to get his arms up in defense, but his sluggish effort faltered before Jason's relentless onslaught — the silverback executed a second bone-shattering double-blow, then a third, each strike more punishing than the last.

All too aware that Trey did not stand alone, Jason slung his long right arm around, clubbing Mallory across his snarling face just before the werewolf would have sunk his sharp teeth into Jason's bowed legs. Jason kept the swing going, kicking off and away from Trey as he attempted to strike Alistaire, too.

But the vampire evaded the attack with unbelievable speed, pulling back before Jason's thick knuckles could connect. Alistaire retreated several more steps, his eyes narrowing as he assessed his gargantuan opponent and plotted his next move.

Stunned almost to incapacitation, Trey labored to rise, but Mallory recovered faster — shaking his head, he shifted from wolf to wolfman and advanced from the opposite side of Alistaire.

"So ..." the Irish wolfman slurred through his half-human mouth, "... this explains why ye didn't smell like a normal werewolf."

"*Indeed,*" the vampire agreed.

"Did ye already *know* the trunk contained the remains of a panwere — like yerself, Jason? Was all that—?"

Jason saw no advantage in chatting. He feinted toward

Alistaire, and when the vampire withdrew another step, he whirled back toward Mallory and shapeshifted again.

Mallory had braced himself to dodge a large gorilla's fist, but the colossal paw of a swift, oversized Kodiak bear caught him full on the shoulder, its thick, deadly claws tearing down through hirsute flesh, rending all the way through the werewolf's still-seething burn from Iyare's flare. As Mallory curse-roared in agony, Jason swept out again with his other paw, catching his enemy on the head once more. Dazed and overwhelmed, Mallory stumbled backward and collapsed.

"*Enough!*"

Before Jason could react, the vampire bounded onto his tremendous back; Alistaire's weight was negligible in his Kodiak form, but the talons that dug deep into his flanks? *Those* he felt, especially when Alistaire flexed them deeper still.

Jason twisted from side to side, even spun in a complete circle, but the vampire clung to him like a tick. In desperation, he threw himself upward onto his hind legs and over backward, hoping to crush Alistaire between his heavy bear form and the unforgiving pavement.

But the vampire again proved too nimble, releasing his hold on Jason and rolling to safety with sinister grace. Then the bastard was on his feet in an instant, talons flexed and fangs gnashing, poised to strike.

Too slow, too bulky! Jason's mind screamed in frantic urgency. Sacrificing the bear's size and strength for agility, he shifted from Kodiak down to an acrobatic white-handed gibbon, converting his backward momentum into a complete roll upright, to stand before the vampire in a less-than-ideal form.

Further shifting into a somewhat familiar form — he could no longer ignore the strain of changing into so many new and different animals so close together — Jason faced Alistaire as a Barbary lion.

The vampire hissed and snarled, and proceeded to circle the imposing cat.

Jason suspected that the monster was attempting to maneuver him to put his back toward Mallory and Trey, so rather than mimicking the revolving pattern, he took one step away for every step sideways, gaining distance as they went — he kept his eyes on the vampire, but focused his ears on the werewolf and zombie, alert for their approach.

But we can't keep this up indefinitely. Anytime now, the cops or some other authority are going to show up in response to that family I terrified. Then all hell's really gonna break loose, and no way innocent people won't get hurt.

An idea struck him. He had no clue if it would work — he didn't know enough about real vampires, damn it! — but he was running out of options, so what did he have to lose?

Your life, idiot.

Not helping!

As if sensing Jason's momentary distraction, the vampire lashed out like lightning — God, he was *fast* — slashing right at his face, targeting his eyes! Jason's reflexes were a fraction too slow to pull back, but he dipped his big head so that the talons raked across his forehead instead. He countered with his own formidable claws, but with fluid elegance, Alistaire danced back out of range.

Jason could feel the hot blood flowing from his wound; if it weren't for his tawny fur, it would have streamed into his eyes and blinded him after all — which, for all he knew, was always the vampire's Plan B.

He and Alistaire continued to rotate around one another. Jason's ears told him that Regina was at last stirring for real, but it sounded like Trey and Mallory were recovering as well. That, plus he was pretty sure he heard radio chatter from somewhere below them.

No more time.

Coiling his great feline muscles, Jason pounced toward Alistaire, swinging down toward both shoulders. The vampire slipped away without much effort, but before he could retaliate, Jason struck out again, this time sideswiping in a blur of predatory precision — the tips of two of his claws snagged the arm of Alistaire's fancy shirt. He snapped his jaws, but the vampire had already moved, so he unleashed a relentless barrage of slashes again, and again, and again, keeping his prey springing side to side, pursuing until he had closed the distance. With a final, powerful swing, Jason's paw sliced through the air toward the vampire's head with deadly intent.

Alistaire's body — skin, hair, even clothing — bleached to the same ivory white as his glowing eyes, then dissolved into that mist he had used to escape Iyare's attack earlier ...

... which was exactly what Jason was hoping he would do.

While the vampire was changing into supernatural mist, Jason also shapeshifted. His mass depleted but his arms lengthened, his fur replaced by feathers, his snout exchanged for a beak, his feline eyes growing beady and bright.

A Barbary lion had forced the vampire to change form, but it was an oversized snowy albatross that brought his record-breaking wingspan of over fifteen feet down full force ...

... right through that gossamer mist.

The stubborn vampiric cloud refused to dissipate at first — it was, after all, the alternate configuration of a sentient being — but Jason swept his unmatched wings as he had his lion's claws, assaulting Alistaire over and over. And, gradually but inexorably, the Triumvirate's vampire lost cohesion, stretching thinner and thinner until he was little more than a ghostly wisp.

But Jason discovered that it was exhausting to flap his wings like this without taking flight, and he teetered forward on his webbed albatross feet, gasping for breath and striving not to fall over.

"J-Jason ...?"

Regina, back in human form, pulled herself across the trunks of cars as she staggered toward him. He also returned to his naked, human self, and met her halfway. They held one another, both in relief and a pooled effort to remain standing.

"I ..." she whispered, "... I am in *awe* of you."

He smiled at that. "Thanks."

"We— oh, no ..."

He felt her stiffen, and shifted his gaze.

Damn it all to hell, the Triumvirate were also recuperating: Trey knelt on one knee, his hands probing his chest; Mallory — a wolfman once more — stood shaking his furry head beside the zombie; and Alistaire's thinned mist grew less translucent with each passing second, gelling together near his cohorts.

All that, plus multiple sirens reverberated through the night, drawing ever nearer.

"We ..." Regina gulped another breath, her free hand holding her forehead. "We have to ... run. Can you ... make it to the car?"

But Jason looked over to their vehicle, judging the distance that had grown over the course of their battle, and knew they would never make it. With Mallory's help, Trey was up on his feet, and Alistaire was maybe a minute, probably less, from reforming to the point of changing back.

What should I do?

God, how often had he asked himself that over this past, insane week?

Focus, Jason, or you're both dead.

His strength was returning, but would it be soon enough? And even if he could reach back into the pulse of the Earth, what other animals were left to try? For fuck's sake, the Triumvirate had already stood up to a gorilla and a bear. Should he try an American bison? Or an African savannah elephant? And even if either of those beasts were sufficient to barrel straight through these assholes, how would that help Regina? Even if she tried to ride him, what would stop Alistaire or Mallory from scampering right up after her?

Trey and Mallory eyed them while Alistaire swirled ever closer to a man-shaped cloud.

Should he turn into a large reptile? Could he draw from the insect kingdom? What about arachnids? Or amphibians? What were his limits? And what would prove most practical for a fight like this? What, damn it, *what*?!

Think, damn it, think, think, think*!*

Jason had devoted so many years to photographing wildlife, and even more studying photos taken by others, yet he could not seem to picture in his mind — here, now — a single animal that could get them out of this. Too much noise, too much pressure, he couldn't picture any of them, couldn't picture—

Picture in your mind.

Those words, Iyare's words, came back to him. He had asked:

So ... I can turn into anything? Any animal?

And Iyare had answered: *As a panwere, any animal you can picture in your mind.*

How literal was that? Was it just a more poetic phrase for "any animal you can remember clearly," or did he really just have to *picture it* in his mind?

He wanted to ask Regina, but would she even know, with certainty? Probably not.

As they watched, Alistaire achieved humanoid form, and the Triumvirate faced them together once more.

"Get ready," he breathed.

She looked at him and nodded. He also saw Mallory perk up and the vampire tense, so he knew they had heard him, too. Good — maybe they would prepare themselves for an attack, instead of this Hail Mary he was about to throw.

Under other circumstances, he would have slowed his breathing and closed his eyes for this level of concentration, but he no longer had that luxury.

Keeping his enemies locked in his sights, he once more stretched out for the pulse of the Earth. He plunged into it, bathed in it, immersed and saturated himself body and soul as he envisioned a dynamic Shire horse, its fur black as night, sleek and beautiful ... *and* he conjured an image of a majestic, powerful harpy eagle, that bird of prey renowned for its rugged wings — the snowy albatross possessed the wingspan, but the harpy eagle boasted the strength.

Shire horse and harpy eagle ...

Horse and bird ...

United as one.

Only when Regina gasped and stumbled away from him did he realize that he had closed his eyes after all, and as he fell forward onto all fours, he heard Alistaire mumble, "*Was ist das?*" while Mallory cut loose with a much louder, "What ... the ... *fuck*?" Trey remained silent, but Jason liked to imagine his mouth agape, his jaw slack.

When his eyes opened once more, Jason lacked any reflective surface large enough to see himself. Not that he had any need; he had felt the transformation, knew the impossible form he had taken. But for posterity's sake, he threw back his head, spread his wondrous wings ...

... and allowed the Triumvirate to behold the awe-inspiring sight of the black-haired Pegasus before them.

I'm not limited to the wildlife of the real world, he marveled in amazement. *I can tap into mythology. The possibilities are* endless*!*

But he also knew they were seconds from the Triumvirate's recovering from their stupefaction and coming at them. He turned his long, muscular neck so that he could make eye-contact with Regina. Given time, he could probably manipulate his body so that he could speak, but for the moment he possessed only a horse's throat, and so he whinnied while willing her to understand: *Get on!*

Regina, tears of numinous joy in her eyes, divined his intent. Any normal human would have had difficulty springing onto the broad back of such a tall horse, but she succeeded on her first attempt, bending her legs so that she could grip him with her thighs without her feet interfering with his wings.

With one final equine "fuck you" glare thrown toward the Triumvirate, Jason reared back and leaped into the air. Feathered wings should never have been able to heft such mass, but between his lycanthropic strength and the inherent mythical nature of the Pegasus, he had no trouble taking flight.

And to think, he had been afraid to attempt flying as an *eagle*!

Flashing police lights flooded the parking garage's ramp as they gained altitude, but he could not have cared less — that was the Triumvirate's problem, and those assholes were welcome to it. Regina leaned forward to embrace his neck, nuzzling her face into his shaggy mane and laughing with delight.

Soaring ever higher into the vast expanse above, they lacked a golden sunset into which they could fly off, but Jason found it more than appropriate to angle for the waxing moon and leave behind the glaring, sprawling lights of humanity. They would rejoin the clamor of the modern world soon enough, but for the time being, all of that remained far below them.

For this fleeting stretch of time, the night belonged to the two of them, *together*, unified in their celestial escape.

SENDER: jason.bakari@igotprivatemail.com
TO: Sebastian and Patricia Samir
SUBJECT: OUT OF TOUCH FOR A WHILE Friday, 3:49 AM

Hey, Mom & Dad!

Sorry for sending you this email from a different address than usual. I wanted to let you know that I'll be out of touch, just for a little while. I'm working on a new story, something bigger than my regular Watchdogs website. I can't go into any details right now, but I didn't want you to think that anything was wrong if you write or call and I don't respond.

Also, if anyone contacts you asking about me, don't worry about that, either — it's probably a competing news group trying to weasel out the story I'm onto! Just tell them you haven't heard from me, okay?

I'll let you know more when I can. Take care! Love you both!

Jason

Sender Unknown

Friday * 4:06 AM

Hey, D. It's me, the watchful weirdo who owes you the most drinks. How's my favorite deputy?

I'm sorry I'm MIA, and I'm sorry about ghosting you. It took some effort to retrieve my phone (long story), because I would *never* have remembered the number for your burner. Let's all just be happy that raccoons have opposable thumbs, huh?! (Sorry, a little self-serving humor there.) As I'm sure you can deduce, this is coming from a burner of my own, so I really, really hope you didn't delete-&-block without taking a peek at this text first!

Seriously, though, I wanted to reach out, so as not to leave you hanging any more than I already have. I can only imagine all the ??? you have at this point, especially with the rumors about that latest incident near Knott's. I promised to let you know whatever I could, but I'm sorry to say that's more complicated than ever.

I can tell you that — for a while — you don't have to worry about any more wolf attacks, or lion attacks, or especially videos of "flying horses" (crazy what they can fake online these days, huh?). [Laughing emoji]

BUT, AS YOUR FRIEND, I HAVE TO SHARE THIS MUCH: THERE ARE FORCES AT WORK THAT CAUSE THESE THINGS *AND* THOSE THAT ARE TRYING TO CONTAIN THEM. I *CAN'T* PROMISE THAT YOU WON'T EVER SEE MORE INCIDENTS LIKE THE SPIDERS LAST YEAR OR THE AIRPORT WOLF A COUPLE OF WEEKS AGO. I *CAN* SAY THAT I, AND MY TALL FRIEND (DUDE, WIPE THAT SMIRK OFF YOUR FACE) ARE WORKING THE PROBLEM. WE'VE GOT SOME TRAVELING TO DO, AND A HELL OF A LOT OF RESEARCH, BUT ... WITHOUT GIVING YOU NIGHTMARES OR PROMPTING YOU TO WRITE ME OFF FOR GOOD ... I WILL ALSO SAY THAT I'VE FOUND MYSELF IN A UNIQUE POSITION TO *MAYBE* INFLUENCE SOME OF THESE BIZARRE EVENTS MORE THAN I EVER IMAGINED IN MY WILDEST DREAMS.

THAT'S ALL I CAN REALLY TELL YOU, FOR NOW. YEAH, YEAH, I KNOW, I'M LEAVING YOU WITH EVEN *MORE* ??? THAN BEFORE. I'M SORRY THAT THIS IS THE BEST I CAN DO AT THE MOMENT. HEY, AT LEAST YOU KNOW I'M ALIVE AND WELL, RIGHT? I'LL BE GOING OFFLINE AGAIN FOR A WHILE, AND MY NEXT TEXT MIGHT BE FROM YET ANOTHER NEW NUMBER (SO DON'T JUST DELETE & BLOCK 'EM ALL!).

TAKE CARE, D. WATCH YOUR BACK ON DUTY *AND* OFF. AND IF YOU WERE AT ALL SERIOUS ABOUT THAT "EARLY RETIREMENT" YOU SOMETIMES MUMBLED ABOUT AFTER YOU'D DOWNED A FEW TOO MANY ... DO IT. YOU'LL SLEEP BETTER.

YOUR FRIEND,
YOUR FAVORITE WEIRDO

P.S. HOLD ON TO THIS BURNER AS LONG AS YOU CAN. IF I'M EVER ABLE TO REACH OUT IN SOME HELPFUL WAY, I WILL. THAT'S A PROMISE I WILL ABSOLUTELY KEEP.

THE TRUTH IS WAY, WAY OUT THERE

MESSAGE BOARD MODERATOR, SHELLEY_O

NEW MESSAGE, PRIVATE — Friday, 4:27 AM

BONJOUR, SHELLEY!

I HAVE NO IDEA WHAT "OFFICIAL" STORY TREY HAS PASSED ON TO THE WATCHDOGS (IF ANY) ABOUT MY ABSENCE OR WHY (I PRESUME) I'M PERSONA NON GRATA, BUT I KNOW YOU WERE ALREADY ... LET'S CALL IT "DUBIOUS" ... ABOUT THIS ODD SITUATION, AND I WANTED TO PUT YOUR MIND AT LEAST SOMEWHAT AT EASE.

AS YOU CAN PROBABLY GUESS FROM MY REACHING OUT TO YOU HERE ON YOUR OWN WEBSITE, I DIDN'T TRUST CONTACTING YOU THROUGH THE WATCHDOGS SITE — ASSUMING MY LOGIN CREDENTIALS HAVEN'T BEEN REVOKED.

I'M WRITING TO YOU, SHELLEY, FOR TWO REASONS. THE FIRST IS SIMPLE ENOUGH: TO LET YOU KNOW I'M OKAY. I KNOW WE'VE NEVER BEEN SUPER-CLOSE OR ANYTHING, BUT YOU WERE THERE FOR ME WHEN I NEEDED INFO ABOUT THE TRIUMVIRATE, AND I WANTED TO SHARE MY APPRECIATION FOR THAT.

THE SECOND IS A LITTLE MORE COMPLEX, BUT I'D FEEL REMISS IF I DIDN'T AT LEAST TRY: I *STRONGLY* SUGGEST THAT YOU NEVER BRING UP THE TRIUMVIRATE TO TREY AGAIN. I MEAN, YEAH, YOU WERE PROBABLY ALREADY LEANING THAT DIRECTION SINCE HE SHUT YOU DOWN SO HARD LAST TIME, BUT ...

GOD, I WISH I COULD ELABORATE; I'M PROBABLY ALREADY WHETTING YOUR APPETITE AS IT IS. BUT I WILL TELL YOU THIS

MUCH, BECAUSE I DON'T KNOW HOW ELSE TO PUT IT: THE TRIUMVIRATE IS DIRECTLY RELATED TO MY BEING "ON THE LAM." I'M NOT SAYING ALL THE RUMORS YOU'VE HEARD ABOUT THE TRIUMVIRATE ARE TRUE — THEY AREN'T. BUT YOU SHOULD KNOW THAT THE TRIUMVIRATE *IS* A REAL THING, AND THAT TREY IS AWARE OF THEM AND IS COVERING FOR THEM, SORT OF.

IF I HAD WRITTEN THAT MUCH TO ALMOST ANYONE ELSE ON EARTH, THEY'D WANT TO HAVE ME COMMITTED. BUT I KNOW *YOU* WILL TAKE ME A LITTLE MORE SERIOUSLY. I'M NOT SAYING YOU SHOULD QUIT THE WATCHDOGS. I'M JUST SAYING YOU SHOULD PROBABLY PRIORITIZE YOUR OWN WEBSITE FROM NOW ON, AND IF YOU DO EVER DECIDE TO WRITE ABOUT THE TRIUMVIRATE HERE ON THE TRUTH IS WAY, WAY OUT THERE ... *PLEASE* USE A PSEUDONYM.

AND IF I EVER HAVE ANYTHING REALLY JUICY THAT I THINK CAN BE *SAFELY* PUBLISHED, I'LL REACH OUT TO YOU.

TAKE CARE, SHELLEY. AND TREAD VERY, VERY CAREFULLY ... BUT, ONE REPORTER TO ANOTHER: *NEVER* GIVE UP THE GOOD FIGHT.

YOU KNOW MORE THAN YOU REALIZE.

JASON

Alistaire opened the panel in the hallway floor, emerging from his hidden coffin for the night. His senses informed him that both Sean and Trey were home, and he was unsurprised to find Trey seated before his computer setup.

Once a single personal computer, since Trey's recent "evolution" as a zombie, Alistaire and Sean had acceded to his upgrading his systems. Alistaire did not understand all of it — he adapted with the times better than most vampires, but even he viewed computers as a technology growing at a mystifying, perhaps alarming, rate. But even the most devoted Luddite would be hard-pressed to miss the addition of two more monitors, a second computer tower, a laptop, and something called a "router," into which all computers were plugged — bypassing the need for the mysterious "WiFi." No longer confined to a simple computer desk, Trey's collective apparatuses dominated most of the western side of their living room.

Trey glanced over his shoulder, nodding with a simple, "Alistaire."

"*Trey.*" After a pause that was just long enough to be noticeable, Alistaire added, "*I trust you are continuing to recuperate from your injuries?*"

Trey shrugged. "Getting there. I'm recovering faster than I would have ... you know, before."

Another silence hung for a long, uncomfortable minute after that. Many months had passed since their encounter with Young Bondye, even longer since the incident with the wolf-weres in Alaska, and while those experiences led to Trey's improved station — his increased mental and physical functionality, his ability to better pass as a living man — to say that the ultimate cost of that transformation weighed heavily upon Alistaire would be a colossal understatement. No longer able to make do with substitutions, Trey required periodic feeding on *living people* to maintain his improved efficiency and fundamental control over his hunger.

Thus far, Trey had limited his "feedings" to the most truly disgusting members of society — which was the *only* reason Alistaire acquiesced to these new circumstances. So long as this remained the case, Alistaire tolerated this reprehensible arrangement.

But he was watching, and Trey knew it. And so, the tension between them persisted.

Seeking to break the disagreeable quiet, Alistaire asked, "*Have you discovered anything new of Jason Samir's whereabouts?*"

Trey shook his head. "Afraid not. In fact, we're a little worse off than before. Remember that brief hit we got from his phone? I'm pretty sure he was just grabbing specific information — probably something from his Contacts list — because he didn't make any calls, send any texts, or access the Internet. Well, shortly after you went down for the day, we got another signal from Jason's phone, but you'll never believe where it was this time."

"*Nowhere in Los Angeles, I take it?*"

"You could say that: It was several miles out over the Pacific Ocean. I've done my best to check for any boats or plane flights that lined up, but I'd bet that he was out flying on his own again — probably as a bird, since there haven't been any more 'Pegasus' sightings. Bottom line is, I figure he dropped his phone out over the water, and that he only activated it so that we would *know* he was doing so. If I'm right, that method of searching is now a total dead end."

"Ye know ..." Alistaire and Trey both turned to regard the Irishman as he emerged from the kitchen and addressed the vampire, "... if those 'visions' of yers could give us a heads-up to watch Jason as a potential werewolf, it woulda been a *lot* more helpful if they'd added that he might be a freakin' *panwere.*"

Alistaire allowed himself a slight sigh. "*Sean, you should—*"

Sean waved him off. "I know, I know, they're never that

specific. I'm just givin' ye grief, Alistaire. I only wish we could've gotten through to Jason, had time to win him over." He shook his head. "I never shoulda left him alone with those two. I was just tryin' to ... to make it *his* choice, ye know?"

"*I understand.*"

"Still, I'll be kickin' myself over that one for a while. Can ye imagine if we'd managed to draft 'im? He'd've made us one hell of a quadrumvirate." He shook his head and chuckled, less in humor as in resignation of an opportunity lost.

Turning back to Trey, Alistaire asked, "*Has there been any further progress salvaging the contents of Doctor Hellqvist's trunk?*"

Trey winced. "Not as much as I'd hoped. I've prioritized getting those shafts analyzed, but the problem is that so much of all the metal objects inside the trunk melted together from the heat of that damned flare, we can't be sure which metals were or were not part of the original alloy." He rotated his chair back to the computer and clicked around with his mouse, then typed a few commands. "I can tell you that the metallurgist's educated guess — and she stresses that it's *only* a guess, so she can't swear by it — is that the shafts were made of silver and unknown amounts of rhodium, niobium, and tantalum. But that leaves us with a number of questions: How critical is it to get the proportions of the different metals exactly right? How, and *why*, would this combination have a greater effect on a panwere than pure silver, and how the hell did the Egyptian lycanthropes figure that out to begin with? And how did they find all these metals anyway? Rhodium, for example, should not have been accessible to ancient Egyptians at the time." He raised his arms in a great shrug. "If we have to oppose Jason again — and I'm really hoping we don't — I'm not sure if we'll be able to use this elixir against him."

"I'm with ye on not wantin' to square off against Jason," Sean said. "He really seemed like a good guy. If only Regina and the rest hadn't gotten to 'im ..."

Trey's computer played a short musical sequence, calling his attention elsewhere, so Alistaire replied to Sean, "*I sympathize. My only direct encounter with Jason was our conflict atop the parking garage, but I share your general impression of him.*"

Sean chuckled. "Not that he didn't screw us right well with the timing of his dynamic exit. If ye hadn't been able to use yer 'powers of persuasion' against the local gardaí when they arrived—"

"Um ... Alistaire?"

The two faced toward Trey. "*Yes?*"

"Someone's sent an anonymous message to the *Watchdogs* site." He rolled his chair back a bit and pointed to his center monitor. "But it's not addressed to the Watchdogs. It's addressed to *you.*"

Alistaire and Sean shared a curious glance — exceedingly few people had any notion of the connection between the German vampire and "Trey Romero's" journalistic website. So who could be sending the message? Perhaps Jason and the werewolf, Regina? But why would they be writing to *him* rather than to Trey, or even Sean?

Alistaire stepped forward to read the message.

ABOUT THE AUTHOR

CHRISTOPHER ANDREWS lives in California with his wife, Yvonne Isaak-Andrews, and their wonderful daughter, Arianna. In addition to his duties as stay-at-home Dad, he is always working on his next novels, and continues to work as an actor and screenwriter.

Excerpts from all of Christopher's novels can be found at www.ChristopherAndrews.com.

RISING STAR VISIONARY PRESS

continues the fine RISING STAR tradition of bringing you only the best and brightest undiscovered authors!

Explore the works of RSVP's featured author
CHRISTOPHER ANDREWS!

PANDORA'S GAME (ISBN #978-0977453528)
Games involving hypnosis and the supernatural unleash the unexpected.

DREAM PARLOR (ISBN #978-0977453535)
The novelization of the independent science-fiction film in the tradition of *1984* and *Total Recall*.

PARANORMALS (ISBN #978-0977453566)
A tale of superhuman wonder in the tradition of the *X-Men* and the *Wild Card* anthologies.

HAMLET: PRINCE OF DENMARK (ISBN #978-0977453559)
The novelization of Shakespeare's classic. Excellent for students or any fan of The Bard.

THE DARKNESS WITHIN (ISBN #978-0977453542)
A collection of disturbing short-stories. Includes "Connexion," the bridge between the *Triumvirate* novels PANDORA'S GAME and OF WOLF AND MAN.

OF WOLF AND MAN (ISBN #978-0982488201)
The **IPPY award-winning** sequel to PANDORA'S GAME.

NIGHT OF THE LIVING DEAD (ISBN #978-0982488218)
The novelization of the public domain horror classic.

PARANORMALS: WE ARE NOT ALONE (ISBN #978-0982488256)
The exciting second entry in Andrews' *Paranormals* saga.

MACBETH (ISBN #978-0982488270)
The novelization of another Shakespearean classic. Excellent for students or any fan of The Bard.

ARAKNID (ISBN #978-0982488294)
The terrifying third novel in Andrews' *Triumvirate* saga.

PARANORMALS: DARKNESS REIGNS (ISBN #978-1736198315)
The intense third entry in Andrews' *Paranormals* saga.

JULIUS CAESAR (ISBN #978-1736198339)
The novelization of another Shakespearean classic. Excellent for students or any fan of The Bard.

Available everywhere books are sold. Visit the author's website: www.ChristopherAndrews.com.

www.ingramcontent.com/pod-product-compliance
Lightning Source LLC
Chambersburg PA
CBHW030356310726
48979CB00001B/329

* 9 7 8 1 7 3 6 1 9 8 3 4 6 *